EVASION

J. R. WAGNER

This book is a work of fiction. Names, characters, businesses, organizations, places, events and incidents are either a product of the author's imagination or are used fictitiously. Any resemblance to actual persons, living or dead, events or locales is entirely coincidental.

Published by Solomon Caw Publishing
Downingtown, PA

Design and composition by Solomon Caw Publishing
Cover design by Todd Berkhammer
Illustrations by Jason Lodeski

Publisher's Cataloging-In-Publication Data
(Prepared by the Donohue Group, Inc.)

Pending

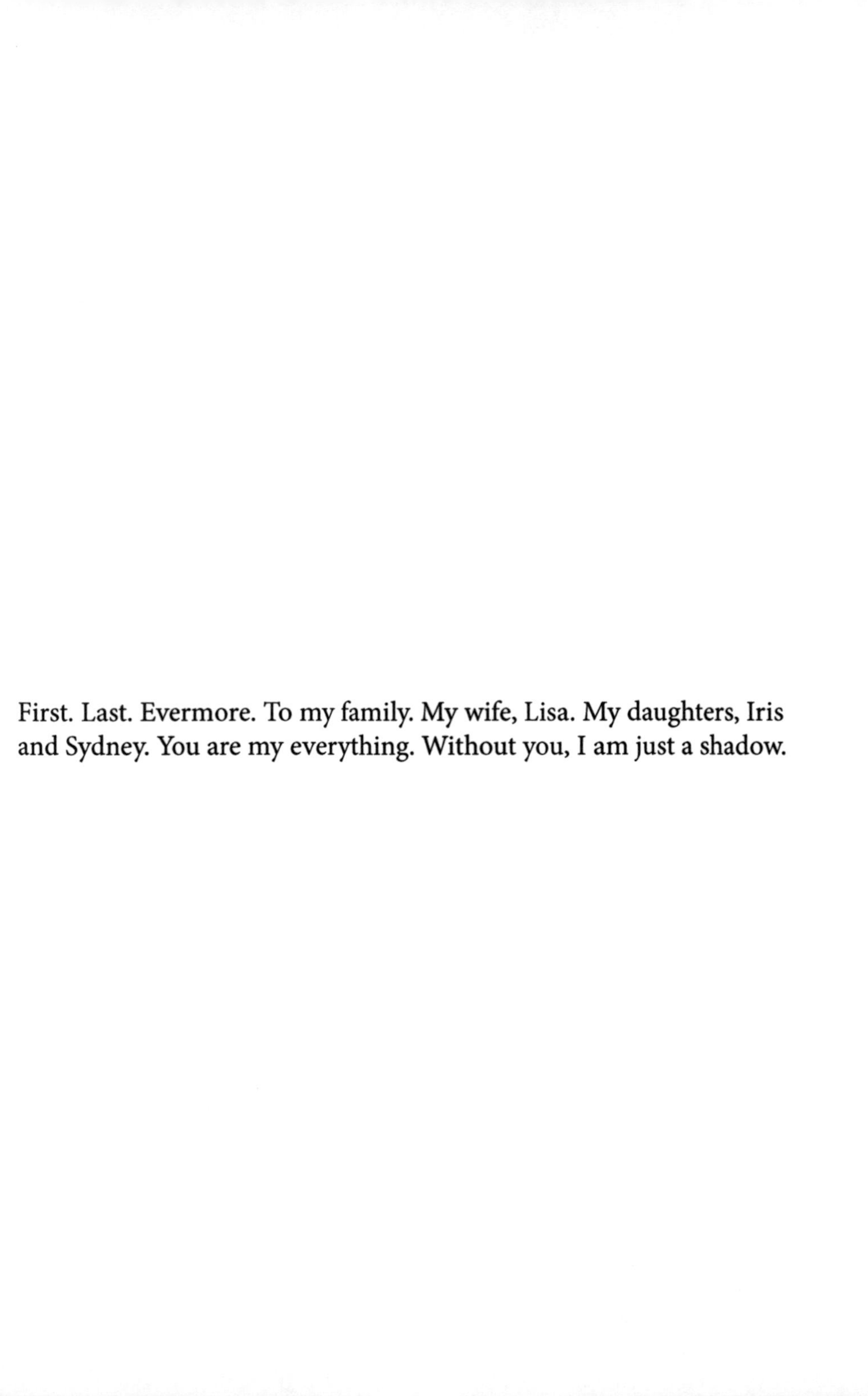

First. Last. Evermore. To my family. My wife, Lisa. My daughters, Iris and Sydney. You are my everything. Without you, I am just a shadow.

The Never

N
W
E
S

1

an unlikely meeting

September 1898, Paris

Akil Karanis strode down the mud-covered cobbles of the Avenue des Champs-Élysées. The hems of his violet robes were soaked and browned despite his best efforts to avoid puddles along the road and splashes from passing carts. The day was grey and dreary with intermittent rainfall soaking travelers daft enough to leave home without an umbrella.

He continued northwest, not slowing for a group of schoolchildren dashing across the avenue directly in front of him. Nor did he slow for a cart that had managed to dislodge a wheel and was surrounded by onlookers and the piqued-faced coachman. He deftly stepped between two men shouting suggestions on the best way to repair the lamed conveyance.

Akil passed under the Arc de Triomphe then turned northeast. He continued for several minutes before turning down an alley scarcely wider than his shoulders and pushed open a green door framed by a hedge at the far end. He stood in a small courtyard with finely crushed stone underfoot, dense foliage around the perimeter and a lone fountain perfectly centered, which spilled clear water from its upper reservoir into the much larger base. "Erakutsi ," he whispered, extending his hand over the cascading water.

The fountain began to spin, slowly at first, then gradually picking up speed until it was a blur. Akil took a step back as the upper basin lowered into the base, which glowed pale blue for a moment before melting away, revealing a spiral staircase that disappeared into darkness. Akil stepped over the rim of the base and onto the first step. He glanced over his shoulder, then descended into the depths.

At the bottom of the stairs, torches stood in brackets on either side of a handleless door set in a stone wall. Akil knocked once. The sound of his knuckles impacting the aged wood reverberated like a battering ram rather than the curled bony fingers of an old man. The door opened. Akil crossed the threshold into an antechamber. A sturdy sofa was occupied by an enormous cat whose tawny fur was covered in patches of midnight black, creating the illusion of shadowed, solid color from a distance. The cat lazily lifted an eyelid revealing a single green eye as the sorcerer passed. "Murk," Akil greeted the cat.

A twitch of its tail was the only acknowledgement Akil received as he passed through a doorway into a small yet cozy drawing room. A fire burned hot and the floor was carpeted, thick and red. Beside the fireplace, a man stood with his back to Akil, fixing himself a drink.

Without a word, Akil hung his cloak on a hook bracketed to the wall. The man turned and handed Akil a drink. "You've proposed many schemes, my friend, most of them harebrained, ridiculous or both, but this, this could quite possibly be your greatest."

Akil raised the corner of his mouth in a half-smile, lifted his glass in an unsteady hand and downed his drink. His expression was severe rather than celebratory. "I would hardly refer to framing young James for my very own murder so he would be exiled to Ak Egundiano a scheme, Ilixo ," he said.

"Fine, fine. But you do realize what a masterful thing you've accomplished, don't you?" asked Alvaro.

"Do not act as though you played no part in this, Ilixo. Your role was as imperative as mine. Perhaps more so."

"Regardless, what's done is done. I truly hope you were right about the boy. I'd hate to think we wasted all those resources for nothing."

"I am certain," said Akil with finality. Alvaro took Akil's glass and turned to refill it as Akil sat heavily on one of the upholstered chairs. Concern radiated from every crease in his bronzed face. He rubbed his snow-white goatee with his thumb and forefinger and closed his eyes. Alvaro turned, drinks in hand.

"Your expression suggests something other than certainty," he said.

"I care for the boy," Akil said without opening his eyes. "It was not an easy thing to do."

"I've known you a long time, longer than the lives of most unfaithful, and I've never known your compassion to get in the way of your obsession."

"For the good of one or the good of all? An easy question until emotions cloud our minds," Akil said, taking the drink. "I am getting old and find myself haunted by my actions of the past…and present."

"We all have our parts to play. It is those of us who play them without question or deviation who find ourselves on the right side of things," said Alvaro.

"Right or moral?"

Both men drained their cups in silence. Akil stood quickly, the fatigue gone from his posture. Alvaro looked at the taller man, concern written on his face.

"Do not let your feelings for this boy stand in the way of stopping the Epoch Terminus. Besides, you have another matter to attend to first."

"I have no intention of helping that…monster."

"You made an agreement, Akil. In all our years as friends, I've never known you to renege on an offer." Akil paused and looked deep into Alvaro's black eyes . "I know you have a sordid history with Alexander. I understand that. I also know that you have an opportunity to move past the hatred that has cost so many lives, and I don't think you'll turn away from that so hastily."

"I can help James," said Akil, reaching for his cloak.

"Help him? He is gone, Akil. The only way he will ever return is if he truly is the Anointed One. Nothing was ever said about interfering with the path he must take to return. Do that and you may damn us all."

"I will not sit idle. I have been gifted great powers. I will not sit and hope. I cannot," said Akil.

"For the good of the many, you must," said Alvaro. "At the very least you must first fulfill your obligation. Then if you still desire to help James, I will assist you if I can."

"He is but one soul, yes; however within him is the potential to save us all." Akil turned and exited the drawing room. Murk slunk past Akil as he crossed the threshold and rubbed up against Alvaro's legs, nearly knocking him over. Alvaro reached down and scratched between his ears.

"I know you're worried," Alvaro said to the cat. "He will do what he feels he must, and in the end, he will be all right. Wait and see."

2

a journey continued

James could feel it. He could feel it as he squeezed the steel key. The black castle drew nigh. The sensation pulsed inside of him, synchronous with his heart yet distinguishable as it ran from his palm to his chest where it infused him with energy and confidence. They had not lingered long in Harbor Town after their encounter with Peroc's former tribe. He had seen to that. James knew the importance of moving quickly lest The Never itself catch wind of his plans and put an end to them all.

He reflected upon his journey as he looked out over the water. Exiled. Banished for the murder of Akil Karanis, his mentor. His entire upbringing had been centered around the belief that he was the Anointed

One, the one believed to have the power to stop the feared Epoch Terminus — the destruction of his kind. His world had been shattered the moment the Grand Master read his sentence and imposed his exile. Banished to The Never, a place for criminals — murderers, traitors and worse. A place where he was powerless and alone.

Yet, he had persevered. James had found others, and power, it seemed, had found him. The need to find a way to return home, to escape from this place, to prove his innocence, drove him on, yet somewhere along the way a new desire had worked its way into his mind. The black castle had become an infestation, an addiction, and James was powerless against its draw.

As the Queen Mary rounded the Third Widow, none of her crew had any desire to stop and explore the island. All had been convinced the answer to escape lay to the south. Only Luno had looked longingly at the cliffs of the Second Widow as they passed. James could see the desire in his face from across the deck. Luno stood at the helm staring out at the island. His desire for knowledge appeared oftentimes stronger than his desire to leave this place. Subconsciously, he turned the wheel toward the Third Widow. Only a shout from Roger, "Water's shallowin' quick, Cap'n!" brought him out of his trance, and he righted the wheel before they ran aground.

At the start of their journey, James had performed an incantation to fill the sail with wind on the otherwise calm and windless day. It wouldn't be long before they passed East Point and could see the black castle. Up in the crow's nest, Kilani looked out over the main island as they passed. She was one of the few who had seen the black castle with her own eyes. The first time she had set eyes upon it, she had felt a sense of foreboding so powerful she was reluctant to speak of it. The memory alone sent shivers down her spine.

James looked up at Kilani from the quarterdeck as she stared out at the island. A naive observer would think she was searching for an object in the distance, but James knew better. She longed for something. Something that mattered above all else. Would she abandon him if she found a way to return? Would he lose her? They were close, but James knew the feelings they shared were not the same. Regardless of their differences, James knew there was something pulling at Kilani — drawing her in a direction that could be her undoing. Whatever it was that Kilani longed for kept her at a distance. For James, this determination made her all the more alluring. He smiled as he thought of the similarities between her and his mother.

It had been years since he had seen his mother, long before he was exiled. She had let him go. She had let him become Akil's apprentice. He knew it hadn't been easy for her, but now looking back he knew it had been the best decision from her perspective. She couldn't have known it would end the way it did. Nobody could have. Everyone had expected him to be the one to stop the Epoch Terminus. The only way his mother could be certain he would get the training required was to send him with Akil. Does she know what happened to me? he thought. Does she think I am a killer? Does she believe I murdered Akil?

James longed to see her again, to hold her, to feel her reassuring embrace. He longed to look into the eyes of someone and feel nothing but love — no judgment or disappointment, simply love. He wanted to feel the kind of love only a mother could give. Her love gave him strength. He needed to see her again.

Luno looked at James as he watched Kilani, smiling. He believed their relationship to be more a convenience for Kilani than anything deeper. James was truly attracted to her, of that he had little doubt. He also knew she had never truly opened up to him, never given herself completely to James. Even after all the time they had spent together, there were still things she did not tell him — could not tell him. It was the same with Luno. The only difference was that he had come to accept it long ago. He had struggled at first but in time had come to grips with the fact that she was not going to share herself completely with him or anyone. As he looked at them now, he felt only pity for the boy.

Could he fault her? Did anyone completely share the ghosts of their past? There were many things he had not shared with anyone in this place. Some things he had confided to Kilani, but not everything. Some things were too painful, too terrible, to share with anyone. And James. He must have suspected how Luno felt about Kilani, yet he pursued her anyway. Could Luno blame him? In his heart, Luno knew the answer was no. He was but a boy — although his time here had aged him considerably. He also knew that Kilani would use James as she had used him. They were but a means to an end for her. Kilani's end was getting out of this place. Luno had realized long ago that if someone came along who Kilani believed could free her from this place, she would leave him by the wayside. When James came, his suspicion was confirmed. He felt for James. Whatever it was that drew Kilani with such force to escape from this place would eventually break them apart as well. Either James would find a way to escape or he wouldn't. But for Kilani, failure would leave an emptiness inside her that would break her to pieces. There would be no putting her back together again.

Luno also knew there was a part of himself that was jealous of James. During his short stay in this place, James had managed to find the two things Luno had longed for his entire life. The island had given James the knowledge that had eluded Luno since his arrival. With that knowledge came the power to manipulate his environment. Magic. It had been given to James in one fell swoop — implanted into his mind. It hadn't required any discipline or learning. Why didn't the island give it to me? Luno thought. Was what James said about the stone tower true or was he hiding something? Before leaving Harbor Town after their encounter with the Belator, James had attempted to teach the small group what The Never had shared with him but had found little success. They were clearly in a hurry to depart for the south, and James had grown frustrated with the group's inability to implement his teachings. Luno was desperate to learn, yet his continued failures eventually wore on him, and he had agreed to make an early departure. James was used to being different. Used to being special. Perhaps he was different because he manipulated others into believing it was so. Did he really try to teach us what he had learned or was he holding back so we would fail?

In his heart Luno knew the answer, yet he allowed this line of thinking to continue despite all the evidence to the contrary. It was this doubt in the face of overwhelming evidence that had seen him banished to The Never all those years ago. However, he was the leader of this group, and despite the power James now held, the crew — and James — still looked to him for guidance. He would not lead them astray — even if that meant withholding information for the good of the mission. They sailed on and only he knew what lay ahead.

The Queen Mary rounded East Point, and for the first time since the day of James's arrival, he set eyes upon the black castle. At a distance, it looked like a void in the landscape, as if an artist's brush had missed a spot on the canvas. It was simply a shadow rising out of the water, devoid of detail or delineation. Desire hit James like a wave, washing all other thoughts from his mind. He needed it. He needed to touch the smooth walls. To walk across the inner ward as the wind blew through his hair. It called to him and he knew he would not turn away from the black castle again.

"There it is!" James moved quickly to the bow for a closer look. Peroc, now garbed in tampere-hide trousers like the men in the group, still looked out of place among them. Having never been at sea, the voyage had proved arduous for the little man. He had spent the majority of his time on board the Queen Mary clinging to the rail and retching over the side. Now he raised his head searchingly in the direction of James's gaze, then let out a cry and turned away from the rail, cowering against the capstan. "Can you see it?" James asked excitedly, not taking his eyes from the castle. "Beautiful, isn't it?"

"I see nothing," said Luno.

"There. Off the starboard bow at the end of the spine."

"Nothing beyond th' last rock 'cept open water," said Roger.

James grew increasingly frustrated. He turned to Kilani who had made her way down from the crow's nest, her skin as pale as the dead.

"Can you see?" James asked.

Kilani would not look. She hung her head and her body trembled. James reached out and touched her shoulder. She abruptly pushed his hand aside and moved to the stern.

As the Queen Mary drew closer to the black castle, the sea became rough. By the time the ship drew even with the end of the spine, the swells rose as high as the deck. Several times, James had to reinforce the hull with protective incantations to prevent it from being broken to pieces. He also increased their speed to prevent the ship from being rolled by the larger waves. She pitched and rolled over crest and into trough. James stood surefooted at the bow looking out at the black castle while the others gripped what they could to avoid being cast into the sea.

The castle rose up out of a bed of rock, studded with sharp rocky protrusions like black thorns. The battlements were higher still — much higher than any man could hope to cast a rope. It was clear that this castle was inaccessible by any conventional means. James gave Luno a nod, and he turned the wheel to starboard, pointing the bow toward the outcropping they hoped would provide shelter for the Queen Mary while they made landfall in the newly constructed dinghy.

A deafening crack from overhead set everyone to action. Halfway up, the mast had snapped. Immediately the sail went limp and fell, pulled by the weight of the broken timber. Jan and William dove out of the way as the mast crashed through the railing and plunged into the sea. The sail, still roped to the base of the mast, caught like an anchor in the water, pulling the ship almost completely onto her side.

"Tertiri zé Manukto ragö," James intoned, his hands extended toward the rope. Nothing happened. James said it again, this time focusing more intently on the rope. It had to be cut or the next wave would capsize them completely. Again nothing happened.

Luno fought with the wheel to right the boat but could only hold it at its current angle. Cries rose up from the crew as they tried to untie the knot at the base of the broken mast, but the tension on the knot was too great.

"Cut the halyard!" Luno screamed.

Roger ran forward waving a hatchet. The others leapt aside as he brought the blade down. The rope split, and the Queen Mary righted herself as mast and sail were lost to the depths. The ship turned and began to move rapidly to the south. She rolled over the massive swells, her bow crashing into each successive wave as she went. James grasped the rail as water sluiced across the deck and threatened to wash him overboard. He continued to repeat incantations in hopes of mounting some defense against the waves.

"Bring 'er about! We're heading out to sea," Roger bellowed. "'Ard to starboard!"

"She's not responding," Luno yelled, turning the wheel, which spun easily yet had no effect on their direction of travel.

They were at the mercy of the sea. The bowsprit splintered as the ship crashed into a wave. Judging from the shudder that ran through the ship after the last impact, Luno was certain one more hit would break her apart and that would be the end of their mission. He braced himself as another huge wave rose up to strike the Queen Mary. It did not strike. As quickly as it rose, the wave fell and the sea became still.

One by one, the crew stood and relaxed their white-knuckled grips on whatever they'd been clinging to. Luno did a quick head count and was relieved to see that nobody had been washed overboard. Both William and Roger laughed and soon Jan joined them. James and Luno exchanged concerned looks. James climbed to the quarterdeck and looked to the north. In the distance, he could make out the dark shadow of the castle. Powerless, he could do nothing but stare at the distant shape he so longed to reach.

"Land ho, Cap'n!" Roger shouted. The Queen Mary was gliding quickly across the water, heading east toward a small island. "She'll run aground. Put about!" Still, they were not in control of the ship.

"Tertiri zé Manukto narvik," James said, attempting to gain control. The boat responded by slowing down. James let out a sigh of relief. Perhaps the lapse he had experienced was because he hadn't been completely calm and focused enough to perform the incantations. With another incantation the boat moved parallel to the shoreline. "We must make landfall so we can assess the damage."

"Agreed," said Luno. "I don't know about you, but I'll be happy to have my feet on dry land."

"Amen, Cap'n," said Roger.

Under James's direction, the Queen Mary followed the eastern shoreline in a southerly direction. They reached a cove cut deep into the island. James turned the boat into the cove in hopes of finding a decent anchorage that was protected from the unpredictable seas between them and the main island. Jan shouted excitedly as he pointed at something in the distance. Luno, still grasping the wheel although he couldn't say why, stared at the shoreline. "My God, he's right!"

"What is it?" James asked.

The rest of the crew made their way to the starboard side of the boat. In the distance they could see a wooden structure built out over the water — a dock. There were no buildings on or along it like in Harbor Town, but the basic construction was similar. Not one boat was moored to the dock and not one person could be seen from the water. Carefully, James guided the Queen Mary alongside. William, Roger and Jan quickly secured the boat. The group of seven disembarked and stood on the dock inspecting the ship.

"A bleedin' disaster," pronounced Roger as he took in the damage.

"I imagine there's a settlement nearby. We will need lumber and canvas among other things if we expect to sail out of here," said Luno. "Be on your guard. Unexpected visitors aren't usually welcome in this land."

After gathering a few supplies from the hold, the crew stepped off the dock one by one and onto the land. James was last and hesitated for a moment. The group looked back at him as he stood paralyzed with indecision. Finally, he stepped onto the land. A wave of cold ran through his body as his foot made contact with the sand. He felt drained and weak. To disguise his sudden frailty, he gruffly ordered the crew to find water as soon as possible.

The group followed a well-worn sandy path that twisted through the jungle. Unlike the main island, which was most often eerily silent, this island teemed with wildlife that made a deafening racket. Birds of all sizes and shapes called to each other and fluttered about. Several strange-looking winged insects hopped from branch to branch alongside the group as they continued down the path.

As they walked farther into the jungle, more and more of these peculiar creatures joined the group. Their wings moved so quickly they buzzed like a bee's, though these creatures were much larger than any bee James had ever seen. Including their wings, they were about the size of his fist. Every time he tried to get a better look as one landed on a nearby plant or tree, the creature would flutter away before it came into focus. James still felt the chill that had enveloped him when he stepped off the pier and walked now with his arms around his body trying to keep warm.

Ahead he watched William draw his short sword and begin to swat at the strange insects. They deftly avoided his flailing blade. William's attack drew more of the little creatures and soon there was a large cloud hovering over him.

The group came to a sudden stop. James looked past William to see that Luno had halted in front of a large bamboo gate that extended across the trail. The strange insects continued to hover above William, mere inches beyond the range of his sword.

"Putain! Vat are zees sings?" he growled, continuing to swing at them.

"Belay th' swingin' o' yer liken to be stung," Roger chortled.

William moved back down the trail away from the group, completely preoccupied with the buzzing creatures. James made his way around William and his swarm of followers and stood beside Luno and Kilani in front of the gate. The bamboo was fitted tightly together, making it impossible to see through to the other side. The gate rose well over James's head and stretched into the jungle on either side. A crude symbol had been drawn on the gate in red. "Not exactly a welcoming sign, is it?" Luno asked.

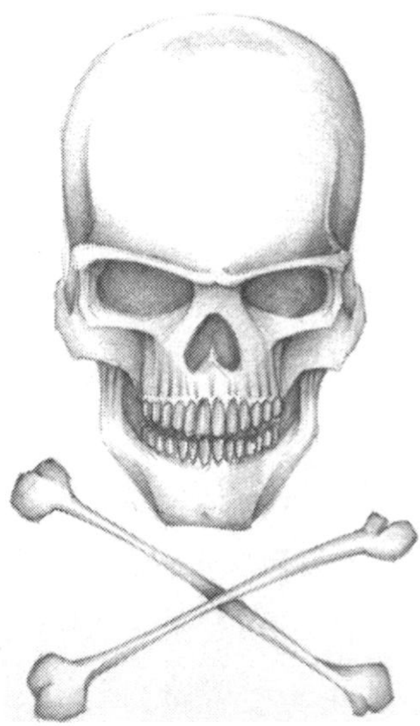

James saw a shadow move at the bottom of the gate, then a second and a third. He silently motioned in the direction of the movement, but neither Kilani nor Luno noticed the shadows.

"What is it?" whispered Luno.

James signaled for him to be quiet and did his best to silently indicate that people might be lurking on the other side of the gate. Behind them, William was still making a ruckus.

"Please tell him to shut the bloody hell up," he whispered to Kilani.

Kilani turned and walked back the way they had come. William was farther down the trail than Kilani had expected considering the racket he was making. She could hear his cursing as well as the trees and bushes rustling well before he came into sight.

Back at the gate, James and Luno had devised a plan. A large dry shell hung by a rope across the front of the gate, and they suspected it was a crude door knocker. Luno gripped it and struck the gate several times, signaling everyone else in the group to be silent as he did so. After a moment, a most peculiar voice called out from behind the gate. It was loud enough for all to hear yet hoarse and gasping like an old man who had spent a lifetime shouting. The eeriness of it sent chills through the group.

"Who goes there?" the voice hissed.

Luno and James exchanged uneasy looks before Luno turned to the gate and said, "My name is Luno of Harbor Town to the north. My companions and I come in peace. Our ship was damaged at sea, and we require supplies to get on our way. Will you kindly help us?" James could hear whispers behind the gate, almost like arguing.

Down the trail, Kilani rounded the bend to a distressing sight. William was now surrounded by no fewer than one hundred of the fist-sized insects. They flew about, continuing to avoid the swings of his blade with ease. One of the insects parted from the group when Kilani stepped into view and flew toward her. It stopped in front of her face and hovered in the air, studying her. For the first time, she had a close-up view of the insect. Its wings were semitransparent with black veins running through them in circular patterns. It was the body of the creature that Kilani found truly fascinating. It looked similar to that of a human, having both arms and legs, but the creature's body was armored with plates of black exoskeleton that exposed only a few patches of brown skin. Its face was also masked by the exoskeleton armor, and long golden hair flowed over its shoulders from beneath an armored helm. It had a long, narrow tail that flared out at the end like a paddle. From its belt hung two miniature blades. Kilani and the creature studied one another for some time.

At the gate, the group waited impatiently for a reply. Stepping to James's side, Peroc set eyes on the symbol for the first time. He immediately turned and cowered behind Roger, clearly frightened. Finally, the same eerie voice called out from behind the gate.

"Only one shall enter," it rasped.

"I don't have a good feeling about this at all," James whispered, looking at Luno.

"Nor I," Luno replied.

Luno glanced back at the others, realizing Kilani and William had not rejoined the group. He shot James a worried look. James nodded and hurried down the trail to see where Kilani and William had gone.

"I shall finish here, and we will be on our way shortly," Luno called after him. He turned back to the gate. "I'm afraid I will have to decline your offer."

William continued to swing at the creatures that swarmed around him. Soon his arms began to tire. He lowered his short sword. One of the winged creatures separated from the group and hovered in front of William's face. The two gazed at each other for several seconds, each equally mesmerized by the other. Then the creature struck.

A searing pain shot through William's eye and he let out a terrible cry, falling to his knees and clutching his blinded eye. His wail broke the trance that had its grip on Kilani and the creature in front of her. The creature zoomed back to the swarm, which now hovered in a tight formation above William. Before Kilani had taken two steps toward her fallen compatriot, the swarm was upon him. The screams were terrible — akin to those of Jan's sister when the searing moonbeams had struck her in their escape from the Severed Heart . Kilani froze, not sure what to do. Before she could decide, William fell silent and the swarm rapidly dispersed into the jungle. She took a deep breath and willed her legs to step to William's side. He lay face down and motionless on the sandy path. His body was riddled with small incisions, each of which wept blood.

Kilani rolled William onto his back and let out a gasp. Both his eyes were gone. Small cuts covered his face and neck. He was not breathing. Not moving. William was dead. She heard a noise behind her. She stood quickly and drew her dagger. James rounded the bend in the path. His eyes went from Kilani with her dagger drawn to William's supine body. He rushed to her side. "Are you all right?"

Kilani nodded and gestured to William. "They attacked him. They slaughtered him," she said, her voice getting fainter with each word. "They took his eyes."

"What are they?" asked James.

"I'm not sure. At first I thought they were insects, but now that I've really seen one, I don't know."

At that moment, Peroc came running down the trail, shouting in his native language.

"Luno is gone? What do you mean?" James asked. Before Peroc could explain, he saw William's body and shrieked.

"It was them, wasn't it?" he asked.

"Who?" asked James.

"The winged creatures. The tymanuk."

"Where is Luno?"

"He went inside. They took him."

Without another word, James ran back up the trail to the gate. There Jan and Roger were pulling at the large bamboo slats in an attempt to pry open the gate. When they saw James, both men stepped aside.

"Tertiri zé Manukto voriko," said James, extending his hands.

The gate rattled and shook violently but did not open. James tried another incantation, then a combination of incantations and finally threw a massive fireball at the gate, which left only charred residue on the bamboo. Frustrated and exhausted, James turned away in an attempt to calm himself. In front of him on the trail stood Kilani, Peroc at her side .

The cacophony of insects and birds had fallen silent. Roger cupped his hands to his mouth and shouted Luno's name several times. There was no response from the other side of the gate. "Where be tha' dun-souled buffoon?" Roger asked, finally noticing William's absence.

"He was attacked by those winged creatures," James said quietly, fighting back the lump in his throat and the tears in his eyes."He…he's dead."

"Dead?" Roger said, his jaw quivering slightly. "I don' understand. The half-masted fool was jus' 'ere."

"Did you not hear the screams?" Kilani asked.

"Screams?" Roger's jaw quivered again.

"It all happened so fast that even Kilani, who was but a few steps away, was unable to stop the attack. I'm sorry, my friend. From the moment I set foot on this island, it has not felt right. We need to retrieve Luno and be on our way as soon as possible – before more tragedy befalls us."

James turned back to the gate. The charred markings blew away like dust as a gust of wind coursed through the jungle. Leaves clattered as it passed then fell silent once more. James looked intently for some kind of weakness in the gate, the posts to which it was mounted perhaps. He stepped closer to one of the posts. Carved into the wood were the same symbols they had found on the stone columns on the First and Second Widows. This time, James knew what they said. He reached out and touched the carving. The moment his skin met the wood, he felt, once again that the island was connecting directly with his mind. Rather than information, he saw images. He saw a dark place — a tunnel. A vast maze of bamboo with stalks black as sackcloth. The last image was the inside of a castle, beautifully decorated with paintings, tapestries and sculptures. The walls and floors of the room in which he stood were…black.

He could hear voices shouting as if from a distance. Slowly they came into focus as did his sight, and he realized Kilani had pulled him away from the gatepost while the others were trying to rouse him.

"What happened?" she asked.

"I saw images, a tunnel, a maze and … a castle. I think I saw the inside of the black castle. It was…beautiful." James said, a faraway look in his eyes. After a moment, he shook his head in an attempt to clear his mind and got to his feet. He strode to the opposite post. There were symbols carved into this one also. This time, James decided not to touch the post but merely read the inscription.

"It says, 'Only those who are invited may enter.'" He quickly stepped up to the center of the gate, grasped the large shell that Luno had used as a knocker, and struck it against the gate. Once again he could see shadows moving behind the gate. Whispers rose like wisps of smoke from an early morning fire. James looked at Kilani, who stood beside him, listening. The whispering stopped. After several moments of silence, James turned and began walking down the trail.

Before he reached the bend, the strange voice called out from behind the gate.

"You may use our dock to make repairs. When they are complete, you must leave immediately," the voice hissed.

"What have you done with our friend?" James asked.

"Your accusatory tone is hurtful," the voice said. "Your friend entered willingly and shall stay until he is ready to leave."

"Will you give me your word that no harm will come to him?"

"I give my word to no man, especially not the likes of you," the voice rasped.

"We will not leave without him."

"You will do as you are told. Now be gone before injury befalls another member of your group."

Night was falling. Against James's instincts, which were telling him he must not leave Luno behind, he turned away from the gate and led the group back toward the beach. As James rounded the bend, he expected to see William's mutilated body but was surprised to find it neatly wrapped in fine white cloth and lying on a crude stretcher. Roger hurried to William's corpse, weeping. In disbelief, he pulled back the cloth covering the face. William's face was clean, his eyes covered with a strip of black cloth. After several moments, Roger pulled the white cloth back over William's face and stood. Jan was already positioned at the foot of the stretcher. Together he and Roger carried the body down the path.

"Who did that to William's body?" asked Kilani. "Where did the stretcher come from?"

"I don't know," replied James as they continued down the path. "The more time we spend here, the more uneasy I become. We must make haste."

"And Luno?"

"I don't know."

3

isolation and reunion

August 1896, The Isles of Scilly

James was alone. The constant pressure of his mother's expectations had finally become too much for him. He wanted a normal life. A home. Friends. He was tired of hiding. Tired of having to learn new skills every day. Tired of constantly having to be the person everyone expected him to be. Tired of carrying around the guilt of his father's death. Tired of listening to his mother cry herself to sleep every night.

James had left nearly three weeks ago, traveling to the small cluster of islands off the southwest coast of Great Britain that he and his father had visited years before. He had always been drawn to this place. It was small and quiet. There was a boys' school at the end of a lane. He thought he would like to go there. However, the reality of settling into a place like this at his age was proving more difficult than he had anticipated. Despite having sufficient funds to rent a place to stay, the prying questions of prospective landlords always sent him away. Although he had always been told that he looked older than his years, they were a nosy lot. "Where are your parents, lad?" he was usually asked.

Eventually, after over a dozen tries, James gave up on finding a legitimate place of residence. He discovered an abandoned cottage not far from the village and managed to make it habitable. The seclusion was not what he had had in mind. He would have preferred to stay in the village proper and become part of the community.

James decided to visit the school to see if he could enroll. On his walk down the cobbled lane, he met a group of laughing boys. They were smartly dressed in their green blazers and black trousers. Each clutched a small stack of books. Their laughter ceased as he approached.

The tallest boy looked at him with a dour expression and muttered under his breath. The other boys howled with delight. James clenched his fists in an attempt to repress the anger he could feel swelling inside him. "Something funny?" he asked .

"What did you say, boy?" said the tall lad.

"I want to know what you found so amusing," demanded James.

"Amusing, eh? Awfully big word for a prat your age, ain't it?" The others laughed.

"Simply because you haven't the wits to comprehend words with more than three letters doesn't give you the right to insult someone," said James. The boy, who stood as tall as James yet far broader, took a step forward.

"Say that again, you bilge-sucking prat."

James's heart raced. This was not how he had wanted things to go. He hadn't even made it to the school and already he'd found that he wasn't fit to be among his peers. He lowered his head and turned away.

"I thought so, you fatherless son of a whore."

James was on top of the large boy before he could react. Reason was replaced by rage. It was all a blur. James couldn't recall how he'd managed to get the upper hand on the boy. One minute, he was charging toward him and the next the boy lay motionless beneath him, his face bloodied and unrecognizable. The other boys in the group looked on in horror as James beat their leader into unconsciousness. He growled like an animal as he threw punch after punch, breaking bone and teeth.

Finally, James got hold of himself. He looked at his bloodied hands. His knuckles throbbed and surged with blood and energy. James dragged his gaze back to the boy's face and quickly stepped off him. He couldn't believe what he had done. He wouldn't believe it. More onlookers had gathered — all of them school students. James saw in their faces what they thought of him. They were terrified. He turned and ran and didn't stop running until he reached his cottage.

That night, he vowed never to harm another human. He was angry at his lack of self-control. He was afraid of what the future would bring. Mostly, James missed his mother. Her soothing voice, her comforting embrace. He cried himself to sleep.

Several weeks passed before he had the courage to come out during the day. James finally stepped out the front door of the cottage and into the overcast early autumn morning. The smell of rotting leaves from the nearby forest reminded him of the place where he and his father had been ambushed. Arenberg. Chills swept up and down his body as the memory of that place washed over him like an arctic wave.

As James walked slowly down the lane toward the village, he had an overwhelming feeling that he was being watched. He paused, scanning his surroundings. Forest to his left, rolling hills and farmland to his right, the village ahead and the sea beyond. He saw no sign of anyone. Strange. Most folks were up and about this time of day. The feeling remained as he continued down the road.

He tried to clear his mind, but as he reviewed the list of supplies he'd set out to collect, James spotted movement in his periphery. The majority of the multicolored leaves had fallen, giving him a clear view at least fifty feet into the forest before the trees grew too thick. He scanned the woods in search of anything out of the ordinary. Probably just a deer. James turned and saw a figure walking toward him with a beast in tow. He felt a sense of relief to see another person.

As the figure drew nearer, he realized it was an elderly woman. She crept closer, leading her heavily laden donkey, hunched under the weight of her own back like a goose scanning the water for its next meal. As he drew abreast of the woman, James greeted her cheerfully. He'd decided he needed to be overly friendly to the townsfolk in an effort to fit in regardless of whatever mood he was in at the time. She looked up at him and grinned a toothless smile that reminded him of a snarling dog protecting its dinner. A show of teeth to say, "Stay away or you'll get a feel of these." In the old lady's case, the gums were simply insulting, and James was taken aback.

Disheartened, he walked on, dragging his feet. He turned back to take another look at the old woman, but she was gone. He was immediately on high alert. There was nowhere the woman could have gone. The road stretched for several miles before it turned out of sight and even a horse at full gallop wouldn't have been able to cover that distance in such a short time.

James was unsure of his next move. He could run for cover in the forest, yet simply looking that direction gave him a bad feeling. He could go back to his cottage but felt as though he would be trapped there. He was always sure to have a supply of transporting powder with him, and today was no exception. In his pocket, he sifted the grains between his fingers, waiting for a sign that he should leave. All was still. After several minutes, he decided to continue to the village. If someone were after him, they'd be less likely to attack among the unfaithful.

He jogged down the road, not seeing another person. As he reached the crest of the hill where the road sloped down into the village, he noticed the fog was unusually thick. It had rolled in from the sea during in the night and completely engulfed the coastline. James could barely make out the school, which was perched on the hillside less than a mile from where he stood. It was eerie — all of it. The sense of being watched, the woman, the fog, and the fact that he had yet to see anyone other than the disappearing hag. Usually by now the harbor was speckled with fishing boats, and the farmers were out tending their fields. Today it was as if everyone had decided to stay in bed.

James stopped at the main crossroads in the village. To his right was the road to the school. He thought of the incident with the boy. Part of him believed he had deserved the beating. Another part of him was terrified by what he had done — and without the use of magic. Once again, he had allowed himself to lose control and, as a result, hurt someone. He reminded himself of what his teacher Mr. Ammoncourt had told him after the death of his father. It was something he remembered to the word. "James, you must control your emotions or they will control you. It is up to you to decide whether you are the master of your own self."

James took one last look behind him hoping to spot the old lady, but saw only empty road. He took a resolute breath and plunged into the fog.

As soon as he breached the mist, he was chilled to the bone. He knew there were buildings ahead, but couldn't make out much more than his own feet beneath him. James heard nothing as he continued cautiously down the road. No sounds of people scurrying about. No activity on the wharf below. Not even sea birds calling as they waited to follow the fishing boats on their journeys. It reminded him of the silence after a heavy snowfall. He shuddered, not sure if it was from the cold or his anxiety.

Finally, he reached the building-lined square. A sound grew from the silence as he cautiously headed toward the center of the square. When the rim of the fountain came into view, he knew the sound was coming from inside. As he stepped to the edge and peered in, James saw that the water was churning and bubbling. The small fish that once swam inside were floating on top of the scalding water, and he could feel the steam on his face.

"A fair bit of magic if I do say so myself."

James spun toward the voice, his hand already withdrawn from the pouch containing his transport powder, the granules pressed between his fingers. Akil Karanis stood a few paces away, a kindly smile on his face.

"You did all this?" James asked.

"Indeed."

"How? How long have you known I've been here?"

"You have spoken of this place on several occasions, which put it near the top of my list of suspect refuges."

James tried to remember mentioning this place to Akil. He remembered Akil asking about his father but couldn't remember specifically naming this place.

"All who desire some sort of normalcy in their lives will return to a place in which they find comfort when they are pushed too far. It is quite a normal reaction. Even though your previous stay here was brief, you associated that time with what you envision to be a normal life."

"My mother sent you then?"

"Your mother came to me when you left. I told her I would do my best to find you and convince you to return."

"She doesn't know where I am?"

"No, she does not."

"How long have you been here?"

"One day less than you."

"So you know about the…incident?"

"I am aware of your altercation with the boy, yes."

"Do you know if…if he is all right?"

"Are you asking me if he lives?"

The thought that his hands might have taken a life terrified James. Since the day of the confrontation he'd longed to know, yet he was petrified that he would discover he had killed the boy.

"He will survive," said Akil. "But his injuries are extensive and without my intervention will take months to heal."

"Will you help him?" asked James.

"Perhaps," said Akil. "First I must know that you understand both men and boys must live with the consequences of their actions."

"I understand, Master. I deserve to be punished. What I did was wrong," said James. He hesitated for a moment, contemplating what would happen to him next. "I don't want to go back to my old life," he said sheepishly.

"Most would not. It is not an easy life. You live under the shadow of an expectation so great that any normal man would break into pieces under the pressure. I am afraid I am to blame for that."

"You? What have you got to do with it?"

"Long ago, I decided to go looking for the person prophesied in our lore. My search led me to conclusions never before reached. I was the first to have specific details about this person. After many trials, those details enabled me to locate you. Everything, every single detail I have uncovered directly relating to the Anointed One, points to you. You have not been chosen. You simply are that person. Whether or not you want to be that person is irrelevant, I am afraid."

"But my mother said if I didn't keep training and studying, I wouldn't become who I needed to be."

"You have made great strides and gained the attention of many powerful sorcerers because of your abilities. Your mother is afraid for you. She believes if you do not continue to advance, you will fall victim to powerful and influential men who seek to use you for their own benefit. In the end, what you decide today has no bearing on the man you will become."

"You've come to tell me this? To tell me that I don't have to return?" James asked.

"James, for far too long you have been given no choice about the direction of your own life. You have grown to resent the expectations placed upon you. A man with a permanent axe to grind can be dangerous and unpredictable. So I am here to offer you a choice for the first time in your life."

"You mean I can decide if I want to go home with you or stay here?" asked James.

"That is the choice I am offering," said Akil. "Many men have felt the burden of responsibility and have not been able to bear its weight. There is little shame in that."

But James did feel shame. He also felt a twinge of anger, and he was certain that was Akil's intent all along. It wasn't as if he feared responsibility; he simply had allowed himself to become worn down. James was tired. Tired of running. Tired of hiding. Tired of being told what to do and where to go. He wanted something, anything, normal and consistent in his life.

As if reading his mind, Akil said, "No great accomplishment comes without great sacrifice. Your father knew this. Your mother knows this, which is why she agreed to let you go."

"What do you mean?" asked James.

"Your mother has agreed to accept the outcome of our conversation," said Akil, sitting on the rim of the fountain, which had stopped boiling. "Before you make your decision, I shall offer you yet another choice. Should you decide to return to the life fate has chosen for you, I will give you what you so vehemently desire to the best of my ability."

"What?" James asked.

"Consistency, regularity, normalcy."

"How could you give me that?"

"I would take you as my apprentice," said Akil. "Know this, James. Nothing lasts forever. Even the comforts of home and family must end as a boy sets out on his own to become a man. I can only offer you these things for a time. Working with me will be hard. Harder than anything you have ever done. Not only physically, mind you, but emotionally as well. It is not an easy path. You would study with me until you are ready."

"Ready for what?"

"I think you already know the answer to that," said Akil.

James did know. His mind was a web of confusion. He couldn't believe, on the one hand, that he could choose to stay here, away from everything. Everything including his mother, he thought with a pang of guilt. On the other hand, he could train with Akil, one of the greatest sorcerers alive. They would be together. He wouldn't be switching from instructor to instructor every time his mother felt they weren't safe and had to relocate.

"Before you make your final decision, know this, James. You will be found. Alvaro wants you more than anything else in the world. Despite your discretion, it would take little time before word of your whereabouts would reach him. He would come for you, and you would live on his terms rather than your own. If he should allow you to live at all, that is. In the end, my boy, nobody can escape their destiny no matter how far they run."

James knew what Akil was trying to say. When he had arrived in the village, he had believed he could live a normal life, free of all the pressures he'd left behind. It had taken Akil only one day to find him. It wouldn't take Alvaro much longer…and then what? Run? Fight? Submit? Die? He'd be living the same life he had wanted so desperately to escape, and he'd be living it alone rather than surrounded by the ones he loved.

James hung his head when he realized how foolish he'd been. Akil stood. The fog lifted and the fish in the fountain began to wriggle back to life. People started to come out of their homes and go about their business. As James looked around, he realized how much power was required to cast such an incantation. In the recesses of his mind, he realized he too wanted to be able to wield a power that great. The corner of Akil's mouth twitched upward knowingly.

"May I say goodbye to my mother before we leave?" asked James.

"Naturally," said Akil. "You will need some of your possessions before we set off. First, I believe we must attend to an injured child."

James and Akil made their way back up the hill toward a cluster of houses. Inside one of those houses lived the boy James had beaten. He was there, surrounded by family all living out their lives completely oblivious to what was coming. James realized, as he looked out over the sea, that the days of his childhood had drawn to a close.

4

missing and mystery

Realizing his intense thirst for the first time since they'd come ashore, James summoned water from the jungle and provided some to each member of the group. He sent Peroc and Jan to find firewood while he and Kilani returned to the Queen Mary for the supplies they would need for the night. As they walked down the pier, Kilani was silent.

"Do you believe Luno went willingly into that place?" James asked.

"Do you?"

"I don't want to believe it, but part of me does," said James.

"Luno hid many things deep inside himself. It would not surprise me if he knew more than he was letting on. I suspect he sent you away to help William so he could go inside," said Kilani. "He knew you would protest had you been there."

"Do you have any idea who dwells beyond the gate?" asked James.

"No. I'm not sure Luno did either. Finding natives is one thing. Finding English-speaking folk protected by the power of the island is something different. The latter is much more … concerning."

"Agreed," said James.

They stepped onto the boat to retrieve the supplies. James paused as he moved the wooden crate containing Luno's map collection out of his way. He unfurled several scrolls until he found the map of the island known as The Resting Man. James noticed that Luno had drawn in the dock with a piece of charcoal before they had disembarked. Otherwise, there was little detail on the map. He rolled it back up and placed it next to a scroll labeled Ammoncourt Map.

Together he and Kilani carried the gear to the beach where Roger was sitting watch over William's body. Peroc and Jan had returned empty-handed. As they drew closer, Peroc ran to meet them.

"This place is undying. It is a land of death that does not die," said Peroc in his native tongue.

"Explain," said James.

"On our walk into the jungle, did you not notice the ground?"

"What of it?"

"Not one fallen leaf litters the jungle floor. Not one fallen branch."

James took several steps into the jungle and immediately understood. Typically covered with several inches of deadfall, the ground lay bare and exposed. Strange indeed.

"What is it?" Kilani asked.

"There is no firewood to be found. No fallen branches anywhere."

"We have no choice but to bring down a living tree," said James, stepping away from the group and raising his hands toward a towering tree. "Tertiri Zé Manukto suomi."

The tree began to shake violently. James thought he saw a dark shadow jump quickly from the upper branches into another tree as he lifted it — roots and all — from the ground and brought it to rest on the beach. Jan and Peroc went to work with hatchets. Despite his urge to get the fire going as quickly as possible, James allowed them to continue to chop rather than using his powers in hopes that the exertion would relieve some of their tension.

The next order of business was to bury William's body. James and Roger found a spot at the edge of the jungle overlooking the harbor. James extended his hands, recited an incantation, and lifted the soil from the ground, making a neat grave. He allowed Roger to tend to the burial while he cast several protective spells around the encampment. Again, James thought he spotted movement in the upper branches of the trees bordering the beach. By the time he was able to focus on the spot, whatever it was had disappeared.

James felt a distinct unease as the sun fell behind the horizon. The roaring fire gave the crew little comfort after the day's events, so he decided to set light orbs around the perimeter to make it easier to spot approaching enemies. James assigned watch shifts and tried to rest. However, the palpable nervousness made relaxation and sleep nearly impossible. In the end, everyone sat close to the fire and waited for the sun to rise.

Eventually, the others fell into restless sleep, save Kilani. She crouched in the sand beside the fire staring into the flames, lost in her own thoughts. James sat apart, brooding over being thrust into the leadership role, battling the anger he felt toward Luno. It was a role he was not ready to assume, but because of his abilities, the others looked to him as the next in line to lead. But already under his watch a man had lost his life.

Another, more determined thought worked its way into James's mind.

The images he'd seen when he touched the gatepost. Throughout the night they'd crept into the forefront of his consciousness, and throughout the night he'd fought to push them away, determined to focus on the present.

Movement out of the corner of his eye drew his attention. He turned his head and saw a most unexpected thing. A boy, no older than twelve, walked along the tree trunk James had felled. The boy wore rags and his skin was filthy. His sandy blond hair stuck out in all directions, and he wore a playful smile on his face. In his belt was a black sword. The boy maneuvered atop the trunk with his arms extended for balance as if his presence were perfectly ordinary. He did not look over at the fire or at any of the people huddled around it. A crash on the deck of the Queen Mary diverted James's attention from the boy. When James looked back at the fallen tree, the boy was gone.

The noise from the Queen Mary brought Kilani immediately to her feet. She ran to the dock. James followed.

"What was that?" she asked as James approached.

"It sounded like something falling onto the deck."

"This place is cursed. We should leave at first light."

"And what of Luno?"

"He's made his choice."

"Will you stay here and keep watch over the others," James asked, "while I go take a look at the ship?" Kilani nodded and headed back to the fire.

James walked down the dock, casting several light orbs along the way. As he stepped onto the deck, it became immediately apparent what had made the noise. The small wooden crate that held Luno's map collection was broken into pieces. The maps were gone. James searched the deck and then below deck to be sure someone hadn't moved them before they settled into camp. The maps were nowhere to be found.

James had managed to convince himself that the boy was simply a waking dream, but now he was not so sure. Perhaps he had been a diversion so someone else could get the maps. But who? Why?

James returned and told Kilani what he had found. She offered no opinion and they discussed it no further. The others began to stir as the eastern horizon brightened with the coming dawn. James took a deep breath and allowed the vision to manifest in his mind's eye. The gatepost, the tunnel, the maze, and the black castle. What did these things have in common? The more he thought about the castle, the more he yearned for it. He needed to find out what it all meant. Could these images hint at a path into the castle? The one way to find out was to get through that bamboo gate. He would try again today. There must be a way inside and he was bent on finding it. The cool steel of the key pressed tightly against his palm as a constant reminder of his goal.

Peroc prepared some smoked meat while the others took note of the repairs that needed to be made to the Queen Mary. She would need a new mast, bowsprit and sail, along with a new section of railing and some planks on port-side aft. The wood could easily be hewn from any tree with James's powers but the sail, small pieces of animal hide sewn together, would be much more difficult to procure. Even if James transported back to Harbor Town, he would be hard-pressed to find enough suitable material to make a sail large enough for the Queen Mary.

While they ate, the group discussed options. Roger suggested letting James power the boat without a sail. James quickly dismissed this idea, reminding him that during the storm he had struggled to perform even simple incantations. He didn't want to rely completely upon his powers — he wasn't confident they would always be available. They discussed several more ideas, each less likely to work than the previous. Finally, they decided to start working on removing the damaged timbers and revisit the sail problem later in the day. James assigned himself the task of retrieving a piece of lumber for the mast.

He set out down the trail, looking for a tree tall and straight. Before he knew it, he had reached the bend before the gate. He saw several of the tymanuk responsible for killing William perched on a branch. James sent a burst of energy from his hands toward the creatures, knocking them from the branch. All but one managed to take to the air and escape into the upper canopy.

James approached the lone creature lying on the edge of the sandy path. He stooped to have a closer look. James could see that the creature was still breathing from the movement of its exoskeleton chest armor. Long red hair streaked with white flowed behind its armored mask. James scooped it up in his hands and lifted it still closer.

James's fear of these creatures immediately disappeared when he was able to see one up close. It was beautiful. Its translucent wings shimmered with a rainbow of colors. James let the creature slide into one hand and held his other over top of it.

"Tertiri Zé Manukto tupasarri."

James felt the energy leave his palm as he directed it to the tiny body. The creature slowly lifted its head. After a moment it rose to its feet. When it realized where it was standing, in the palm of James's hand, it leapt into the air and flew into the upper branches of a nearby tree where the others in its group were waiting. The small group watched as James continued down the path. James noticed their posture had changed from defensive to curious.

James rounded the bend and once again stood before the gate. He saw the same group of creatures fly over the gate and into the place he believed held the answers he sought. The red skull and crossbones remained, looking brighter, as if recently repainted in scarlet ink.

James stepped toward the rightmost post — the one he had touched the previous day — and reached out his hand, his desire to see the images again drawing him closer. As his fingertips reached the wood, he was thrown backward. His feet left the ground and he landed hard on the path. Brushing his dark hair out of his face, he stepped up to the gate once again.

After inspecting the symbols on both posts, he stepped in front of the leftmost post, which he had not touched the previous day. Slowly, cautiously, he extended his hand. Rather than throw him away, a force drew his hand closer. As soon as his hand made contact with the wood, his vision went black. James could only feel. He felt great sorrow, followed by trepidation and then triumph and joy. James smiled as the happiness spread through his body. The feeling of joy quickly turned to rage — a rage like he'd never felt before. Despair soon followed and lingered longest. Then, nothing. He could neither feel nor hear nor see. It was as if he no longer existed at all.

A jolt of energy brought him back to the present, and he was once again sailing through the air, repelled by the post. He struck the ground, landing on a root that breached the earth like the knuckle of a great hand. A wave of pain coursed through his back. He was slower to get up this time, and as he approached the gate, he thought he heard, of all things, laughter. He froze, listening, but all had fallen silent save the rustling of the leaves and the scraping of the door knocker shell against the gate set in motion by a light breeze. James reached for the shell.

"What are you doing?" James turned and saw Kilani behind him. She did not look happy. "Are you planning on abandoning us as well?"

"I believe the answers lie inside here," said James.

"What answers?"

"The answers to everything," James said, his voice growing louder. "How to find Luno, how to reach the castle, how to finally get out of this place."

"What makes you think the answers lie here?"

"The images I saw earlier, they are the way inside the castle. I know it. I think the places I saw — the maze and the tunnel — are beyond the gate."

"It doesn't concern you at all that even your powers aren't strong enough to break through the gate? If you can't even gain access to this place, what makes you think you'll be able to handle whatever is inside?"

"Why are you afraid? You, who want to leave this place more than anyone?"

"This place is cursed. That castle is cursed. I believe we will find only suffering in either. We've been here for less than a day and have already lost one of our own. And Luno has abandoned us. We should leave immediately and never return."

"Luno did not abandon us. If I know him, he's probably in there trying to get to the castle himself or negotiating with whoever dwells inside," said James.

"Do you know Luno? Do you truly know him? I don't, and I've been with him much longer than you have."

"All of us have parts of our past we'd rather not share, Kilani. That doesn't make him a deceiver. He's always acted with our best interests in mind."

"And whose best interests are you acting in? Seeing that castle again appears to have poisoned your mind. All your will is bent on getting into it."

"If that is the road that leads us home, isn't that for the good of us all?" James asked. "Luno has spent a lifetime seeking a way out of this place, and he believes that way lies inside the black castle. I believe the way into the black castle lies inside this gate. Think of it, Kilani. A way home."

"That's all I've thought about since I've gotten here. That's all I ever think about. If a feeling is so strong that it convinces me to abandon the only suspected way out of this place, perhaps you should consider not rushing into the unknown."

"I must go inside. I know that now. If you do not wish to join me, return to camp. Roger is more than capable of sailing the Queen Mary once she is repaired. He will take you back to Harbor Town. Perhaps I will enter and find nothing, in which case I will join you on the beach. If I do find something, I promise you this: I will find you and I will take you with me. We will go home together."

James stepped toward Kilani. As he did so, he heard a creaking behind him. Kilani's eyes widened as she looked over James's shoulder. He turned. The gate had opened. It was open only wide enough for one person to pass through. Beyond the opening thick foliage blocked further view.

"I must go," James said. He leaned closer to Kilani, but she backed away, never taking her eyes off the gate.

"I hope you find what you are looking for in there, I truly do," she said. Without another word, she turned and walked away.

5

moving on

September 1896, Corsica

Margaret sat waiting impatiently. Akil had told her that James was coming to see her. He was coming to say goodbye. He would go with Akil and learn from him. She trusted Akil implicitly with her son, and it had become clear that she couldn't protect him any longer. He had to learn how to protect himself.

James had run away out of fear — fear of confronting his destiny. Margaret knew that running from destiny was futile. It had a habit of finding you. It hadn't taken Akil more than a few days to locate James. Akil had told Margaret about the confrontation with the schoolboy. James was an angry child and she feared for him.

Margaret had insisted that Akil not strong-arm James into returning.

She wanted him to make his own decision. Whatever decision that was, she would accept it. She had been holding on so tightly since her husband's death, she was afraid she would never be able to let him go. It took him running away to make her realize the time had come. She must let go and have faith that everything she had done for him would help him flourish. She hoped one day he would understand that it was all for his own good — and that it was all done out of love. Margaret believed no one could escape destiny, as had her husband. For this reason, they were determined to impart as much knowledge and skill to James as they possibly could before his destiny came calling. It hadn't come yet, but Margaret knew the time was near.

Margaret could hear the clopping of hooves on the cobbled lane on the far side of the house. She sat in the garden sipping her tea. It was an aromatic mixture of dried peach and black Chinese, which soothed her mind and body as she inhaled the steam. The cup warmed her hands on this unusually crisp autumn morning. The flowering Mediterranean garden surrounding her brought Margaret back to a time when, if she had a good book on her lap, she would have been utterly relaxed and at peace. Times were much different now and although the garden soothed her, the business at hand would not be easy. She had lost her husband. Now she was about to say goodbye to her only son. She mustered all her strength — it would be only moments before James rounded the corner of the house.

Margaret sat up straight, trying to look relaxed yet proper. She had never been so nervous to see her boy before. The last time she had been this nervous was the day she and her husband had married. Not their traditional wedding, which had taken place years before, but the wedding celebrated by two lovers from the magical world to seal their unity.

Most of that day was a blur. Only two other people had been there,

James, who was but a child, and the officiant. She couldn't remember the incantations he'd cast that day nor could she remember what she or Stuart had worn. She could recall being nervous before the ceremony — petrified, actually. In the world of the believers, a new world to her, she knew that there was a match for everyone — only one match. If you weren't with your match, the incantations would fail and the ceremony would not continue. Part of her was confident that Stuart was indeed her match. Part of her was afraid of what would happen if he were not. Still another part, buried deep down where not even Stuart had reconnoitered, questioned whether she could love at all, whether she deserved to be loved. Then it happened. In a swirl of silver smoke, the bond was created and she could feel her husband — truly feel his heart, his love for her. The smoke connected their bodies like a web between branches. Her nervousness abated and she knew he was the one. Despite the hardships during their early years, the new sense of togetherness they had found — a product of the life-altering news about their son — rekindled a love between them that had been covered by the dust of time. They forgave the past and forged a stronger relationship as a result of that forgiveness. Through their acceptance of each other, they had rediscovered the love of their younger years.

Everything save the love between them had melted away in that moment. All the pressures that had come into their lives were gone in an instant. There was a white flash and the smoke disappeared. They were asked to close their eyes. Margaret could feel her husband still. She knew he was there, still part of her. The officiant declared that as long as they both lived, they would always be able to feel each other, regardless of physical distance. Only death would sever the connection.

Now, sitting on the weather-worn wooden chair, Margaret felt as though she were about to sever another connection. Resolute that she would be strong, she took another sip of her tea as James walked along the bricked path that wove between the grenadier dahlias and the achillee. He did not smile as he approached, and she immediately feared he was angry with her. She placed her cup on the table and stood. The blanket that was draped over her shoulders slid onto the chair.

James hung his head, not meeting her eyes. He was tall now, nearly as tall as she. His shoulders were broad, and Margaret could see the beginnings of whiskers on his cheeks. He looked older. Could that happen in one month's time? Perhaps she had not been paying attention as her son grew into a young man — too busy protecting him to see what he had become. The thought saddened her. She reached over and lifted his chin until he met her gaze. She gave him a warm smile.

"I'm sorry, Mother," he said quietly.

"James, you have nothing to be sorry about. I should be the one apologizing. I've finally realized the time has come. You will learn more about yourself in the coming months than I could teach you in years. I am proud of you, my son, and I always will be. When you are ready to return, I will be here for you. Until then, make the most of this opportunity. It has been offered to very few."

"I will do well, Mother. I will honor you, and I will honor Father."

They embraced. Margaret held her son for the last time as a boy. James kissed her on the cheek and turned away, walking quickly down the path, not wanting his mother to see his tears, his weakness. Margaret let her tears come.

James fought off the tightening in his throat. He fought hard to suppress what easily could have been tears of loss and sorrow had he still been a boy. He wiped the corners of his eyes before rounding the corner of the house. Akil stood beside his horse, waiting to begin their journey together.

Akil had insisted that they travel by horseback rather than transporting to their destination. He spoke of missing the benefits of being immersed in one's surroundings when transporting from place to place, but to a fourteen-year-old, anything other than the fastest way from one place to another made little sense. Save the rather precarious boat ride across the Ligurian Sea, they traveled north solely on horseback for eight days. The bone-chilling rain had started not long after they departed and had not stopped. After several hours, James recalled the weather incantation his father had taught him. He glared at Akil for not reminding him to use it, and noticed that his mentor appeared content to let the rain soak him though. Several times James looked over and saw Akil shivering but said nothing.

On the ninth day, they arrived in Cherbourg where they crossed the Channel to Portsmouth. Another seven days saw them to Edinburgh. The rain dissipated as they reached the outskirts of the city and was replaced by dense fog. Akil led James through the city to a small building not far from the train station. Inside they met two men, broad in shoulder and plug-ugly, along with a woman. The woman had seen many turns, yet maintained the beauty of her younger years. James and Akil followed the trio as they made their way into a small room at the back of the building and descended a narrow set of stairs. A lone portrait hung on the wall above the railing. In it, a young girl and boy stood side by side, both grinning.

The stairway opened into a sitting room packed full of musical instruments. A large piano, which would have never fit through the door let alone down the stairs, stood in the center of the room. The woman walked to the fire and stood with her back to her guests. She turned slowly, her kind countenance marred by worry as her eyes washed over James.

"I suppose, Akil, that this is the boy?" she asked, motioning to James.

"Indeed."

"I will ask that you excuse us then. My sons will accompany you upstairs until I have need for you."

"Of course, Alene," said Akil with a slight bow. As the trio retreated up the steps, James wondered who this woman was and why Akil had left him alone with her.

"I'm not sure what he's told you, boy," she said, looking at James, "so allow me to enlighten you. I have a gift, but it isn't a gift that I can share with others. I myself am not sure how it works. I simply know that every time Akil brings someone by, he's led that person to believe he is the Anointed One. I have the unenviable job of telling them they've been misinformed. That's how it works."

"But the Seer said..."

"You've been to the Seer then? Well, that makes you a rarer breed but not entirely unique. Of all the 'Anointed Ones' I've seen, only two have been to the Seer. One of them turned out the same as all the others. The other...well, we don't speak of him."

James couldn't believe what he was hearing. He had spent the last nine years of his life being told that he was without doubt or question the Anointed One. Akil had never mentioned any others he'd suspected, and he had certainly never mentioned having any doubt about James. Yet here he stood, before what appeared to be another Seer.

"Let us begin so I can go about my day. This won't take long at all," she said, ignoring James's look of confusion. She took James by the hand and led him to a large cushioned chair. She placed her hands on his shoulders and sat him down while stooping to his eye level. "What's your name, boy?"

"James."

"A good name, James. A strong name. I'm going to ask you some questions, and I want you to answer them as best you can." James nodded, glancing nervously at the staircase, wishing Akil would return. Alene rubbed her hands together, blew in them, and then opened them as if offering a gift. Droplets of purple liquid wept from her palms and gathered into a pool. The liquid trembled, then began to rise and take shape. A chess piece, a bishop, shimmered in the firelight.

"What shape do you see, James?" Alene asked.

"Where?" James asked, confused.

"In my hands, what shape do you see?"

"I see nothing in your hands."

She smiled at James nervously, allowing the purple liquid to fall to the floor. She began rubbing her hands together again. She opened them, palms up, and cupped them together in front of James.

"Describe what you see," she said.

"I see your hands. They look as if they're holding something that isn't there," said James.

"Very good. Now, watch closely and tell me what you see. Look right into my hands."

Once again dark violet droplets gathered on her palms and slowly rolled to the low point where her hands met until a small puddle formed. James remained silent. Again the liquid shuddered and rose up from her palms, this time in an arch. Alene said nothing, but looked deep into James's eyes as he concentrated on her palms.

"What do you see?"

"I see only your hands," said James. Again Alene let the liquid splash to the floor and began rubbing her hands together.

"What does that mean?" James asked.

"It means nothing," Alene replied, but the conviction in her voice was gone. "How old are you?"

"Fourteen," replied James.

"What is your mother's name?"

"Margaret."

The woman opened her hands once more. This time a white fog slowly rose from her palms and began to swirl around James's head. He looked straight through it, closely watching the eyes of the woman.

"Describe your mother for me," she said.

In a very tired voice, James began to describe his mother. His words became slow and labored until he fell completely silent.

"He is all right, I've done him no harm," said the woman, looking over her shoulder at Akil, who was now standing at the bottom of the stairs. "I have put his mind at rest and will now speak with his inner spirit. This is my gift, as you well know." The fog continued to swirl around James's head as the woman looked deep into his vacant eyes.

"Tell me your true name," she said in a slow, almost musical, rhythm. James was silent for several moments. Finally, a deep, strange voice that did not belong to him replied. It said one word.

"Haravik."

Alene started at the sound and looked up at Akil. She quickly returned her attention to James.

"Tell me your purpose."

Once again, James replied in a voice like the creaking of a door untrue on its hinges. None of the words he spoke were familiar.

"Ue nöla suopelon ve norante."

"What did he say? What language is that?" the woman asked. Akil ignored her, focusing intently on James. She put a hand on each side of his head and closed her eyes. A deep sound rippled the fog that surrounded James's head, like a bow sounding the lowest note on a bass viol. Again and again it sounded, sending ripples through the mist like pebbles dropping into a pond.

Without warning, the woman was thrown backward onto the floor. The mist immediately dissipated and James's vacant demeanor with it. He stood quickly when he noticed the woman lying on the floor and offered her a hand, which she refused. Slowly, she got to her feet and walked to the fire where she stood silently for several moments. James looked to Akil, searching his face for a hint of understanding. Akil returned his gaze, revealing nothing.

"What happened?" James asked. Finally, the woman turned and faced her guests.

"Please leave," she said, looking at James.

"Why are you upset?" James asked anxiously. "I'm entitled to answers." James turned to Akil who remained silent with a faraway look in his eyes.

"You are entitled to nothing, Mr. Stuart. Be comforted by the fact that you haven't been living another one of Akil's lies, for that is the only comfort you will find in what I have to say. As for the rest, I shall not speak of it in the presence of a child regardless of his destiny."

"James, step outside," said Akil. About to object, James saw by the look on his mentor's face he had no chance of convincing him otherwise. He turned and climbed the rickety steps, closing the door behind him. He stepped past the woman's sons and out the front door. It had begun to rain.

"Iraitzi ur," James said, using the incantation to keep himself dry. Movement at the end of the narrow alley caught his attention. James watched as the person drew closer. After a moment, James realized it was a girl not much older than he. She smiled, peeking out from the side of a stack of discarded wooden crates. He returned her smile, feeling immediately drawn to her.

"What's your name, boy?"

"James. What's yours?"

"Cypress."

"Do you live here?"

"Aye."

"So you're her daughter?"

"Aye. Tell me James, do you believe in magic?"

"Don't you?"

"I see things. Things I can't explain. Mother has visitors that do things that other people cannot do. I ask her about these things, and she always tells me I'm being nosy and should mind my own business. I notice people, different people that everyone else seems to ignore. I even had a brother once. He was close to my age. Mother showed him all sorts of magic…then he was taken away. Now, Mother insists that there is no such thing as magic and to believe otherwise is childish."

Alene's reasons for keeping a thing of such magnitude from her daughter meant little to James, for an opportunity to impress someone — especially a pretty young girl — should never be taken for granted.

"It is real," said James. "You see it or don't see it because you believe or don't believe. He looked over his shoulder at the doorway and then turned back and cupped his hands together. "Biztu ," he said quietly. He opened his hands, revealing a small flickering flame between them. Cypress stepped closer. Wonder and joy lit up her face as she reached for the flame. She recoiled slightly from the heat of the flame and smiled at her foolishness.

"I want to learn," she said.

"I wish I could teach you," said James, "but we aren't from around here."

"Neither are we," she said sadly, "but my mother says we can't return to London. She refuses to say why. Will you visit me someday, James?"

The door creaked open and Akil stepped out into the rain. James nodded at Cypress as he brought his hands together, extinguishing the flame. She smiled and quickly ran past Akil and through the door, closing it behind her. Akil appeared to have aged considerably since their arrival less than an hour earlier. Akil put his arm around James in a rare display of affection and gave him a weak smile.

"Are you quite well, Master?" James asked. Akil did not reply but squeezed his apprentice's shoulder a bit tighter. "Do you think we could return here sometime?"

"No, I don't think that would be a good idea. Our business is done and it is time to move on." The door opened and Alene's two sons stepped out into the rain. Akil nodded to them. "They shall escort us to our next destination."

"Where do we go from here?" asked James.

"Not far."

The four men made there way down the alley and onto the main street. It had grown busy since their arrival, and James felt out of place among the well-dressed official-looking men scurrying about, but they took no notice of the travelers as they continued down the cobbled street. The group turned up a sweeping marble staircase and into the largest and busiest building on the block.

The cavernous lobby echoed with the footfalls of people moving hither and thither as the foursome continued upward. The third floor consisted of nothing more than a long hallway. Both floors and walls were bright white marble. A single wooden door stood closed, recessed in the marble wall at the far end of the corridor. Akil fished a large black steel key from his pocket and unlocked the door. The two men had taken up positions on either side the entrance and appeared to James that they had no intention of coming inside. Akil extended his arm, inviting James to push open the door and continue inside.

Rather than finding himself inside a place of business, James stood in a stunning conservatory. Any urge James had to question Akil about the events of earlier in the day faded away. He was completely engrossed in his surroundings. The walls were lined with tropical trees and vines, which stretched several stories up. Nestled in the crooks and crevices of the trees were orchids of stunning color and fragrance. In the center of the conservatory was a perfect rectangle of grass bordered by flowers of every color James could imagine. Grazing within this perfect rectangle were two horses. He recognized Archos, once his father's.

Stone columns wrapped in purple, blue and white flowering vines stretched overhead, supporting the frame for the glass ceiling. Upon closer inspection, James realized shelves had been sculpted into the columns and each shelf was stuffed with books, books from floor to ceiling.

Akil took a deep breath and smiled. James hurried to keep up as Akil strode along a stone path, letting his extended hand brush along the low-growing flowers as he went. The path twisted around a group of pink flowering shrubs to reveal a wrought iron table and three cushioned chairs. Akil sat heavily in one of the chairs and let out a sigh. James remained standing, taking in his surroundings. The glassed walls were fogged over, preventing James from seeing what was on the outside. Scores of hummingbirds made their way from flower to flower. Not far away, James could hear the trickle of water. "Is this place real?" he asked.

"You are standing in it, are you not?" replied Akil.

"I should ask, 'How is this place real?'"

"In our world there are doorways that simply lead into adjoining rooms. Others lead to rooms adjoined by incantations. With the proper incantation on either side of a doorway, one can create a connection between two destinations. There are limitations, of course — we are all bound by the seven laws, but some of us are more creative than others," Akil smiled.

"You made this?"

"I did. It is one of my finest creations."

"Where is it? I mean, where is this building? We aren't in Edinburgh."

"You are correct. We are in western France. I came into ownership of this place long ago and have been working on perfecting my indoor Eden ever since. Using the Crystal Palace constructed for the Great Exhibition of 1851 as my inspiration…and adding some of my own personal touches over the years. I collect exotic plant species during my travels and bring them here. I am particularly proud of my Tyrian convolvulus." He gestured to a trumpet-flowered vine.

"In more than a dozen cities I have managed to create doorways that lead back here. Quite impressive, if I may say."

"So if we can travel through doorways anywhere, there isn't always a need to transport," said James.

"The laws, boy, do not forget the laws. Transporting is the only means of instantaneous travel between locations. Yes, we are inside a building in France, but our doorway is in Edinburgh, and back to Edinburgh is the only place we may go once we exit this room."

"But you said you have doors from other cities to here."

"I do. Every time I walk through them I come here, and every time I leave I return to the city where I originated. I could be in Stockholm and you could be in London and we both could meet here, but neither of us could return to any place other than that which we came from, and neither of us could leave this building and be in France."

"I've never heard of this type of magic," said James.

"There are few who have. It is very complicated and takes a long time to perfect — longer than most are willing to invest. As you can see, the result can be — ”

“Amazing,” said James.

“Sit down, James. Relax. Let us drink tea and rest before we begin your instruction.” Reluctantly, James obeyed. Akil conjured two cups of tea out of thin air. James opened his mouth to ask how he had done it when he noticed that Akil had closed his eyes. Akil held his cup close to his nose and inhaled several times before taking a sip. James, not wanting to ignore part of some type of ritual, did the same. Immediately, he felt a sense of clarity and sharpness he'd never felt before. His mind felt…open.

After they finished their tea, Akil stood and strode down the stone path. James rose and hurried to catch up. Akil stepped off the path and onto a tight-knit ground cover then between plants with leaves bigger than either of them. Beyond these plants a space opened up, revealing a small pond. Akil stood at the edge and James joined him.

James looked into the water and was shocked to see a school of what looked like swimming bats. Rather than brown or black, these creatures were clear — very similar to the jellyfish James had seen wash up on the coast from time to time. Their organs glowed red and purple inside their translucent bodies as they circled the pond.

“What are they?” James asked.

“They are called water bats. A not-so-elegant name for a rather elegant creature.”

“They're incredible.”

“There are so many things we take for granted in this world, James. People make assumptions and have beliefs that are so steadfast and resolute that the mere possibility of anything contradicting those beliefs frightens them into completely ignoring the truth. These small creatures are quite common but rarely seen and often mistaken for something else, especially when they take flight.”

"They can fly?" asked James.

Akil extended his hand. A speck of light rose from his palm. He sent it into the water where it darted around until it held the attention of the school of water bats. The orb propelled itself from one side of the pond to the other and the school followed. It then shot out of the water and up into the canopy above. The water bats followed in a glowing blur as they pursued the orb.

"Never become so rigid that you will not accept the possibility of something out of the ordinary — especially if that thing shakes the very foundation of your belief system — for those are the things we must consider most often," said Akil. "Tell me, James, when did you know you were a sorcerer? When did you know you could perform magic?"

"I guess I always knew. I can't recall a specific event or time."

"That is right. You grew up knowing that you had this ability. Did your parents ever tell you that they did not?" asked Akil.

"My parents were unfaithful?" James asked, shocked. His parents had never mentioned this to him. Not even once.

"You can imagine your father's surprise when Mr. Ogilvy told him he had the power inside himself to perform magic. At first, he did not want to believe it at all. You see, James, your father and mother had both been raised to look down upon anything they called supernatural. They thought those who spoke of it seriously were strange — even mad. 'Only children speak of such things,' your father said to Mr. Ogilvy. The idea that sorcery is nothing but a fairy tale is so engrained into the fabric of today's society that we, the ones who know better, have become the outcasts. We have become the exiles. We have become the danger to those who don't believe — those who will not allow their minds to open and understand that this power we wield is not unique to us but unique to the human race. Instead of pushing us apart, it could just as easily bring us together."

"So much time has passed that I am afraid we may never be able to coexist peacefully with the unfaithful. Most of them ignore us. There are some who want to rid the world of us. They want to wipe the history of our kind away and pretend we never existed. Occasionally, they murder our kind."

"But we are so much more powerful. How can that be?" James asked.

"It is against our laws to kill the unfaithful for any reason — punishable by death."

"I don't understand. Even if we can't kill them, we can still defend ourselves against whatever crude means they use to try and harm us, can't we?"

"How many laws of sorcery do you know, James?"

"Seven," said James.

"Tell me the laws as you know them."

"You cannot transport alone anywhere you haven't physically been. Time cannot be altered or manipulated. A killing incantation will also kill the one who casts it . You cannot conjure something from nothing. All magic flows through the hands. Only true lovers share the bond. Healing saps the strength of the healer equal to the extent of the injury healed."

"Very good. You have been taught well." Akil smiled. "Now what if I told you there was an eighth law? One that is known only to those in positions of power."

"What is it? Will you tell me?" James asked excitedly.

"I am strictly forbidden to tell anyone who has not been approved by the council to receive this information. Therefore, of course I shall tell you. The eighth law states that an incantation is as powerful as the belief of the person upon whom it is cast."

Akil let James absorb what he had been told. James scrunched his face in thought then finally relaxed as he began to understand what that meant.

"But we perform magic on unfaithful all the time. How is that possible?" asked James.

"If by we, you mean our kind, then you are mistaken. I dare say you've never seen an incantation cast directly upon the unfaithful. The majority of incantations we perform around the unfaithful are deterrents and distractions to keep them from seeing evidence of our existence. If I were to try and lift one of them , for example, it would have little effect. I will show you the next time we are among the unfaithful so you can understand completely," said Akil. "Now, let us take rest, James. Tomorrow brings a busy day."

James's mind raced with the information Akil had shared. Question after question swirled around in his mind as he was led into a courtyard wreathed by a thick coniferous hedge that stretched well above his head. As they stepped between two stone pillars and into the courtyard proper, the light dimmed and the questions, now on the tip of his tongue, began to dissipate as his mind slowed. Akil ushered him to one of several beds arranged around the perimeter like markings on a clock. He smiled knowingly as James tumbled into the bed and faded off to sleep.

6

the governor

James had a vague notion of what might lie behind the gate before he entered, but the reality of the environment into which he was immersed was beyond his wildest imaginings. An entire city block appeared to have been uprooted and dropped on this desolate island. The main thoroughfare was an smartly cobbled street. The buildings were constructed of materials consistent with those in western European architecture.

Storefront signs, too far in the distance to read, creaked on their cast iron posts as they swung in the breeze. Two- and three-story buildings neatly painted in shades of red and green stood side by side a stone's throw from the gate. The rectangular windows on the shaded side of the street were framed by intricately carved woodwork. Flower boxes overflowing with colorful blooms adorned the windows. The window glass was flawless. James couldn't recall ever seeing perfectly clear glass. On the opposite side of the street where the sun was brightest, canvas awnings prevented the light from intruding into the windows.

Roughly halfway down the street stood two three-story buildings connected by an enclosed arching bridge that allowed passage from one side of the street to the other without ever stepping outside. This passerelle de cel had purple and green stained-glass panels that created an ephemeral glow on the cobbles below as the sun passed through the panes. Pairs of lamps atop black iron posts, burning despite the daylight, stood in the center of the street every dozen feet with just enough room between them for a small cart.

James was so enamored with the buildings, that the absence of even a single person walking about did not spark his regard. A sense of foreboding prompted him to look back toward the gate. Rather than the tightly fitted bamboo, a solid iron gate blocked his retreat. Wrought iron fencing ran off into the jungle on either side of the gate. The owner of the voice he'd heard was nowhere to be seen. He turned back toward the cobbled street where an oddly familiar circular fountain sprayed water from the spires of a miniature castle set in the center. Before James could inspect the fountain, a slight movement directed his attention to the corner of the closest building where two figures stood silently, watching. Slowly, they walked toward James.

At first glance, James thought they were short men like Peroc, but as they drew closer, he realized they were not men at all. They were children. Neither boy could have been older than twelve. Both were filthy and wore ragged, threadbare clothes. Each carried a short sword in his belt but made no effort to draw it in the presence of the stranger. The taller of the boys had dark brown hair that stood out in all directions and was caked with mud . He had a long scar beginning above the top of his ear and terminating in the cleft of his chin. The other boy, shorter and broader, stood with a stern and confident demeanor. Both continued forward until they had positioned themselves between James and the fountain. Neither said a word as they inspected the visitor.

"Boys," James said, crouching slightly so he didn't look so tall and intimidating, "will you take me to the leader of your village?

"So you want to see the Guv'nah?" the shorter of the two boys asked tersely.

"Aye," said James.

"Are you sure you want to see the Guv'nah?" the taller boy said in a tone indicating that seeing the Governor was not a good idea.

"Aye," James replied. The pair looked at each other and smiled as if sharing an amusing secret. The shorter boy turned back to James wearing his stern expression once again.

"Then follow us — if you can!" He turned and took off at a run.

The taller boy raced after him down the cobbled street. James, taken by complete surprise, hastily closed the gap between them before they got too far ahead. They passed under the passerelle de cel, dodging lampposts, carts and barrels before the street turned sharply to the right and abruptly ended at a large stone house.

The house itself appeared completely out of place among the surrounding structures. The other buildings they had passed were well crafted and well maintained. This house, while impressively large, looked as if whoever built it was an amateur at best. None of the exterior walls stood straight, nor were they even in length or came close to level. James was surprised the structure managed to stand at all. Even the large wooden front doors were misshapen, leaving gaps between door and frame on both top and bottom. The two boys stopped at the uneven steps leading up to the doors. The taller of the pair pointed to the doors.

"The Guv'nah is inside," he said, breaking into a fit of laughter as he looked back at his friend. The boys took off running and were out of sight before James could question them. Everything about this place, this modern village, put James on edge. Everything felt so…wrong. What are children doing in this place? How did they get here? So many questions. An ill-fitting door, ominous in every way, held behind it the possibility of answers. James cautiously climbed the steps. Only when he reached the top step did he notice two other boys flanking the doors. Each held a long bamboo staff and glared off into the distance, ignoring their visitor. As James lifted his hand to knock on the door, he heard a humming noise behind him. Turning, he saw several of the tymanuk hovering inches out of reach. He looked at the boys guarding the door expecting some type of acknowledgement, but they continued to stare straight ahead.

James pounded on the wooden door. The sound echoed like he had taken a battering ram to the door, shaking the entire house. A cloud of dust fell from the frame with his last knock. After a moment, a series of concussions sounded as if someone were beating the door from the inside. James heard one of the guards snigger. When he turned to see what was so amusing, the boy simply stood, once again, looking out into the distance. A hint of a smile on the corner of his mouth was all that gave him away.

James turned back to the door and lifted his arm to knock once more. Before he could land his blow, the door swung inward with a groan. James glanced at the stone-faced guards as he ducked beneath the doorframe. He could hear both boys laughing, then the door closed behind him and all was silent. The entry hall of the house was also without a straight line. Several doors occupied the uneven walls, each a different size and none of which James could pass through without ducking. To pass through one particular door, he would most likely have to get on his hands and knees.

"Is anyone here?" James called. The echo was surprisingly loud — so much so that it made him jump. When no response came, he decided to take the largest of the four doors on the left side of the foyer. As he reached for the handle, James thought he could hear the beating of the tymanuks' wings nearby. He leaned his head closer to the door to better listen, but all was silent. James reached for the handle and realized that, in fact, there was no handle. He glanced at all the doors and realized none had handles or knobs. He turned back to his chosen door and gave it a push, sending it to the floor with a boom. Dust billowed up in a filthy cloud.

Stepping on top of the door, James continued into a long hallway. The walls zigged and zagged and the floor pitched up and down in the queerest of directions. It was covered in thick red carpet and held decades' worth of dirt and dust. The walls were unadorned except for a lantern here and there and the occasional scrawled writing — clearly in the hand of a child. The red characters were indecipherable.

He continued down the hall, calling out from time to time and receiving no reply. Oval and circular windows at random heights allowed enough light inside to see. The beams of light penetrating the passage were thick with floating dust that danced in miniature vortexes. James continued until he reached what appeared to be a dead end. No door or side passage gave any indication that the corridor continued. He took several steps back and surveyed his surroundings. After a moment, James noticed one thing out of place. The carpet in front of where he stood was free of dust and dirt. Upon closer inspection, he found a steel ring embedded in the center of the clean area.

James slipped his finger into the ring and gave it a pull. A chain attached to the ring extended from a small hole in the floor. As he continued to pull slowly, James heard a loud click and a circular trap door dropped away at his feet. Rather than a set of stairs, a crudely built wooden ramp pitched downward into the darkness. The sound of feet shuffling across a wooden floor echoing up from the darkness prompted James to call out. No reply.

"Tertiri Zé Manukto vinka," James said, extending his right hand while attempting to coax a light orb from his palm with the other. Nothing happened. "Tertiri Zé Manukto vinka," James said again, clearer, louder, hoping that perhaps he'd mispronounced the incantation. Again, nothing happened. James's heart began to beat faster inside his chest and his breathing quickened. No, he thought. I will not give in to panic.

He closed his eyes, thinking of the exercises Akil had pounded into his brain day after day during their time together. In moments, his heart rate slowed along with his breathing. Every fiber of his being was telling him that nothing but danger lay ahead through the trapdoor, yet he couldn't convince his body to turn and retreat. He fingered the smooth black steel key in his pocket, bolstering his resolve.

The silence in the corridor was broken with laughter from below. Down the ramp — somewhere deep beneath the house in the darkness — someone was laughing. A child. What do I possibly have to fear if a child is laughing? This rationale quickly supplanted all feelings of foreboding. James carefully stepped onto the ramp no wider than his shoulders. Immediately, he lost his footing and landed hard. As he slid downward into the darkness, the laughing continued. It grew louder as James descended. A light in the distance managed to keep complete darkness at bay. James sped toward the light, which, he realized as he drew closer, was a small hole at the bottom of the ramp. James winced as he approached, not knowing if he would fit through such a confining opening, yet somehow he did. He fell for only an instant before landing on a large cushion.

James rolled off the oversized cushion and jumped to his feet as he surveyed his surroundings. The large room was lined with torches and dominated by a central fire pit where embers glowed red. A small animal blackened on a spit above the embers. The floors and walls were roughly hewn stone. The ceiling appeared to be a tangle of roots. Numerous holes the same size as the one through which James had fallen spotted the ceiling and upper walls, all well out of reach. Beneath each hole was a cushion. On the far side of the cooking fire were three chairs. The center chair was significantly larger and more ornate than its sentinels and was carved from midnight-black wood. A large wooden table stood perpendicular to the wall littered with the dirtied dishes of half-eaten meals.

James walked slowly across the cold floor toward the three chairs. Even at a distance, the craftsmanship was notable, especially that of the center chair, which James considered more throne-like than the others. Swiping the long black hair from his eyes, James was surprised to find himself sweating profusely. As he stepped closer still to the trio of chairs, he heard a noise behind him. Instinctively, he drew his sword and spun around. His sword clanged against the steel of another blade. The sword's owner stood no higher than James's chest and wore a grin that quickly faded when he realized his swing would not land true. James thrust his blade forward, pushing his attacker to the ground.

It was a boy, no older than the others he'd met on his journey to the house. He was as dirty, if not more so. His clothes were also ragged and filthy. However, the blade in his hand set him apart from the others. It was a thing of beauty — forged from black steel and adorned with black jewels along the hilt. James tightened his grip on his own blade as he eyed the boy's.

"Where is the Governor?" demanded James.

"Who's asking?" the boy replied in an awkward preteen voice as he rose to his feet.

"My name is James. What is your name, boy?"

"They call me Gai. And I am no boy."

"Indeed," said James. "Now take me to the Governor. I have little time for games."

"What is it you want from our honored Guv'nah?"

"I was not brought here to bandy words with the likes of you, child. My business is with the Governor."

"You will bandy words with me. Now, what is your business in Adelphi?" asked Gai, standing as tall as he could, the tip of his blade now pointed at James.

"Adelphi? Is this what you call your home?"

"No you witless burugabeko, Adelphi is my land and all it encompasses. Every tree, every building, every grain of sand within its borders belongs to me."

"So the entirety of this island is not yours to control?"

"Foolish man! I brought you here. You are on my island! From the waters off her shores to the dirt between your toes, this place does my bidding. My land is called Adelphi, and my island has a name — a name you will not be privy to. If you want the Governor, speak now, for that is what they call me," pronounced Gai defiantly.

"You? Impossible."

"Men who doubt my powers only doubt them once. I'm feeling kind today and shall afford you that single warning. Now, what is your business?"

"If you brought me here, I should be asking you that question."

"My purpose for bringing you to Adelphi is in no way related to your reason for seeking me. Now tell me quickly before I spill your entrails on the floor."

"I believe that on this side of the gate, somewhere in this town, is the way to the black castle. I'd like you to show it to me," said James.

"All men who come here, every one, desire entry into the black castle. Do you know how many make it inside?" He paused, waiting for an answer. When it was clear James was not going to reply, Gai continued. "None. Never once has a man set foot inside that castle. She is a temptress . She sits and calls and waits and lures and destroys. She tempts in so many ways – leads men to believe they can reach what they so long for – to breach her walls and move on from this place. In that way, we are symbionts, the black castle and I. She lures all men toward her and when they are close, I take them from her."

"Take me to the black bamboo forest," said James.

Gai laughed and turned his back on James. He hopped deftly onto one of the long uneven benches then onto the table, paying no mind to the plates of spoiled food as he traipsed through the rubbish with his bare feet.

"You are a prize, Captain James. I've met very few men with knowledge of the native tongue. Still fewer who can perform magic in my land. But none of them, including you, have powers inside my own house. I would have been utterly disappointed if my blade had struck true. Long I have searched for an adversary, and I believe my search has ended."

"I am neither your adversary nor your enemy. I come in peace. I simply want to pass through this place and reach my destination. Perhaps we could arrange some sort of trade for safe passage."

"You are sharp tongued for a man. Not quite as sharp tongued as your comrade, but your determination is far greater than his."

"Then you have spoken to Luno. What have you done with him?"

James asked.

"I have done nothing with the man who calls himself Luno. I simply saw him on his way."

"And will you not do the same for me?"

"There is something about you, Captain James. I can't quite put my finger on it, but you have a certain aura that I am incapable of describing. The old man you call Luno is of no use to me. He will never escape the maze nor see the entrance to the tunnel. All for the best, if my powers of foresight are of any value. He is destined to walk the paths of that never-ending labyrinth for eternity. You, on the other hand…I daresay I need you, and you will soon realize that you need me as well."

"Let us help each other. Give me what I want, and I shall give you what it is that you desire."

"I'm afraid your desire is the antithesis of mine. Giving you what you want would mean that I will never get what I want. And of course, I will not have that."

"Perhaps we can make an arrangement," said James.

"I cannot think of anything you have that I would even consider a substitute for what I so desire."

"How is it that you know I will be or even can be he whom you desire, Mister Gai?"

Before James could blink, Gai leapt from the table and struck him on the head with the hilt of his sword. Pain shot down his spine, sending him to his knees. James's grip on his own blade involuntary relaxed. The sword fell clattering on the floor.

"Never call me mister. I am no man, and you shall not refer to me as one. The next time it won't be my hilt you feel on the top of your head. You may address me as Governor or Gai."

"My apologies," James said, rising unsteadily to his feet. He couldn't believe how quickly Gai had moved. He was beginning to doubt his chances of fighting his way out of this place. Gai was back on the table, pacing through the trash and swinging his sword through the air, fighting an invisible opponent as James's vision cleared.

"Your sword, I've never seen anything like it," James said.

"Spellbreaker steel forged in the fires of the black abyss," Gai said, proudly allowing James to have a good look.

As he looked at the black steel blade, James's hand instinctually slid toward the pocket where he kept the key. He forced himself to stop and hoped Gai hadn't noticed. They were forged from the same steel. This boy — this devil — must know the way into the black castle.

"Even if I were to let you go, show you to the maze, and even lead you through it, you would die within minutes of entering the tunnel. That is a place even I dare not go alone."

"Then perhaps we might go together. Tell me, Mis…Gai," James said, catching himself before he blurted out what surely would have been his last word. "Have you ever been inside the black castle?

"Never. I have no desire to travel there. Only men are foolish enough to try. I am content to remain here. All that I have ever desired has come to me."

"Perhaps inside lies more. Something you haven't imagined. An even better life than the one that you now live."

"Impossible. That's the nonsensical thinking that gets men killed. More, better, bigger. They lead lives of perpetual discontent. Regardless of how great what lies inside might be, it does little good if you never reach it. Why try? Why risk everything for the unknown? It is folly."

"It is not unknown. I have set eyes upon it. It calls to me. I alone have the ability to enter, and I seek your assistance."

"And what do you offer in exchange?"

James felt as if this conversation would circle round indefinitely. He wasn't sure what was standing on the table looking at him at this moment, but he knew it wasn't a boy. His hopes for getting into the black castle were quickly fading. He felt tired — exhausted — and he didn't believe he'd ever have the power to determine his next course of action. He was at the mercy of this…creature. He stumbled to the three chairs, turning his back on Gai, and considered each of the seats one at a time. He let out a sigh as he dropped into the center chair. Simultaneously, Gai shouted, "No!" and appeared in front of him. Despite the terror and anger on Gai's face and his empty, reaching hands, James felt calm and relaxed. Gai reached out to touch James, then hesitated as one reaching for a hot skillet.

"How is this possible?" Gai gasped in panic.

James could see the rage and confusion in Gai's face, but it did not affect him as it would have a moment ago…before he sat in the chair. The feeling of euphoria was too strong for him to be concerned with whatever was troubling Gai. James could feel a slight vibration in the chair as he watched the boy-creature, who was now pacing and muttering to himself. The vibration grew stronger — strong enough that James had to grasp the arms of the chair to keep his teeth from chattering.

Then, without warning, the chair splintered into a thousand black wood shards, leaving James lying supine on the ground. Gai rushed to his side and yanked him to his feet. James's head immediately became clear. Gai took several steps back. "Find your friend and leave. Never return."

"Will you take me to him?" asked James.

"You will find him without me. Leave this place before I change my mind," Gai demanded, with a look that that left James unconvinced he spoke the truth.

"What was that chair? Why are you afraid? Why do you change your mind?" asked James.

"I do not fear you or any man, and the chair is nothing but a chair — my favorite chair, in fact, which you have broken. I should run you through for destroying it, but I'm feeling gracious today. I am allowing you passage, so you had best accept it before I reconsider. You have until sunset to find your friend and be gone, or I shall begin killing members of your group. I'm sure eventually I'd kill someone you care about. Daylight fades fast on my island, so make haste."

In an instant, Gai was gone. He moved so fast James had not seen which way he had exited. Something had frightened him, James was certain, although he found little comfort in it. He walked back toward the hole that he had fallen through and noticed Gai's black sword lying on the floor beside one of the benches. As he reached for the sword, he knew beyond any doubt that the key and the sword were forged from the same steel. The instant his fingers touched the hilt, James could feel the call of the black castle. It was stronger than ever, and in that moment, he knew he was getting closer. James wrapped his fingers around the hilt, letting his desire consume him as he admired the unusual black steel blade, black jeweled guard and black leather-wrapped handle. James decided it would make a good replacement for his own sword, which lay abandoned on the floor not far away.

James looked up at the holes in the ceiling and considered trying to jump up and reach for the ledge. After a moment of consideration, he realized the effort would be futile. He searched the room for anything that might help him reach a hole.

"Tertiri Zé Manukto suomi," James intoned, and to his surprise, the table rose upward.

James directed it on end, spilling the rotten food onto the floor, then righted it and brought it beneath the largest hole. He stepped onto the table and then lifted it off the ground until he could easily reach the lip of the hole and climb inside. Sending two light orbs ahead of him, James pulled himself through. The passage was steep and narrow but climbable. A small doorway opened at the base of one of the stone turrets that rose from the rear of the house. In a moment, he was outside.

Blinking in the sunlight, he saw one of the tymanuk on the low branch of a tree. The creature made a noise like two smooth stones rubbing together. James stepped closer and could now see that it was gesturing toward the front of the house.

"Can you understand me?" James asked in the native language, feeling silly for trying to talk to the winged creature. The tymanuk immediately bowed and took to the air, hovering beside James's face. "You want to show me something?"

Again the creature bowed and gestured toward the front of the house. It flew around the house and toward the main thoroughfare with James a step behind. The streets were vacant as James accompanied his odd companion. The creature turned into a gap between two buildings. The gap was so narrow, James would never have noticed it had he been walking by himself. The small alleyway opened into a courtyard ringed by stone benches and small ornamental trees. In the center of the courtyard, several more tymanuk stood in a circle. A handful more hovered above.

As James drew closer, he could see they were standing around one of their own, who was lying motionless on the ground. Its head rested in the lap of another that was gently stroking its hair. The creature James had followed gestured at the motionless body. James crouched. The circle parted, allowing him unobstructed access. Across the torso of the creature, a deep wound spilled not blood but what looked like clear grains of sand. James understood why he had been brought here and thought it couldn't hurt to have allies in this forsaken place. He gently scooped up the creature in his hand.

"Tertiri Zé Manukto tupasarri." With his other hand he directed the healing energy to flow into the injury.

The wound was slow to heal and sapped more energy than James thought possible for such a small creature. After several minutes, the gash across its thorax was gone. The creature sat upright and took to the air. Others joined in congratulating it on finding health again. James rubbed his hands together, letting the nearly invisible grains fall to the ground. He could easily pick out the creature that had led him here by the purple coloring of its wings and legs.

"Will you help me?"

The creature bowed.

"I need to find someone. I believe he is in the black maze. Will you show me the way?"

Again the creature bowed. It spoke quickly to the others then gestured for James to follow. At the far side of the courtyard, James pushed open an iron garden gate as the creature flew above. They passed through a row of dense shrubs beyond which a vertical wall of rock rose high into the air. Its face was choked with vegetation. The tymanuk paused at the base of the cliff and indicated that James must climb.

"Tertiri Zé Manukto suomi ragö," James said, extending his hands.

The stone cliff vibrated for a moment, then slabs of rock slowly pushed out from the cliff face, forming a crude staircase. James rapidly ascended the makeshift staircase, then the pair traversed a narrow section of rock before halting at an impossibly deep chasm with a swift river at the bottom. Ahead was a rope bridge. The creature gestured to the bridge, and James made for the crossing. The wooden planks secured across the bridge looked sturdy and the rope intact. James crossed, hardly feeling the sway of the bridge beneath his weight.

The tymanuk led James along a narrow path at the very edge of the gorge until it turned into the dense jungle. At the far end of the path, daylight indicated a large open space. As James emerged from the jungle, he caught his first glimpse of the maze. Midnight-black bamboo stalks stretched into the sky as high as the tallest trees. They grew so close together it seemed as if a storm cloud had settled in the middle of the field. Only toward the top did they sprout green leaves. James guessed the maze was several miles across.

He ran to catch up with his guide, who hadn't paused, and together they made their way across the low-grassed field. When they reached the maze, James could see no obvious entrance. The stalks were as big around as his leg and nestled too close for even his guide to pass between them. The guide gestured to his feet. James looked down at the large flat stone he was standing on. The stone was engraved with a single word: Inari. He spoke it aloud.

The bamboo directly in front of him parted like curtains. The path was paved with similar flat stones. All was illuminated by a diffuse blue light. James was astonished that any light at all managed to penetrate the dense canopy above. He looked over at his guide. "My friend is in there?" he asked. The guide nodded. "Will you help me find him?" Reluctant at first, the guide finally agreed with a nod, and together they entered the maze.

7

unspeakable loss

May 1792, Glencolumbkille, Ireland

He held her and he wept. She had been his love and he hers. Only one person was responsible for her death. He could only blame himself He had known the road would be fraught with danger, yet he allowed her to come. She had insisted upon it. He couldn't bear the thought of being away from her for such a duration, so he had agreed. Now, in an instant, she was gone.

Her death was the worst kind. Terrible in and of itself, yes, but almost unbearable for him because he could have prevented it. He had created the monster that had taken her life. She had left this world screaming in pain and fear, and he had been powerless to help her. By the time he had reached her side, she had quieted. The long, thin hands of death were already pulling her away, and there was nothing he could do.

Akil Karanis wept as he'd never wept before as he cradled the body of his love in his arms. The brightness in her eyes dimmed as they stared for ever after into nothing. Those spiritless eyes that had once been the doorway to her soul now reflected only the moon. Her face was a mask of terror, as if even in death she would not know peace. She had been his everything: his motivation to be a better man, his inspiration to do great things, his source of strength when his own had been sapped. She had loved him, all that he was and everything he aspired to be. In all his solitary years he had never found love, and he had come to peace with the idea that he would be alone — until he met her. Now she was gone, and Akil could only blame himself.

Stricken with grief and misery, he saw no reason to go on. He saw no reason for anything. All of his life was a waste. What had he truly accomplished? Chasing what most believed was a myth had led him here. He had told her it was for the greater good. She had believed him. She believed he was acting selflessly for the good of all when, in reality, he was here because he wanted the prestige that would come along with his discovery and, even more so, redemption for his previous failures. Being ordinary had never been acceptable for Akil. Now his quest to be exceptional had led to his greatest loss.

He held her in his arms and wept until his eyes hurt. He wept until his tears ran dry. Hours passed. The sun began to rise in the east, and still he would not let her go. Rain fell from the grey, cloud-stricken sky, and he continued to hold her. He held her until he exhausted all the strength in his body and slept, still cradling her in his arms.

Akil awoke with a start. The rain had stopped. He felt a presence nearby, yet saw no one. Her body was gone. He was alone in the spot where she had been slain. Frantic, he tried to rise but was unable. His vision was blurred. He closed his eyes and rubbed them with the heels of his hands. When he opened them, the world was in focus again. A heavily wrinkled old woman in ragged clothes stood less than an arm's length away. Akil knew not how she had gotten there, yet for some reason, he was not afraid. She hunched over a wooden cane and her mouth hung open as she pulled in air with effort. Her teeth had long ago abandoned her infected gums.

"You have a choice," she said in the voice of a much younger woman, "as do all who walk this earth and some who walk beyond. You can let your grief determine your destiny, or you can determine your own destiny," she said, jabbing a finger into his chest. "Your love is gone. That is an indisputable fact and one that you must come to terms with soon, for this world doesn't allow men such as yourself to wallow in self-pity very long before it swallows them whole. I will tell you two facts before I go. First, and probably the hardest for you to believe, is this: you will love again. Second and most important: you are not and never will be an ordinary man."

Then she was gone, and Akil found himself lying in someone's arms. He was bloodied and broken. The pain was terrible. He struggled to see who was holding him, but the bright sun shone into his eyes. A voice spoke, a voice he knew all too well. "It will all be over soon." Akil realized the person holding him was…himself.

Thunder so loud it shook the earth roused him from sleep and welcomed him back to the world of misery and sorrow. He turned his head and saw her body lying next to him in the mud, her eyes staring vacantly. Akil had never dreamed. Not once in all his years could he recall having a single dream. Today in his grief he had experienced his first — or perhaps it was something else.

He tried to find his misery, to force it out, but the tears would not come. He had grieved a lifetime's worth in mere hours, and never again would Akil Karanis shed a tear. As he lay there in the deepening puddle, he thought about his dream. He believed it was his mind's way of trying to cope with her death. For a moment, he considered the notion that it had indeed been a prophecy. However, all his study of prophecies, of how they were made, and the Seers who made them would not allow him to believe that he himself was a Seer.

He needed to get up. He needed to take her body somewhere dry. He tried to stand. As he pushed himself off the ground, the muscles in his body contracted with all the force they had left in them. Had he any voice left, he would have cried out. As it was, he simply fell back into the mud and water beside the body of his love. After a moment, he tried again, but with even the slightest movement, his muscles contracted painfully. Akil knew it was no use. Every time he tried, his body betrayed him. He could not move.

Then he heard a noise, a sound other than the falling rain. It was the sound of sodden hooves trekking through the muddy field. He dared not lift his head to see who it was. The horse stopped so close Akil could hear its breathing. It let out a whinny as the rider stepped to the ground. Footfalls in the mud drew closer.

He felt a presence beside him and heard a gasp — no doubt at the sight of their bloodied and ruined bodies. The footsteps retreated, and Akil realized the observer must have thought he was dead also. Once more he built up the courage to endure another bout of pain and lifted his head and arms, letting out a cry before falling back to the ground. The footsteps quickly returned. He could now see the outline of a young boy. The boy knelt beside him and placed his hands on Akil's forehead and throat. He whispered, "Sendatu ," a healing incantation. Akil could feel a rejuvenating warmth surge through his body. He tried to sit up, and for the first time he was able.

"Are you all right, sir?" the boy asked.

Akil was far from all right, but the boy need not hear of it. Akil nodded and thanked him.

"What happened?" asked the boy, looking over at the body that had once been his love.

"She was attacked," said Akil. "I had gone into the village for supplies and foolishly left her alone. By the time I returned it was too late," he lied. Pain gripped his chest as he spoke the words. He could feel the void of the missing connection between them, the bond that would never return.

"Do you know who it was?" asked the boy. "The murderer, that is."

"Yes," said Akil. He did not elaborate and the boy did not pry.

"I live just over that hill," the boy said, pointing to a rise not far away. "You must come inside out of this rain."

"Thank you," said Akil. "I think I will." He got to his feet. Once he was certain of his stability, he stepped beside her body and extended his palms over her. "Jaso ," he said. Her body rose several feet into the air. "Iraitzi ur ." The rain stopped falling on her, spilling over the invisible barrier he conjured. The boy, he realized, had taken off his cloak. Ever so gently, he draped it over her body. Together they walked toward the boy's house in silence as her body floated between them.

When they reached the top of the hill, Akil could see the house, smoke rising from the chimney. When they reached the stable, the boy tied up his horse. Akil decided he would leave her in the stable as well. He set her gently on the straw and cast a protective incantation that would keep any hungry vermin away. The thought made his chest and throat ache. Once he was sure her body would be safe, he turned, and together they walked to the house.

The low doorway forced Akil to duck in order to cross the threshold.

They were greeted by the bluster of a concerned mother.

"Where ye been?" she demanded, not looking up from her stitch work, yet somehow knowing he had come in soaked through. "Look atcha, dripping wet all over m' floor. Wha's t' matter wit' ye, boy?" Finally, she glanced up from her sewing and noticed the stranger standing in her doorway. "Who t' 'ell is that?"

"Ma, this is…" The boy realized they'd never exchanged names.

"Akil Karanis," said the sorcerer, extending his hand. "How do you do?" She stood, placed her fabric and needle on her chair, and stepped forward, taking his hand while drinking him in. He was soaked and muddy from head to toe. His short grey hair and beard dripped water onto the floor along with his rain-soaked clothes. If not for the mud, his clothes would also have shown the stains of blood, which Akil was glad was not the case. He noticed the woman eying her wet floors morosely.

"Allow me," Akil said. "Haize xukatu ." A gust of warm wind began to swirl around the two sodden travelers. In a matter of seconds they were dry and the puddles on the floor were gone.

"So," she said, turning her back on him and walking toward the fire, "yer one of them."

"Pardon?" said Akil.

"She means a sorcerer," the boy said, moving to Akil's side. "Ma hasn't met many."

"You mean your parents are not sorcerers?" Akil asked, intrigued.

"Ma thinks me pa was but just didn't tell 'er. He went missing before I was born."

"And what is your name, young sir?" Akil asked.

"Ciarán," the boy said with a smile.

"Ciarán. A strong name. Destined for greatness." Akil smiled.

"His pa named 'im." The woman turned to Akil. "I wanted t' name 'em after me pa, but tha' bloody fool insisted on callin' 'im Ciarán, so Ciarán it is, eh boy?" She grinned at her son.

"Aye," he replied.

"Where are me manners? Tea, Mister Karanis?" she asked.

"Please," he replied, stuffing his shaking hands into his cloak.

She lifted the black kettle from the stone hearth and looked inside. "Fetch some water, will ye, boy?"

"Aye, Ma." Ciarán looked clearly disappointed with the idea of leaving the warm, dry house. He picked up the kettle and opened the door.

"Allow me," Akil said, looking at the boy. "Ur etorri ." He gestured toward the rain as if beckoning it to enter. Raindrops came together to form a small ball that floated through the air to the kettle where it dropped inside. This process repeated itself several times until the kettle was full. Ciarán smiled and took the kettle to his mother, who sighed with exasperation.

"I suppose ye can sit till the tea's ready," she said. Akil sat beside the boy on a long wooden bench he'd pulled from the table. They all sat in silence for several minutes. Akil fought to distance his mind from the earlier events. Each time he tried, he could only see her body, bloody and broken, lying in the mud.

"So wha' brings ye our way, Mister Karanis?" Ciarán's mother finally asked.

"Simply passing through," said Akil.

"Where ye headed? If ye don' mind sharin'…"

"Belfast," he lied.

"And how did ye cross paths wit' me son?"

"It was actually your son who found me," said Akil. "My wife and I were traveling together. We were attacked by robbers. She was killed," he said, swallowing hard. "And I was injured. Your son healed me and brought me here out of the rain."

"Oh my," she said. "Good fer nuthin' robbers think they own th' roads from 'ere to Londonderry. No travelin' alone any more 'round these parts. I am sorry fer yer loss, Mister Karanis."

"Thank you," replied Akil, his voice breaking. Ciarán's mother started slightly when she saw how truly broken he was.

"Ye could use a warm meal an' mayhap a bed fer a few winks. No sense in goin' nowhere while it's still rainin'," she said.

Rather than argue, Akil shared in the hospitality of this kind woman and her son who had most likely saved his life. He ate warm stew with bread and ale before she insisted he rest in her bed. Akil lay down after performing a calming incantation on himself to help empty his mind for the next few hours. He fell asleep almost instantly.

Clouds of smoke and flashes of light add to the melee of thunderous explosions as Akil runs across the courtyard and through the gaping hole that was the curtain wall moments before. He notices three bodies, two to the right and one to the left, as he hurdles a pile of debris. He does not slow down to identify any of the fallen. On the opposite side of the wall, the air clears and the cacophony of explosions quiets. Three figures come into view beside a small stream that twists beneath a massive tree. The tree's bark is mottled white and green with patches of brown that are peeling away from the trunk. One of the figures is kneeling. The second has his arm on the third. All have their backs to Akil. No!, he thinks. This cannot be!

"No!" he screams .

Akil sat bolt upright, drenched in sweat. Slowly, he slid his legs off the bed and stood. It was nearly twilight. Ciarán's mother was fast asleep in an uncomfortable chair by the fire. Her mouth hung open and a string of spit stretched from the corner of her mouth, dangling precariously above the floorboards. Ciarán was nowhere to be found. Akil quietly exited the house and made his way to the stable. The long shadows of sunset painted the hilly terrain in shades of gold. Akil could hear ocean waves crashing ashore in the distance. As he reached the stable, he heard an odd sound coming from the other side. He cautiously made his way around to investigate.

A small garden with flowers in full bloom around the perimeter glowed orange in the setting sun. A vine-choked trellis with gourd-shaped white blooms welcomed visitors. Akil immediately spotted the source of the noise and was touched yet again by Ciarán's kindness. The boy was digging a grave at the edge of the garden. He had made considerable headway despite encountering several large rocks he had pulled from the ground and tossed beside the pile of dirt. He stood in the hole up to his waist. So focused was he on the project at hand he didn't notice Akil approaching. For his part, Akil thought if he had a tear left to shed, the sight of this boy he had met but hours prior digging a grave for his wife would have coaxed it from his eyes. When Ciarán noticed Akil he stopped. Akil smiled warmly at the boy.

"I thought she'd like it here in the flower garden," said Ciarán.

"She would indeed, young master. I cannot begin to express my gratitude. You have truly been my savior, a debt I will not take lightly. Now, step out from there, and I shall teach you."

The boy climbed out of the partially dug grave and stood beside Akil. Akil opened his hands. "Askatu ." The earth at the bottom of the grave jumped slightly. "Jaso ," and the newly loosened dirt rose from the grave and fell neatly in a pile beside it.

"Anyone can learn the incantation — the words, that is," said Akil.

"The skill is in being able to manipulate it to do what you want once you have said it. That takes practice and intense focus. You have to allow your mind to travel with the magic. Let it flow beneath the dirt and break it apart. Then let it lift the dirt. This is not an easy task but one that will come with practice." Ciarán nodded, but appeared confused. Akil smiled, wishing he had more time to teach the boy.

"If I may ask, where did you learn the healing incantation you performed earlier?"

The boy paused for a moment. Akil could tell he was struggling with whether to tell the truth.

"A man in the village. I saw him use it on his injured gelding. He asked me if I wanted to learn how to do it myself. I have not done it on anyone, I promise, Mr. Karanis, just a few animals and you o' course. I know folks react strange when they see things of that sort."

Akil smiled as he realized the boy felt reprimanded.

"Not to worry," said Akil, setting Ciarán's fears to rest. The pair stood silently for a moment before Akil glanced at the grave and said quietly , "I believe it is ready." The boy nodded and silently walked back toward the house, knowing that burying his wife was a task Akil would want to do on his own.

And so Akil laid her to rest beneath the dirt beside the small flower garden. She had loved flowers, and he thought she would be quite content to rest in this small, out-of-the-way place. He used one of the rocks Ciarán had unearthed and carved a single word into it. Bake — peace. Gently, he laid it as her headstone. He then knelt beside her grave and said his goodbyes, promising to return and visit from time to time.

Now it was nearly dark, and Akil knew it was time to move on. He made his way toward the house to express his thanks to Ciarán and his mother. The moon was bright despite the early hour and was already casting shadows. Before he reached the front door, Ciarán's mother stepped outside.

"May I have a word, sir?" Concerned, Akil stepped to her side. She stopped, took a deep breath, and looked up at him.

"Will ye take 'im with ye?" Akil had not expected this. Not at all. He was stunned into silence. "I have so little to offer 'im 'ere. I cannot teach 'im what ye know. The boy needs a proper teacher," she pleaded.

"Madam, I am afraid my destination is no place for a boy, even one so talented as Ciarán. I promise you this, though; when I return, I will take young Ciarán as my apprentice."

"Thank ye, sir," she said, nearly falling to her knees with gratitude. "I knew fate brought ye 'ere fer a reason. He is a good boy and will not let ye down."

"Your confidence in my return is reassuring considering where it is I travel. If I do not return, please do not take it to heart. There are few who have," said Akil. The woman did not reply. "If you do not mind, I would like to bid farewell to the boy."

"O' course," she said, leading him back into the house.

Ciarán sat pulling flames from the fire as Akil had with the water earlier in the day.

"Most impressive," said Akil. "Improvisation with a different element. Most impressive." Ciarán smiled proudly, sent the flame back into the fire, and stood.

"You're leaving," he said, his voice thick with disappointment.

"I must be going. There is a task that I must attend to. Continue to practice and remember what I have told you. We shall meet again if the fates desire. Until then, I must ask a favor of you," Akil said. "I noticed a third horse in the stable."

"Of course, Master Akil," Ciarán's mother said before Akil had a chance to finish. Th' grey one will suit ye best. His name is Nibs. 'E's a bit of an independent spirit, if ye know what I mean, but 'e'll take ye far 'n' fast."

Akil fished in his pocket until he retrieved a small cloth sack. He set it on the table.

"It is not much, but it is the least I can do for your hospitality."

With this he turned and walked out the door. Ciarán reached for the bag and emptied its contents on the table. Two dozen gold coins spilled onto the wooden tabletop. Ciarán's mother gasped.

"I thought he said he was attacked by robbers," said Ciarán, looking at his mother.

Akil hastily made his way to the stable and untethered the grey gelding. He saddled him quickly and made for the lane along the stream at the base of the hill. The moonlight was bright enough to see by, helping make his exit discreet. Akil looked over his shoulder at the small garden behind the stable and bid his love farewell. He then closed the door on his emotions, determined not to open it again for a very long while .

Inside the small house, boy and mother sat staring at the largest pile of money either had ever seen. They would live quite comfortably for some time.

8

the maze

The diffuse blue light cast eerie shadows, making it nearly impossible for James to see more than a few steps ahead into the bamboo maze. Each stone on which he stepped was identical to the last. When the pair reached a T-junction, James looked both left and right for clues that might indicate which direction Luno had gone. He strained his eyes to spot a sign — anything, a bent blade of grass, a misplaced grain of sand.

The tymanuk interrupted his scrutinizing search with excited stone-rubbing chatter. He looked and saw it was pointing at one of the stones leading to the right. He crouched and saw several grains of orange powder — transporting powder. Luno had gone right, James was sure of it. He hurried down the path, then stopped abruptly. He returned to the intersection and extended his hand.

"Tertiri Zé Manukto ragö." In a swirl of fine dust, a shape slowly formed on the surface of the stone. After a moment, it became clear. James had engraved an arrow into the stone pointing toward the exit. Again, he turned and headed down the path. This particular section continued uninterrupted and unintersected for such a long distance that James started to think there was some sort of enchantment that would keep him walking forever. Finally, the path turned to the left. Several steps beyond the turn, the path intersected another.

James could keep straight or turn. He crouched again and studied the ground, searching for the orange powder. Once again it was the tymanuk who found it first and excitedly gesticulated its discovery. Again, James marked the stone by engraving an arrow and the pair continued, taking the left path. Every few steps another path intersected. Each time, James and the tymanuk stopped to confirm which direction they needed to travel, making progress slow.

After countless turns, James and his guide reached an clearing. A circular courtyard spread out before them. It was lined with stone benches and was virtually identical to the courtyard in the village where James had healed the injured tymanuk. On one of the benches sat Gai. The guide quickly flew behind James in hopes of not being seen. Gai stood. He glanced down at the black sword that James now carried, then looked into James's eyes.

"I see you and the traitor are progressing nicely."

"Are you here to distract me?" asked James.

"I could tell you where he is, you know. He isn't far, just on the other side of one of those doors." Gai pointed to five doors on the far side of the courtyard somehow nestled tightly between the bamboo canes.

"Tell me," said James.

"What is the challenge in that? I'm quite looking forward to sunset."

"I'd have thought one as intelligent as you wouldn't enjoy murder for its own sake," said James.

"I'm not sure whether to take that as an insult or a compliment," said Gai.

"Simply an observation," James replied, studying the five doors. They were identical in size and color, but the hardware was unique. He stepped forward for a closer inspection, leaving Gai standing alone.

James stood in front of the wooden door on the far right. The knob was dull and round. It was made of black metal and otherwise unremarkable. James ran his hand over the knob before moving to the door immediately to its left. This door had a long ornate handle with a thumb latch. It too was forged from black metal. He touched the handle, then continued to the center door.

Gai stood behind him looking irritated. He made a series of noises that sounded like the language of the tymanuk, and James's guide quickly flew behind him.

The center door had but a flat silver finger plate where a knob or handle should be. James expected to see his reflection as he reached toward the panel but saw only an eerie reflectionless shine of polished silver. He touched the cool metal, allowing his palm to slide down it before stepping to the next door.

This door had two hefty metal brackets mounted on the door itself supporting a bressumer that extended completely across the door and overlapped the frame on either side. The mechanics of it made no sense at all. This type of anti-entry mechanism was typically used in a castle, where wall-mounted brackets held the board in place to prevent a breach of the door in the event of an attack. Here it looked as if the board simply prevented the door from being pushed or pulled open, which could easily be done by sliding the board off the brackets. James touched the board and stepped in front of the last door.

This door had a small round knob similar to the door on the far right. However, rather than black, it was polished gold, and rather than positioned to the side as a typical knob might be, this was dead center. James ran his hands along the wood of the door and around the golden knob but did not make contact with it. He turned and faced Gai.

"Well? What is your choice?" asked Gai.

"I have a proposition for you. Call it a challenge if you will."

Gai's eyes lit up with excitement. "Continue."

"I will allow you to pick a door for me…"

A smile crept across Gai's face.

"…if you allow me to pick a door for you."

"Done," said Gai.

"You choose first," said James, stepping back from the doors.

Gai grinned a cunning and knowing smile as he slowly walked beside the row of doors, making no sound as he padded across the crushed grey stone.

"I choose this door." He stood before the door with the heavy wooden board seated in iron brackets. Then he raised his hand and pointed, not at the door in front of him but at the door with the silver finger plate. He laughed mirthlessly and stepped back beside James. For the first time, James realized Gai was wearing the sword he had dropped during their initial encounter. They had exchanged blades by choice or by fate.

"Now for your selection, Captain James," said Gai.

Without hesitation, James pointed to the door on the far left – the one with the small golden knob in the center. Gai slowly stepped to the door James had chosen for him while James positioned himself in front of his chosen door. Each looked over at the other. James nodded and reached for the silver panel. In his periphery, he could see Gai reaching for the knob.

James's guide perched on his shoulder, gripping his hair. James closed his eyes and imagined a lever handle centered on the panel. The cool metal against his fingers prompted him to push the handle down. With a click, the door swung open. James stepped over the threshold without looking to see if Gai had kept his end of the bargain.

Familiar stone felt smooth and cool underfoot, and James realized it was the very same that lined the pathways throughout the maze. The tymanuk hovered in the air beside him. The door clicked shut and vanished behind them, leaving a wall of bamboo in its place. James quickly reached into the pouch that hung from his belt. He motioned for his guide to hold onto him as he sprinkled transporting powder over his head, half-believing it wouldn't work. James was surprised when he was engulfed in a swirl of orange smoke.

In an instant, he was back in the courtyard of the five doors. Sitting on one of the benches, lost in contemplation, was Luno. He stood with a start, clutching a large roll of parchment in his hand. James was at his side before the surprise of seeing his friend had settled in.

"We need to go. Now," said James.

"How the bloody hell did you get here?"

"I'll explain later. Hold onto me," said James.

Luno wrapped his arm around James's shoulders and in a flash they were gone. To their surprise, they transported to the large iron gate that marked the exit to Adelphi. James heard shouting and turned to see two boys running toward them with swords drawn.

"Pirates!" one of the boys shouted.

"The Guv'nah said they might come!" said the other.

"The Governor is not who you think he is," shouted James. "He is neither boy nor man."

"He told us you'd say that," the taller of the two boys replied, finally coming to a stop a cautious distance from the men.

"Where are you from, boy?" asked Luno, looking at the smaller of the pair.

"What's it to you, pirate?"

"Enough talk!" the taller boy said. "Kill the pirates!" They lunged at the men with their swords.

"Tertiri Zé Manukto norge," James intoned, blasting the taller boy with a burst of energy that sent him to the ground. At the same moment, the smaller boy swung his blade at Luno, who raised his forearm to block the blow. The result was effective but painful as the sword cut through the flesh and embedded into the bone. The scroll of parchment he'd been clutching fell to the ground as Luno let out a cry. James sent the boy into the air with an incantation of such force that neither he nor Luno saw him land.

Behind them they heard shouts. Both men turned and saw nearly a dozen boys running down the street brandishing weapons and shouting, "Pirates!" James turned back to the gate, searching for a release mechanism.

"There," Luno said, nodding toward a black wheel on the far left of the gate. James ran to the wheel and fought to turn it. A cog behind the wheel meshed its teeth with the gaps of another in an intricate system that lowered several large steel counterweights. The gate groaned open.

"The map!" Luno shouted, diving to the ground to pick up the roll of parchment. James gripped Luno's good arm and pulled him to his feet as he clung to the parchment with his injured arm, blade still embedded. Together, they stumbled through the gate.

"Tertiri Zé Manukto Aroy," James said, sending a burst of energy at the wheel, spinning it back in the opposite direction as they stepped through. The gate closed silently behind them.

“Why didn’t you transport us back to camp?” Luno asked through gritted teeth .

“I tried,” said James, pulling the parchment from Luno’s injured hand and shoving it into his belt. Behind the gates the shouting grew louder. For the moment, the gate did not open. James extended his hand over Luno’s injury. “Tertiri Zé Manukto tupassari.” Nothing happened. He tried again. Still nothing. He couldn’t understand. He had been able to heal one of the winged creatures in this very spot not long ago… James looked to where his tymanuk guide had stood on his shoulder before they transported. She was gone.

9

arenberg

October 1896, Northeastern France

Margaret walked hastily through the forest, bent upon reaching her destination. The small village she had passed hours earlier had been the last sign of civilization for miles. Since the day she had felt their bond ripped from her chest, she had pushed the memories deep within herself. But now that James was gone, off training with Akil, Margaret allowed the hauntings of her husband's death , buried deep for nearly two years, to resurface. After much contemplation, she had decided she must visit the place where Alvaro's men had captured her husband. She wanted to see with her own eyes where his last battle had been fought. Her hands trembled with anticipation as she continued deeper into the forest.

Not long after it happened, what seemed like a lifetime ago, James had pointed out on a map where they had been. Even at thirteen, James was a master navigator. A small wooden dowel floating above her palm pointed the way to her destination. The memory of her trip alone to visit the Seer nearly ten years ago resurfaced as she strode through the forest. A small wooden dowel hovering over her palm had guided her on that journey as well.

It was nearly dawn, but the first light of the day had not yet penetrated the thinning autumn canopy. Mist still clung to the forest floor, making it difficult to see the stones and roots embedded in the ground. According to James, he and his father had purchased supplies in the very same village Margaret had passed. The pair had given a false destination to anyone in the village curious enough to ask and had abandoned the road for the forest not long after losing sight of the last house. Margaret knew it was too dangerous to enter the village herself. She had long suspected that one of Alvaro's loyalists had spotted her husband and son in the village and sent for reinforcements that fateful day. James had recounted the events preceding his father's death more times than she could remember, but for reasons even Akil could not explain, James still could not conjure a memory orb containing the incident.

Almost an hour passed before the wooden guide-stick began to spin feverishly above her palm. She had arrived. The mist had lifted, revealing scant low-growing brush and a thick layer of leaves that crunched underfoot. Without her silencing incantation, Margaret would have been heard by all manner of creature and man during her trek across the forest. She looked around. Any signs of the skirmish had long been erased by the coming and going of the seasons.

Margaret strode in ever-widening circles, studying the ground for any evidence of her husband's passage, determined to find something. Anything. Every day since his death she had fought to keep his memory alive inside her. She clung to everything he had owned. She had purchased the last chair her husband had sat in before he and James left for Arenberg. The owner of the inn had sold her the bedding as well, which she slept on every night. It was unclear to Margaret what she was seeking out here in the forest. Closure? To Margaret, finding closure meant forgetting, and she did not want to forget. She would never forget. Since that memory-laden winter day when her husband came bursting through the door going on about magic, the pair had grown steadily closer.

The tip of her boot struck something, yet when she searched the forest floor, nothing substantial had been disturbed. She stooped to investigate. The tips of her fingers began to pulse with energy, a sensation she hadn't felt in many years. She began to move the leaves one at a time. With every leaf she removed, the sensation in her hands intensified until it felt as if the energy were going to burst from her fingertips. The last few leaves appeared to hover in space several inches from the ground. Margaret brushed the leaves away and slowly lowered her hand. A force pushed back. Something was there, hidden by an invisibility spell.

Margaret involuntarily looked around to be sure she wasn't being watched, and then quietly said "Eraskutsi. " She gasped as the invisibility spell melted away. Resting on the ground was her husband's leather-bound journal. She slowly lifted it, surprised by its weight and thickness. She didn't remember it being this large. Her hands shook as they held the precious book. She smelled it, hoping for some trace of her husband's scent. Unsure if she was ready to see what he had written, Margaret decided she would look at the first page and no more. The inside cover read,

James Lochlan Stuart III

For those who succeed me, so that my efforts are not in vain.

Margaret immediately recognized the sloppy, child-like writing of her husband. She continued to the opposite page.

Twenty-first of May, 1887

Everything has changed. Up is down. Left is right. Many important lessons have I learned over the course of this past year. The most important is this: never hold on to a belief so tightly you will not allow yourself to be open to the possibility that you're wrong. Being wrong can be, and usually is, simply a result of ignorance rather than lack of intelligence. Highly intelligent people can be, and most often are, extremely ignorant in many regards. On these pages I hope to leave thoughts and lessons others may find useful. To my beloved wife, with whom I've fallen in love a second time over the past year, and my dear son , who carries a burden far too heavy for any one man, let alone a child , I hope you may find solace and truth within. Life begins and ends with hope.

J.L.S.

Margaret looked up from the journal. Tears rolled down her cheeks as she smiled. She had stumbled upon the greatest treasure she could imagine. She scanned her surroundings nervously, reminding herself that it wasn't safe to linger in this place. Disappointed that she could not continue to read, she tucked the journal inside her traveling cloak. Before she made her way back, there was one other place she must visit.

The sun was setting over the distant hills as Margaret looked out upon the small church from the edge of the forest. She had continued through the forest after finding the journal until she reached its boundary where the grassy hill tapered down to the village. She decided to wait until dark before entering the place where her husband had died, and she had spent most of the afternoon perched on a large rock in the forest not far from the tree line. She sat, her hands shaking, as she looked at the journal resting upon her knees. Many times throughout the afternoon she had reached to pull open the cover, and each time she had retreated. It didn't feel right, she finally decided, to read it here, so close to where her husband had been killed. With that, she tucked the journal into her cloak and focused on the task at hand.

Smoke from the chimneys in the village caught the last rays of red sunlight. Little stirred in the village. The horses had been tended to; the people had all gone inside for the night. A small pack of dogs roamed the streets looking for scraps. An owl hooted in the forest, beckoning the night. Only one person had left the church since Margaret had taken up her watch. The village priest had shuffled down the street, head bowed and shoulders hunched as if he carried the burdens of his entire parish.

Finally, darkness enveloped the land. Margaret advanced quickly, needing no light as she made her way to the church, having memorized her path during the hours before sunset. She knew coming here was particularly dangerous. Every several paces she whispered, "Estalgabetu ," to reveal the presence of any hexes or curses. When she reached the church, she placed her hand on the wooden door. She had read in one of Tabitha's books that when someone dies, their soul leaves a trace of itself behind. Margaret believed that if any trace of her husband's soul remained, she would know — she would feel it — not because of her skill as a sorceress but because of her love for her husband. Margaret whispered, "Estalgabetu, " one final time and reached for the handle. It was unlocked, as were most church doors in these untroubled times. She soundlessly slipped inside and closed the door behind her.

Several candles flickered at the far end of the church, casting eerie shadows as the flames danced in the drafts coming through the ill-fitting windows. The furniture was arranged exactly as James had described. Margaret had been sure it would be different after the terrible event that had taken place there — an acknowledgement of the horrors. Now that she pondered it, she realized it was likely that no one in the parish was aware that anything at all had happened in their beloved church. The only evidence of her husband's demise was those left behind to cope with the loss.

She scanned the room, repeating her revealing incantation. She was alone. The floorboards groaned as she walked toward the front of the church. "Isildu ," Margaret whispered, and her footsteps fell silent. With each step, Margaret tried to feel for any trace of her husband. This was not magic but instinct. She willed her senses to expand beyond her body. Her body felt like a force rather than flesh and blood as she continued forward. She felt as if she were floating across the floor as she searched for him.

A step away, a group of ornate wooden chairs was arranged in a semicircle. Each had an upholstered seat, blood red. Margaret couldn't recall James describing cushions this color, and she knew his attention to detail was preternatural. He had memorized nearly every detail. She reached out for the closest chair, not with her hand but with her mind and her senses.

"You should not have come here," a voice said.

Margaret immediately jolted back into her body and spun toward the voice. She saw a figure standing in the shadows. Her hand went instinctively inside her transporting pouch, but she hesitated.

"They have been expecting you or your son to come back here. Their patience is infinite. You know this, and yet you came, risking your life and your son's future." Margaret pinched the powder between her thumb and forefinger, but did not react.

"You cannot transport in this place. Had I not arrived before you, you would be in the hands of the enemy and your son would soon be an orphan." A weary and perturbed Akil stepped into the dim candlelight and glared down at Margaret. He towered over her, and for the first time, she was afraid of him. "Why have you come? What is worth risking so much?"

Margaret could not speak. She suddenly realized how foolish she had been — coming here had become an obsession. She had clung to the idea of feeling the bond again, the magical bond all lovers share until the end. Yet she had known the bond had been broken the instant it happened. It was as if someone had taken a knife and severed her heart.

She had been sitting by the fire in a London library skimming a manuscript her husband had sent her to find. She was sipping a cup of tea as her finger ran down the page. It was the delightful tea she had brought back from India after her travels with her husband to visit the Seer. The cup was almost to her lips when the breath left her body and her blood ran cold. The cup fell, shattering into a thousand pieces on the marble floor. She felt as if her heart had also shattered into a thousand pieces.

She lay there on the floor gasping for air, benumbed. Tears spilled from her eyes with such force that the fire in front of her was nothing but a yellow blur. Her spine arched and she let out a shriek as the pain shot through her heart. A moment later — a moment that felt like hours…days — the pain was gone. It had been replaced by a raw emptiness.

Margaret refocused on Akil. The displeasure on his face changed to sympathy as he watched her relive that night. Akil had known that loss. He had known it more than once in his long life, and he recognized it when he saw it. What would he give to feel that bond again? Almost anything. What would he risk? Almost everything. He saw and understood. What Margaret had come here to do, Akil had tried as well. He had tried numerous times as his powers grew, yet he had never been successful at feeling even a glimmer of his lost love. It was a specific kind of magic, and very few had the skill and natural ability to do it. Akil had met several sorcerers during his travels who claimed they had the power, but he refused to seek help. It was an incantation most personal in nature. One would not simply ask a stranger to perform an act of magic so intimate, so revealing. He would not let others know he still clung to the loss so tightly. Weaknesses were meant to be exploited, and he could not trust this knowledge to anyone, especially someone he met in passing. He felt pity and sympathy as he reached for Margaret's shoulder.

"I am sorry about your husband, Margaret. I truly am. He was a great man. He loved you dearly. His love for you will endure as you pass it to James. We must remember those who precede us by passing along the imprints they have left in our hearts and minds to the ones still with us. In this way we honor them." He gave Margaret's shoulder a gentle pull. "Now, let us be done with this place once and for all.

"You can do it," she whispered.

Akil did not respond. He knew what she was asking and knew it would only result in disappointment. He pulled her shoulder again, more forcefully this time.

"Margaret, we must go. We must leave this place."

"Please. I need to feel him once more. Just once more. Then I can move on. Then I can focus on the future rather than the past. Please, Akil. Help me."

"My dear, while I am familiar with the incantation, I have tried more times than I care to remember and have failed every time. It will only exacerbate your disappointment and emptiness."

"Will you try for me?" Margaret begged. "If it does not work, I will understand. I will accept that it is not my destiny, and we will leave this place. I give you my word I will never return. All I ask is that you try. Please."

Akil sighed and removed his hand from her shoulder. He knew they had time. The counter-spells he had cast were far superior to the incantations cast by Alvaro's men. The only one he had been unable to reverse was the anti-transporting incantation, one of the few that could be undone only by the person who cast it.

"Very well," Akil whispered, raising his hand. Immediately, a black orb appeared over his palm. It expanded and swirled like smoke as it grew. With a flick of his wrist the smoke left his hand, separated in midair, and clung to the windows. Another motion of his hand shot the bolts on both doors. Akil walked slowly along the semicircle of chairs, whispering to himself, his hand extending over each as he passed. He stopped at the second to last. A flick of his wrist slid the chair forward silently.

"Sit," Akil said, motioning to the chair. Margaret sat. Instantly, the candles went out, and the small church was consumed by darkness. Margaret could hear Akil whispering, but he was speaking too quietly for her to discern the words. Small orbs of red light, each no larger than a grain of sand, rose from the floor. As Akil stepped to the back of the chair, the glowing red orbs danced like dust particles caught by the rays of a fiery sunset.

Margaret thought they would settle once Akil stopped moving, but instead they began to swirl anti-clockwise around the chair where she was seated. The speed increased with each revolution until it was no longer a collection of individual points of light but a ring surrounding her chair. Margaret shivered as the temperature inside the ring dropped. Wind blew, a storm raged. She could no longer see Akil. The pressure inside the ring increased, causing a shooting pain in her ears. Margaret clamped her hands over her ears as if covering them would somehow ease her agony. The chair beneath her began to rattle and shake.

Margaret stood, afraid the chair would break beneath her. A brilliant light flashed and Margaret was blinded. Then, she felt it. A presence. A hand. Someone was touching her shoulder. The hand slid across her back to her other shoulder. She reached out for it but felt nothing. The hand was on her cheek, gently cradling it. She reached for it once more and again felt emptiness. She smelled a familiar scent. Margaret stepped forward, both arms extended, attempting to grasp this energy — this presence felt so near. Energy in her hands created a pressure at her fingertips so intense she felt as if they would split apart. She allowed herself to send it forth. The power of its release pitched Margaret backward against the chair. She fought against her own blindness, willing herself to see. Dark shadows danced in front of her. Margaret heard a whisper. A familiar voice. She turned quickly and saw a shadow moving into a bright light. She lunged toward it, reaching out to catch the shadow. A surge of energy shot from her fingertips and prevented the shadow's escape. Before Margaret knew what was happening, she was clinging to the shadowy form, and it embraced her. The apparition slowly came into focus, and Margaret let out a blood-curdling scream.

Instantly, the room returned to its previous state, and Akil stood over her.

"What is it? What did you see?" he demanded.

"I saw him," she gasped. Her eyes watered as she attempted to regain her composure. "James."

"You saw Stuart? It worked?" Akil asked.

"No, not my husband. I saw…my son," she cried and her tears began to flow. Akil met Margaret's gaze.

"Impossible," he whispered.

"It was him. He was here. He was a man, but I know it was my son. How can that be?" And for the first time since Margaret had known him, Akil muttered the words; "I do not know."

10

retribution

James ripped off his shirt and wrapped it around both blade and arm. Blood was flowing heavily from the wound. James threw Luno's good arm over his shoulder and dragged him down the path toward the camp. Behind the gate came the eerie chanting: "Pirates! Pirates! Pirates!"

The sun had nearly set when James and Luno cleared the jungle and stepped onto the beach. Kilani, Roger and Jan, huddled around the fire, jumped to their feet. Kilani was the first to reach them. Luno had gone ghostly pale. James's shirt was drenched in blood.

They laid him down carefully. Both Jan and Roger had already removed their shirts and were packing them against the wound.

"Got to get th' blade out," said Roger.

"Can't you heal him?" Kilani asked.

"I tried," said James. "It isn't working."

"What do you mean it isn't working?" she replied angrily.

"It's not working. I don't know why. We have to get the blade out. I think it may be hexed. Roger and I will hold his arm. Jan, pull out the blade." James looked at Jan and motioned his instructions. Jan nodded and grasped the hilt. Roger and James gripped Luno's arm while Kilani held his other hand and tried to distract him. Luno's face had changed from white to grey, and he struggled to keep his eyes open.

James nodded at Jan, who pulled upward on the hilt of the small sword with all his might. With a horrifying cracking sound, the blade broke free. Jan dropped it in the sand as James tied one of the shirts over the wound as tightly as he could. He stood over Luno and extended his hands. "Tertiri Zé Manukto tupassari." A light green glow rolled like a wave from James's palms and wrapped itself over both bandage and arm. Luno's color immediately improved.

Jan shouted excitedly. "Er kommt," he said again, pointing down the trail. Roger looked up.

"Wha' the bloody 'ell?"

Kilani immediately rose to her feet. "James." James looked to see what had gotten everyone's attention, Luno momentarily forgotten. Walking down the trail was Gai, hand outstretched as if something delicate sat in his palm, anger cast on his boy-face. He halted in front of James.

"Here is your traitor," he shouted, tossing something to the ground. His lips were wreathed with clear granules. The tymanuk, bitten into two pieces, landed at James's feet. Chills ran down his spine as he realized what was on Gai's mouth. It was the tymanuk's blood. "You killed my lieutenant," Gai said more calmly.

"We were protecting ourselves," said James. "Look what he did to my friend." James pointed to Luno, who was beginning to stir as he regained consciousness. Gai glanced toward Luno.

"He will live," said Gai. "My lieutenant is dead. Retribution must be paid."

"Ain't got nuthin' t' pay ye with," snarled Roger.

"One of you will stay behind. The others must leave by sunset tomorrow. I will provide you with what you need to repair your vessel." Gai took a step toward James. "And the one who stays," he said, pointing a finger at James, "cannot be you, and it cannot be him." He pointed at Luno, who was now awake and alert.

After a moment of shocked silence, Kilani lunged for Gai, who quickly sidestepped and pushed her to the ground. James released a burst of green energy at Gai, hitting him square in the chest and sending him spinning into the air. But rather than falling back to the ground, Gai remained airborne, hovering just below the treetops. He flew toward the group, stopping just out of arm's reach.

"You have no power over me, pirate. This is my island. Now, I will have your decision by sunrise or none of you will leave." Gai smiled triumphantly at James. As he grinned, a shadow fell over his face, and for an instant the boyish features turned dark and ugly. James found himself shaking with anger. He fought to conceal it. Catching a glimpse of the rage in James's eyes, Gai flew nose to nose with him. He whispered so that only James could hear. "She will be mine."

"Tertiri Zé Manukto reisa," James shouted. A stream of fire burst from his hands, but Gai was too quick and flew into the jungle before James had even finished the incantation. James turned away from the jungle and looked out over the water. The Queen Mary stood in the harbor, still without a mast but otherwise in good repair. The long shadows of twilight stretched from the shore onto the water. Despite all that had happened, James's desire to return to the maze to seek the black castle had grown stronger. The only obstacle was this mysterious boy-demon. He released his grip on the black-bladed sword, unaware that he had even grasped it, and turned back to the group.

Jan and Roger were helping Luno to his feet while Kilani stood staring at the spot in the jungle where Gai had disappeared.

"What is that creature?" she asked, not turning her gaze from the treetops.

"I don't know," said James.

"It seemed to know you," she replied. James said nothing, trying to gauge what was truly on her mind. "What did it whisper to you? "

"He said, 'Sunrise, pirate,'" James lied.

Kilani finally turned and looked into James's eyes. James could feel her searching for the truth. He didn't know why he had lied to her. To protect her? Perhaps. Part of James believed Kilani would want to go with Gai, and he knew he couldn't let that happen.

"We are long overdue for a fireside palaver, are we not?" Luno said, poking at the flames with a stick. Each member of the group nodded in agreement and took positions around the campfire as James cast protective incantations. Everyone settled around the fire, silently reviewing the day's events. Roger was the first to speak.

"Sommon' mind tellin' me wha' the bloody 'ell tha' thing was?" Everyone turned to James who continued to stare into the embers.

"It is a demon," said Luno.

"How do you know?" asked Kilani.

"I have seen its other face. It takes the form of a boy because it chooses to, but that is not its true form. The demon calls itself Gai."

"Why did you leave us, Luno? Why did you go?" asked Kilani, anger rising in her tone.

"I had no choice," said Luno. "He invited me in. There was something in his voice that ensnared my reason."

"He has powers over this place," said James, "inexplicable powers, as you saw. He claims to have brought our ship here."

"For what purpose?" asked Kilani.

"He said he was lonely," replied James.

"Lonely?" scoffed Roger.

"He seeks an adversary," said Luno. "He told me as much as well. When I disappointed him, he sent me to the maze."

"The maze?"

"He said the maze leads to a tunnel and the tunnel to the black castle. Unfortunately, he also said the maze is unsolvable and the tunnel impassable. I was lost for weeks wandering through that bloody thing until James found me."

"Weeks? You've been gone less than a day," said Kilani, but she took in the beard on Luno's cheeks and the dark shadows under his eyes. He looked older — not by days but by years.

"I was led to the maze by, of all things, one of the creatures that killed William," James said. "I don't believe they are murdering fiends, only that they protect themselves. They are intelligent. They can communicate. This creature led me to the maze where I was able to find you." He nodded at Luno, who unconsciously rubbed his arm where the blade had struck him. "This demon must have some kind of anti-transporting incantation cast around his domain. I attempted to transport directly to the beach, but we appeared just inside the gate. That's where we were attacked by the other boys."

"Other boys? There's more of 'em?" asked Roger.

"I don't believe the other boys are demons like Gai," said James. "They appear to be…normal boys."

"But you killed one of them?" asked Kilani.

"They attacked. James was simply defending us. You don't attack unsuspecting adults with the intent to kill and expect to be smacked on the arse for misbehavior," said Luno. "This demon must have them under some sort of hex or spell."

"Does that excuse the murdering of a child?" Kilani asked in a strained voice.

"No," said James, looking deep into the glow of the fire. "It doesn't."

All sat in silence, mulling over the events of the day. James thought of nothing but Kilani's accusation. Murderer, she had called him. And she was right. Regardless of whether or not he'd intended to do it, the boy was dead by his hand. James unsheathed the black-bladed sword and laid it across his knees. It appeared to absorb the light of the fire, rather than reflect it. He ran his fingers along the blade.

"Where did you get that?" Luno asked.

"Gai left it behind after our encounter at his house," said James.

"Bloody evilest thing I ever saw," said Roger.

"He called it spellbreaker steel. He said it was forged in the fires of the black abyss." Kilani and Luno exchanged knowing glances.

"And just how did he come to leave it behind?" asked Luno.

"I followed two of the boys to a stone house at the end of the street to meet the Governor, as they call Gai. He told me I was a worthy adversary. But then something strange happened — something that seemed to frighten him. There was a grand chair that I felt compelled to sit in, so I sat. The chair broke under my weight. Before that moment, I don't believe Gai had any intention of letting me go. But when the chair broke, something in him changed. He was fearful and angry. He told me where to find you and that I must get you and leave immediately. Then he disappeared, leaving his sword behind. I thought it looked like a good blade, so I took it." And it will guide me to the black castle, he thought.

Luno eyed him skeptically.

"Enough about the sword," Roger said. "The demon said one of us is to be left behin' — tha' be me, Peroc, Jan or Kilani. I'd volunteer myself, but wit' William gone, I'll be needed to crew th' Queen Mary."

"I stay," Jan said boldly. "I am strongest, no?"

"You are indeed the strongest, my friend; however, I don't believe it should be you. Your sister needs looking after, and we will need all the hands we can get on board," said James. Peroc, who had been silent since the discussion began, stood and began to speak. James translated.

"There was a story I heard as a child — the story of a demon that lived on this very island . All of the children would gather on the shore of my island in hopes of catching sight of this demon, but none ever did. Our mothers grew angry if we even mentioned this demon. I am a native of these lands. I know them better than any of you. If anyone is fit to survive this place, it is I." Peroc sat down with finality.

"I agree," Luno said, all too quickly.

"Aye," concurred Roger. "'e's little 'elp on board." Kilani stood and walked toward the dock without saying a word. "Wha's on 'er mind?" James stood and followed, sheathing his sword as he made his way across the beach to her side. The moon hung just over the tree line , bathing the entire area in a blue light. Kilani did not turn as James approached.

"I know what you're thinking, and it isn't true," said James.

"It is true. I am most fit to stay. Peroc's intentions, while noble, will not satisfy Gai. I heard what he whispered to you. It is me he wants. And he wants you to have to make that decision. He wants you to feel the pain of giving me up."

"I don't intend to honor any agreement with that devil," said James. I will transport all of us to Harbor Town. We will have to abandon the Queen Mary."

"I am not certain I want to return to Harbor Town," said Kilani.

"What?" Shock spread across James's face.

"Something here is different. I feel closer to them. I'm not sure how to explain it."

"Kilani, what are you talking about? Closer to whom?"

She sighed and finally made eye contact with James. The tears were there, ready to spill onto her cheeks. "James, I am not the same person I was before I came here. I had a life. A family. My boys — they are twins, you know. I was taken from them. They are babies, my boys, and they need me. They need their mother, and you're right, I will do anything — anything to get back to them. That includes leaving all this behind with everyone I've come to care about here."

James looked at Kilani and understood. Luno was right. Kilani would attach herself to the person she thought most likely to help her return. A moment ago, it was James. Now, it was the demon Gai.

"I don't understand why you believe the answer to getting home lies here with Gai. He can't travel through the tunnel that leads to the black castle. He said so himself. He may have powers — inexplicable powers — but I have powers too, Kilani, and I do not fear the tunnel. My only fear is losing you."

She looked at him and smiled. The smile was wrought with sadness and pity. Kilani reached up and laid her hand on his cheek. James flinched as if she had slapped him. He stepped back, his hand immediately going to the hilt of his sword. Kilani took a step back, projecting fear where there had been empathy. It took James a moment to realize what he'd done, and he quickly lifted his hand from the hilt.

"You don't know if that demon will help you at all. It is very likely that he intends to kill you, Kilani. I've looked into his eyes, and I've seen the malice that lies behind the boyish face. Gai cannot be trusted. But you can trust me. You know you can trust me. And you know I'm equally bent upon getting home."

"There is something happening to you, James. The others may not see it, but I do. You are obsessed with getting into the black castle. You have been since the first time you saw it. I believe finding a way home and getting into that cursed place are mutually exclusive. One does not beget the other. You seem to believe that all the answers lie within those dark towers."

James's hand unconsciously slipped into the pocket where the key rested. As he touched the cold steel, he knew that the way home had to pass through the castle. He couldn't understand why Kilani wouldn't trust him — why she would rather trust this demon, this monster in a boy's body, over him. She was leaving him. He was losing her right now. Anger surged through his body as his hand slipped back to the hilt of the black sword.

"Look at you," said Kilani. "Even as I speak, you stroke that key and don't have the wits to realize I notice. I notice, James. I notice everything you do. Ever since you and Luno found it, you haven't let it out of your sight. I dare say it is poisoning your mind. You are a good man, James. Yet you seem to be slipping away from reason as time passes. And that…that thing you've gotten from Gai that you now grip without even knowing it," — she pointed to the sword with a look of disgust — "is as poisonous as the key. It's as if they're made from the same ore or with the same purpose. You cannot control yourself, James! You are no better than that demon."

"It is you who have lost control, Kilani!" James shouted. "These trinkets mean nothing to me. Nothing! I am in control. It is you who does not listen to reason. It is you whose obsession with returning home at all costs has again and again torn to pieces the relationships you've

forged here. Now, once again, after feigning interest beyond friendship with someone, you forsake them for your next best option for salvation. You are cold and self-centered. Tell me, Kilani, if you run away with this demon and he shows you a way home, will you come back for us or will you simply turn your back on those who have loved you all this time?"
Kilani began to speak, but James quickly interrupted.

"There is no need to answer. It is clear where your loyalties lie. And while I understand your need to return, I don't understand — will never understand — the selfishness that surrounds your obsession. It has clearly driven you to madness if you believe salvation lies in there," he said, pointing toward Adelphi. "As always, Kilani, you will decide for yourself what is best for you and to hell with the rest of us. I hope your children never know of your betrayal or they may not look upon you with visions of angelic perfection. They may see you for who you really are."

Kilani stood, absorbing the daggers James thrust at her while tears rolled down her cheeks.

"You have no idea what it is like to be a mother torn away from her children. Left to wonder every minute of every day whether they are safe. Whether they even remember what you look like. Whether they cry out your name every night as they go to sleep. You cannot possibly understand the love that is shared between mother and child. How could you? My only concern is for my children. If that is selfish of me, so be it. I cannot be responsible for the greater good when my children are left to fend for themselves. I do know this, James. I am no good to them or anyone else dead, and that is what lies at the end of the path you propose." Kilani's weeping reduced her voice to a hoarse whisper.

"I have seen your heart, James, and it is true, as are your intentions. You are a better person than I could ever be. Do not let this place take that away from you. Do not let your singular focus squander the lives of those who follow and trust you." James began to speak, but it was Kilani who interrupted now.

"Yes, James, you are their leader, and that makes you responsible for each of their lives. I am not a leader. I never have been. Please, James, allow me to follow my instincts. They have never failed me. I ask for permission to go, and as our leader, only you are able to give it. I cannot say I will honor your decision if you tell me to stay, but I nevertheless ask for your leave. I will say this and then I will say no more. I do feel for Luno. He is the father I never had. It breaks my heart to leave him. I do feel for you. Despite your youth, James, we have a connection. I cannot deny that. I've longed to explore that connection — to understand what roots it and where it might lead — but I can't. My mind, my focus, my determination will not allow it. Not when my children are out there waiting for their mother. Before dawn, I will go to the gate. I beg you not to tell the others until I am gone."

Kilani looked at James for a response. His head was down, his hair dangling in front of his face like a black curtain. For a long time, he was silent. As Kilani was ready to turn and walk away, he lifted his head and looked at her with dry eyes.

"Godspeed, Kilani."

11

tea and theories

December 1896, London

Ahe bell tinkled every time someone stepped through the heavy wooden door into the cramped little shop. A shelf full of clocks ticked by the seconds in maddening cadence. The footfalls of several shoppers caused the wooden planks to groan, making Margaret wince, haunted by memories of her past. She reached the end of the aisle and turned to make her way to the opposite end for what would have been the thirteenth time. Avoiding the watchful eyes of the shopkeeper, who no doubt considered her a potential thief, she strode down the aisle pausing to inspect the porcelain dolls.

"There is a tea room across the street that serves the most magnificent Earl Grey. Would you care to join me?" Margaret jumped. She had been so alert for his arrival — how had she missed it? Without waiting for an answer, he turned and made his way to the exit. Margaret followed at a distance, smiling in response to the accusatory stare of the shopkeeper as she passed. The cobbled lane was strewn with patches of ice, making travel, even across the street, treacherous. People stepped haphazardly; some gripped desperately onto whatever they could find to prevent themselves from falling. He was already on the opposite side of the street and descending the stairs into the tearoom.

Carefully, she made her way across the street. A wooden sign swung in the cold wind. Solomon Caw Books, Tea & Curios. Glancing over her shoulder, she descended the stairs and stepped inside. Akil was already sitting at a small table in the corner of the room. He was busy stirring a small silver spoon in one of the two steaming cups on the table in front of him. The man behind the counter did not look up as she passed. He appeared transfixed by whatever was printed on the side of a small wooden box of tea that rested on the shelf. Save the proprietor, the shop was empty.

"Good to see you," Akil said, stirring his tea with a silver spoon. Margaret nodded, removing her traveling cloak and hanging it on a hook on the wall. The fireplace on the opposite wall burned low and hot. Margaret did not have to ask if this place was secure. She had long ago learned that Akil would never conduct a meeting in any location that wasn't. Based on the doleful gaze of the shopkeeper, Margaret surmised that Akil had cast a distractive incantation that would keep him from overhearing or disturbing them. He had most likely also cast a deterrent incantation at the top of the stairs. If anyone should attempt to enter the tearoom, they would think it wasn't a good idea for one reason or another. Perhaps they would suddenly remember something — an appointment elsewhere, their spouse's birthday — or simply forget where they were heading to begin with. They would continue on, forgetting they had ever desired to enter in the first place.

"What did you find?" Margaret asked.

Always straight to the point with her, Akil thought. He couldn't blame her for wanting to know, although she certainly would not like what he was about to tell her. Her generation appeared to have lost the graciousness of inconsequential conversation. He did miss discussing the simple things — the weather, flowers, tea — all of which held great interest but little importance in the grand scheme of things. He believed that discussing such trivialities was a type of mental refreshment — a good way to clear one's mind of all the stressors of daily life. At times he would go into a pub or tearoom and strike up a conversation with an unfaithful simply for that purpose. He had great difficulty finding anyone in his world who didn't know who he was.

"Not much, I am afraid. What little I did find comes mostly from word of mouth rather than the archives. Very few sorcerers have delved into this subject because of its fruitless nature."

"Anything will be better than the complete ignorance I'm living with at the moment," said Margaret testily.

"I want to start by telling you what I know about the soul itself. I realize I may have already told you some of this, but I believe it is important to hear it again." Margaret nodded anxiously. The burning log in the fireplace snapped as the flames pulled at the wood grains. Only Margaret flinched at the sound.

"When a person dies naturally, her soul passes peacefully into the afterlife, or so the story goes. When a person dies an unexpected or violent death, her soul is torn from her body. Sometimes, when this happens, the soul does not pass on and will remain earthbound until it can make its way to the afterlife. In very rare instances, the soul itself will tear. When the soul is torn, a trace of that person is left behind. Even now, however, I'm not fully convinced this theory is entirely correct. The incantation I performed in the church attempted to help you see if your husband left a trace of his soul. As I said previously, I have tried this myself several times without success." Akil paused briefly, taking a sip of his tea before he continued.

"Now, if this theory is correct, what you saw in the church means that somehow your son managed to tear his soul while he remained alive. I suppose it is possible that the magic James spoke of was so powerful that it did tear away part of his soul while killing everyone else in that room. "

"What does that mean? What does it mean to live one's life with only part of one's soul?" Margaret asked.

"We often hear stories about people — villains mostly — who are said to be so evil that they are without a soul. Does this mean that the soul is the center of all good in a person? If this is the case, what does that mean for James, whose soul is now incomplete?"

"Are you saying he will never be able to pass on?" asked Margaret.

"In my travels of late, I met a man who claimed he lives with a fractured soul. He told me during his childhood he witnessed things so horrible that he buried himself deep inside his own mind — so deep in fact that he lost the function of his physical body. Mind and body were so far separated at that point, the man professed he could travel beyond his body with only his mind. The more proficient he became at this process, the further he could travel. Despite his increasing ability to distance mind from body, he always reached a point where a force pulled him back. One day he decided he did not want to return to his body. He alleged he fought the force so fervently that something ripped away. He said his soul had been torn."

"And what is this man like? Does he live a normal life?"

"The boy, who became the man that I met, never had what we would consider a normal life, not from the day he was born. He was never loved as James is and spent most of his early years living in fear. I met him in Boulderfield Manor."

Margaret gasped. Boulderfield Manor was where they sent dangerous and often deranged criminals and stripped them of their magical abilities — or tried to. Was James destined to be like this man — a criminal? He had already killed four people! Margaret forced her mind to stop. She would not allow that horror to befall her son. He was a good boy, not a criminal. She would do everything in her power to prevent him from becoming like that man.

"Most people would believe that to live without a complete soul makes one more susceptible to the lure of evil. If they knew of James's past, they would think he was destined to live a cursed life. My theory, however, is quite different than what I have presented to you." Akil lifted his teacup and inhaled deeply.

"I believe what you saw was not part of James's soul at all. Take a moment and try to remember the image of your son you witnessed that day. What did he look like?" Margaret thought hard. She remembered seeing the face and knowing it was her son, but there had been something different about him. He was a man, not the child he had been the night his father was killed.

"He was a full-grown man," she said.

"Why would the soul of a boy take the image of a man?"

Perhaps she was wrong, Margaret thought. Maybe it was her husband after all. No. She was sure it was her son. While they had similar characteristics, there was no confusing the two. She had no doubt it was James.

"I'm hoping you can answer that question," said Margaret.

"Fortunately, I believe I can. The soul, whether traveling onward or left behind, always assumes the image of the body it occupies at the time. Always. Therefore, what you saw was not the soul of your son as a child."

"I don't understand," said Margaret. "Are you saying that what I saw was the soul of my son as an adult? But James is only 15 ! How is that possible?"

"I do not think it was his soul at all but an imprint."

"An imprint? From the future?" asked Margaret.

"Not in the literal sense. I believe your son will find a way to influence past events when he becomes a man — a form of magic many have strived to accomplish with no success."

"Have you ever tried?"

"I do not believe in tampering with the past even though there are many events in my life I would like to change." Akil seemed to fade as he stared off into the distance. He shook his head slightly and looked back at Margaret.

"So, do you believe James's soul remains intact?"

"I do," Akil said with a reassuring smile. "I do not believe your son has a future in villainy or evil. Rest easy, dear Margaret. He is a product of good parenting and will grow to be a good man."

Relief swept over Margaret. Her shoulders relaxed and she picked up her tea for the first time. "You truly believe James will find a way to influence the past — specifically that event? The death of my husband?"

"I do," replied Akil. "That single event is without a doubt the most influential in his life. It has changed his very being. You said yourself he hasn't been the same since. And in truth, what child would be? Despite our best efforts to convince him otherwise, James still holds on to the guilt and the blame. Carrying such a burden his entire life could destroy a man."

"If he has been able to influence the past, why hasn't the present changed?" asked Margaret.

"Perhaps he was unsuccessful. Perhaps the present is a manifestation of those changes. We, as bystanders, would not know the difference."

"Is there any danger in this form of magic? Should we dissuade James from using it?"

"My dear Margaret, James is but a boy — a boy who is struggling with even the most basic of incantations as a result of this event and the self-imposed guilt surrounding it. Even mentioning that he may one day have the power to alter the past would mostly likely fall on deaf ears. Or worse, it could be the seed that precipitates the action sometime in the future. I suggest neither of us mention it at all. As he is currently in my care, I will see that it does not reach his ears. Perhaps in the future we will address it once again."

Margaret nodded. This meeting could have gone so differently, but she had found solace in the answers Akil had provided. She warmed her hands on her cup as the fire cracked and popped.

"What news of Alvaro?" Margaret asked, always curious as to the goings on outside her sheltered existence.

"He gains strength in the council. While the majority are not in agreement with all his proposed legislation, the fanaticism of his constituents continues to grow, as does his popularity. He will no doubt continue to rise in power."

"And with his rise will come an increased pressure to get his hands on James."

"Indeed, which is why it is so very important that James make up for lost time with his training," Akil said. His brow furrowed as if the very words he spoke somehow pained him.

12

love lost

It was well before dawn when James awoke. Dreams of his father crying out for help while James looked on, frozen in place, left him feeling more exhausted than when he'd shut his eyes. James rose and walked toward the tree line. There Kilani stood as if expecting him. James was hopeful that she'd changed her mind, but as he began to speak she silenced him with a finger to her lips. Her eyes were glassed over but no tears fell.

Slowly, she reached out and placed her hand behind James's head. Warmth radiated from her touch and flowed down his spine. In that moment, the draw of the black castle had no power over him. Only one desire consumed him. He marveled at the strength of it. She suddenly stepped forward and pressed her lips against his. Every dream he'd had of touching his lips to hers, of running his fingers through her hair, of feeling the smooth skin of her neck as he kissed her, was nothing but a dream, hazy and unclear, compared to the reality of it. He could get lost in this place and never have need to return.

She pulled away without meeting his eyes and hastily advanced toward the jungle path. James could see the sorrow in her posture as she walked away. He wanted nothing more than to stop her, to make her stay, but he knew his efforts would be in vain.

"Where is she going?" James turned to see Luno standing not far away. He had seen everything. James tried to reach out and stop him as he pursued her, but Luno easily broke free. He shouted her name, sounding more and more desperate as he followed the path out of sight. Meanwhile James remained firmly planted to the spot, his mind reeling with utter shock and confusion in the aftermath of Kilani's kiss. A moment later, Luno stormed out of the jungle, anger written all over his face. "What have you done?" he demanded.

"I let her go."

"You let her go? You let her go to that devil to be murdered?" Luno shouted, stepping closer to James.

"It was her choice. Once she has made up her mind, you know as well as I that there is no talking her out of it."

"Aye, but just because she's stubborn doesn't mean you let her walk off and commit suicide."

James could feel his defensive rage boiling beneath the surface. He tried to push it away. He did not want to fight with Luno. Luno's shouts now had the rest of the group stirring around the campfire. The first light of dawn peeked over the eastern horizon.

"Kilani has every right to chose her own path."

"You don't get it, boy. Gai has ensnared her mind. That's what he does.

Think about how easy it was for him to direct you where he wanted you to go. Do you really think that was your choice or his will?" The color drained from James's face as he realized what Luno was saying. "Yes, that's right. You've allowed her to walk into the custody of that murderer."

"How dare you call me a murderer," said Gai, appearing as if from thin air. "Only one of us has spilled blood," he said, looking at James. "Now, you've held to your end of the bargain so I shall hold to mine." He snapped his fingers and no fewer than a dozen boys walked out from the jungle with armloads of supplies. Each dropped his load on the beach and quickly retreated.

"Make your repairs. You have until sunset to be on your way. If that floating abomination remains in my harbor after the last rays of light fall behind the western sky, your people will know death. And I'll start with the one who has given herself to me."

"Like hell," Luno snarled, lunging at Gai. He easily sidestepped the older man and pushed him face-first into the sand. James's hand immediately went to the hilt of the black sword. Gai's eyes followed. Gai stepped closer, close enough to whisper.

"Soon, Captain James, soon we shall cross swords. But do not think that you have a chance of beating me with a blade."

James felt something in the back of his mind, almost as if Gai were drawing from his desires, pulling at them like threads. James put up a mental barrier as Akil had taught him. Gai's expression changed subtly. No, not his expression but rather his features . He appeared more feminine, James thought. This change was manifested in a fuller frowning mouth, smoother skin and wider eyes. Then he smiled and the boyish face returned, save a mouth full of needle-like teeth.

"You are different, aren't you, Captain James?" whispered Gai. "So much pain in your past, such a burden in your future. And still, barely a man. Yet, you've chosen to rise rather than crumble. That is, if the black castle doesn't pull you into its grasp. If you hear nothing else I say," Gai continued in a whisper, "hear this: that place — the lure of it — warps the minds of men. Even the greatest of your kind. Even you. You will become so consumed with it that all else will be forgotten. Soon, you'll even see it as a means of escape, which couldn't be further from the truth. Once the black castle has you, there is no escape. There is only pain." Gai turned and walked toward the jungle path, then called over his shoulder to James. "Perhaps you are the adversary I've been seeking, Captain James. The chair isn't right all the time." James could only stare at the spot where Gai had vanished into the foliage. So consumed was he by what he'd been told that he didn't notice Luno rushing toward him.

"You've killed her!" Luno shouted, fists flying, as they grappled in the sand. In seconds, Roger and Jan were pulling Luno off James. Luno continued to scuffle with the two of them until they finally shoved him back toward the fire. James lay motionless, staring up at the sky, blood trickling out of the corner of his mouth.

"Ye all right, Cap'n?" asked Roger, standing over him.

It was too much. All that he'd heard in the past several minutes, each opinion contradicting the other. He needed time to think. He slowly got to his feet and nodded at Roger who returned his nod with a quizzical expression.

"Make ready to set sail. I shall return before midday."

13

hope found

February 1710, Northern Mongolia

Akil Karanis crouched in a cave, his cloak drawn tight, his bare hands extended over a small fire. He was less than a day's journey from his destination, yet now, after he had traveled so far, doubt began to creep into his mind. It felt like a lifetime since he had spoken with Okon ak aintzinako. For some, it had been a lifetime. She had given him the book that contained the bloodline of the one he now sought. She had given him the Aldi Jaitsu that wound down as the Epoch Terminus approached. She had given him these things, and then the great Siren had banished him to Ak Egundiano — The Never.

Akil had considered abandoning his search for the Anointed One not long after arriving in The Never. He had quickly realized the futility of looking for an escape and lost himself in a depressive spiral. Years passed. He survived because surviving was the only thing he could do. His magic had left him. Then, one day, there was a bright flash not far from his primitive camp. He cautiously approached and found a woman, naked and powerless, lying on the bare earth.

He removed his cloak, fashioned from several small animal pelts, and tossed it over the disoriented woman, then helped her to her unsteady feet. Akil led her to his camp and sat her by the fire. As she became more lucid, he handed her a wooden cup of tea he had dried from herbs found on a hillside not far from his camp.

"Thank you," she said. Akil started. It was the first voice, other than his own, he had heard in nearly a decade.

"What is your name?" he asked.

"Abigail," she replied. "Abigail Ammoncourt."

"My name is Akil."

Abigail nodded and smiled but said nothing as she stared into the depths of her tea. Akil began pacing in front of the fire, his mind racing. He needed information, and finally here was someone who could provide it. Abigail placed a hand on her forehead.

"Will you stop your pacing — my head's near exploding as it is."

Akil froze and studied the woman. She was short with wide shoulders and thick limbs. Her dark hair was pulled back in a tight bun, and not a strand appeared to be out of place despite the arduousness of her journey to Ak Egundiano. Her olive skin was flawless save the wrinkles on her forehead and at the corners of her brown eyes.

"I need to lie down before I vomit." Akil quickly took the tea cup and tossed it onto the ground, then helped her to her feet. He led her around a strange stone formation and into the small hut he'd made from stone, mud and wood. He eased her onto the bedding and stepped outside, knowing she had fallen asleep instantly.

He waited impatiently for her to wake. Nearly two full days later, Abigail stepped out of the hut looking more rested but just as frightened. Akil immediately stepped to her side and offered her more tea.

"If that's the same swill you gave me earlier, I'll pass. I could do for something to eat, though."

Akil chuckled and retrieved a skin of water and some smoked meat from his food stores while Abigail surveyed her surroundings. Before she had turned completely around, Akil thrust a piece of meat in her face, startling her. She slowly took the meat and stepped back several paces.

"You're not exactly right in the head, are you?"

Akil took a deep breath trying to find calm before responding.

"I apologize, Abigail. You are the first human I have seen in three thousand six hundred and seven days. As you can guess, I am quite eager to discuss how it is you have come to be in this place."

Abigail sat on a stone beside the fire, pulling the cloak tight around her body.

"First, Akil, I need to know, what is this place?"

"It is called Ak Egundiano. You may know it as The Never."

"It is true then," said Abigail, hanging her head.

"What is true?"

"The council said that's where they were sending me. I didn't believe them ."

"Impossible. The council has neither the knowledge nor the power to banish someone to Ak Egundiano," said Akil. "Most are unaware of its existence."

"Clearly, they have found a way," she replied.

"But why? Why would they banish you?"

Abigail lifted her head. Tears rolled down her cheeks as she looked into

Akil's eyes.

"I killed a man."

Not long after Abigail's arrival, another person arrived, then another. Within a year, nearly two dozen people had been banished to The Never. With each new arrival, Akil's spirits rose and his thoughts began to stray to his purpose — finding Gai ak zangar. With the aid of several volunteers, Akil began mapping the main island and what could be seen of the satellite islands. With his maps, he conducted his search grid by grid, but the Siren continued to elude him. What he found instead was an escape from The Never. When he returned to his own world, seventy years in the time of men had come and gone, yet age had not touched him. He had returned with one focus: finding the Anointed One.

Akil stood, stretched his stiff muscles, and let his doubts fall from his shoulders like snowflakes. Slowly, he made his way to the mouth of the cave. The snowstorm that had chased him out of the open had passed and a new day was dawning. A red sun shone through the distant peaks, washing the snow-covered land in a crimson blanket. A bad omen, he thought.

He extended his palm. "Urtarazi." The snow that had blown into a drift higher than his chest during the night quickly melted. Akil stepped out onto the mountainside and continued his journey upward. Once he reached the summit, he followed the ridge line over three more peaks before descending onto a plateau to the village. He had traced the nomad tribe with relative ease because other tribes were quick to share stories of an unusual boy with strange powers.

In less than an hour's time, four young, wide-shouldered men escorted him into the chief's ger and took up positions around the perimeter with watchful eyes. Akil sat at a rickety wooden table across from one of the largest men he'd ever seen. Beside the man sat a woman with strong

Mongolian features, but one aspect that made her stand out from the others in the room. Her white-blonde hair was pulled back from her face into a waist-length braid. Her narrow eyes bored into Akil as he studied her tanned, youthful face.

"Speak, foreigner, for we have little time to receive guests. A storm approaches," said the chief.

"I have come for your son," Akil said in perfect Mongolian, still looking at the woman. Akil could see her knuckles turn white as she gripped the chair.

"He is different. He is like me. I can take him where there are others like us. He will be safe. He will be nurtured there." Akil turned to the large man. "He will no longer cause your tribe any trouble."

Akil sat back and let the pair discuss what he had told them. He knew the chief was not the boy's father and would be happy to be rid of the difficult child. The woman, on the other hand, was not relenting to the man's argument. Finally, the chief puffed out his chest and bellowed at the woman. She instantly fell silent and her eyes reddened. The man looked at Akil.

"And what do you have in exchange for the boy?" Akil reached into his cloak, removing an item wrapped in burlap.

"I shall give you the crown of Tolui Khan," Akil said, unwrapping a golden crown. The front was centered by a tall scalloped peak that descended to meet folds curled into ovals resembling owl's eyes. He placed it on the table and lifted his cup of tea. The chief's mouth dropped open. One of the guards lost hold of his pike, which clattered loudly against the back of Akil's chair. After a moment of silence, the chief hardly glanced at the woman beside him before making his decree.

"Take the boy."

Akil Karanis stood, carefully placing his teacup on the table. He bowed to the chief and then to the woman at his side. The man returned a wide smile, but the woman refused to make eye contact. She was red faced and watery eyed.

Akil stooped as he pushed aside the blue and white blanket that hung across the doorway of the ger and stepped out into the cold. The village was small, only a few dozen structures, all of them the temporary shelters of a nomadic people. Worn paths in the snow led from one to the other. The absence of mud mixed with the snow indicated that temperatures had been below freezing long before the tribe arrived. Rising up on three sides of the plateau, ice-capped mountains provided shelter from enemy tribes. The fourth edge of the plateau fell away into the clouds and beyond.

Akil made his way past several of the round , thick-walled felt tents with domed roofs. From afar, the village appeared to be a cluster of giant mushroom caps. The only thing giving them away as habitations was the smoke from their vented roofs. At the last ger, the wide and well-worn path tapered to a single set of footprints. They were small — a child's. Akil grinned to himself and continued on in pursuit of the person who had laid the tracks not long ago. The wind raged, blowing his hood back and causing his white beard to swirl like a cat's tail. He whispered, "Blindatu," and the wind ceased to pummel him. He paused long enough to pull his hood back over his receding hair and then continued following the tracks.

As he neared the edge of the plateau, it appeared as though the tracks simply vanished into the void. Upon closer inspection, Akil could see a narrow stone ledge where the violent winds had not allowed any snow to settle. He stepped cautiously down onto the ledge, taking a moment to peer at the swirling grey clouds below, and then continued on. The ledge descended and widened until it stopped abruptly where the face of a glacier towered above both ledge and plateau. Akil looked up the sheer cliff in front of him. He smiled and held his hand against the icy surface.

"Erakutsi." The ice melted away into a narrow opening, revealing darkness within. "Bizitu." A pink orb rose from his palm and hovered in the dark entryway, lighting the narrow stone corridor. Akil turned, not able to fit otherwise, and sidestepped his way inside. The fissure opened into a small cave where a boy no older than ten crouched beside a small fire. He held his knees tight to his chest and rocked slightly while staring into the flames. He did not look up at Akil.

"Your protective incantations are impressive. Highly advanced. You should be proud," Akil said, once again in perfect Mongolian. Still, the boy did not look up. Akil stepped closer to the fire, carefully avoiding the roof of the cave as it dipped down. He stooped across from the boy and extended his hands, warming them beside the flames.

"You are different than the others. You have a gift. You desire to be special. I will see to that — it is why I have come. If you stay, you will become more of an outcast as time passes until even your own family pushes you away. What I have to offer will harness your great potential. You will find community and comfort among our kind."

"Will I ever return?"

"That is a choice left to you. I have received permission from the chief of your tribe to take you as my apprentice. I will teach you what I know and bring you before my people and all will rejoice in your coming."

"Why? Why will they rejoice?" asked the boy.

"You are special. My kin have been waiting for you for quite some time," said Akil.

"I don't understand."

"All in time, my boy. First, you must gather what you wish to bring along, and we must leave this place." Akil's face gave away the urgency of his statement. The howling wind outside the cave grew louder with each second. He glanced over his shoulder as a clap of thunder shook the walls.

The boy stood, his tanned face partially hidden beneath his white-blond hair. He warmed his hands over the fire for a moment, then turned and picked up the bearskin coat he had set neatly on the stone behind him. As he shrugged it on, it became obvious it was much too large for him. Akil smiled as he pulled a matching cap over his head, lifted a sack from the ground, and slung it over his shoulder. Strung to the outside of the sack were the curved blades of two scimitars.

"They were my father's," the boy said as Akil examined them.

"I have been told he was a great warrior," said Akil. To that the boy did not reply but walked around the fire and stood beside Akil.

"Our chief fears these blades. He says they are cursed because my father never lost a fight with them, but because they were passed down from my father's father, the chief could not take them from him. Not many moons ago, the chief led a hunting party of all the tribesmen. My father did not return. The chief said he had fallen from a cliff while fighting an enemy tribe that had been hunting in our territory. I asked the chief about the blades. He said the gorge was too deep to retrieve them. I went to the site of the battle. The only tracks I found were those of my tribesmen. I climbed down into the gorge, and I found my father's body. There was a dagger in his back — the dagger of the chief. My father's swords had never been drawn. I buried my father as best I could after taking his swords. I hid them in this cave.

"The next night, while the tribe slept, I snuck into the chief's ger and stabbed the dagger into his wooden table. I covered my tracks in the snow. The next morning, the hunters were searching the area but they wouldn't say why. The chief looked afraid for the first time I can remember. He will live in fear until I am old enough to face him as a man. Then he will die."

"When you learn what I have to teach you, those blades will seem like toys."

"I shall pass them to my son and he to his," the boy said, ignoring Akil's statement.

"I will take you to bid your farewells and then we shall leave."

"It is best if we just go," the boy said, thinking of his mother and the brother he would leave behind. Akil paused a moment, allowing the boy to reconsider. Resolutely, the boy looked up at Akil, his eyes glassy but his face determined. "The storm will only get worse."

"Very well, Alexander. So shall we begin our journey. May it be as prosperous as foretold."

With that, Akil reached under his cloak and produced a pinch of purple powder. He sprinkled it over his head while pulling the boy close. In a brilliant flash of smoke and light, they were gone.

14

adelphi

James stood on the long rocky outcropping that stretched from the main island into the sea toward the black castle. He hadn't returned to this place since he'd arrived in The Never. He stood on the spine — the cluster of vertebral boulders that stretched from the main island out into the sea. The black castle was frustratingly close, yet far enough away to make gaining access impossible from where he stood. The moment he arrived he could feel it calling him, beckoning him to come and enter. Instinctively, he reached for the key in his pocket with one hand and the black steel sword with the other. His body jolted as his connection with the castle amplified. His need for it surged. James felt himself moving toward the drop-off between the stony vertebrae as if he were being pulled by an invisible rope. As he walked, a flicker of clarity told him his quest had become an obsession. Still, his conscious mind, rapt with desire, was able to ignore all logical thought by rationalizing the importance of getting inside the castle. For a brief moment, he couldn't remember why it was so important to stand on the battlements overlooking the courtyard. Then it came to him — to find a way home, of course. Yes. That was more important than anything else.

As he willed himself to turn away from the castle, James thought of Kilani. Had Gai killed her or was she safe? Perhaps she had been shown the way through the maze, maybe even escorted into the black castle itself. She could be looking out at him from one of the towers right now. A pang of jealousy swept through James. He shook it away. If he managed to discover a way inside before he could find Kilani, he would come back for her. He promised himself he would not forget.

James inhaled, filling his lungs with the clean sea air as he looked upon the shore. Before he allowed himself to become transfixed again, he reached into his pouch, removed a pinch of transporting powder and disappeared in a flash of orange smoke and light.

He appeared on the wooden dock in the same spot from which he had vanished. The repairs to the Queen Mary were well underway. Roger and Jan had been able to set the new mast and rig up the sail. Peroc was doing his best to repair the railing while Luno paced nervously across the deck. "It's about bloody time," Luno growled. James halted as he noticed the long shadows stretching from the pilings. The sun hung low in the western sky. When he had left, it had not yet crested the trees. This is impossible, he thought.

"Where the bloody hell have you been, boy? If we don't get everything wrapped up and set sail within the next hour, we'll most likely find ourselves at the bottom of the harbor," Luno shouted, a strange timbre to his voice. James noticed the change immediately. He focused on Luno and realized he wasn't moving with his typical vibrancy. James nodded to Peroc as he stepped onto the deck and then froze. From his vantage point, he thoroughly inspected the entirety of Luno's person, then focused on his hands. They were shaking, not in anger or frustration, simply shaking. His skin had a sickly pallor. His unsteady gait was more of a shuffle than a stride. When Luno finally reached the rail and turned, James started. Luno's face had aged by years. He was a bent old man. Their eyes met for the briefest of moments before Luno broke contact, looking off into the distance as if something had caught his attention.

"Care to explain where you've been for half the day while the rest of us were scrambling to get 'er seaworthy?" asked Luno in a voice that matched his decrepit appearance. James tried to speak, but words would not come. He could only gape at the old man standing in front of him. Roger approached the ship with an armful of lumber.

"Tried to tell 'im, but he don' want to listen. Been pacin' since you left, mutterin' to himself."

James stepped into Luno's path, blocking his progress. Luno met his eyes. "That's a bold look, boy! Speak your piece quickly before I smack the hair off your head." James lifted a hand in an attempt to convey that he hadn't come to argue.

"Do you not see?" he asked in a hoarse whisper.

"I see perfectly well. I see an arrogant child standing before me and three of the most incompetent deckhands that have ever crawled this land scurrying around like rats before a flood." Luno's once bright and intelligent eyes were clouded and bloodshot under wrinkled, drooping lids.

"Don't you see?" asked James. "It's gone."

"What's gone?" shouted Luno.

"Your eternal youth, your agelessness. Time is no longer your ally but your enemy."

"What is this nonsense that you speak?"

James extended his hands. "Tertiri ze Manukto inari." Between his hands a silver orb grew. "Inari." The orb became reflective, mirroring Luno's wizened features. James watched as his mouth slackened and the fire went out of his posture.

"No. Impossible. This is a trick," he said, trying to clench his fists. His swollen, knobby knuckles would not allow it. He looked down at his hands and, for the first time, realized they were covered with wrinkled, loose skin. Jan put his arm around Luno's shoulder. James hadn't had much of an opportunity to get to know Jan during their brief travels together, but by this one gesture, he knew Jan was a good man.

"Iz true, boss. James vould not lie to you," he said. Luno looked in the reflecting orb again then into the eyes of Jan whose strong arms made sure his weak legs didn't give.

"This is your fault!" he spat, pointing a bent finger at James. "You let her go. You had the power to keep her here. We all had decided who would go, and you went against our decision!" Luno's knees started to wobble and Jan half-carried, half-dragged him to the steps of the quarterdeck where he sat with his head in his hands.

"Look at me," groaned Luno. "I'm useless. I'm…dying." Then, to everyone's surprise, the old man who had been the indefatigable Luno, began to cry. James turned away, unable to face the emotional breakdown of the man who'd been so steadfast and strong since his arrival. Roger joined him as he walked astern.

"We got to get him out o' this place, Cap'n. Mayhap things will slow down or even turn 'round if we get back t' Harbor Town," Roger said, searching James's eyes for any glimmer of encouragement or hope.

"Did Gai take Luno's unnatural long life?" asked James. "Does he have that power? Something took it away, whether Gai or this island or

The Never itself." The men looked over at Luno, who was still weeping into his hands as Jan attempted to console him. "You're right though, he needs to be as far from this island as possible. How close is she to being seaworthy?" he asked, gesturing to the Queen Mary.

"S'long as she don' run into another one o' them rogue storms, she should make the journey."

"Very well. Let us gather our things from the beach and depart immediately."

Roger nodded and they made their way onto the dock where they found Peroc already piling their belongings beside the ladder. It took less than an hour to prepare for departure. To their relief, Luno had fallen into a deep sleep.

Once everything was on board, James stood on the beach looking longingly at the jungle path that led to Adelphi. He knew what he must do. His stomach clenched in anticipation of what would come. Resolute in his decision, he turned back toward the Queen Mary. The wind had picked up over the past several minutes — a good sign for a swift sail. A voice, ever so faint, blew from the shore. Soon. James was certain he was hearing the call of his adversary. Yes, soon, he thought.

James boarded the Queen Mary after releasing the mooring lines. He nodded to Roger who pulled the halyard line as Jan stood behind the wheel. The instant the sail was fully raised, it billowed outward, jolting the ship forward. They were out of the cove in minutes and rounded the point headed in a northeasterly direction that would bring them to Harbor Town long before sunrise. The moon was already well on its way into the sky as the Queen Mary cleared the point. The setting sun at their backs illuminated the peaks of the main island. In the distance, the black castle came into view.

James could hear its call in the recesses of his mind. His hands subconsciously reached for the key and the hilt of his sword. As his fingertips contacted the black steel, his mind was transported. He was standing on the smooth stone of the keep. His colors flew atop the turrets and along the curtain walls — their black cloth rippling in a fierce wind. A doorway at the far end of the keep spilled a bright, inviting light, but James ignored it and strode to the short staircase at the opposite corner of the keep.

He mounted the steps into the square enclosure where he found a second set of narrow wooden steps leading to the wallwalk, which ran the perimeter and no doubt provided a clear view for lookouts and archers in the event of an attack. James climbed the worn wooden steps despite their groan of protest and stepped between the merlons of the battlement. He was looking out over the sea. The sky was a cloudy grey mass with lighter patches where the sunlight fought to penetrate. Not far away was a group of islands: The Never . He could see the spine as it rose from the water and curved back toward the main body of the island. James could make out the very spot upon which he had stood on the day of his arrival. The same spot he had occupied hardly an hour prior.

He stepped to the opposite side of the square to the crenel, his hand resting on the top merlon as he gazed out at the open sea stretching to the horizon. The sea was rough. Waves broke into whitecaps in every direction. The water, a reflection of the sky, was grey, imperious and forbidding. Then he saw something. Like a piece of flotsam, the Queen Mary rolled and pitched over the waves. He wanted to call out to it but he knew even on a calm day, the distance was too great. She sailed north toward Harbor Town. A smile crossed his face as he carefully made his way back down the rickety wooden steps then the stone pie-steps that twisted around and out onto the expanse that was the top of the keep. The light from the doorway at the far end of the keep continued to shine — to beckon. James thought he could hear music inside. He forced himself to turn away and found himself back on the deck of the Queen Mary. He slid his hand from his pocket and realized he'd been squeezing the key so tightly that it had left an impression in his palm.

James surveyed his surroundings, wondering how long he'd been lost in his vision. None of the others appeared to notice anything at all. As he looked off the port side of the ship, James wasn't surprised to find that they had indeed passed the black castle and had the easternmost point of the main island off the bow. He turned and headed toward the quarterdeck steps. As he lifted his foot onto the first step, James heard a sound from the cabin beneath. Curious, he peeked through the small window set into the door.

Luno was pacing back and forth in the small cabin. He shuffled his feet as if they were too heavy to lift. His shoulders hunched forward while his head remained perfectly erect, reminding James of an ancient tortoise. His face was even more wrinkled and the hair on his head had turned thin and white. Luno neurotically rubbed his hands together as he muttered.

James wanted to go to him. To try and explain what had happened with Kilani. To explain why he now had to leave as well, but he know it would be to no avail. He turned away from the doorway and mounted the steps. Roger stood behind the wheel with a watchful eye on the bowsprit, keeping it aligned with the easternmost point of the island.

"'E's getting worse, in't 'e?" asked Roger.

"Aye," replied James.

"And I reckon you'll be leaving us soon as well?"

"Aye," said James, impressed with Roger's perceptiveness.

"Do ye think 'e'll get any better once we reach Harbor Town?"

"I truly hope so."

"But ye don' know fer certain, do ya?"

"No, Roger, I don't."

"I still believe in ye, Cap'n. Remember tha' when yer starin' down tha' demon."

James smiled at Roger. He was truly touched that after all they'd been through, even after losing his best friend, this man still had confidence in him. James extended his hand. Roger gripped it tightly.

"I will bring her back," said James.

"Course ye will, sir."

"And when I return, I shall lead us all from this place."

Roger nodded, stoic. At the bow, Jan showed Peroc how to coil a length of rope.

"Look after him, Roger. He'll be upset when he learns that I've gone."

"Aye, aye, Cap'n."

James removed a pinch of transporting powder from his pouch and was gone in a flash of orange light and smoke.

James appeared on the main street of Adelphi. His experiment had worked. He now knew that he could transport into but not out of the village. James saw no sign of Gai or any of his lieutenants. Ahead was the passerelle de ciel that spanned the width of the street. He proceeded slowly, inspecting each building as he passed. A tearoom with two stories of flats overhead boasted windows adorned with flower boxes. Each box overflowed with hyacinths, daisies, primroses and snowdrops . James smiled as he recalled the horticultural lessons Akil had forced him to sit though as he inhaled the intoxicating scent of hyacinths.

Beyond the tea shop was the alley where the tymanuk had led him on their way to the maze. As he was about to turn down the alley, he paused and surveyed the next shop, which stood beneath a green awning. A gold-lettered sign read G. Dragon Apparel. He looked down at the rags he was wearing, at his bare feet, black with dirt, and stepped inside.

To his left was a hat rack covered in bowlers, top hats, fedoras, porkpies, and Tyroleans. On the right side were rows and rows of faded boxes stacked nearly to the ceiling. A three-paneled mirror stood in the far corner and several Sheraton sofas occupied the center of the shop along with a countertop buried beneath a pile of fabric. Everything in the store was covered in a thick layer of dust. James stepped toward the shortest stack of boxes and slid the topmost from the pile. He laid it on the floor and carefully opened the lid, allowing the bulk of the dust to slide to the carpeted floor. James lifted a neatly folded piece of grey fabric only to realize that it was simply that — fabric. Frustrated, he threw it to the ground and repeated the process several times with the same result. Finally, after going through nearly a dozen boxes, he stepped to the counter.

A pile of tan cloth unfurled in the shape of a pair of trousers. He smiled and held them up to his waist. They look to be about right, he thought. James removed the dirty rags he'd been wearing and found the trousers to be slightly large in the waist and very short in the leg. A chill ran up his spine as the soft fabric caressed his skin. He smiled as the urgency of his task subsided. After going through the rest of the piles on the counter, he managed to find a black waistcoat and a pair of braces.

James tried on several pair of boots but could not bear confining his feet. He made his way to the dust-covered mirror and using one of the pieces of fabric, swiped away the dust. He couldn't help but laugh. The tan trousers held up by braces and the black waistcoat with nothing beneath were an odd costume to be sure.

A yell from outside sent James running toward the door. A boy stood outside the shop window looking in. James recognized the boy as one of the guards from Gai's house. James slid the key into his pocket and fixed his black sword around his waist, moving awkwardly against the weight of the new clothes. The bell clinked as he pushed through the door and stepped out onto the street. The boy stood and stared as James approached. His mouth hung open in a state of gape-jawed shock.

"State your business, boy, or tell me where I can find Gai." The boy remained silent, mouth open. His expression did not change. "Speak," said James, drawing his blade "or I'll have your tongue." The boy did not flinch as the tip of the black blade came within inches of his face. He simply stared at James as if he were a ghost. Frustrated, James sheathed his blade and began to walk down the street.

As he reached the brick building that supported the passerelle de cel overhead, he peered over his shoulder at the boy, who hadn't budged. As he turned back, James noticed a sign hanging above the solid oak door of the building: Oliver Bailey, Gunsmith. James took one last look at the boy and then turned the knob and stepped inside.

This shop also appeared to have been abandoned. The dust was thick and the air stale. Beautifully crafted pistols and rifles hung on racks along the wall. James drew a pistol from its resting place and studied it. He felt its weight in his hands. Ran his thumbs over the smooth ironwood grips with gold inlaid designs on each side. Despite his unfamiliarity with such a weapon, he smiled. Not wanting to be overburdened, James selected two lighter weight pistols and two beautifully crafted leather belt holsters. He also found a small pouch of pre-made shells which he slung over his shoulder. Something picked at the back of James's mind as he belted the holsters and slid the pistols home. A feeling of urgency tugged at his consciousness, but he pushed it back as he stepped out the door.

James turned, looking for the boy, and was surprised to see that a small group had formed. Some stared at him silently while others talked amongst themselves. James strode toward them confidently. He stopped within arm's length of the group and looked down at them, towering over the largest boy. The group stepped back when James spoke.

"Where is your master?" he asked. No reply. "Why have you gathered here?"

"We've never seen anyone go in before," piped a small voice from somewhere in the middle of the group.

"In where, that shop?" James asked, pointing to the gun shop.

"In any of the buildings."

"Are you unable to enter the buildings?" asked James. Several of the boys nodded but none spoke. James realized it explained their handmade clothing and crude, carved spears.

"So you've returned," a voice said from the back of the group.

The crowd of boys swarmed around Gai. James heard one of the boys exclaim wonderingly, "He's gone inside!" A shadow of consternation fell across Gai's face.

"Do you see that, boys?" asked Gai. "That is a pirate. Remember what he looks like. They're big, they're ugly, and they want nothing more than to kill us all. What do we do when we see a pirate?"

"Kill it!" the boys shouted.

"Very good," said Gai, continuing his lesson as if James had voluntarily come to serve as a visual demonstration. "Remember what you have learned. More will come. None of them can be trusted and all shall be killed…except for this one. If you ever see this one again, find me. This one belongs to me. Do you understand?"

"Yes, Guv'nah !" they shouted.

"Good," said Gai. James stepped toward him.

"I am not here to fight you. I do not want to hurt any of your lieutenants. I simply seek to locate the woman who passed through your gate and find passage through the maze. If you bring her to me, if you take me to the maze, I will not bother any of you again."

"Look at you," Gai said, clearly disgusted. "Half-dressed in that dreadful attire…and those crude weapons strapped to your sides. Do you really think they'll do you any good here?" James reached down for the pistol grip only to find an empty holster. He checked the other and found it empty as well. Gai smiled at his frustration. James released the belt, threw the ammunition pouch to the ground, and unsheathed his sword.

"Where is she?" he demanded.

"What makes you think your friend wishes to see you?" asked Gai.

"She is well aware of your powers of manipulation. You would find it difficult to ensnare her with your poison words," replied James.

"I shall take you through the maze, Captain James," said Gai. "Let us go."

"I go nowhere without Kilani," replied James.

In a flash, Gai was nose to nose with James. Startled, James stepped back.

"You dare give me orders on my own island! I will tell you how it will be, and you'd be wise to keep your demands to yourself. If you want your childish infatuation to survive, bite your tongue and come with me. There is no salvation for that one."

"What do you mean, salvation?" asked James.

"My patience wears thin, pirate. We go at this very moment or you will be haunted by the screams of your love for all eternity. The decision I leave to you."

Without waiting for an answer, Gai walked down the street and vanished into the alley. James looked up and down the street in hopes of seeing some sign of Kilani but saw none. Even the boys had disappeared. Letting out a deep breath and pushing down his anguish, James gripped the hilt of his sword and strode into the shadows of the alley where Gai stood waiting.

Gai led James into the courtyard where several tymanuk were gathered on the edge of a stone bench. They instantly rose into the air and swarmed around Gai's head. He spoke to them in their peculiar tongue, like stones rubbing together. All but one of the creatures flew up and out of sight. The lone remaining creature settled comfortably on Gai's shoulder.

Gai nodded and James stepped through the wrought iron gate at the far end of the courtyard. In front of them were the cliffs. James deftly ascended the stone staircase he had created for himself earlier. At the top of the cliff, James looked over his shoulder. Gai was no longer behind him. Assuming he would catch up with his inhuman speed, James continued through the jungle and stepped onto the field of grass.

In the center of the field stood Gai. Even from a distance, James could see the sparkling remnants on Gai's mouth and chin. His winged companion was gone. "Keep up, pirate, or this will take all day," Gai said, taking to the air as if he had wings himself.

Feeling the urge to show Gai he wasn't as powerful as he thought, James sprinkled transporting powder over his head and instantly appeared at the entrance to the maze. He saw Gai searching behind him.

"Keep up," shouted James. Gai turned in mid-air looking frustrated and flew to the entrance, hitting the ground hard as he crossed the threshold. He took off at a run, no longer able to fly. James followed closely, trying to count the turns they were making. There were several sections that appeared identical, and when they passed an owl sculpture for the third time, James believed they were either lost or Gai was intentionally trying to confuse him. Finally, they reached the courtyard of the five doors. Gai turned to James and smiled.

"Each door will eventually lead to the tunnel. They are equally challenging, equally dangerous. I shall pick the one I know best and have traveled often," Gai said in the language of The Never. The grin on his face made James think he would choose anything but the easiest route. Gai walked slowly toward the doors. He stopped in front of the center door then continued to the door immediately to its left, looking over his shoulder several times to make sure James had followed. He attempted to lift the massive timber that rested in the black metal brackets, keeping the door from opening. After a moment, it became clear that Gai could not lift the large board by himself.

"Tertiri Zé Manukto suomi." James sent the bressumer up out of the brackets and crashing to the ground beside the door. Gai looked back at James, obviously attempting to control his frustration and humiliation.

"I always bring my lieutenants when I travel the maze," huffed Gai. The door swung open with a groan as the two of them stood shoulder to shoulder staring into the darkness. The air was putrid. About to take a step, James paused.

"After you," he said, extending his arm. Gai looked at James and, for the second time, his features appeared more feminine than masculine. Before James could confirm that it wasn't an illusion of light, Gai stepped through and into the blackness. James lit several orbs, which rose from his palms, and crossed the threshold. The instant James passed through, the door slammed shut.

A long, wide corridor lined with the massive black bamboo stalks stretched away into infinity. The two of them stood staring into the depths of the maze. Underfoot was grey stone. A horse-length from where they stood, the stone ended and white sand covered the path into the distance.

"Lead on," James said, looking down at Gai, who was obviously as unfamiliar with this area as he. Gai stepped forward, shooting James an irritated glance. His weight had not yet shifted onto his lead foot when he began sinking into the sand. Quickly, he pushed off and away, returning to his position beside James. "Devil's sand," he said. "We are trapped."

"You've killed us both, you arrogant fool," James said, looking at him disgustedly.

"Wrong, pirate. You may be too slow for the devil's sand, but I am not." Gai took off running, quickly becoming but a blur in the distance. James stood alone.

"Tertiri Zé Manukto reisa." James extended his hands, palms facing each other. A small flame ignited between them. It quickly grew until it was too large to contain between his outstretched arms. It turned over on itself, growing in intensity with each rotation until the flames became blue. James cast the rolling orb of flame at the ground in front of him. It hovered there for a moment, the heat forcing James to turn away as black smoke rose from the ground. James thrust his hands towards the flaming ball, sending it wheeling down the path.

He stepped forward to inspect the sand at the edge of the stone. The sand had melted under the intense heat, then hardened as the flaming orb moved down the path, leaving a glass trail in its wake. After a moment, James stepped forward, cautiously placing his foot on the opaque layer the heat had created. It was surprisingly cool and hard, and it held fast under his weight. He nodded to himself and cautiously advanced onto the pathway, keeping his distance from the blue flames that made it passable.

In not much time at all, he reached the end of the path. The endless trail must have been an illusion, he thought. The maze turned left where it transitioned from the cauterized sand to a grass-choked stone path. This path continued, twisting and turning, until finally opening into the courtyard of the five doors. On a bench sat Gai, patiently waiting.

"I underestimated you," he said.

"Apparently a habit of yours," replied James. He stepped into the center of the courtyard and stared at the five doors, ignoring Gai. He'd traveled through two of the five doors so far without making much progress. There must be some clue, some indication on the door itself that revealed which one led to the tunnel. "I thought you said all doors lead to the tunnel."

"Are you not standing in front of the doors again with the opportunity to make another choice that may take you there?" asked Gai. "None of the doors open into a grassy flower-filled field full of signs that point you to the entrance of the tunnel, if that's what you're expecting."

"You said you would guide me there."

"One cannot be led through the maze until he understands the maze. Do you think you understand it yet?"

In truth James, wasn't sure he did. He could find no logic in how it was laid out. Nor had he detected any common indicators that he could use to guide him toward his goal. He was becoming frustrated. James looked up, trying to see through the leafy canopy to determine how much daylight he had left.

"Time stops in the maze. There is no night or day. As I said before, you could wander forever in here," said Gai.

James stepped forward and inspected each of the doors once again. He ran his hand across the wood and hardware of each before moving on to the next.

"This looks vaguely familiar," Gai said with a smirk.

After James finished his inspection, he walked to the door on the far left — the very same door he had taken the first time. He placed two hands on the door. He breathed in deeply through his nose and exhaled several times before turning to Gai.

"You fool, you've already been through that door."

James turned back to the door and let his hands run over the wood and the frame again, this time even more slowly than the last.

"This is my choice," said James.

"I am your guide, am I not?" asked Gai in an irritated tone.

"The only guiding you have done has led me to a place I have already managed to find on my own. Unless you're ready to offer a sound suggestion, I will move along."

"This maze will only grant passage to those who understand it. I cannot inject that understanding into your dimwitted mind. You can choose every door and make little progress until you grasp how it works. Once you understand, you will no longer need a guide," said Gai.

"I learn best from experience, I'm afraid," said James, reaching for the finger plate. The door swung open, revealing darkness inside.

"You may learn by your own death," Gai said anxiously, rising to his feet.

James took a step forward then turned to Gai. "Death is simply another doorway. One perhaps even you cannot avoid passing through." Without another word, he turned and crossed the threshold into darkness. James heard the door close behind him. The sound echoed in the darkness. Already James was aware that despite having previously traveled through this door, he was in a different place.

"Tertiri Zé Manukto vinka," he said, lifting his palm as the light orb rose from it. It grew brighter, revealing his surroundings. Stone walls curved around the room . Above him was a brilliant canopy of stars. The wall in front of him began to ripple, as if it were covered in a shimmering layer of water. Tiny points of light, reflections of the stars above, perhaps, speckled the rippling stone. Like a curtain dropping, a door descended silently in front of the wall, identical to the door James had entered. Cautiously, he stepped toward it. Each footfall echoed as if he were in some great hall. James wiped his sweaty hand on his trousers and pushed the finger plate. The door swung open, revealing a room that had a distinct familiarity.

He knew this place. His mouth dropped open as he stepped through the doorway and took in his surroundings. He had been here many years ago as a boy. He was in Akil's conservatory.

15

betrayal

March 1897, Kraków, Poland

James and Akil stepped through the oversized wooden door and into a small, dimly lit room. They looked at each other in silence before Akil spoke.

"Are you ready to begin your training, James?"

"Yes."

"As with all my apprentices, I am going to ask something of you that you may find difficult to agree to," Akil said in a hoarse whisper as he leaned in to James's ear.

"I am ready," James said resolutely.

"When I ask you to do something, you must do it without question or hesitation. Do you understand?"

"Yes."

"And do you agree?"

"I do," said James, looking curiously into the old sorcerer's eyes.

"Very good," Akil replied cheerfully.

He reached into his cloak and removed a pinch of transporting powder. Akil lifted his hand above both their heads, gave a slight nod to James, and in a flash of purple light and smoke, they were gone.

The pair reappeared in a dense jungle beneath an ancient tree with buttress roots that tapered from several feet above their heads to the ground over three horse-lengths away. Orange and black lizards tried to hide themselves in the crevices of the bark as James looked up in wonder. His love for trees had been spawned by his father's infatuation with them.

"Magnificent, is it not?" asked Akil, running his hand along the top of one of the roots. James simply nodded.

Akil smiled and then turned and began walking. After a moment, James noticed Akil had gone on without him and hurried to catch up.

"Where are we going?" he asked when he finally reached Akil's side.

"I must ask that you do not speak another word until I have given you permission. It is of the utmost importance. All shall become clear in time," said Akil.

James nodded. He began to feel a twinge of nervousness in his stomach. The jungle had an odd familiarity to it. After several more minutes of brisk walking, he knew why. Ahead was a set of stone steps he'd seen no less than three years prior. It was the beginning of the walkway that led to council headquarters. James was now standing in the very spot where David Ogilvy had approached him and his mother after his father's memorial service.

Akil continued, reaching the base of the steps, but James stood frozen. Akil Karanis, enemy of the council, was escorting him into council headquarters where most likely Alvaro was holding court. There was a bounty on Akil, signed by Alvaro himself, yet Akil was briskly jogging up the steps as if he were visiting his grandmother on a Sunday afternoon.

James began to tremble. His skin was immediately soaked with sweat. So much had changed since his previous visit. There was open aggression between Akil and Alvaro, as Alvaro had made public his desire to get his hands on James so he could disprove that he was the Anointed One. Safe travel, once merely difficult, was now nearly impossible. There was even a rumor that a bounty had been placed on the capture of James. As he stood there, James was certain Akil was bringing him to the council to collect the bounty. He had been betrayed.

Akil turned when he reached the top of the steps. He smiled compassionately down at James.

"Come here, boy, and I will explain something to you."

James did not want to go to Akil. He wanted to turn and run. If Akil hadn't taken his transporting powder, James was certain he'd already be gone. He didn't understand why this man, who had been nothing but kind and protective, was leading him to his doom. James remained frozen in place. Akil muttered something to himself and descended the stairs. Carefully stepping over the tangle of roots at the bottom, he approached James.

"I realize I have ordered you not to speak, and I expect you to continue to obey my command, so you may nod if you understand. Do you understand?"

James nodded slowly.

"Settle yourself. Repeat the primer incantation in your mind. Say it thrice and look into my eyes."

James did as he was told and looked up. Akil's green eyes were brighter than James had ever seen them. Youthful. James immediately felt relaxed.

"Your father trusted me. Until the day he died, he trusted that the path I had set him upon was the right one. He fought vehemently for my cause and risked his life countless times simply because he blindly believed what I was telling him was the truth."

At the simple mention of his father, James's eyes glassed over and a lump formed in his throat. He willed the tears not to spill from his eyes as Akil spoke.

"He died for my cause, James. If anyone is to blame for your father's death, it is I."

James closed his eyes, but despite his best efforts, a single tear escaped and rolled down his cheek. Akil had not been there the night his father had died. He did not know what had happened.

"James, you are my cause. You. The implicit trust your father gave me I also require from you. Without it, we will not progress. You must trust that my every action is in your best interest. Always. Your father believed this, and I must ask you to do the same."

James opened his eyes. Another tear escaped, and James began to get angry with himself. He balled his fists as he looked at Akil. When their eyes met and he read the sincerity on the old man's face, James again relaxed. His hands unclenched. Akil leaned down until his face was even with James's.

"Son, are you ready to trust me as your father once did? As your mother still does?"

James nodded. Akil put his hand on James's shoulder, gave it a gentle squeeze and turned toward the stairs. James stepped forward quickly, wiping away the tears with his sleeve.

"And so it shall begin," said Akil.

They ascended the steps together, Akil again briskly jogging, his aged body unaware of its frailty, while James, in an attempt to keep up, took long strides, skipping every other step until they reached the grey stone cloister.

The flagstones stretched away into the distance untrodden by anyone save James and Akil. It must be after midday, James thought as they continued toward the central building. Despite the overcast skies, the sun managed to cast the slightest of shadows on the rectangular columns. At the end of the walkway stood two white-robed guards who were chatting with each other until they noticed the approach of James and Akil.

Immediately, their bodies tensed. Akil did not slow, and James had no choice but to keep moving at his side. One of the guards began to speak, but Akil waved him away with a dismissive hand and passed through the same entrance Alvaro had used when James and his mother attended his father's memorial. James looked back at the guards, who argued between themselves — over what, exactly, James was not certain.

"Keep up," said Akil.

James turned and realized he'd fallen behind. He hurried to catch up as the crowds roaming the halls started to thicken. Without exception, every person the pair encountered stopped and stared gape-jawed, first at Akil and then at James, as they passed. James could hear the whispers of the sorcerers behind them. "It's him." "What is he doing here?" "It's Akil and the boy!" "Have they come to surrender?" "Where are the guards?"

James so desperately wanted to speak to Akil but remembered his instructions and said not a word. His hands clenched into fists as he prepared himself to fight.

Akil took turn after turn, continuing to startle everyone who was deft enough to recognize him. James looked over his shoulder and realized that many of the sorcerers they had passed were now following at a distance. Two large wooden doors stood recessed in the stone wall at the terminus of the hallway. Akil extended his hands, whispered, and the doors groaned open.

Inside the room scores of sorcerers sat on stone benches surrounding a raised marble dais. On it stood two women, and behind them, in an ornate black wooden chair sat Ilixo Alvaro. Every head turned at the interruption, and the crowd reacted immediately. Some gasped, some shouted, and some even screamed at the sight of Akil and the boy.

The two women on the dais exchanged glances then looked back at Alvaro with matching expressions of utter confusion. Alvaro, whose face had gone several shades paler, got to his feet unsteadily and stepped to the lectern. He raised his arms and prepared to speak. While his posture indicated uncertainty, his voice revealed nothing.

"Silence," he commanded the roaring crowd.

The room immediately fell silent. During the commotion, Akil had not stopped moving, James still at his side. They reached the lowest step of the oval dais and stopped. James looked up at Akil, who wore the anticipatory look of someone visiting an old friend. Alvaro nodded to someone in the back corner of the room before looking down at the pair. James noticed he had a white-knuckled grip on the lectern and sweat was beading on his forehead. A fourth person James had not initially noticed stood from a squat wooden stool tucked close beside Alvaro's garish perch on the dais. Slightly built yet muscular, the boy with white-blonde hair seemed somehow familiar. James met his cold blue stare, and a shiver coursed through his body. Akil drew in a deep breath, giving James reason enough to break eye contact with the boy for which he was glad.

"So, Akil, you have come."

"So I have, Ilixo ."

"I presume you are aware that your position on the council has been forfeited."

"So I have been told, although I fail to understand the circumstances that justify such an action," Akil said, his eyes sweeping the room with a chastising glance. "However, that is not the reason I am here."

"What is the reason a wanted man and his puppet so boldly enter my chambers?"

Akil turned, again facing the crowd.

"The Epoch Terminus draws ever closer," he said, his voice booming across the great hall. "Tell me, members of council, what has your leader done in preparation or for the prevention of this event? Drawn your attention elsewhere? Created a non-existent conflict that will take the lives of thousands of innocents?"

Akil turned back to Alvaro whose teeth were clenched so tightly James thought they would break. A noise at the end of the hall drew James's attention. Scores of white-robed guards marched through the far doors and took up posts around the perimeter of the chamber. Alvaro smiled down at Akil.

"Because of your years of service to this council prior to your betrayal, I'll allow you to state your business before you and your pet are taken away," said Alvaro.

Akil turned to James and whispered, "Stay by my side." He then stepped up onto the dais. James had no choice but to follow. The boy behind Alvaro began to advance, as did the guards. Alvaro held out his hands.

"I will give my old friend a moment to speak his mind."

Old friend? James thought. How can this be? But before he could dwell on it, Akil stepped to the lectern and addressed the council.

"I would be lying if I said it was good to be back under these circumstances. The majority of you have voted to place that ridiculous bounty on my head. I am not here to browbeat you for your poor decision making or your lack of vision. I am here for one reason and one reason alone. The Epoch Terminus."

James could see the shock still engraved on the faces of the council members as they stared up at Akil. Out of the corner of his eye, he noticed the light-haired boy had stepped to Alvaro's side.

"This council still manages to ignore what will most certainly be the end of each and every one of you if no action is taken. You are all well aware of my belief that the boy standing beside me is the Anointed One. James has met all the criteria spoken of by the Seer and still you do not act." Akil paused for a beat.

"Or do you? James has been hunted nearly his entire life because of my suspicions. His father was murdered because of my belief, and I go so far as to say that some of you here today had a hand in his death."

Several gasps rose from the council members. James heard one man shout, "How dare you! Remove this liar immediately." The man fell silent as both Akil and Alvaro raised a hand to silence him.

"Despite this," Akil continued, "despite all of your betrayals, despite your perpetual insistence on ignoring the rising tide, I stand before you with the one person who will put an end to the Epoch Terminus and ensure the survival of our society. The survival of each and every one of you. And as a token of my good faith, I offer the council what it is you so desire yet have had neither the opportunity nor the aptitude to attain."

James followed Akil's words until his last sentence. Unsure of his meaning, he turned to face Akil, who had done likewise. James looked into Akil's eyes and saw something there. Pain? Sadness? Regret? Akil reached out and placed his hand gently on James's shoulder. He gave a slight nod before turning to Alvaro. As he turned, James noticed the light-haired boy was staring at him, his face a mask of utter shock. A feeling of foreboding swept through James as Akil began to speak once more.

"Time passes too swiftly not to work together. This is not about power, it is about survival. To that end, I offer Grand Master Alvaro the Anointed One so that he may confirm for himself that he is indeed the one who will put an end to the Epoch Terminus. You have one month. No more."

As Akil spoke, Alvaro's jaw dropped, as did the light-haired boy's. Alvaro's eyes darted from Akil to James in disbelief. So intent was he on the reactions of the others, James did not comprehend the words Akil was speaking — but he knew something wasn't right. He could feel it.

"Now," said Akil, "I take my leave."

James stepped forward, expecting Akil to join him as he stepped off the dais. When he did not, James turned and looked back at his mentor. Akil slid three glass phials from a pocket hidden deep within his cloak and tossed them into the air. Everyone surrounding the dais stepped back as the phials went buzzing over their heads and crashed into the far walls. The room went completely black. James could hear screams and saw flashes of light within clouds of grey smoke. Several concussions shook the room and sent James to the ground. As he hit the floor, it struck him. He realized what was happening. He was being left behind. Anger grew inside him as he struggled to find Akil in the darkness. Betrayal. Longing. Abandonment. Pain. He was being left behind. He was being left behind.

James struggled to stand but could rise no further than his knees. His body shook and tears rolled down his cheeks as he fought to breathe. No, he thought, I will not be left again. A red glow emanated from his body as the hurt and rage enveloped him. More flashes of light erupted in the darkness. More screams echoed through the chamber. But they were distant — muted. He felt someone close but saw only a shadow — blackness in the darkened room. Sound rose from his constricted throat as he reached out for the shadow he believed was Akil.

"No!" James croaked. "Don't leave me!"

He managed to get to his feet and took off at a run toward the black shadow. As he ran, the room cleared and with it, the shadow.

"Father!"

And then it happened. Energy pulsed from his body, spreading in every direction like a wave. As it rolled, destruction was left in its wake. The stone benches fell to powder, the lectern to splinters. The energy rolled until it washed up on the walls like waves on a cliff and dispersed. James remained on his feet for a moment before his mind began to cloud and his legs gave way, sending him onto his back.

He lay supine on the cold floor trying to catch his breath. No, he thought. Come back. He struggled to lift his head. His eyes focused and he saw what was left of the chambers. Nothing. Destruction. Then he saw it. Out of the corner of his eye. A body.

He had done it again. He had killed. James screamed frustration and rage until his voice failed. As the noise echoed off the high ceilings, something drew his attention. Movement. The body beside him was not dead. Slowly, it rolled and the hood fell away, revealing white-blond hair. The boy perched himself unsteadily on his elbows and looked at James. Not dead, James thought and then slumped onto the cool stone floor as unconsciousness took him.

16

flora and glass

James refused to believe his eyes. Except for the growth of the plants and the addition of several species of flowers, the conservatory hadn't changed at all since his last visit. Either the maze had drawn this image from his mind or Akil had managed to create a doorway from The Never back to his world.

How is this possible? He wondered. Am I home? He hurried down the stone path, hopping over the trimmed grass sprouting between the stones. He rounded the bend and saw the wrought iron table where he had frequently palavered with his mentor. There, sitting in the very same place he had so long ago, was Akil Karanis.

James stepped closer, surprised that Akil hadn't risen to greet him. As he drew within an arm's length of the man, James couldn't repress a smile.

Akil was sound asleep. An empty teacup lay in the grass beside his chair. His face had changed very little during the time they had spent apart. His quiet breath whistled faintly as it passed through his crooked nose. The old man's muscles twitched and his eyelids fluttered as he slept. He whispered something over and over. No. James placed his hand gently on Akil's shoulder.

Akil immediately awoke and stood abruptly, knocking the heavy chair to the ground behind him in the process. He looked at James, startled at first, but then a smile slowly worked its way across his face and he began to laugh. James began laughing as well. The pair embraced as they continued to crow. They laughed until tears streamed down their cheeks. When finally all the laughter had been released from their bodies, Akil sighed heavily then slowly bent and picked up his chair. He sat wearily.

"I was beginning to have my doubts, boy. I see you found my door," he said, smiling. James suddenly found himself exhausted and fell into a chair .

"Yes. Even now, I'm not certain why I chose it. It's almost as if it called to me."

"You have an innate ability to detect particular types of magic. Always have." Exhaustion gripped James's mind, which began to swim as his body rocked in that pre-sleep motion common among children who have spent the day playing under a hot sun. When his chin hit his chest, James's head snapped up and he opened his eyes. Akil was smiling at him, a smile that would not fade.

"It appears as if the strength given to you through the water of Ak Egundiano is wearing off. I suggest you take rest before we discuss all that needs discussing," said Akil.

"I have so many questions," James said, fighting to keep his eyes open.

"As do I. All can wait until you've been refreshed. I must insist, for your mind must be clear and strong."

Before James could object again, he fell into a dreamless and undisturbed sleep. When he awoke, he could not recall how he'd ended up in the comfortable bed upon which he found himself. The scent of cooking food filled the air. He sniffed hungrily at the wonderful smells as if they could sate his growling stomach.

James sat up in bed and, for a brief moment, he believed his encounter with Akil had been a dream. Only when he took in his surroundings did he realize the truth. Eight smartly made beds were nestled in a small circular clearing wreathed by a coniferous hedge speckled with pink blooms. Every several feet the hedge was neatly trimmed around moss-covered pedestals upon which sat sculptures of various animals. Behind James's left bedpost sat an owl, behind the right a lion. Pathways of polished marble tiles, brown veined with black and white, radiated from the center of the clearing like the spokes of a wheel. Between the tiled pathways grew a dark green moss dappled with yellow flowers. He followed the marble pathway between the sculptures of a snake and a dragon onto the grassy area in the center of the conservatory. The grass was perfect, uniformly trimmed and weedless across the expanse of the large rectangular lawn. At the perimeter of the lawn rose stone columns that held the arching glass ceiling over one hundred feet above. Each column was wrapped with vines that bloomed purple, blue and white flowers shaped like miniature Meerschaum pipes. Shelves had been sculpted within each column, and each was stuffed with books, books from floor to ceiling, precisely as James remembered from his previous visit.

James continued across the grass through a vine-draped trellis onto the small patch of grass where sat the iron table. There, Akil was humming to himself while tending to several pans cooking away atop the table. No fire heated them from below. Without turning his attention away from the food, he asked, "Well rested, are we?"

"Yes. That smells delicious," said James, eyeing the food as his stomach growled.

"Good. I am sure you have been longing for some proper food. Tea?"

"I'd love some," said James.

While working the cooking spoon with one hand, Akil extended the other over the table. Two cups of steaming tea appeared in a flash of light. Three more flashes brought cream, sugar and honey.

"Sit, boy. We shall not say a word until you have eaten, so there is no use hovering like an outsized hummingbird," said Akil.

James sat on the cushioned iron chair and lifted his cup. Breathing deeply, he allowed the intoxicating smell to work its way into his nose and wrap itself around his brain. The result was an immediate sense of focus. At the moment, the only thing James could focus on was the food Akil was preparing.

Akil scooped eggs onto one of several serving dishes that were stacked beside his pans while humming a tune. Moving that dish aside, he scooped bacon onto the next. With the wave of his hands, the dirty pans were gone. He placed an empty plate in front of James and took a seat beside him. James looked at the food with an anticipation he hadn't felt since he was a boy.

"It is all yours, boy. Best eat while it is hot," Akil said, sinking a serving spoon into the eggs. James gently set his cup of tea onto the table and spooned himself some eggs and bacon. He scooped a forkful of eggs into his mouth. The taste was extraordinary. The next bite wasn't nearly as proper, and as the meal progressed, he abandoned the fork altogether and shoveled eggs into his mouth with the serving spoon while stuffing in bacon between bites with his free hand. Akil looked on, clearly pleased.

James consumed everything in front of him. Akil offered to prepare a second batch, which James declined for fear that his distended stomach would burst. With a wave of Akil's hands, the table was clear. James shook his head, still amazed at the ease with which his mentor was able to perform incantations without needing to speak the words. Akil grinned at James's reaction.

The pair stood and Akil led James along a narrow path paved with a single row of circular stones that passed between low-growing thornless rose bushes. At the end of the path sat wicker chairs with purple cushions. Akil extended his arm, gesturing for James to sit. After conjuring two steaming cups of tea upon the table between the chairs, Akil lowered himself beside James.

"I suppose now you are ready to talk," Akil said.

"How did you get back? Through the conservatory doorway? Did you get to the black castle? What's inside? Is the way to the castle through the maze? Who is Gai?"

"Slow down, boy. One question at a time."

"How did you do it?" James asked.

"I presume from your barrage of questions that you are aware of my visit to Ak Egundiano and that you have met dear Luno." James's face fell as he recalled what was happening to Luno.

"What is it?" asked Akil.

"Luno is dying."

"No. Impossible," whispered Akil, almost to himself.

"I would have thought it impossible if I hadn't witnessed it myself. His age is rapidly catching up with him. Over the course of a day, he looks to have aged thirty or forty years."

"How can this be? What were the events leading up to Luno's decline?"

"I believe it happened when he entered Adelphi. I think Gai did something to him."

"Gai? Impossible. She is not a murderer."

"The Gai I know is a cunning savage," said James, not registering Akil's gender reference. "He nearly killed me on several occasions, threatened to kill all in our group, and took one of our members captive."

"She is cunning, there is no doubt about that. I suppose she could have turned savage after all that time spent alone on her island, but I do not believe she has the power to ungift that which has been given by Ak Egundiano. That power lies with the land alone. I suppose the question is why has Ak Egundiano seen fit to take back the gift it bestowed upon Luno. Why now? Something to do with your meeting Gai, perhaps? She and Ak Egundiano have always been at odds. Perhaps taking Luno's gift puts Gai at a disadvantage."

"Master, why do you refer to Gai as a woman?" asked James.

"Because she is Gai ak zangar, a Siren. Perhaps you should explain how you've come to believe her a man," said Akil, lifting his teacup and twisting it in his hands as he leaned forward.

"He is a boy. At least, he has taken the form of a boy. There are moments, flashes really, when I can see that he…she is something else. On occasion he did look more feminine and once, I swear to the gods I saw a mask of darkness pass over his face. He surrounds himself with other boys of the same age. They are not nearly as powerful as he, and I daresay they do not know what he truly is. A Siren…incredible. That explains much of his ability to manipulate the thoughts of others."

James's mind immediately went to Kilani. Perhaps her choice to go with Gai hadn't been her decision after all. Perhaps her determination was simply the crafty manipulation of this Siren. A new urgency to return and find Kilani rose up in his chest.

"Other boys, you say? What are they like?" asked Akil.

"None are older than Gai — twelve or thirteen. They are dangerous for their age. All are able to brandish a sword. One managed to wound Luno quite severely, but I was able to heal him."

"Heal? So Luno has managed to discover more of the language? Did he teach you?"

"No. I alone was gifted this knowledge."

"By whom?"

"By The Never," replied James.

Akil leapt to his feet, ignoring the hot tea that spilled over the rim of his cup and down his fingers. He began to pace in front of James.

"Show me."

James had forgotten he had the ability to allow others to view his memories. The native language of The Never lacked the words to produce such recreations. He cleared his mind and extended his hand."Oroitu." The orb rose from his palm and began to grow. James tossed it between them them as it expanded. Inside the orb, a scene came into focus.

James was walking toward the tower in the center of the water-curtained cavern. He paused within arm's reach of the stone spire. Immediately, his eyes lost their focus and the expression melted from his face, leaving a blank mask. Slowly, he reached up and touched the spire. The scene faded away.

Akil stared pensively as the shimmering orb disappeared.

"What did it say? What did you hear?" he asked, pacing once again.

"I felt as if the spire awakened something in my mind that had been there the entire time. Once that happened, I knew everything. I knew the language of the land. I could perform incantations. I was powerful again."

"Incredible," Akil said, deep in thought. "I believe you have been chosen."

"Chosen for what?" asked James.

"To destroy Gai ak zangar."

17

alvaro

March 1897, Burgos, Spain

James awoke in a soft yet unfamiliar bed. He struggled to remember where he was and how he had gotten there, but the memory simply would not come to him. He looked around the room. It was windowless but bright. Tapestries hung from metal brackets mounted to the walls. A strange rumbling caused James to start. It lasted a few beats then stopped. James searched for the source of the noise but saw nothing out of the ordinary. The noise sounded again as James sat up. This time he was certain it was coming from the shadowy corner.

He slid out of bed and stood, unsteady at first, but quickly gained his balance. Again the noise sounded. James took an uncertain step toward the corner and then another. This time, the shadow appeared to expand and contract with the resonance of the sound. James stepped forward.

"I would not step any closer. While he is a deep sleeper, he doesn't like to be startled and may latch onto whatever or whomever disturbs him. I have the scars to prove it."

James turned quickly. Alvaro stood in the entryway. His posture was neither threatening nor aggressive. Everything came flooding back. Akil had given him over to Alvaro under no duress. Akil had abandoned him.

"Believe me, James, I was as shocked by Akil's actions as you. Strolling into council headquarters during a meeting. Only Akil Karanis could get away with something so brash. He is a man of his own rules, that is for certain."

James wasn't listening to Alvaro. His hands were raised, ready to cast an incantation at the first sign of trouble. Anger swelled in him as he thought about Akil. Now he was the prisoner of the man who had murdered his father. He would never see his mother again.

"Now that you are here, I'd be a fool not to take advantage of the opportunity it affords me." Alvaro stepped into the room. James stepped back, bumping into something behind him. A low growl redirected his attention. As he turned, the shadow rose, baring white teeth, forget-me-not blue eyes staring into his.

"Murk!" admonished Alvaro. "Leave our guest alone."

The oversized black cat immediately slunk toward Alvaro, rubbing against James as he strode across the room. Alvaro began scratching the cat under the chin, producing the same resonating rumble James had heard earlier — the cat was purring. Its tail flicked back and forth, nearly reaching James.

Murk turned toward James and sauntered in his direction. James froze as the beast approached. Again he rubbed his black coat against James's side, circled behind him, and repeated the process. The cat paused, looked back over his shoulder at James, and held eye contact.

"I believe he would like you to give him a scratch," said Alvaro, nodding reassuringly. James slowly reached out and gently rubbed behind the cat's ear. The cat immediately pushed against James's hand, coaxing him to scratch harder. James obliged and the monstrous cat began to purr. A smile fought its way onto James's face. This was the largest predator he'd ever seen, and here he was petting it like a house cat.

"He likes you, James. Highly uncommon. Until today, I'm the only one who's ever gotten a purr out of him. I believe this is a sign of good things to come," said Alvaro.

James extended his other hand and began scratching the cat behind both ears. Murk turned his head slightly and licked James's arm with his sandpaper tongue. James laughed at the sensation. Murk was so enjoying James's affections that he turned and pushed against the boy, sending him into the wall. The cat stepped after James and rubbed his long body against James who obligingly scratched along his spine. When James reached his haunches, Murk stretched them upward while extending his forelegs as far as the room would allow. Fur sloughed off in fistfuls as James continued to scratch. The purring continued as Murk's long tail gently whipped back and forth occasionally hitting James in the face.

"Murk! Baketsu !" The cat grudgingly stepped away from James and slunk out of the room, shooting Alvaro a perturbed look. "Bloody thing thinks he's the master," Alvaro said, looking up at James who was trying to rid himself of the layers of fur stuck to his robes. "My apologies. As you can imagine, he isn't the easiest creature to groom. Most of the stable boys refuse to come near him, and I'm afraid every anti-shedding incantation I've tried doesn't seem to affect the brute."

Alvaro held up his hands. "Haizatu ." A gust of air flowed from his hands and began swirling around James. It increased in speed until his clothes and hair rippled as if in a windstorm. Alvaro lowered his hands and a large ring of black fur fell to the floor.

"You've been asleep over twelve hours. You must be famished. I've had breakfast prepared. " Alvaro continued to the doorway, but turned back when he realized he wasn't being followed. "I understand your apprehension. I also understand your hurt. Akil's unorthodox methods rarely take others' feelings into consideration. You have my word, as I have given it to Akil, that no harm will come to you whilst you remain in my care. Now, come and eat something before Murk manages to get his paws on it."

They finished eating in silence. "I trust your stomach is full," said Alvaro, rising. James nodded. "There are many things you need to see, James, and very little time in which to show you. And there are things I require of you as well."

James remained seated, looking pensive. "Akil called you his old friend. I thought you were enemies. I thought we were enemies."

"James, you and I are not enemies. Of that, I shall explain more later. As for Akil and I, we have a complicated past. A past that began with a friendship." James's furrowed brow made it obvious that he did not understand. "Before one can become a member of the council," said Alvaro, sitting back down at the table, "there is a training program every prospect must complete. It weeds out those ill suited to lead. Very early on it was clear that Akil was the most gifted of all the sorcerers in the program. As I have a tendency to be drawn to those with superior abilities, I made it a point to become close with Akil. It didn't take long to form a friendship. Ironically, we also became rivals due to our philosophical beliefs. Regardless of our differences in opinion, however, our friendship has endured."

"When you say differences in opinion, you mean how you believe the unfaithful should be treated, don't you?"

"That was the fundamental difference, yes," said Alvaro, picking up a piece of bacon and biting off the end. "Since we've stumbled upon this topic — one that I'd hoped to broach at a later time — I might as well provide further explanation. Akil, no doubt, has told you and all his followers that I wish to see the unfaithful destroyed so that the faithful may come out of hiding. He says that I want a war between the faithful and unfaithful. This couldn't be farther from the truth." He paused. "I was born into an unfaithful family, James. Did Akil ever mention that?"

James shook his head.

"I thought not. It wouldn't do his cause much good to share that I visit my unfaithful mother every Sunday, would it? Akil is a master manipulator. His half-truths and subtle innuendos enable him to rally forces to his cause, a cause that if seen to fruition would spell the destruction of our kind. It is the very nature of humanity, faithful and unfaithful alike, to destroy each other. The unfaithful have become particularly adept at taking the lives of one another. When it became clear that the faithful and unfaithful had reached a philosophical crossroads, and the unfaithful were too stubborn and proud to stop and consider the ramifications of their actions, the faithful decided to take another path, one of peace. While it may be in our nature to destroy ourselves, we usually have the foresight to choose temperance. Never has there been a time of peace among the unfaithful, not once since they gained the intelligence to put ink to paper. All the advances in language, engineering and art over centuries have taken place under the cloud of war. A man will tell you he would never wish war for himself or his family, yet that same man is the first to take up arms at the slightest provocation. Now, imagine teaching these men our ways. That is what Akil proposes. Imagine what war would become. It would be terrible, James. We would not survive. It would result in the Epoch Terminus."

James's head was spinning. Hustasunetik . He tried to clear his mind. As he listened to Alvaro, he felt detached from his body. He felt as if he was looking through someone else's eyes, hovering in the cramped interior of another mind that pressed against his own, slowing his ability to think, to understand.

Alvaro stood.

"I see I've given you much information in perhaps too brief a period. Especially on a topic with such dire implications. Too much for a mind of your age to process in one sitting, I imagine. Let us go for a walk, James. You look like you need some fresh air."

Alvaro led James out of the small room, through a narrow passage and out an arched wooden doorway. They stepped out onto a brick walkway bordered with waist-high white flowers. As James attempted to pull the door closed behind him, Murk pushed his way outside. He took a few steps then turned, looking at the boy. James pulled the door closed and followed.

Murk waited until James was at his side before continuing their procession behind Alvaro, who was rounding a bend in the path not far ahead. When James reached the bend, he stopped. At the end of the path was a circular courtyard with several stone benches. Familiarity he couldn't quite place nagged at the back of his mind. After a moment, he disregarded the sensation and stepped into the courtyard. Murk crouched down — his eyes focused on something beyond the border flowers. A low growl rose from deep in his chest.

"Not to worry, he's only playing," said Alvaro, sitting on one of the benches. "Why do you believe Akil left you with me, James?"

"I don't know," replied James, despite having his suspicions.

"He wants me to believe that you are indeed the Anointed One. With my support, all the bickering between sides would come to an end. We would unite behind a single cause and, of course, Akil would get all the credit for having discovered you, not to mention be positioned quite nicely as the advisor to the Anointed One. He's left you here so that you may prove yourself. He believes you will do just that."

James had been listening, but his mind caught on one word. Bickering. Was that how Alvaro classified what had been happening between him and Akil? People had died — good people, his father among them — and Alvaro described it as if two children were arguing over a toy. James's hands balled into fists as he shut out every word Alvaro was saying. Finally, Alvaro noticed his distress and paused. James's breathing was rapid; his eyes bored into Alvaro's.

"Bakestu ," Alvaro said, extending his hands toward James. Wisps of white smoke glided from his palms and gently encircled James, who continued to stare at Alvaro with contempt. "Boy, what is it?"

James closed his eyes and fought down the anger. If Akil had sent him here, there was a good reason. He would learn all he could. I must not lose control again, James thought, allowing himself to absorb Alvaro's calming incantation.

"I am troubled, Master Alvaro," said James, choking on the propriety of his words.

"Please be candid, James. We will not get anywhere if we hold back," said Alvaro.

How wrong you are about that, James thought, recalling what had happened in the council hall.

"How is it that you can describe the dealings between you and Akil as bickering when lives have been lost as a result? Lives I care about."

"James, why don't you have a seat," said Alvaro, extending his hand toward the bench across from him. James hesitated. He didn't want to sit. He wanted to remain standing face to face with the man who had killed his father. He wanted to remain at the ready. When he realized Alvaro wasn't going to begin speaking until he sat, he had little choice but to perch on the edge of the bench.

"This will not be easy for you to hear, I assure you. What vexes me is why Akil would put you in a position where you would ever be able to hear it. Sometimes, even I do not have the ability to know Akil's intentions. But I guarantee you this, James, Akil has thought this through — the conversation we're about to have, as well as everything that could possibly happen during your stay here. He's reviewed every possibility in his mind and still believes it was the right decision to send you to me. The very notion boggles my mind." Alvaro sighed heavily. "After all you've been through, you have a right to know the truth. My adversarial relationship with Akil is a farce. All of it. Do you understand what that means, James?"

James didn't reply. He couldn't reply. The magnitude of the statement wasn't easily digested by his fifteen-year-old brain.

"Your lifetime in hiding has been completely unnecessary. I have not been hunting you down. I've never sent any of my men to capture you, and I did not order the murder of your father."

"How can that be?" whispered James, his head spinning.

"Above all things, Akil Karanis desires power — as most men do. When he discovered you, he was certain he'd finally found the Anointed One, the one who would put an end to the Epoch Terminus. Akil knew that controlling you, influencing you, would put him in a position of unimaginable power. Despite all his abilities, which are quite possibly unmatched by any sorcerer who has ever lived, Akil has always struggled to build a following because of his failures. He takes great risks, and time and time again, he fails because of them.

"What better way to control you than to make you believe you're in constant danger, danger from which only he can protect you? His plan was progressing well until your abilities began to develop at an alarming rate. He needed to stay close to you in order to see you through your final years of training. He needed to become the most influential man in your life. Do you understand what I'm saying, James?"

James did not understand. Any of it. As Alvaro continued to speak, his head grew more and more clouded until he wasn't able to process any of what he was being told.

"Akil realized he'd never have the influence he needed over you while your father remained such a strong presence in your life. James," Alvaro said, leaning forward and looking deep into James's eyes. "Akil arranged the murder of your father."

"No!" James leapt to his feet. As the single word escaped his lips, the stone benches in the courtyard cracked and fell in chunks to the ground. James ran across the courtyard, through a vine-wrapped trellis and into the gardens beyond, leaving Alvaro lying on his back in a pile of broken stone. A smile crept across his face as James ran out of sight.

18

answers and warnings

"Why would The Never need me to kill Gai? I don't understand." James had always assumed he had been gifted his knowledge so he could find a means of escape.

"Gai is an abomination in the otherwise perfect land that is Ak Egundiano," replied Akil. "Gai's ability to manipulate the very laws upon which the entire place has been created will eventually lead to its destruction…unless, of course, she can be stopped. I do not believe Gai fully realizes her abilities."

"And I am expected to destroy a Siren?"

"I believe there may be another solution."

"How do you know this? Were you really there, Master? In The Never?"

"I was. A long time ago."

"How did you get there? Were you banished? How were you able to return?"

"To appropriately respond to each of your questions could consume an entire day. I will begin with your last question because I believe it is the most important. I have spent more time on that island than anyone has a right to. Just as I was beginning to believe solitude would drive me mad, others started arriving, and I quickly learned that the council had discovered a way to send condemned sorcerers to Ak Egundiano. Eventually, I found Luno and we began the construction of Harbor Town.

"Still bent on finding a way home, I often wandered to the coast to collect my thoughts and re-evaluate my situation. One day, I headed northwest until I reached the sea. As I stood looking across the channel at the Severed Heart, I saw a child looking back at me. He was a native. Naturally, I waved at the boy, and he waved back, albeit hesitantly.

"I decided to set up camp not far from the place where I had seen the boy, and every morning when I walked the beach I would see a child standing on the shore across the channel looking back at me. Each morning it was a different child. Sometimes it was a boy, sometimes a girl. None older than ten. Finally, my curiosity got the better of me, and I decided to attempt to cross the channel.

"It was not very far, so I stripped off my clothes and slid into the water. About midway across, I heard a sound behind me. At this point it no longer made sense to go back, although in hindsight it did not make sense to be in the water to begin with, so I continued swimming. The water churned as if it were boiling all around me, but I pressed on and made it to shore. The will of Ak Egundiano was in my favor that day. The child I had seen earlier was gone. The tracks of the children, however, remained on the beach. I followed them into the jungle where they disappeared at a clearing. I decided to wait nearby and see if another child would pass through.

"The following morning, I heard a noise in the clearing. At first I saw nothing, but after a moment a hand appeared, emerging from the jungle floor. It was quickly followed by the head and body of the child to whom it belonged. I rushed to help and as I stepped near, I fell through the opening that the child was attempting to extricate herself from.

"I fell through a tangle of vines until I reached the ground. Unharmed, I stood and realized I was in a small cavern. A tunnel led away from the place I had fallen. Having never been one to deny my inquisitiveness, I followed the tunnel, which was not much higher than me in most parts, and in some places I had to stoop and even crawl. The tunnel stretched on and on for miles. Stores of food had been strategically placed along the tunnel, which was lit by the glowing green sap of the roots that snaked through the hardened soil of the ceiling. Eventually, I passed another child who was making his way in the opposite direction. I attempted to communicate with the child, but he simply stood frozen with fear. I moved on. For eleven days I walked. Each day I passed another child, but after the first, I made it a point to try and avoid being seen, hiding in shadowed corners or small alcoves so as not to frighten them.

"Finally, the cave floor sloped upward. I was in the jungle again. Exhausted, thirsty, and nearly blinded by the natural light, it took me the better part of a week to recover both my strength and my bearings. During that time I did not see another child. I climbed to the highest ground I could find and was amazed at what I discovered. I was on neither the Severed Heart nor the main island. I was far to the south on Prey Island."

"So you traveled all that way underground? Beneath both the main island and the sea?" asked James excitedly. "A native I've befriended spoke of a rite of passage the youth of his tribe had to go through in order to join the adults at their camp on the Severed Heart. I never considered the idea that it entailed traveling from another island."

Both men were silent for a spell. James tried to let everything he'd heard sink in. He was desperate now to return and free Kilani from Gai's spell. It was at this moment that he realized how the black castle had blinded him. He had cut her off emotionally the instant the castle came into view when they rounded East Point what felt like years ago. There was a chance she was alive. She was the only woman, other than his mother, James had ever loved. And she was alive somewhere in Adelphi. He instinctively reached into his pocket for the black steel key. Empty. His heart begin to pound with anxiety. Reaching down for the hilt of the sword, James realized it too was gone. He looked up at Akil. Panic turned to a feeling of betrayal.

"Bakestu ," Akil said quietly, extending a hand toward James. Immediately, calm washed over him. "Your trinkets are fine, my boy, although I daresay they are more than mere trinkets. Regardless, you shall have them when you are ready to leave. Now, let us continue our conversation."

Akil sat and crossed his legs. He sipped his tea and began turning the cup between his hands. James felt a moment of confusion before remembering where they had left off. Thoughts of the black castle faded into memory.

"What happened when you reached Prey Island?" asked James.

"I discovered natives, mostly women, encamped in a beautifully camouflaged, heavily fortified enclosure not far from the entrance to the tunnel. It turned out to be a nursery of sorts where the youngest of the tribe were raised safe from the dangers that plagued the elders on the Severed Heart. Once they came of age, they were sent off to complete a task of which I am still uncertain. When they successfully completed the task, they were granted passage through the tunnel. When I asked about the island to the east, the Resting Man, the elders among them spoke of a cursed place. They would not even approach the eastern shores of Prey Island for fear of setting eyes on the Resting Man.

"Naturally, my mental inquisitiveness got the best of me, and I decided to attempt to make landfall on the Resting Man. By this time, an elder female had introduced me to transporting powder along with the necessary incantation, which I found to be quite useful in several incidents involving tamperes wishing to dine upon my flesh. Numerous times I attempted to construct a seaworthy craft but did not make it far beyond the shore before my journey was thwarted. I was beginning to believe the stories I had heard from the elder natives about crossing to the Resting Man, which up until that point I thought were nothing more than generations-old tales told to prevent children from being harmed.

"Finally, I constructed an outrigger with a small sail and gave the crossing another try. I launched from the point closest to the western shore of the Resting Man and paddled as hard as I could. I was even able to power my boat with a wind incantation using the vocabulary the elder matron so kindly pounded into my thick skull. When I got halfway across the channel, waves started coming in from the south. This in and of itself was a mystery, because the channel is protected from winds by both the southern tip of the Resting Man and Prey Island. I continued eastward, hoping against hope that I could cover the short distance before a giant wave sent me and my small vessel to the bottom of the channel. I spotted my landing point on The Resting Man. It was so close I could have swum the distance in minutes. My desire to reach it overtook any and all logic, and I did what I never believed possible and would never do again during my stay in Ak Egundiano. I transported to the shore."

"It worked, obviously. So the law is not a law after all," said James.

"Remember what I told you about Gai's ability to manipulate the very laws upon which all magic is founded?"

"Indeed," replied James.

"I believe my close proximity to the place where she dwelt enabled me to transport to the shore — a place I had never physically been. The sea rose up as if it was angry that I had made it of my own accord. Yet despite the fury of the waves and wind, it could not reach the shores of Gai's island. Long before I was banished, Ak Egundiano had lost control of that place. Gai rules her island, but fortunately for you, her ignorance keeps her power in check."

"So you met Gai, found your way through the maze, and proceeded through the tunnel to the black castle?" asked James.

"It was not quite as simple as that. I did eventually reach Adelphi and was invited inside. To this day I have no explanation for the village street that exists there as if it were plucked from downtown Zurich and dropped on the island. I do know that, for some reason, not even Gai can enter any of the buildings that line the main street. They sit full of life-changing supplies and weapons, but never has any man been able to enter…with the exception of one."

"Who?" asked James.

"I may be getting long in the tooth, my boy, but I like to believe my powers of observation are not dulled quite yet."

James smiled, looking down at his accoutrements. "I thought you were talking about someone other than me," he said. "Yes, I have entered the buildings."

"It appears as though between your ability to master and manipulate the language of Ak Egundiano and its acceptance of you vis-à-vis your entry into the buildings, you have proven yourself a worthy adversary of Gai."

"Why does she so long for an adversary? She spoke of it when we first met." James told Akil everything that had happened in Gai's house. He sat and listened, completely enthralled by the story. When James finished, he thought Akil would attempt to explain the meaning of the events that had occurred within the sunken room, but he did not.

"When I met Gai for the first time, she was not the hostile creature you encountered. She did not disguise herself in the body of a child nor did she attempt to control my mind. In fact, it took me quite some time to realize she was a Siren at all.

"Eventually, she showed me the maze, and we walked its passages together, mapping a way through to the final doorway after spending months exploring. By this time, I had grown quite fond of Gai and she of me. Or so it appeared. We reached the final doorway, neither of us knowing where it would lead. I suspected it simply led to the main island as part of the underground network, but I was wrong. Despite her desire to enter, Gai could not cross the threshold. She once described the sensation as walking through a substance that thickened with each step until finally when she reached the threshold, her limbs would not respond at all."

"So I went on alone through the doorway and into the passage. It was quite different than the tunnel the children travel to the Severed Heart. This was not roughly bored dirt and roots but meticulously hewn black stone…the stone of the black castle. The instant I stepped inside the tunnel I knew it would take me there."

"Then you traveled through the tunnel to the black castle?" James asked excitedly.

"I have seen many things in my life that have instilled fear in my heart, and I have felt pain both physical and emotional. I tell you now they pale in comparison to what lies in that tunnel. By the time I made it through,

I was a different man. I implore you, James, to seek another way. No man should suffer what I have endured. I made it back, yes, but the price I paid was high. I have never been the same. I have not slept without blood-curdling nightmares since my return — and that was many, many rotations ago."

James spoke impatiently. "But you made it back! You're free. How can you tell me not to use the same road that brought you your freedom?"

"I have seen what that passage can do to a man, James. I have seen it with my own eyes, and it is a terrible thing to behold. I am a gifted sorcerer — gifted beyond most. Do you believe you are equally as gifted, James?"

"Of course not. But what's that got to do with passing through the tunnel?"

"Everything. Everything." Akil looked deep into the bottom of his teacup, pensive. James tried to understand what he meant, but it was a fruitless effort. "Listen to me, James. You must listen to what I have to say. You must not interrupt, and when I am done speaking of it, you must not speak of it again. Do you understand?" James did not understand, but he knew Akil too well to protest.

"Yes, Master."

"I am not the only man to travel from Ak Egundiano — The Never — through the tunnel and return home. There is another. One other. He was gifted as well. Just like you. I lament to say it was I who instructed him to use the very same route I had traveled. When he returned, he was not the same. At first, it was but a look in his eyes that made me suspect something was wrong. Over time, it became apparent that he was irreparably damaged. As a result, many good sorcerers died by his hands. It is for this reason that you must find another way."

James suspected he knew of whom Akil spoke but did not press the matter.

"Master, how did you come to The Never?"

"A tale for another time, my son. Know this: what I sought, I did not find, but today, for the first time in over a century, I believe it is within my grasp once again."

"What did you seek?" asked James.

"I am not ready to distract your mind with the desires of an old man. Ak Egundiano is a place fraught with mysteries that no man is likely to unravel. One could go mad simply thinking about it. You must maintain your focus. You must find another way to return."

"But you were able to make a doorway from The Never," protested James.

"Making doorways is my own brand of magic, if you will. Very much like transporting, I am able to make a doorway to a place I have been before. When you leave through the door that you entered, you will return to the maze. When I leave, I will step onto the street of a rapidly growing city in America. There is no way for either of us to walk out of my conservatory and onto the field in which it sits in France. It is this limitation that I believe enabled me to bridge one world to the other. I created the doors in the maze to — "

"You? You created the five doors?"

"I did — with Gai's help. She is easily persuaded and guided. The more I interacted with her the more I understood how ignorant she was to her potential. I was able to guide her to do my will while allowing her to believe she was the one in control. The doorway required incantations I could never have done myself."

"But Gai acted like she'd never been through the doors," replied James.

"The doors change. Every time someone passes through them, they change. Only a sorcerer can predict where they will lead. Only a sorcerer can pass through this door and into my conservatory." Akil sat back in his chair and gazed off into the distance for a moment.

"Once we created the doors, I was able to return with my books and shared many works of literature with Gai. She was most captivated by fictional stories and begged me to read to her as often as possible. Unfortunately, my supply of books was limited. A doorway can only be opened to a room that has been prepared with the proper incantations on the other end. Had I known, I would have connected it to the Vatican library. Once we found the entrance to the tunnel and realized Gai could go no farther, I promised I would return after I had completed my exploration." Akil sighed, clearly pained, a look of regret and loss on his face. "Very little in this world could ever get me to travel through that tunnel again — I dare say nothing."

"You spoke of a map of the maze," said James.

"You have already gotten to the courtyard of the five doors. You can simply transport there if you would like to return," said Akil. As he looked at James, he knew his desire was not the five doors but the entrance to the tunnel. "I left the map behind. What became of it, I do not know."

"Does one of the doors lead to the tunnel?" asked James.

"Bloody fool, listen to what I am telling you!" The sorcerer raised his voice and clenched his fists. "Do not go into the tunnel. It does not matter how much you want to get back, the man who returns to this world will not be the same man who sits beside me now. I strictly forbid it. You must find another way."

Akil had never chastised James in such a manner, let alone forbade him from doing something. His mind reeled with the knowledge of how to get to the black castle, and it was almost unbearable to be told in the same breath that he couldn't use that knowledge. Akil's eyes bored into James.

"I suggest finding the woman Kilani before you seek another way to return," Akil said. He hoped if James did find her, she would help deter him from making a bad decision. "Use me as a resource. I can be quite clever for an old man. Once you have found Kilani, return and we will discuss other ways to get into the castle."

The thought of Kilani momentarily crowded out James' obsessive desire to gain access to the castle. The pair sat in silence for a moment.

"I will continue to ponder another means of escape and record my thoughts in my journal, which I will leave upon the table in the event I am not here when you return. If we miss each other, record your progress as well, so I may be able to help." James nodded as Akil stood. His weary body did not want to return to The Never, but he knew he had no choice. So many questions still needed answers, but he could hear the black castle's call.

"How do I return to this place?" asked James.

"You know which door to use," replied Akil.

"Yes, but I walked through the door once before and ended up on the other side. And you said yourself the doors are always changing."

"Now that you are aware of this place, my doorway will always grant you passage."

James and Akil slowly walked back toward the door. James noticed his possessions lying on the table where he had broken his fast.

"A most curious blade," Akil said.

"Gai calls it spellbreaker steel. I imagine the name says it all."

"How dreadful."

"Indeed."

"And the key?" asked Akil.

"Luno and I found it inside a cave not far from Harbor Town. I believe it was forged from the same steel as the blade."

"So Luno found the key, did he?"

"You are familiar with this key?" James asked.

"Yes. You will have no need for it, James, and I must ask that you leave it here."

James's hand immediately reached for the key as if Akil had attempted to snatch it away. The instant his fingers touched the cold steel, his mind went racing to the black castle. He was on a long, steep, narrow staircase hewn into black stone and illuminated by torches bracketed to the black walls. Below he could hear the crashing of waves. Above, the inviting sound of music beckoned him. A voice called to him. He took a step upwards. Against his bare foot the stone felt a degree warmer, a touch drier. The voice called again, its musical quality undeniable. James continued up the steps. A light at the top of the stair began to brighten.

James felt a pressure in his chest. It steadily increased from uncomfortable to painful to unbearable. He let out a cry as he fell. Beneath him was not cold stone but warm grass. The pain was gone. Akil stooped over him, shaking him vigorously.

"Let me help you up." James took a deep breath and accepted Akil's hand.

"What happened?" he asked.

"I was hoping you could tell me," said Akil. "The moment you picked up that key, you appeared to leave your body behind. It took a seldom-used incantation to bring you back."

"I…felt strange. My mind did wander, I believe, yet I cannot recall to where," lied James. Akil bowed his head as if defeated and stood silent for a moment.

"We are here to help each other, are we not?" asked Akil.

"Yes, Master."

"If I am to help you, James, you cannot withhold any information from me. Do you understand? Every detail is essential. What you believe to be minor detail could be the most important information of all."

"I understand, Master."

"Then tell me, James, what you have omitted."

"I was inside the black castle," James replied sheepishly. "There was no way to be certain, but somehow I know that's where I was. I stood on a long black staircase that wound down to the sea. At the top, I could hear music…and someone calling to me. Then, a terrible pain in my chest and I fell."

"Mysteries. Hints and clues, all related, all intertwined, like unraveling a tapestry . Every time I believe I have a better understanding of Ak Egundiano, something happens to shatter my suspicion. As I said earlier, I believe that Gai and Ak Egundiano are opposing forces. Gai is like a foreign invader, and she fights, unknowingly I believe, against the will of Ak Egundiano. Her very existence in Ak Egundiano has changed its elemental construct. Now, you speak of a vision in which the black castle, a place I long believed to be a manifestation of the power of Ak Egundiano, and Gai are working together to call you." James's brow furrowed with concentration as he tried to understand.

"The music, the voice calling to you, beckoning you, all hallmarks of a Siren. The stairs, the black stone, along with your certainty of the location. Gai ak zangar and Ak Egundiano — The Never — are somehow working together."

"You're able to infer all that from the description I've provided?"

"Know this, James, there are no coincidences on Ak Egundiano. None. Everything happens because Ak Egundiano wants it to happen."

"Everything except Gai," replied James.

"What was once clear has been clouded, I am afraid. I shall think on it while you are away. Now, one final topic before you depart. I believe there may be a way to save Luno," said Akil, moving down the path toward the doorway.

"How, Master?"

"Are you familiar with the falls?" asked Akil.

"Of course, Master."

"At the bottom of the falls is a healing pool. If you can get him there, the aging process may reverse itself."

"But Master, didn't you say Luno's aging was a result of the will of The Never?"

"Sometimes, James, going against the will of Ak Egundiano will yield results in your favor. However, there is always a price to pay."

"Price?"

"Nothing someone with your abilities cannot handle," said Akil, pausing in front of the door.

"Very well, I shall take Luno there upon my return," said James.

"And find Kilani before Gai manages to warp her mind, making her irretrievable."

"Of course, Master."

"Let us monitor each other's progress in the journal. I shall return here as often as I can, and it would be wise of you to do the same. Until we meet again, dear James." Akil pulled James into an unexpected embrace, then before another word could be spoken, opened the door and stepped into the darkness.

James turned back to the table, looking over his shoulder to be sure Akil's knowing eyes weren't peering in from the darkness of the open doorway, then quickly pocketed the key. He gripped the hilt of his sword, ensuring it was secure in its scabbard, and followed Akil over the threshold.

19

serik

James ran far and fast until his legs burned and his lungs screamed. Finally, he gave in to the pain and slowed to a walk. He took in his surroundings.

White-barked trees stretched high above his head. As he continued to walk, he saw a large marble column lying on its side. Broken and moss-covered, it had clearly lain on the forest floor for a long time. He hopped on top of the column, careful not to slide off the other side, and began to walk along it, paying no attention to the ancient runes carved into the marble beneath his feet. His mind swam from the deluge of information Alvaro had shared. All the truths he had come to believe were now shaken, turned upside down in a matter of minutes. He needed clarity.

The column sloped upward slightly, and James saw that the far end rested on a circular stone base beside the broken plinth that had once supported it. He lifted his head now, noticing other broken columns splayed outward from the platform. In the center, Murk crouched as if he were tracking prey; however, the playful whipping of his tail suggested otherwise. James took a step forward, and Murk's ears swiveled slightly as if listening intently to James. He stepped again, and again Murk's ears turned, this time in the other direction.

"Murk, I don't want to play," said James.

Murk did not change position or give any indication that he understood what James had said. James took a third step and Murk sprang, easily bridging the distance of at least twelve feet with a single bound, and landed squarely on top of James. He rolled at the last minute, distributing the force of the impact across his broad shoulders and pinioning James's arms to his sides. The cat glared up at James, baring his fangs, and for a moment James thought he had met his end. But rather than taking a bite out of his prey, Murk stuck out his long black tongue and ran it up James's cheek and across his mouth and nose. James spat and rolled out of Murk's embrace onto the platform.

Murk rolled onto his stomach and again assumed the hunting position, head and chest down, haunches slightly raised, ready to pounce. James smiled as he extended his hands toward his attacker. "Blindatu! " He then turned and sprinted toward the edge of the platform. Murk lunged, but this time struck James's invisible barrier, and, for a moment, appeared to sink his claws into it before sliding to the ground. He paced back and forth, swatting at the invisible barrier, testing its width. Murk continued moving along the barrier until he reached a large tree at the edge of the platform. Giving the barrier a final swat, Murk leapt into the tree and climbed up into the canopy. James looked back over his shoulder to see the giant cat stretching his paw outward from one of the upper branches. He smiled and increased his pace.

Having found the top of the barrier, Murk leapt to an adjacent tree, slid down the trunk, and took off in James's direction. By the time Murk hit the ground, James had come upon a group of large stones set into a hillside. Moss and small plants grew in the crevices of the dark multi-layered stone. Midway James saw a break wide enough to squeeze into.

"Ikusezin eta kontra -suma. " James cast incantations to ensure he would not be seen. As the last syllable left his lips, James heard the gentle brushing of leaves as Murk's paws caressed the ground. The walking shadow had his nose to the ground. Murk stopped at the spot where James had concealed himself and peered into the crack. James held his breath while trying to suppress a smile.

Murk's eyes inspected every inch of the gap before continuing past. Having lost the scent beyond the gap in the stones, Murk turned back and began to retrace his steps. The moment his hindquarters were in view, James jumped out from his hiding place. The instant he broke through his own protective incantations, Murk turned and spotted him hurtling through the air. But the cat was fast, much faster than James, and he rolled, gripping the boy as he fell and bringing him gently to the ground before straddling him menacingly. James let out a laugh that felt as purifying as a drink from a cool spring. He had found a friend here after all.

The shadows stretched out toward the east as the pair finally began their long walk back. Suddenly, Murk's hackles rose and a low growl sounded from the depths of his throat. James spotted a lone figure standing at the base of a tree.

"Identify yourself," he said, extending his hands in a defensive posture. The figure stepped forward and lowered his black hood, revealing white-blond hair that contrasted with his Asian facial features.

"I am Serik. I am also under the care of Master Alvaro, although I doubt he has said as much." James lowered his hands and stepped forward. Murk advanced to James's side, but his hackles remained up and he continued to growl. Serik glanced at the giant cat. "Bloody thing never liked me after I accidentally set his tail on fire." Serik grasped his right fist in his left hand and bowed. James returned the greeting.

"You are Master Alvaro's apprentice then?"

"I am. I was at the council meeting. I've never seen a room clear so quickly." He smiled. Now James remembered his face. It was the last face he'd seen before losing consciousness in the council chambers. "You're the one Akil Karanis left behind."

"Yes. I'm James."

"Not a good feeling, to be abandoned by your mentor like that," Serik said.

"And what would you know of it?" asked James.

"More than you might suspect" replied Serik.

James clenched his fists as the memories flooded him, and he looked away. Murk nuzzled one of his fisted hands as if he sensed James's anguish.

"Sorry, friend, I wasn't trying to be hurtful. Truly. It's been a while since I've gotten to talk with someone close to my own age." James's hands relaxed, and he looked up at Serik.

"It's not your fault," he said. "Do you come into these woods often?"

"Nearly every day. There is something about them, a peacefulness I can't find anywhere else."

"Have you seen the ruined temple?" asked James.

"Aye, it's one of my favorite places." James smiled. He could like Serik. Murk finally stopped growling and sat at James's side. "The beast really has an affinity for you. He's very picky when it comes to people."

James scratched between Murk's ears. "So I've noticed." He focused on the cat. "How long have you been with Alvaro?"

"Nearly seven years," Serik replied.

"Do you trust him?"

"Of course. Master Alvaro is wise and good." Serik said, but there was something about his posture that made James think he was holding back. The frogs began their predusk cacophony. "Come on," Serik said. The pair walked in silence as they made their way through the forest.

When they were in sight of Alvaro's manor, Serik paused, looking around. He turned to James with a stern expression.

"Akil Karanis told you you're the Anointed One, did he?

"Aye."

"How long have you known?"

"Nearly my entire life," replied James. Serik looked as if he'd been struck.

"You all right, mate?" asked James.

Serik turned away from James, took a deep breath and turned back, his casual demeanor returning. "Fine. It was a strange sensation. I get them sometimes. Feels like someone elbowed me in the jaw."

"What do they mean?"

"Haven't been able to figure it out. Strangest thing."

James feigned a smile, but once again was troubled by Serik's manner.

"You'd best get back before dark. I'll make my own way." Serik stood and watched as James and his shadow headed toward Alvaro's house. "Perhaps we should meet again tomorrow after Alvaro releases you from lessons," he called out. "We could meet at the temple. Bring the beast if you must."

James turned and nodded, then continued toward the house, smiling to himself. He had made two friends today.

James skirted fallen trees and stones as Murk trotted alongside him. As they approached the ruined temple, he spotted Serik sitting on a column, his bare feet dangling. Murk began a half-hearted growl as he caught sight of the blond boy. "It's all right, Murk," said James, scratching between his ears. The cat's hackles smoothed, and he licked James's arm with his rough tongue.

Serik stood and shed his traveling cloak. It was warm for early spring. A slight breeze rolled the few remaining dead leaves across the forest floor. He grinned as James approached.

"I was hoping we could spar," said Serik. "I haven't learned much in the way of combative incantations under the tutelage of Master Alvaro, and I've heard you are quite good."

"And where have you heard that?" asked James, climbing onto the fallen column and atop the ruined temple platform.

"Everybody knows who you are — who you're supposed to be. I've heard rumors of your abilities for years."

"If you've heard I'm good, why would you want to spar?" asked James with a smile, surprised to find himself excited for an opportunity to perform incantations.

"You learn best from those more skilled than yourself, no?"

" Very well," said James, "let us borroka egin and see what happens."

"I am indebted to your generosity," said Serik.

James also removed his traveling cloak and tossed it over a broken column. He noticed two blades lying beside the column. "What are those for?" he asked, pointing.

"I will show you something in exchange for my lesson." James nodded and positioned himself roughly ten paces from Serik. He turned his body, revealing the smallest profile possible, and extended his hands. Serik did the same.

"Lur -destolestu ," said James, spreading his fingers and allowing the incantation to flow from his palms. The ground beneath Serik's feet slid forward, knocking him to the ground. He began laughing as he lay on his back. James stepped cautiously to his side as Serik's fit of hysteria continued. "Are you all right, mate?" Serik finally regained control of himself and rolled onto an elbow, looking up at James.

"That was bloody brilliant. Let's do it again." James helped Serik to his feet, and they took their positions on the temple platform.

"Are you ready?" asked James to the still-smiling Serik. Serik nodded.

"Blindatu ," said James, putting up his invisible barrier. At the same time, Serik sent a burst of energy at James. The red burst struck the barrier and dissipated. Next, he sent a torrent of flame. Again the barrier blocked the incantation.

"Suntsitu ," said Serik, frustration creeping into his voice. The barrier trembled but did not break. James smiled. "Apurtu -oztopo ." Again the barrier trembled, but this time it flexed, distorting everything on the opposite side. Small cracks appeared in the barrier. The cracks began to widen. "Suntsitu, " Serik said again. This time the barrier shattered like glass, each piece disintegrating before it touched the ground.

Before James could react, Serik sent a burst of energy at him. It struck him directly in the chest but only knocked him back a few steps. James stepped forward, his hands extended.

"Bloody hell!" exclaimed Serik, panting.

"You are the first person ever to break one of my barriers — aside from Master Akil, that is," said James. "Where did you learn that incantation?"

"I made it up," replied Serik.

"Very good. Improvisation is the key to outwitting your opponent," said James, parroting one of Akil's lessons. "When they can anticipate what you're about to do, they can perform a counter-incantation." Serik smiled and nodded as James explained his tactics.

"Now it is your turn to be the teacher," said James glancing at the blades.

"Very well." Serik picked up the blades, still inside their scabbards, inspected each one for a moment and then tossed one to James, who nearly dropped it. James looked up at Serik to see if he had noticed and was relieved to see that he was busy inspecting the hilt of his sword. The scabbard and hilt were tightly wrapped black leather over hardened steel, and the sword seemed to fit James's hand perfectly as he pulled it from the scabbard. The blade was long and curved, narrow at the hilt, then flaring wider and ending in a fiendish point. It was very light, honed razor-sharp, and marbled with two metals, the lighter swirled throughout the darker, giving it a beautiful and deadly appearance.

"I've never seen a blade like this," said James.

"There are few who have. It was crafted by my ancestors who were the greatest blacksmiths of their age. They used a combination of metals never seen prior or hence and incantations that died when the entire tribe was wiped out in an avalanche during the Great Winter. These blades are said to be among the rarest in the world. Also some of the best."

"How did you acquire them?" asked James.

"They were passed down from my grandfather to my father and then to me," said Serik, a distant look in his eyes.

"This is a one-handed sword?"

Serik broke out of his reverie and looked up at James. "Aye. It is light, maneuverable and cuts through flesh as easily as air," he said, swinging and jabbing the blade in a fashion James could only guess was that of a highly experienced swordsman.

James studied the blade in his hand. He'd seen men wielding swords before, but none had been sorcerers. Throughout all his training, no one had ever mentioned swordplay as an area of study.

"First," said Serik, interrupting his train of thought, "you need to stand properly. It is very similar to our barroka egin stance. Body turned, exposing as little as possible. Sword hand leads, your empty hand is used as a counterbalance while thrusting."

James turned his body and held up his sword, mimicking Serik's posture. The blade felt good in his hand, and he had a sudden desire to swing it. James brought the blade out and around in a sweeping cut through the air. Serik laughed.

"Not bad," he said. "A few problems with that move, of course, but nobody is an expert the first time they pick up a blade. When you swung, your entire body was exposed. A good opponent could have skewered you a dozen times before your blade came around. The second was the strength of the cut — too much power in it. If an opponent managed to sidestep your attack, which they would have with relative ease, you wouldn't be able to defend yourself before stopping the momentum — again being skewered." James nodded, immediately less confident.

"Now, I've found the best way to learn is to spar, so I've enchanted the blades to prevent us from killing each other. The worst they will do is leave a nasty bruise if one of us manages to land a blow. Are you ready?"

Again, James nodded. Serik returned to the starting position and James mirrored. Serik came in quickly, blocking a blow by James, and with a flick of his wrist sent his sword flying through the air. James stepped back and tripped over a vine that had grown up through a crack in the platform. He landed flat on his back. Serik stepped forward and pointed his blade at James's throat as he lay helpless on the ground.

"You must always be aware of your surr—"

In an instant, Serik was on his back with the giant cat on top of him, teeth bared, a low growl rising from deep in his chest. James quickly jumped to his feet.

"Get your bloody cat off me," Serik grunted.

"Murk!" James yelled. "Release!" Slowly, the black shadow retreated, never breaking eye contact as he positioned himself at the edge of the platform. James helped Serik to his feet. "Murk, you cannot interfere. Do you understand?" Murk hung his head slightly but kept his eyes fixed on Serik. "Go hunt," said James.

The big cat turned and slowly made his way off the platform, but not without looking back at Serik several times. Once he was gone, James turned back to Serik.

"You were saying?" asked James.

Serik's chest was heaving, and for a moment, James thought he was crying…until a smile crossed his face. James grinned at the sight of his new friend in hysterics, and soon the pair were laughing like unburdened youths.

20

en garde

James stepped into the courtyard of the five doors. He nervously looked around for any sign of Gai. Nothing. He quickly removed a pinch of transporting powder from his pouch and disappeared in a flash of orange light and smoke. He reappeared on the main street of Adelphi, a stone's throw inside the jungle gate. Despite having stood in this very spot on more than one occasion, as James looked down the cobbled street and at the buildings that lined it, he found himself marveling at this place that should not be. He noticed that down the street, beyond the arched passerelle de cel, stood a lone figure. James instantly felt drawn to the figure. He walked down the street, expecting one of Gai's lieutenants or even the boyish Gai himself.. But as he drew closer, James felt a frisson of surprise. It was a woman. He quickened his pace.

The figure passed under the passerelle de cel, which arched over the street, meeting James at the teashop. He froze. It was not Kilani as he had anticipated. This woman was shorter, her hair a shade lighter, and her skin milky white. She smiled at James as if they were old friends. Caution bells sounded in the back of his mind. He gripped the hilt of his sword. The pair looked at each other in silence until finally James spoke.

"Who are you?"

"You cannot see through my exterior, Captain James? I thought you more perceptive than your predecessors." James looked more closely. He looked past her physical features and deep into her eyes.

"Gai?"

"Perhaps you are not a complete loss after all," she said, stepping forward. James immediately stepped back. "I have taken the form of my true self. Does that bother you?"

"Why have you chosen to do so now?"

"I know who you've been speaking with. I can smell him on your clothes, which, I must say, look quite ridiculous." Gai stepped toward James once more, and this time he held his ground. Her dress brushed against her pale ankles as she stepped soundlessly across the cobbles. Beautiful, James thought, watching her sinuous, graceful stride. She circled behind James, running her hand gently across his shoulders. James felt a warmth course through his body as her fingers brushed across his hair. Her striking eyes gazed into his own as she paused at his side. James felt relaxed, comfortable. She smiled. James smiled back. "How is my old friend?"

"He is well," James replied, lost in her eyes. The blue irises were wreathed with a brown ring that seemed to swirl like mist.

"And what did dear Akil have to say about me?" James blinked and shook his head in an attempt to regain clarity. Gai continued to smile, her eyes never leaving his.

"He grows concerned. He said your behavior of late is not typical of the Siren he'd known for his part."

"He believes I have changed, does he?"

"He is concerned," James repeated, once again lost in the mesmerizing motion of her irises.

"There is no cause for concern," she replied in her musical voice. She stepped around in front of James, running her fingers over his arm and across his chest. "I must protect myself and my lieutenants. In order to do so, I am able to take the form I believe will be most effective against our enemies."

"Why then have you chosen to return to your natural form?" asked James.

"The minute you returned from your palaver — that's what he likes to call his little chats if I remember correctly — I knew you had been with him. His trace is so very easy to detect. I knew he would have told you what I am, so the pretense was no longer necessary. Besides," she said, running her fingers down his sternum, "you like me better this way, don't you?" James stepped back, breaking eye contact. His mind cleared.

"You attempt to infest my mind with your powers of enchantment." Gai feigned shock, which quickly turned to a knowing smile.

"Tell me, James. How is it that you know Akil Karanis?"

"He is my mentor."

"Is he now? Most intriguing. And how much did he tell you of Siren lore?"

"Enough to know I must tread cautiously," James replied.

"He is correct. We are dangerous creatures," she said with an air of innocence. "And did Akil mention his time with me?"

"Briefly."

"Did he mention the nature of our…connection?"

James's eyes darted away as he thought how best to respond.

"He said it wasn't relevant to the task I must perform." This time, Gai stepped back. Anger — or was it hurt? — swept over her face for but an instant before the smile returned.

"Not relevant," she repeated, once again beginning to circle James. "Tell me, James. What does Akil Karanis know of hurt and loss?"

"I — I don't know. We never really discussed it."

"It is something with which you are quite familiar, isn't it?"

"Aren't all who are sent here?"

"Indeed. But you've suffered more than most. I can see it in your eyes. I can hear it in your voice. It is obvious by the way you move."

"Perhaps, but I fail to understand the motives behind these inferences."

"I, too, have lost those closest to me. I lost many when death took them by the hand. I lost one through betrayal. The last simply abandoned me without a word." James could see the pain written on her face. Her eyes were glazed, and the odd motion of her irises had stopped. "Do you understand what I'm saying, James?"

"I do. You have lost, as have I. You have my sympathy and my empathy."

"I want neither!" she shouted. "I want you to understand."

"I am trying, but you're speaking in generalities."

"Humans can be so very limited at times," she said, taking a deep breath.

A wind began to blow down the street, rippling her clothes and casting her hair out behind her. The thin fabric of her dress pressed against her, revealing the beautiful rounded lines of her body — a stark contrast to Kilani's lean and muscled physique.

"Look at me, James," she said. James lifted his gaze to her eyes.

"I was betrayed once and it tore me apart. Akil helped me find the pieces and stitch them together until I was whole again. We had something rare and beautiful. And then he left without a word. He left without a promise of return. He was simply gone. All I had invested in him was wasted. All he invested in me, tossed aside like a child's broken toy. And that was how I felt…how I feel. Broken. Akil Karanis is right, James. I am not the same as I once was.

"I remain here in this cursed place, broken and alone. I never thought I would encounter Akil again until, a moment ago, you appeared by my gate, and I could smell him on your clothes and feel his aura surrounding you like a cloud wreathing a mountain."

"You're telling me that you and Akil were lovers? A Siren and a man, lovers?"

"You know very well he is no mere man."

"Agreed, but I was not aware…"

"Don't be so nearsighted, boy. Many things are believed to be impossible. Most of those impossibilities, despite the fervor of the belief and the certainty of its infallibility, are simply not so."

"Aye, I suppose so."

"Tell me, Captain James, why do you believe Akil Karanis left this place?"

"As long as I've known him, Akil's singular focus has been finding the Anointed One and preventing the Epoch Terminus. I imagine his desire to continue his work fueled his desire to leave."

The Siren balled her fists and grimaced. A moment later, her demeanor was relaxed, warm and curious. "I suppose the fool believes you are the Anointed One?"

"Perhaps."

Gai raised a curious eyebrow and stepped forward. She looked into his eyes. Again the brindle rings of her irises were turning. James did not flinch as she brought her hands to his face. Warmth surged through his body as her smooth fingers touched his cheeks.

"You are different, James. Yes. You have power in you. I can feel it coursing through your body. But other things dwell inside as well. Anger. Yes, much anger seethes inside, and you are unable to let it go." Gai ran her fingers through James's hair as she spoke, never breaking eye contact. "You've used this anger together with your power and the results were… devastating," she said with a smile.

James stepped back and drew the black sword. "I will not fall under your spell, Siren." Gai began to laugh as James stood, sword drawn, breathing heavily. His anger mounted as she continued to laugh. "Whatever it is you find so amusing may be the last thing that courses through your twisted mind."

"Do you really believe you could kill me with my own blade?"

"Tell me where she is," said James.

"I've sent her on her way," said Gai.

"Where is she?"

"You fool, she volunteered to come here. She doesn't want to be whisked away by the returning hero brandishing a sword. I've given her what she needs, and she won't let it be taken from her — especially by you."

"You will show me where she is," replied James, fighting to push away the draw of the black castle as he gripped the blade. His internal conflict manifested in his position, his expression.

Sensing his struggle, Gai turned her thoughts inward. Deep concentration creased her face. She cast her eyes down as she paced back and forth.

"I must ruminate upon these events," she said, finally looking up at

James. "Much has changed. Return in three days, and I will take you to the one you desire."

"I am not here to negotiate. I will not hesitate to give your head leave from your body," James said, the sword beginning to shake ever so slightly.

"You truly are ready to strike me down. Intriguing. And your anger… untamed, unchecked. He was right about you."

Gai extended her arms. A mist enveloped her left hand, then dissipated, revealing a black scimitar forged of spellbreaker steel. Its curved blade was etched with familiar symbols. Where had he seen them? "We shall battle simply because I am curious as to your abilities. After I have bested you, return in three days as I have instructed," said Gai.

James didn't wait for her to attack. He brought his blade down, slashing toward the curve of her neck. She stepped back and parried the blow easily. James swung again, but well before the blade crossed half the distance to its intended target, Gai stop-thrusted, forcing James to traverse in order to avoid her counterattack.

"For a sorcerer you are quite handy with a blade," said Gai.

James attacked again, lunging with a quick series of low thrusts, trying to find purchase beneath her blade. Gai sidestepped each of the thrusts, finally using an iron lamppost as a barrier. Before James could round the obstacle, Gai swung her curved blade diagonally up from her hip through the lamppost at James's head. He could only block as the strength of the impact rattled his shoulders. The lamppost swayed for a moment before the upper portion crashed to the cobbles.

In an instant, their blades crossed again, and Gai stepped forward, pinning the blades between their bodies. She pressed closer still as she released her blade and caressed his back with both hands. Their faces, their lips, were closer than they had ever been. James was consumed with overwhelming desire. He knew, in that moment, that he had lost. He struggled to clear his mind, to push away the desire enough to enable a retreat. He tried to speak, but words would not come.

"It's all right, James," she said in a soothing voice, "there is no need for anger. Let it go. We need not fight when we can be allies. Don't you think there are better uses of our talents than fighting one another?"

"Tertiri zé Manukto ahlnãs," James whispered, releasing the transporting powder he'd managed to remove from its pouch. In a flash of orange smoke and light, he was gone.

21

cetus

April 1897, Cetus

James walked down the long, dark corridor with Alvaro at his side. Neither had spoken since they'd arrived. James could smell the seawater in the musty passage lit only by Alvaro's dim white orb. As they approached the arched wooden door, Alvaro turned to James. James could feel the unease behind his forced smile.

"Your time with me is nearly at an end, James. In order for me to fulfill Akil's request, there is one final test I must perform." He extended his hand toward the door. "Ireki. " It groaned open, revealing a large hall. The floors, walls and ceilings were hewn from the same grey stone. On the left, open archways led out to a balcony overlooking the sea. A damp breeze blew in, sweeping James's hair into his face.

Several black-clad guards, their faces concealed in shadow, stood silently around the perimeter of the hall. A single piece of furniture stood in the center, a worn high-top table littered with glass vials and carafes of various sizes and contents. James tensed. This place was unsettlingly familiar.

"Something wrong, James?" asked Alvaro.

"I've been here before."

"Impossible. Perhaps you've been to a similar…"

"This is Cetus." Alvaro blanched.

"How do you know of this place?" he demanded in an angry whisper.

"This is where you brought Mr. Ogilvy, is it not?" Alvaro was silent for a moment before responding.

"James, you have my word that I will explain everything you wish to know as soon as we complete this final test. He does not like to wait, and I do not want to have to contend with one of his tirades."

James recalled Akil's meeting with David Ogilvy in the ruined castle and the harrowing memories he had shared. His mind reeled as a man stepped from the shadows.

"You're late," he croaked. The hooded figure was cloaked in crimson and black and walked with a slight limp. A tuft of white-blond hair streaked with grey escaped the man's hood and draped across his pale forehead. Two livid mirror-image scars slashed his face from cheekbone to mouth. The man paused as his eyes focused on James, and what little color he had drained from his face. James could see fear in his eyes.

"You realize this may kill the boy," the man said. "In fact, it is likely, considering what we already know."

His words betray him, James thought. He fears me. Alvaro looked nervously at James, then back to the man.

"He has passed all my tests, save one. I am confident he will pass this one as well."

"I've heard that before," the man grumbled. He muttered something

James couldn't discern, and the room dimmed. "Two, actually," he said, looking at Alvaro. "Two tests remain." Alvaro scowled.

"Carry on, and speak only when necessary. I haven't the time to bicker about your theories."

The man grinned unpleasantly as he turned to the table of potions. "I hear you've introduced him to my grandson."

"They seem to have found each other. Let us begin, shall we?"

"I trust the boy is doing well," the man said, ignoring Alvaro's prompt.

"Of course," said Alvaro impatiently.

The hooded man extended quivering hands over the glass containers as he contemplated his choices. He muttered, picked up a flask, and quickly tossed down the viscous yellow liquid, swallowing it with a grimace. He threw the flask to the floor where it shattered and stepped toward James, pushing Alvaro aside.

"What is your name, boy?"

"You know my name," said James. The man froze, his renewed confidence crumbling. He looked hesitantly at Alvaro.

"What is it?" asked Alvaro. The man shook his head as if clearing doubt from his mind.

"Very well, James. Tell me your full name."

James looked at Alvaro. "How can you possibly expect to maintain any measure of my trust when you bring me to see this monster? I know who he is and what he does." James turned back to the man. "I know your grandson well, and he has nothing but disdain for you. You have ruined your family name and forced Serik to live under constant guard for fear of retribution by those whose lives you've destroyed." Again, he looked to Alvaro. "Why would you bring me here?" he pleaded. "To what end?"

Without warning, the man reached up and engulfed the side of James's head with an oversized hand. James tried to step back but found he was frozen in place. He felt a strange pressure inside his mind and wanted more than anything to be somewhere else.

"Will he recall anything?" asked Alvaro.

"Not if this works," the man replied curtly.

James tried to speak — to demand to know what this man was doing to him — but found that he was unable to use his voice. The man muttered several unintelligible words, then, with obvious difficulty, lifted his other hand and placed it on the opposite side of James's head. James resisted the assault. He pushed back against the pressure and closed several doors in his mind's eye as Akil had taught him.

He could see the physical manifestation of the man's effort. His face was bright red, beaded with sweat. His brow furrowed in deep concentration. As his attack began to waver, James seized the opportunity and expelled the invader. The man flung up his hands and stepped back with a curse. James's body and mind were free. He bolted toward the door, but a firm hand on his shoulder spun him around, and he found himself facing Alvaro.

"Just a moment, James."

"Why did you bring me here? To let him break into my mind and change my very being like he did to David Ogilvy?"

"James, I don't know what Akil told you about David Ogilvy, but I — "

"I saw Ogilvy. I spoke to him myself. I know who this man is and what he does here."

"James, had I known you knew of this place, I would have taken the time to explain to you what it is that goes on here and why David Ogilvy was here at all. Unfortunately, we are running out of time, and this final test must be performed. Master Vinokourov is simply trying to ascertain — "

"That man will not enter my mind." James pointed at the elder

Vinokourov. "I know what you've done to people and why you hide away like a coward."

Vinokourov stepped toward James. Alvaro raised a calming hand.

"Remember what I have told you over the past month, James. Nothing Akil Karanis has told you is as it seems. This man, Alexander Vinokourov, grandfather of the boy you've come to know, is one of the greatest sorcerers of our time — of any time. He is not a villain. He has no ill intent. He has a gift that very few possess — the ability to see the path one is destined to tread. He is not a Seer. His is a different type of magic altogether, and it requires the greatest care and skill. I, myself, have allowed Master Vino— "

"And what path are you set upon?" demanded James. Alvaro was silent for a moment, then put his hand on James's shoulder.

"If I tell you, will you allow him to perform the test?"

James considered the implications. Knowing with certainty that he was the Anointed One would give him both freedom and bondage. All self-doubt would be gone. All the naysayers would be silenced. He wouldn't have to hide anymore. He would be respected, perhaps even feared. But he still had his doubts about this man — this man whose very name instilled fear in the hearts of all who mentioned it. The Alexander Vinokourov. Yet there was his grandson… Serik was his friend — his best friend. He had rarely spoken of his family, and James never pried but had managed to piece together his connection to this man.

"He will not damage my mind?"

"James, have I given you any indication during our time together that my mind is damaged?"

The boy shook his head. "No, you haven't." He hesitated. "Very well. If you tell me, I will allow him to perform the test."

Alvaro smiled slightly, but James could see the pain in his eyes. The sorcerer bowed his head for a moment. When he raised it again, his face seemed to have aged by years. James started.

"My path leads to an untimely death." Alvaro sighed.

James didn't know how he should feel. He cursed himself for letting his emotions cloud his mind — something he'd struggled with since the death of his father.

"I'm sorry," said James. Alvaro nodded his acknowledgement. He turned to the elder Vinokourov, still unconvinced despite what Alvaro had shared with him. "Be quick about it."

In an instant, Vinokourov's hands were gripping James's head, thumbs on his temples, fingers wrapped around the back, almost touching. He muttered an incantation, and James's body stiffened. James could feel the sorcerer attempting to invade his mind once again. With every ounce of energy in his body he tried to resist. James could hear Alvaro muttering — an incantation? He could feel a betraying hand on his shoulder. He fought against the combined attack, but it was too much. His energy waned and his barriers collapsed. James's world fell dark.

Alvaro stood watching as the elder Vinokourov completed his task. When he had finished, the hooded man stepped away from James's body.

"Do you have it?" asked Alvaro.

"Yes."

"What will he remember?"

"Nothing."

"Will you be able to do what I've asked?"

"Yes."

Alvaro turned to leave.

"There is something you should know," Vinokourov called out.

Alvaro turned back.

"This boy…he is not like the others. This will not end well."

22

into the depths

James stood at the edge of the jungle not far inland from Harbor Town. He needed to collect himself – to prepare for what might be waiting for him. He tried to clear his mind of Gai and all she had divulged. He had one focus: saving Luno. James took a deep breath and stepped onto the beach.

He quickly made his way to the pier . The gates were closed, barring any access to the pier as well as to the houses that lined it. Never in all his time in Harbor Town had the gates been closed. He saw no sign of life anywhere. James lifted the latch and the gates creaked open.

"Hello?" he shouted. Only the gentle lapping of the water against the piles replied. He ran halfway down the pier, pausing at the steps that ascended to Luno's flat. After shouting once more, he ran up the steps and flung open the door.

The smell was so strong that James began to retch, but he was determined to have a look around before leaving and fought the urge to retreat back to fresh air. "Oibestu." A breeze emanated from James's hands and swirled across the room, collecting all the foul, stale air as it traveled. It hit the far wall, rolled over onto itself, and blew out the door. James stepped aside as the air escaped, leaving the room in a much more tolerable state.

"Thank the gods for that," a weak voice said. James started at the sound. "So you haven't left after all." Behind the low wooden table was a haphazard pile of blankets on the floor. James scanned the blankets until he identified a face so wrinkled and grey that it was camouflaged among the folds and bends of the cloth.

"Luno?" asked James.

"Aye, fool, who else were you expecting?"

"Why are you here, like this? Where are the others?"

"I'm here because this is where they abandoned me. I lack the strength to stand, you see . As for the others, well, I believe they've gone inland, to the clearing."

"I don't understand. Why would they abandon you? Why would they abandon Harbor Town?"

"After your departure, the remnant of our crew sailed the Queen Mary back to Harbor Town to find it empty. Not a soul remained. I managed to convince them that if any of our people were alive, they would have fled to the clearing."

"And so you sent Roger, Jan and Peroc to look for them?"

"In a manner of speaking." James easily scooped up Luno, blankets and all, and placed him in a rickety wooden chair. Luno looked out through the waxen, wrinkled mask that was his face and gazed deep into James's eyes.

"What is it?"

"I found him, Luno. I found Akil Karanis."

"You what?" Luno attempted to rise, which sent him into a coughing fit.

"Ulan dal gouvi." James placed his hands on Luno's chest. His coughing slowed, then stopped altogether.

"How? Where? Tell me, boy!" Luno demanded with as much strength as he could muster.

"In the maze there is a doorway. One of Akil's doorways." Luno began to laugh, which quickly set him to coughing again. James repeated the incantation, bringing an end to the fit.

"The old codger actually managed to do it, eh?"

"There's more," said James. Luno smiled and closed his eyes, affording James his first opportunity to absorb how much he had aged since their last meeting.

"Tell me, boy, before I expire in front of your very eyes," Luno said in his raspy voice.

"He believes there may be a way to reverse what's happening to you." Luno didn't reply. He slowly opened his eyes and waited for James to continue. "Akil said if I take you to the base of the falls, I may — "

"The base of the falls?" Luno interrupted, fighting back a cough. "Have you ever been to the base of the falls?"

"No," replied James. Luno drew a long, deep breath, again mustering his strength.

"Do you want to know why you've never been to the base of the falls?" asked Luno. "Because there is no bloody base. They drop into forever."

"You've seen this? You're certain?" replied James.

"As certain as need be. Certain enough to know we'd waste what little time I have left traveling down the most treacherous terrain this land has to offer."

"Gai also spoke of the bottom. She said that's where she forged the steel of this blade," James said, removing the sword from his belt. He immediately felt the call of the black castle as his hand grasped the hilt, but he pushed the thought away, buried it in the recesses of his mind, and focused on Luno's age-ravaged face.

Luno's eyes went to the blade. His pupils contracted and expanded as if they were trying to focus. His lips moved, yet he spoke no words. James knew Luno was being pulled toward the black castle as well. He sheathed the sword, hoping to take advantage of Luno's current stupor, scooped up the old man and removed a pinch of transporting powder from his satchel. A flash of orange light and smoke, and the room stood empty .

The pair appeared at the edge of the pathway that overlooked the falls. Kilani had taken James to this very spot the day they'd met. The support line previously strung across the chasm was gone. Water spilled freely from the center of the cliff and, as before, made no sound as it fell into the darkness below. James carefully propped Luno against a tree along the path.

"Tertiri zé manukto suomi ragö," James said, extending his hands. The ground rumbled beneath his feet as the last word escaped his lips. Stone slabs protruded from the sheer wall below forming a shoulder-wide path that sloped into the darkness. James sent several light orbs down his newly created pathway where they hovered, providing just enough light to make out the steps. He gently eased Luno over his shoulder like a sack of meal and hurried downward.

After what seemed like hours, the path leveled and widened. Luno began to murmur something James couldn't make out. As the pair continued to descend, the power of his orbs lessened until all but one were extinguished completely. The blue light of the orb hovering above his shoulder allowed James to see only a few feet ahead before the darkness smote it. He now understood why Akil suspected that Luno's cure dwelt somewhere in this darkness. The powers gifted to him by The Never were weakening with every step.

James looked up. The daylight above was but a pinpoint. Luno's short breaths came at sporadic intervals, and James knew he was running out of time. He continued toward where he imagined the water spilled noiselessly downward. The orb dimmed noticeably with each step until James could no longer make out his feet. He attempted to coax the orb lower but it no longer obeyed his commands. It hovered uselessly beside Luno's face.

James pressed on blindly. Luno shifted his weight and grasped James's shirt, moving voluntarily for the first time since their descent began. James's relief was short-lived as he took a step forward and found nothing upon which to place his foot. With Luno over his shoulder, he was too off balance to stop their momentum.

"What's happening?" Luno murmured as James clutched his frail body. Warm air rushed past them.

"We're falling," said James calmly.

"Excellent. Drifting off into a peaceful forever sleep was much too painless a way to die," said Luno. It was then that James realized Luno was speaking in his own voice – not that of an aged and dying man.

"You're back!" he exclaimed.

"Just in time, it seems," replied Luno.

The pair continued to fall, seeing nothing but the blackness and hearing nothing but the wind rushing past their ears. James could feel Luno's body changing as he held it. The frail skeleton was quickly filling out with the mass of his previous self.

Below, the darkness lightened. A red glow and the heat associated with it increased in intensity as they drew closer.

"I don't suppose you'd like to try an anti-falling incantation before we meet what appears will be a painful, fiery death," said Luno.

James tried an incantation, but nothing happened. In the ever-brightening red glow, the worry on Luno's face was clear. After all that's happened, would Akil lead us to our deaths? Over Luno's shoulder James watched the water of the falls cascade down at the same rate as their descent. James followed its path with his eyes until it disappeared in a cloud of steam. If Gai had forged the spellbreaker steel in this place, James knew the bottom would consist of only one thing. Molten steel.

As he hurtled down, James noticed the chasm was rimmed with columns and statues carved into the walls, but by the time it registered in his mind, they had fallen well beyond. The light and heat were becoming intolerable.

"Immolation via falling into in a pool of molten steel wasn't on my list of ways I'd like to die," said Luno.

"Good, because we'll be dead long before we catch fire."

"Very true," Luno replied in his casual tone.

Then, in a moment of perfect clarity, Luno extended his hands and said "Gelditu ." Their descent was immediately arrested. James stared at Luno in shock. "Eragin zehar. " The steam beneath their feet began to ripple like the surface of a pond in a warm summer breeze. The pair began moving toward the chasm wall.

"There is a ledge not far above," said James.

"I saw it as well," said Luno, reciting another incantation. The pair began to rise slowly. "I hope it isn't too far. This incantation isn't good beyond — " Before Luno could finish his sentence, James wrapped his arms around Luno and rolled toward the ledge. They slammed into the chasm wall and fell several feet onto the stone.

They lay there side by side, panting like dogs. Finally, Luno began to laugh and after a spell, James found himself joining in. Their cachinnations echoed off the chasm walls with ear-splitting volume. When they had laughed themselves out, the men stood and took in their surroundings. The ledge, wide enough for three horses to gallop abreast, ran the entire circumference of the chasm. Intricate carvings adorned the walls and stretched well above the men's heads. A stone tampere lunging toward its prey was sculpted into the wall beside them.

"How did you know?" asked James.

"A lucky guess, I suppose," replied Luno.

"In all the time I've known you, you've never attributed anything to luck."

"True," said Luno, running his hand over the gaping stone jaw of the monster. "I've been thinking about it ever since I stepped into Adelphi and began to age. My suspended youth was a gift given to me by The Never. Everything about Gai and his realm — the buildings, the street, his blade — " Luno pointed to the black steel sword on James's belt, "seems to oppose the will of The Never. When I realized a few moments ago that the incantations gifted to you by the land were no longer effective, I surmised that this place is not under the control of The Never, so standard incantations would work."

"Your theory makes sense until we get to the part where you've regained your youth. It was gifted to you by The Never and then taken by Gai. Why then would travel to this place restore it?"

"A valid point," Luno said as the pair began to walk along the ledge. "I can only presume that this chasm is under neither the control of The Never nor is it under Gai's influence. I believe it is a passage between The Never and our world."

23

a hesitant reunion

April 1897, Tanganyika, Africa

James stood on the shore of Lake Victoria looking out over the water. He had been to this exact location on two prior occasions — both times with Akil — but felt some other inexplicable bond to this place. When his time with Alvaro had concluded, Akil had sent word that James was to meet him here. Although James obliged, he felt less secure in his relationship with his mentor and unsure of his intentions.

Several men cast fishing nets from their boat offshore as James moved along the water's edge. Several dozen white birds watched the fishermen from a nearby rock that jutted out into the water. Their long, orange bills spilled color onto their plumage in a vivid stripe of feathers

"So it is that you have come back to me." James, surprised by the silent approach, turned quickly, his hands raised and ready to cast an incantation. Akil smiled, completely disarming the boy. After a moment of studying his face, Akil stepped forward and gripped James in an awkward embrace.

"It is good to have you back, my son," said Akil.

With those words, simple as they were, the anger James had mustered for their meeting melted away.

"A stunning place, is it not?" he continued. "Rich in resource and community. Such a shame the Germans decided to colonize and terrorize these people. Although, before the Germans it was the Arabs. Before the Arabs it was the Portuguese. A long line of invaders have kept generations of natives from living in peace, so I suppose casting blame on the current occupiers isn't entirely fair. I do have a feeling all the invasions and occupations will come to an end before long. Now then, to the task at hand!" He clapped James on the shoulder.

They proceeded down a dirt path and into a clearing where several crude wooden structures stood on the perimeter. At the sight of Akil dressed in his long red robes, which somehow managed to look both foreign and native at the same time, dozens of knee-high children came running with squeals of delight. Akil crouched and allowed the children to barrel into his open arms and embrace him. After he had sent the children on their way, he led James toward a structure in the far corner of the clearing. Akil pulled back the cloth that draped the doorway.

"After you," he said. James ducked under the low doorframe and stepped inside. He was immediately enveloped in darkness. "Argitu ." Two white orbs rose from Akil's palms and into the air far above where the thatched roof should have been. They paused, vibrated and broke apart into thousands of smaller orbs that flew off in every direction, illuminating Akil's conservatory. James gaped at the sorcerer, who simply smiled.

"Now," said Akil, "we shall indulge in a rare delight. I have brought with me tea leaves from the southern part of the country. They are as rare as they are delicious."

He dug into his robes and extracted an oblong piece of folded cloth. James could smell the fragrant leaves contained within. Akil followed the flagstone path toward the wrought iron table and chairs hidden among the foliage on the far side of the conservatory. As they passed the grassy area, James noticed strange birds pecking at the ground. Their long, thin legs held stubby egg-shaped bodies. Neither the bodies nor tails of the creatures were feathered but covered in scales. The whip-like tails were poised upright, reminding James of a rearing snake, and they undulated like ocean waves as the creatures ate. At the end of each tail was a puff of black filaments like a blooming flower. Their necks were similarly long and flexible as they stretched to the ground, dancing from side to side and pecking at the soil with needle-like transparent beaks. Akil retraced his steps when he noticed James was transfixed by the creatures and no longer following.

"Fascinating, are they not?"

"Aye," replied James. Akil cleared his throat, sending James a not-so-subtle message that it was time to move on. James turned away from the fantastical birds and continued down the path. When the pair reached the table, Akil conjured a teapot and kettle, happily dropped several pinches of the tea leaves inside the pot, and filled it with bubbling water from the kettle. Two cups and saucers appeared and placed themselves on the table with a quiet clink. James sat at the table struggling to wait patiently as the tea steeped. Finally, with a smile, Akil poured the tea into the cups and took a seat across from James.

Akil inhaled the steam rising from his cup. "I imagine you have many questions for me after your time with Ilixo." James nodded. Akil smiled. "Excellent. I am glad to see the purpose of this exercise has been fulfilled."

"Exercise!" James was caught off guard. "Is that what you call leaving me with the man I believed to be behind the murder of my father?" he asked angrily.

"Son, before you become overly accusatory, please allow me to explain myself."

"You are not my father. Please stop calling me 'son.' Your hands are not clean in his death and my trust in you has been shaken." James said, trembling.

"James, take a moment and consider. Would I send you into the lion's den without expecting him to plant seeds of dissent? That is what Ilixo Alvaro does. That is his gift. Misdirection and half-truths are his weapons."

"And what are your weapons, Master? You didn't exactly prepare me for this so-called exercise. What was your intent if you knew what would happen once I was a captive?"

"Captive? Trust me James, you were never a captive. I could have retrieved you at any time."

"How? How is it that you are so powerful compared to others on the council ? What is it you want from me? Why have you taken me as your apprentice?" James demanded. In response, Akil extended his right hand. An orb of blue light no larger than a pinpoint grew above his palm. When it reached the size of his hand, Akil spoke.

"First, you must see what I am about to show you. Then I will answer all your questions." He gently tossed the orb into the air and watched it expand until it engulfed the pair in blue light.

Inside the memory, Akil sat alone in a dark tavern. He sipped his drink while inspecting the room. A full glass sat on the table beside him at an empty seat. The fire was dying in the hearth. A barmaid wiped the counter with a wet rag. It was near closing time. A man stepped out of the shadows behind Akil. Alvaro.

"I thought you had gotten lost," said Akil.

"I've eaten something that doesn't agree with me," said Alvaro, rubbing his trim stomach. He sat beside Akil looking tired and pale. Akil studied him for a moment, set his drink on the wooden table, and lifted his hands.

"Sendatu ," he said, sending a wisp of white smoke toward Alvaro. The instant it touched him, his pallor receded and he smiled. "Better?"

"You never cease to amaze, Akil Karanis."

"You should not be so amazed by a simple healing incantation."

"Aye, it is simple in essence. In practice, however, it is rather difficult. Even the council instructors struggle with that particular incantation." At this, Akil simply smiled. Alvaro picked up his glass and drank slowly. "Now, why is it I was so urgently summoned the day after my wedding? I trust you have a good excuse for missing the ceremony, by the way."

"I have found him," Akil said with the merest of grins that was ready to grow with the slightest encouragement.

"Found who, damn it?"

"The Anointed One."

Alvaro slammed his drink down on the table and sat back in his chair.

"Not this again. How many times are you going to take some poor boy under your wing after convincing him he is the Anointed One, only to be rejected by the Seer? And what of the Stuart boy? Have you so quickly changed your mind?"

"The Stuart boy was promising except…"Akil paused, lost within his mind for a moment. "Never mind that, this boy has been to the Seer."

Alvaro leaned forward, looked around and whispered,"And?" Akil simply nodded. Alvaro slammed his hand on the table and let out a bark of a laugh. "You bloody fool, you finally found him. I truly doubted you ever would. Everyone doubted." He grew quiet and once again leaned in close to Akil. "His powers?"

"Like nothing I have ever seen."

"Where is this boy? I must meet him."

"He is here, at this very inn waiting in a room down the hall." Alvaro looked to the corner of the tavern where a passageway twisted behind the turn of the bar. Akil cleared his throat. "There is more. Something you must do for me."

"Anything, my old friend."

"You must take him as your apprentice. You must keep him as far from me as you possibly can. I fear what might happen if he were able to influence my powers or I his. Too much power is not good for any man. It twists minds and distorts reality."

"Since when are you adverse to too much power?

Akil sipped his drink, ignoring Alvaro's question.

"I am no mentor, Akil. Why do you ask this of me?"

"It must be you, my friend. I believe you are meant to train this boy. There is one thing you must know before — "

Alvaro turned ghostly pale as he looked across the room. A boy, no older than twelve, with tanned skin and white-blond hair stood watching the men. Alvaro's fright turned to rage as he looked at Akil.

"Is this some kind of farce? You dare bring him here? You dare profess he is the Anointed One? It is no wonder you want me to mentor him! I will look a fool when I bring him before council, and he will be banished where he belongs." Before Akil could say a word, Alvaro turned and stormed out of the tavern and into the snowy night. Akil beckoned the boy over to the table. He quietly made his way to Akil's side with relief on his face.

"Not to worry, Serik. All is proceeding as planned. He will change his mind and soon, you will be that much closer to fulfilling your destiny."

The scene faded, revealing a gape-mouthed James staring at Akil.

"Based upon your deportment, I surmise you have met Serik Vinokourov," said Akil.

"He is Master Alvaro's apprentice."

"So you see that Ilixo conceded after some convincing."

"Yes, that much is obvious," replied James, grabbing his head as if trying to straighten out all the thoughts that swirled inside. "Akil, I need to know. Who do you believe is the Anointed One?"

Akil nodded. "I understand your confusion. What you have just witnessed, along with what Ilixo has no doubt told you, would confuse any man. I tell you now, despite what you have seen and heard, that the Anointed One sits across from me at this very moment. It is you, James. It always has been you."

"You say that with such confidence, yet after you came to my parents, you brought Serik to Master Alvaro. You told him he was the Anointed One. You told Master Alvaro he'd been to the Seer. That he'd been confirmed."

"It is for precisely that reason you needed to see this memory. How many times has Ilixo brought Serik before the council? You would not know the answer unless Ilixo — "

"Zero," James interrupted.

"So he has told you," replied Akil.

"Yes. Master Alvaro believes that while Serik possesses great power, he does not possess all the traits of the Anointed One," James said, staring into his teacup. "Why did you ask Master Alvaro to take Serik as his apprentice and not me? Why did you even consider Serik after you told me I was the Anointed One? If your reason for not wanting to mentor Serik was your fear of his powers, why would I be any different? Were you prepared to throw me by the wayside if Serik proved more worthy?"

"My quest to find the Anointed One has not been easy, James. Fraught with missteps, oversights and failures is an accurate way to begin to describe the journey. I am far from infallible. It is true that I went to your parents four years ago and told them that you were, without a doubt, the Anointed One. Not long after, I found Serik and he, too, met the criteria spoken of by the Seer. I had recently begun to doubt the accuracy of the prophecy's interpretation, and despite my apprehension because of Serik's less than desirable lineage, I could not discount the boy outright. In order to convince Ilixo that he must be the one to mentor Serik, he had to trust it was my unwavering belief that Serik was the true Anointed One.

"I asked Ilixo to mentor Serik not because I feared my own influence, but because I needed to focus on you. You were, in my mind, always the best candidate, and in the end, it is you who will stop the Epoch Terminus."

"Why didn't you tell me about Serik, about the others before him?" asked James.

"Doubt in the mind of a sorcerer is a disease. This is especially true among those born into an unfaithful family. Your unclouded and unwavering belief and focus were essential — as they still are. When your father was killed, I knew I must complete your training."

"And what of Serik's father?" asked James, intentionally directing the conversation away from the topic of his father — one he was not yet prepared to discuss.

"Serik is a different story entirely. You have heard me speak of his grandfather. The reputation he created for himself has forced him to spend the remainder of his unnaturally long life on the outskirts of society. But Serik's father Hanot traveled a different path. He was an honorable man. Several years after Hanot and his wife Myriam had their first and only child, Hanot and his father had an explosive argu ment. Hanot disappeared and was never heard from again. Serik's mother died a year later, leaving him an orphan.

"A kind sorceress agreed to take in young Serik and raise him as her own. She had great powers and was able to teach Serik much before he was ready to be mentored. When I came to collect him, she had one condition. She insisted I could not mentor him. I agreed."

"Serik's grandfather still lives. You said it yourself. You believe he is helping Master Alvaro develop a mind alteration incantation. He was the one who performed the incantation on Mr. Ogilvy."

"You are correct. He lives at Cetus and is working for Ilixo."

"Serik does not know his grandfather. He believes he is dead or exiled."

"Does he? Intriguing," replied Akil as he took a sip of his tea. "And what do you know of exile, James?

"I know that is for the worst criminals in our society."

"True, very true. That is its intent, I have little doubt." Akil sat back in his chair, turning the teacup in his hands, allowing it to clink against his rings as he spun the porcelain. The pair was silent for a spell until James finally stood and began pacing. "What vexes you, boy?"

"Everything. Everything I've heard. Everything I've seen. Everything Master Alvaro has told me. It is nothing but a tangle of contradictions, yet each explanation seems rational and reasonable. The truth is buried somewhere amongst the lies, and I haven't the mind to separate one from the other. I feel pulled in opposite directions."

"How long have we known each other, James?"

"Roughly five years."

"Correct. I formally introduced myself to you a shade under five years ago. We first met over a decade ago, but I hardly expect you to remember that first meeting," said Akil. He paused for a beat, lost in recollection, then continued. "And how long have you known Ilixo…Master Alvaro?"

"I'm not sure I know him at all. Either of you, actually."

At this, Akil looked as if he'd been struck. He cleared his throat.

"James, I needed you to see from his perspective. I needed you to understand what it is like to know doubt. You must understand the power of manipulation. In order to prevent the Epoch Terminus, you must be exposed to all forms of combat."

"But I don't want to fight him!" shouted James. "He isn't the monster you've made him out to be. He hasn't been hunting me down my entire life in an attempt to gain power. He had nothing to do with my father's death. It was all lies." His shouts echoed in the high glass ceilings. Akil remained silent, allowing James to finish his tirade. In the distance, they could hear the flutter of wings as birds took flight.

"Do you believe that to be the truth, son?"

"I've yet to be convinced otherwise," said James in a more subdued tone.

"James, I will assure you of this: before the end, you will know the truth beyond any doubt. There is nothing wrong with questioning what it is you believe to be true. It makes wiser men of us all. My only fear is that your acceptance of the truth will come too late."

"Too late for what?"

Akil reached into his pocket and withdrew the ornate timepiece James had so often seen him inspecting. When he flipped open the cover, a blue glow danced across his face. Akil shook his head as if he'd been given bad news and quickly snapped the lid closed. As he went to put it in his pocket, James reached across the table and took hold of his wrist.

"You've been staring at that watch of yours since I've known you, and during all that time, you've never given me the courtesy of telling me what it really is. Tell me, please."

James released Akil's wrist and sat. Akil looked down at the watch cupped in his palm. A blue light seeped out from around the edge of the cover. Akil let out a defeated sigh and leaned back in his chair.

"This is no ordinary trinket. It was gifted to me long ago — by whom is not important at the moment. It does not tell the time of day but tells the time that remains — the time that remains until the Epoch Terminus. When I first received the Aldi Jaitsu , it counted down centuries, then decades, and now years. How many I do not know, for it is not a precise instrument. Perhaps as many as nine. Perhaps as few as one. Imagine, James, one year until the Epoch Terminus is upon us. One year and we remain ignorant of nearly everything surrounding the Epoch Terminus. How, where, what is the cause — all these things we know nothing about. We speculate, but speculation is simply that. The Seer foretold of one person who could stop the Epoch Terminus. I believe that person is you, James. If Ilixo also believed, we would have the power of the council on our side, which is why I sent you to him."

"How much time is left?"

"I told you this instrument is not precise. I suppose I could extrapolate from the — "

"How much?"

"That knowledge is a burden no man should bear."

"No man except you," replied James.

"I understand your frustration. If you are the Anointed One, why would I keep such a vital piece of information from you? You must focus on the task at hand, James. Once we leave my conservatory, you must sequester your emotions and focus on your preparation, your training. I will tell you this much, James. The end draws nigh."

24

between worlds

James was incredulous. "Are you telling me you believe there is a way home down here?"

"Aye. If you eliminate the things that don't make sense, that is the only explanation that does." Luno began walking along the wide ledge that circled the chasm, inspecting the countless sculptures of the frieze carved into the living rock. He ran his fingers over each as they moved past. "The stone is surprisingly pliant."

"Who do you believe constructed this place?

"I dare not say. The sculptures come from numerous periods in history. That one there is Roman," Luno said, pointing to a lion, teeth bared and poised to attack. Standing out of reach was a man wielding a pike in one hand, a shield in the other. They rounded a bend. "And this one..." Both men stopped dead, silent.

The walls of the black castle rose well above the rest of the towering frieze, yet James knew it was but a fraction of the size of the true castle. Between the two towers of the outer bailey was a tall arched doorway. Rather than stone, the doors were made of wood, and both were ever so slightly ajar. James instinctively reached for his sword. As his hand grasped the hilt, he felt nothing. No luring pull, no mental transport to another place. Nothing.

"Dare we step inside?" asked Luno.

"It may be our only option," replied James, as his eyes searched for another means of egress along the pathway.

Luno strode onward, and James reluctantly followed. The desire that had pulled at him since his arrival was not drawing him into this place. There was no familiarity here, no comfort. As they reached the large doors, Luno shouldered one, forcing it open. The hinges protested with a groan that echoed in the shadows beyond. Firelight flickered dimly on the arched ceiling stories above.

"Argitu, " Luno said as he extended his palms outward. A small pink orb rose from his palms and grew in size and intensity until it revealed their surroundings. Piles of furniture extended as far as they could see, each stacked precariously high above their heads. It looked as if a slight breeze would send them toppling to the floor. Several plain wooden chairs lay on their sides surmounted by a wardrobe, its thick wooden doors disgorging a jumble of clothes. Behind it, a pile of small tables rose up beyond the light of the orb, each table carefully balanced on the one beneath.

"Egin-argi-menderatu, " said James. Several dozen pinpoint orbs rose from his hands and flew off into the distance, lighting the cavernous room. Their light revealed more furniture in varying states of disrepair piled to impossible heights.

"Is this navigable?" asked Luno, eying the mess for a way through.

"Albora egin ." The stack of furniture in front of the men split down the center and separated, leaving a shoulder-width gap. Several of the higher towers collapsed upon themselves with an echoing crash, spewing up centuries' worth of dust. "I dare say it is navigable," James said with a half-smile.

"Let us hope you haven't woken any long-dormant terrors with your reckless methods," said Luno.

"Haizatu ." A gust of air blew from James's palms and swirled along the newly formed path, taking the suspended dust with it. When the air along the path had cleared, James nodded, and the two men started forward, only to freeze as a sound broke the silence. James likened it to a heavy piece of metal being dragged across a stone floor. They exchanged concerned glances. When all fell silent, they continued.

"Odd," Luno whispered.

"What?"

"No echo."

The pair followed the path until it curved to the right beyond a stack of bookshelves. As they reached the shelves, they heard the noise once more. This time, they were able to determine that the origin was somewhere to their left. They advanced quickly around the bend. As if in reply, a second noise sounded somewhere in the darkness ahead, then a third from behind. It was followed by the easily recognizable groan of door hinges and a sonorous boom. The large wooden doors had been closed.

The men hastened on, continually looking over their shoulders as they made their way through the ever-narrowing pathway. James noticed a small, half-moon alcove to his left where five marble globes lined the perimeter. It seemed somehow familiar, but the ominous sounds, now much closer, drove the pair onward. As they rounded another bend, Luno stopped short.

"Look." Through piles of credenzas and stiff-backed chairs, they could see a large golden brazier hung from a thick chain that stretched up into the darkness. Flames danced above the rim and illuminated the chamber's nearest wall. Close behind them, the screeching, scraping call jolted them onward. A second, to their right, originated behind a tall stack of oaken desks.

They continued to jog as the path turned away from the brazier and back toward the entrance. Luno reached out and pulled on James's shoulder. He pointed back at the brazier.

"Our way out is there, I'm sure of it," he said.

James sent a burst of energy in the direction of the brazier, demolishing the furniture between them and the exit they longed for. The pair continued before the dust could settle. Luno sent a burst of wind, clearing the air and revealing the source of the noise. It stood between them and a black steel door recessed in the wall behind the brazier.

The creature was like nothing either of the men had ever seen. It was tall — twice as tall as a man, thin and covered in large red scales that sparkled in the firelight. The creature had four legs, none of which bent and all of which seemed to hover above the floor in a cloud of dust. The mass of its cylindrical upper body sat atop the convergence of its four branch-like legs. As it watched them, its winged torso spun, rotating at the joint above the legs and below the neck as if it weren't connected to either. Its wings were long and thin — almost like the blades of a windmill. Its head was similarly narrow, as if someone had placed an oblong shield on top of the creature's neck, and fringed with thousands of finger-length tendrils that rippled in all directions as if caught by gusts of wind.

Luno extended his hands in preparation to cast an incantation.

"Wait," said James, stepping forward. "We must pass," he said to the creature. If the creature heard or understood James, it did not acknowledge him. James took another step forward. Luno advanced as well, shoulder to shoulder with James. The creature did not react. Again, James took a step forward until he was within inches of the creature's wings as they spun past, billowing a gust of warm air on his face.

Then, without warning, the creature froze. Luno slowly peered over his shoulder. Two identical creatures had taken up position behind them. They were trapped. James stepped forward again, his hands outstretched in a display of peace. Luno turned slightly, keeping his back to James and his eyes on the two creatures now blocking any possible retreat.

"Apotēket," said James, forgetting that the language of The Never was ineffective. The creature did not react. "Bakedun ," he said, digging the magical language of home from his memory. A wisp of green smoke rose from his palms and encircled the creature. The tendrils on the creature's head began to sway from side to side in unison. Glancing over his shoulder, James saw that the other two creatures were exhibiting the same behavior.

"Let's go," he said, moving stealthily toward the door. Luno followed. The pair kept their distance from the creature as they made their way around it to the black steel door. A large wooden bolt sat in brackets mounted to the frame, preventing it from being pulled open.

"Igo ," James said, commanding the bolt to rise while Luno kept watch behind him. As James quietly maneuvered the bolt to the floor, he noticed oddly shaped protrusions in the steel of the door. They weren't concave as he would have expected, but convex, bulging out toward him.

"Now or never, boy," whispered Luno.

James gripped the looped handle and pulled. The door silently swung open. Luno was instantly at his side, and together they passed through and closed the door behind them. A shudder went through James's body as he instantly recognized where they were — the inner chambers of council headquarters.

"There is something familiar about — "

Luno's statement was interrupted by a rumbling growl from the shadowed balcony seating area. Only when its massive forepaw easily reached the marble floor of the chamber from the balcony, was the tampere's size apparent.

"That's the biggest bloody croc-monster I've ever seen," said Luno.

By the time it descended from the balcony, from head to tail its body spanned over half the width of the oval amphitheater. Its movements were nearly silent save the continual growl that shook the entire room.

"Let's call this one a draw, shall we?" said Luno, turning and pushing on the door. It did not budge.

"Move!" James shouted as he shoved Luno along the wall.

The tampere was in mid-lunge as the pair darted out of its path. It crashed into the wall, its jaws snapping closed. Slightly dazed from the impact, the creature shook its head, allowing pieces of rubble to fall from its mouth, including the steel door, which scraped along the ground throwing sparks in its wake as it slid past the men and crashed into the far wall.

"I believe we would have fared better with the winged beasts," Luno grumbled as he watched the creature shake itself free of the wreckage.

"Mundu igo ," James said, his hands extended. The ground began to tremble then settled back into silence. James didn't have time to think about why his incantation had failed as the creature whipped its tail and sprang along both wall and floor in their direction.

"Sute, " Luno said, attempting his own incantation. A large ball of flame formed between his palms. He flung it at the tampere. The flaming orb reached a considerable size by the time it struck the creature in the face but did nothing to slow its approach. It leapt into the air as James and Luno cut back toward the other end of the chamber.

"Inarjavai !" James shouted as the creature descended on them. It let out a roar, expelling a stench potent enough to knock the men backward, but before the creature could snap its jaws closed, its forward momentum ceased as it struck an invisible wall. James and Luno wasted no time moving in the opposite direction.

"What was that?" asked Luno.

"A tampere," replied James.

"I know full bloody well it was a tampere, you fool. I meant, what was that incantation you cast?"

"The tampere are creatures of The Never. Reason would stand that one would need to use the language of its land in order to combat one," said James as they continued to run. "We must find another way out." They scanned the perimeter as the shaken creature regained its footing and began to batter the invisible barrier.

"There!" said Luno, pointing past the tampere to a small, round green door set at an odd angle into the wall, halfway between a doorway and a hatch.

"I'll lure it over here. Make your way to the door. I'll be right behind," said James.

Luno nodded and the men separated at a run. Unsure which of its prey to pursue first, the creature finally decided on Luno and slowly turned in his direction. James sent a blast of energy at the tampere, causing it to reel and turn. It let out an angry roar and James took the opportunity to send another blast of energy — this one directly into the creature's gaping maw.

Infuriated, its throat vibrated as a steady rumbling growl relayed its frustration. The creature more warily advanced upon James who sent several more blasts of energy in its direction. As James continued luring the creature toward him, Luno reached the door. He stooped, searching for a knob or latch. When he found neither, he gave the door a push, followed by a kick, to no avail.

"Ireki ," shouted Luno in frustration. The door remained closed. Luno looked over at James, who still managed to distract the tampere. James rolled to the side as the creature took a swipe at him. He threw another burst of energy at the tampere while trying to adjust the sword in his belt for better maneuverability. The beast caught a glimpse of the blade and stepped back. Immediately, James drew the spellbreaker blade and waved it in the air. The tampere squealed in fear and quickly retreated to the far end of the chamber. James took the opportunity to join Luno.

"It won't bloody open," growled Luno.

James placed his hands on the brass finger plate, and the door swung silently open. Luno hung his head. He and James stepped over the threshold, and the creature let out a roar of frustration as its meal disappeared.

25

the journal

October 1897, Littlemore, Oxfordshire, England

Her hands trembled as she cautiously opened her husband's diary. Margaret wasn't sure why she had waited over a year to look through its pages. She supposed she was afraid of what she might find written inside. Part of her knew that in order to move on, she must either read its contents or destroy it altogether, yet part of her wasn't ready. Why must we move on? she thought as she returned her hands to the steaming cup beside her.

The fall leaves were thick at her feet, still holding on to the vibrant colors they'd turned before the cool air blew them from their branches. This was her refuge, her escape. She had discovered this secret garden as a lonely, introverted child. A string of events had led her away from her enchanted haven, and it had been lost to her for many years. Margaret adamantly and justifiably refused to return. Over the years, she had managed to make peace with the events of her past and had recently returned for the first time.

Only one other knew of this place. She had mentioned it to neither her husband nor her son. A woman needs her solitude from time to time, she'd often tell herself, keeping the guilt of secrecy at bay. She sat on the stone bench next to the small red tree whose branches spilled down into a dome, giving it the appearance of an umbrella. The lower branches grazed tight-knit pink flowering plants that spread away from the base of the tree forming a perfect circle where they met the fine crushed stone path.

Most often, Margaret would sit quietly and read, allowing herself to escape whatever it was that pulled at her mind to enter into another world. Sometimes, she would simply sit and listen as the wind coursed through the giant beech and oak trees, brushing them together like hesitant dancers. On still days, she would listen to her own breathing or the beating of her heart.

Margaret's heart had been shorn in two at the moment of her husband's death. Now, when she got particularly excited, she could feel the injury in her chest like a file against raw skin. So much has happened since you left. You have missed so much. You are missed so much. If only things were different, you'd be alive. What I wouldn't give to feel you again — your hand in mine, the prickly, unshaven skin of your face. The soft tenderness of your lips against my lips. To hold you again. To smell you. To hear your voice — that soothing, calm voice.

The tears came and she let them. Despite the enduring pain, they seldom lasted long. She took a sip of tea and returned her cup to the bench. Margaret looked down at the journal sitting in her lap. She exhaled and opened it. Her hands shook as she quickly reread the inscription inside the cover.

James Lochlan Stuart III

For those who succeed me, so that my efforts are not in vain.

Margaret then turned to the first page.

Twenty-first of May, 1887

Greetings,

Everything has changed. Up is down. Left is right. Many important lessons have I learned over the course of this past year. The most important is this: never hold on to a belief so tightly you don't allow yourself to be open to the possibility that you're wrong. Being wrong can be, and usually is, simply a result of ignorance rather than lack of intelligence. Highly intelligent people can be, and most often are, extremely ignorant in many regards. On these pages I hope to leave thoughts and lessons others may find useful. To my beloved wife, with whom I've fallen in love a second time over the past year, and my dear son, who carries a burden far too heavy for any one man, let alone a child, I hope you may find solace and truth within. Life begins and ends with hope.

J.L.S.

Margaret read the entry twice more before turning to the next page for the first time. Her breath came faster as she lifted the page with her moist, trembling fingers. The paper was thick and crisp, perfect for absorbing the ink. Stuart had always insisted upon writing on the highest quality paper.

Margaret turned the page. It was blank. She turned to the next page. She could scarcely make out where the lines of writing had been. The ink had faded as if it had been washed in sunlight over decades, rendering the page unreadable. Her consternation increased as she turned page after ruined page.

Impossible, she thought, incredulous that all her delay and anxiety had been for nothing. Margaret flipped to the back cover, also a smear of faded ink, and let the pages fall away from her thumb as she searched for something, anything, readable. A glimpse of blue ink caught her eye as the pages fanned past. She stopped, flattened the journal, and slowly turned the pages searching for the marking she had spotted.

One word was centered on the page. Blue letters inscribed over a pool of blue ink appeared dimensional — as if they were floating. Margaret read the word aloud.

Hementxe

The journal flew from Margaret's hands and landed roughly on the leaves at the base of a vine-choked stone wall, still open to the same page. The word appeared to liquify and began to swirl until it rose from the paper entirely. As it rose, it formed into a globule, then expanded into an orb of blue light. Margaret stood as the orb engulfed her and the garden, taking her to another place and time.

She stood in a small room lit only by a fire in the hearth and two candles on the mantle that dripped and guttered. Bookshelves lined the opposite wall. A cushioned rocking chair was the only other piece of furniture in the room. The heavy wooden door swung open, causing Margaret to jump back despite knowing she was viewing a memory. Stuart walked into the room, his eyes on the floor.

"Please stand facing the center of the bookshelf," he said. He gave her a moment, then lifted his head and looked right into Margaret's eyes.

"There," he said with a smile. "Akil told me it would be easier if I were to look directly at you rather than take a guess as to your position. I hope you find this suitable."

Margaret's heart was pounding. Of all the things she had expected, this was not one of them. She had been told that when a person died, their memories died with them.

"Hello, my love," Stuart said with a wry smile.

"Hello, my love," Margaret replied, tears spilling onto her cheeks.

"Well," he sighed, "I suppose my passing was inevitable. With any luck, you're an old woman, and I've died as an old man peacefully in my sleep. If that isn't the case, then I am truly sorry. Do not mourn long, my love, for you must live your own life, and you must look after James.

"This, above all else, is of the utmost importance: see that our son reaches his full potential. I truly believe that in order to do this, you must be at peace with yourself. You must find happiness within yourself, and you must begin anew. Our boy needs his mother now more than ever in my absence. I know how you are, my love. I've grown to understand the extraordinary and complex person that you are. I believe you will allow this loss to make you question all that is important. Grief makes us all question what truly matters in our lives. I know that you, of all people, are more familiar with the face of loss and hurt than most. I also understand that this makes you both more resolved and more vulnerable. You must rise above this loss — any loss — and see that our son becomes who he is destined to be."

He knows, Margaret thought, recalling her haunted past and her tight-lipped silence when Stuart had queried. He knows and he never spoke a word of it.

"I will not ask you to move on as if I were but a distant memory, for that would be folly. Grief, loss and pain make us who we are and who we will become. Many say they can let go or move on, but that is something that I strongly deny. A great loss cannot simply be tucked away as if it were an outgrown coat or a prized blanket."

Margaret smiled, recalling when, early in their relationship, she had discovered the blanket that Stuart's grandmother had knitted for him as a toddler tucked smartly beneath his pillow. She had thrown the ragged thing in the dust bin. When Stuart had questioned its whereabouts, what a row had ensued.

"It becomes part of us," Stuart continued. "We must accept this new part of who we are and continue down the path that has been chosen for us — or the path that we decide to take. Duty or choice, both respectable foundations for any beginning.

"So Margaret, my love, let my loss become a part of you. Take me in. Absorb my love for you. Let it give you strength. It is here," he said, gesturing to his surroundings, "in this very room, and it is there," he said, pointing to Margaret. "Beside you. Above you. Around you. Take it. It is yours. It always has been. This you must do not only because I ask it of you, but because your son will not thrive if you do not. For that reason alone, you must see the logic in my request and acquiesce.

"So many lies will you hear, my love, especially once I am gone. Lies that will make you question the very path we set upon all those years ago. You must remain steadfast, my dear Margaret. It will not be easy to tell fact from fiction. Explanations provided to you will be so full of intricate detail and supporting evidence that, at first glance, they will appear as irrefutable fact.

"Agree to nothing hastily, Margaret. Take the time that is needed to understand what you are being told and what the teller's intentions truly are. Never, despite any urgency that may be placed on such a thing, rush to a decision that puts you or James in a position that is irreversible. I realize I am being obscure in my references, my love, and I wish nothing more than to be able to convey this information with more clarity; however, I know not the full extent of the lies spun against us, nor do I wish to cloud your judgment with my assumptions.

"You are a great woman, Margaret, and I, I was a lucky man. Twice blessed, for I fell in love with you two times, the second so much stronger, deeper and more meaningful that I dare say I did not deserve it. I did my best to make the most of it, my love. Men don't often get a second chance like that, and upon realizing this, I lived each day knowing what a blessing my life had become. I have no doubt that without our love, James would not be the remarkable young man he has grown to be.

"Love is the foundation of all who achieve greatness, and James is destined to be among them. It is due to our love that he has coped so well with this responsibility, but because I've left you, I'm afraid the onus is upon you to see it through to the end.

"I'm sorry I cannot be there for you, my love. I'm sorry I cannot be there for James. I'm sorry I will not be there to celebrate all that he achieves in his life, to meet the one he calls his love, to witness the strength our love has emboldened within him. Mostly, I'm sorry that I cannot live out my life with you by my side, Margaret. I had a vision of our future together, my love, and it was simple and wonderful. A small cottage on a quiet lake where we would share warm cups of tea on cool mornings while looking out at the mist rising from the still water. Our children and our children's children would occupy our time with their regular visits, and during our time alone, we would cherish each other's company while trying not to drive one another mad." Margaret chuckled and dabbed at her eyes with her sleeve.

"Our son gets his strength from you. I have no doubt that you will rise above this loss and continue to meet all obstacles thrust in your path with a hardened determination that I could never muster. Others may have thought you cold or distant, but I have always known the truth. It was your strength that kept you at arm's length from those who didn't know you. It is this strength that will see our son rise to meet the challenges in his life.

"I must go, Margaret. I wish it were not the case, for I have so much to say — so much to tell you about my love for you, my thoughts, my dreams, the lessons I wish to pass on to you, to James. But as I prepared this speech, I realized that who I am — who I was — can be understood from the life I have lived, the people with whom I have surrounded myself, and the choices I have made. I have found peace knowing that the answers I so often sought from my own father after his death were indeed there all the time. It simply took a bit of unraveling to discover who he really was. We have created a legacy not built on wealth or power but built upon the love of two people. That legacy can never be destroyed and will never fall to ruin. I may be gone, but my love for you will endure.

"I patiently walk the path and enjoy the gods ' beauty. Do not hasten our reunion, for you have much to do, and time passes swiftly for one awaiting his beloved. Until then, my dear Margaret, may you find peace with my passing and summon the strength to do what must be done. Goodbye, my love."

The scene faded as Stuart nodded into the distance. Margaret reached out for him but felt only the crisp air of autumn between her fingers. She stood in front of the long, ivy-choked wall where the journal had landed what felt like hours ago. Overwhelmed and shaken, Margaret sat against the wall and let the tears continue to spill until they ran dry. She then stood, resolute and confident. It was time to begin anew. Margaret retrieved the journal and strode with the gait of an unburdened woman toward her destination.

26

old friends

James and Luno stood open-mouthed as they took in their surroundings. The lush greenery, high glass ceilings, and strange yet beautiful flowers in all stages of bloom could only mean one place: Akil's conservatory. Luno began to laugh, and the tension that plagued James quickly dissipated.

"Do you know where we are, my boy?" asked Luno.

"Aye," replied James.

"If you only knew how long it has been since I've stepped through one of Akil's dooways. How in the bloody hell did he manage to create one in that godforsaken place?"

"More than one, actually," Akil said, appearing from around the corner on the flagstone path. Luno's chortles turned into hysterical laughter at the sight of Akil.

"Of all the certainties in my life — and there continue to be very few — I knew without a doubt that I would never lay eyes upon Akil Karanis again," gasped Luno.

"Yet here I stand," said Akil.

"Yet there you stand," repeated Luno, his smile melting away. "Just as arrogant as when you left us all those years ago, and not a day older by the looks of it."

"You have not aged much yourself, my old friend," said Akil.

"Friend? Is this how you treat your friends? You left us all behind to rot in that place and have the audacity to call me friend?"

"Dear Ciarán. Always rash with your conclusions, even in your old age. The path I took was not an easy one. Not one of our group would have survived the journey."

"Not one except you, of course."

"I was willing to take that chance, and I tell you, the path I traveled has damaged me in both mind and body even though you may not see it. My every day is fraught with pain and guilt."

"Well, that's a relief, isn't it, James," said Luno, elbowing James in the side. "Akil feels guilty about leaving us behind. I'd be surprised if the bloody old fool didn't send you here intentionally. Pain and guilt — please. Every day in The Never is pain and guilt. You will find no sympathy here."

"It is apparent that your ability to listen to reason has diminished since my departure. That being the case, let us have some tea and fill our bellies. Then we can discuss what ails you," said Akil.

Luno's demeanor immediately changed. It was clear that, for the only one of the trio who hadn't had a proper meal in recent memory, the thought of food was a sufficient distraction to temporarily delay his tirade. "Very well. Let us eat and then discuss the matters at hand," he said, still eyeing Akil suspiciously.

"An excellent idea!" said Akil. "What better way to begin a conversation than with food in our bellies and drinks in our hands, would you not agree, James?"

"Aye," James said cheerily as Akil gave him a wink. He would have said practically anything to break the tension.

Having Luno and Akil together in this place, which James associated with his world back home, was bizarre. Never before had the two worlds — his two lives — come together. It gave James hope to watch Luno and Akil walk side by side down the flagstone path, Luno nattering the entire way, to the wrought iron table in the clearing. With a word and a flourish of his hands, Akil summoned an entire meal to the table. Luno wasted no time pulling up a chair and digging in.

"I imagine you have quite an appetite yourself, James, after all you have been through since our last visit," said Akil. James nodded. He didn't feel particularly hungry but would eat nonetheless if for no other reason than to appease Akil. He sat beside Luno, who was tearing into his meal like a ravening dog, and began moving several of his favorite foods onto his plate. Akil took a seat and watched with a grin of satisfaction on his face.

After the meal, Akil waved away the dishes and left in their place a steaming pot of tea and three cups. He filled the cups, sat back in his chair, and inhaled the rising steam.

"I was hoping for something a bit stronger than tea," said Luno.

"I imagine you were," replied Akil with a smile. He offered no explanation or apology, and Luno understood that tea would be the only drink served at this meal. Indignant but satiated, Luno sat back in his chair and sipped his tea. After a moment of silence, it was James who spoke first.

"When we arrived, you called Luno by a different name"

"A name I would rather not hear again. That person was left behind many years ago," said Luno.

"As you wish, Luno," said Akil. James watched as the pair exchanged curious glances.

"How is it, Master Akil, that you were able to create yet another doorway and in that place?" asked James, breaking the strange tension between Akil and Luno.

"I presume you are referring to the door at the base of the falls," said Akil.

"Aye. How in the bloody hell did you manage your way down that bloody hole, into that particular room with those bloody winged tree-looking things, past that bloody giant tampere and make a doorway there, of all places?"

"First, those bloody winged tree-looking tree things, as you so aptly put it are called the Galmaàrden, and you should be glad they were there. Now, I imagine, my dear Luno, that my travels to that place were not much different than your own. Once I realized that I had passed through a barrier of sorts that enabled me to use earth-bound language to perform incantations, it was quite simple. The Galmaàrden are guardians very much like the guardians of Ak Egundiano. They are quite harmless, and the fact that you saw them at all implies their intent to protect you."

"Good thing we didn't run 'em through then, isn't it, James?" said Luno.

"Guardians? Like the guardians we saw by the cave? " asked James.

"Yes, the very same," said Akil.

"What do you mean they wanted to protect us?" asked James.

"The guardians only appear for two reasons: in order to convey an important message or to provide protection. Either they failed to pass on the message or, more likely, they were protecting you."

"Protecting us from what?"

"I shall say this and then I shall not speak of it again. The Galmaàrden were not there when I passed through, and I barely made it beyond the entrance."

"We weren't sure what they were," said James. "We didn't know if they were — "

"And what about that bloody tampere?" interrupted Luno. "How did you manage to cast the necessary incantations with that big bastard running around behind you?"

"Time in Ak Egundiano passes at a different measure from time in our world. When I traveled to the base of the falls, many years would pass until the two of you made the same trip. During my time, there were dozens, if not hundreds of tampere roaming the great halls above the molten lake. The smaller tampere were easy to handle with a simple shielding incantation. I suppose that the food supply dwindled, so eventually they turned on each other, and only the strongest and largest survived."

"I don't understand, master, why or how there could be tampere or guardians below this barrier of which you spoke. If the power of The Never ceases below the barrier, wouldn't all its inhabitants remain above the barrier?"

"I don't believe the power of Ak Egundiano has a finite limitation. I believe this barrier is simply a temporal manifestation of where our world and Ak Egundiano come together, which is why we are able to perform incantations in the magical language of our land with a high degree of effectiveness. I also believe that the powers of both our world and Ak Egundiano stretch beyond the barrier like the roots of two great trees intertwining with each other, thus allowing creatures from either side to pass over."

"Are you saying that we could pass through and return to our world somewhere within the halls of the black abyss?"

"I do not believe so, James. I believe that, like the roots of a tree, one could only travel so far in either direction above or below the barrier. You both arrived in Ak Egundiano by different means, and it is by those means that you must return."

"Are you ever going to explain how the bloody hell you managed to get out and why you don't believe either of us could make the same journey?" asked Luno.

"As I have already explained to James, that path is no longer open to us. If you attempt to take it, I can guarantee one of two outcomes. One, you will die. Or two, you will become so raving mad that you will not be able to function in society. You will become a danger to yourself and others, and, I have no doubt, you will soon find yourself in Boulderfield Manor."

"If this dangerous path is the very same that you traveled all those years ago, and here you sit perfectly sane and visibly uninjured, how can you expect us to believe what you tell us?"

"First, because I have given you no reason to distrust me, and second, because my powers far exceed those of either of you. I can say that I did not escape undamaged. However, because of the strength of my powers, the damage is not apparent to the casual eye."

"Then there is no escape," said Luno, dejected.

"There is. We have yet to discover it, but I promise you there is an escape."

"And do you believe this, James? Do you believe Akil's story?"

James nodded. "I do. I must."

"Why? Why must you?"

"Because I will escape."

"Because of some bloody prophecy? The Epoch Terminus draws nigh, and you're trapped in The Never. What good can you possibly do from here? How can you believe the Seer spoke of you when, as the time for the great event winds down, you are as powerless as everyone else?"

"Tell me, naysayer, of James's powerlessness in Ak Egundiano," said Akil.

"Aye, he's been gifted powers. That doesn't mean he's any more likely to find an escape."

"This boy has saved your life on more than one occasion, has mastered the language of Ak Egundiano, and has crossed blades with Gai ak zangar. You doubt his ability to free himself from this place? My dear Luno, your lack of vision saddens me." The anger melted from Luno's face, changing to puzzlement with the furrowing of his brow. Then realization lit his features.

"Gai ak zangar. The Siren?" asked Luno.

"Yes."

"You?" asked Luno, looking at James.

"Aye. Akil believes she takes the form she believes will benefit her most. In our case, it was that of a child." Luno's mouth hung open as his mind raced.

"So she is the answer," he said quietly.

"I believe we must base our course of action upon that assumption," replied Akil.

"A bloody Siren," said Luno, shaking his head.

"Sirens are complex, powerful and often beautiful creatures. They deserve more than our loathing." James avoided eye contact with Akil as he spoke these words, remembering his conversation with the Siren. "James," said Akil, interrupting his thought. "Had you any more interaction with Gai since our previous meeting?"

James hesitated. How would Akil react if he spoke of his relationship with the Siren?

"James," repeated Akil, as if waking him from a deep sleep.

"Yes, I saw her minutes after our last meeting," said James.

"Tell us of your encounter. Every detail is essential and could reveal the answers we seek."

Reluctantly, James recounted his meeting and subsequent confrontation with Gai. When he finished, both men's faces registered disbelief. Luno began to laugh, causing him to spill his cup of tea. He jumped up as the hot liquid scalded his legs. After wiping away what liquid remained with a string of curses, he looked up at Akil.

"Since when have Sirens taken to lying?"

"They have not," replied Akil, his face emotionless. Luno's smile faded.

"So it is true?"

"It is," said Akil. "It turned out that I had as much influence over her mind as she did mine, in effect canceling out each other's powers of manipulation. After we determined that such was the case, we were able to forge a relationship of sorts."

"Why did you leave her? If you had feelings for her, why did you leave without even saying goodbye?" asked James.

"It is one decision among many that causes me pain to this day. However, no regret accompanies it. I had discovered what I believed was the way back and was determined to find the Anointed One and stop the Epoch Terminus. I was bent upon it, as I still am. It is my singular focus, my only passion, and above all and everyone else, including myself, it takes precedence. If the Epoch Terminus is not prevented, there will be no opportunity for any of us to enjoy the good that life has to offer. Gai is one of many sacrifices I have made to this end."

Neither James nor Luno spoke for a time, simply exchanging glances as Akil became introspective. James finished his tea and gently placed his cup on the table. The sound roused Akil from his thoughts.

"As much as it pains me, we must use her to that end once more. She is the key to your return, James, not the black castle. You must ignore its call and focus on Gai. You may find others you seek along this path as well."

"Kilani," said James.

"Indeed."

Luno looked doubtful but held his peace.

"You will both need your rest before returning. I suggest you take it now lest the voices in your minds never quiet."

"I will not take my rest without more explanation. I have questions, many of them, and they cannot wait until we've rested or until our next meeting, which, in all likelihood, will convene with one fewer of us," admonished Luno.

"I understand your frustration, impatience and anxiety, dear Luno. And I cannot say it comes as a surprise. I must insist, and I apologize."

"Insist? Apologize? You have not the — " Luno slumped in his chair, his breathing deep and relaxed.

"Stubborn fool." James looked at Akil in surprise as he rose to his feet. "Not to worry, it was a simple sleeping incantation. He will wake fully rested and pleasant in several hours. I imagine, James, you are more than ready for some much needed rest?" James nodded and followed Akil to the sleeping area.

"I notice you have disregarded my insistence to leave your weapon behind and can only surmise the key sits in your pocket." James flushed, his hand immediately over the impression of the key on his thigh. "I neither require nor am inclined to listen to an explanation from you at this time. Know this, James. I am an old man, and each word I speak comes with great care and thought. While the reason may not be clear to you, it is imperative that you grasp the importance of my words and understand that perhaps the motivation behind them is beyond your current ability to reckon. That is all."

Akil said a quiet word, extended his hands toward James, then exited through the gap in the circular hedge. An instant later, the calming incantation struck James and he settled into a deep sleep.

James awoke well rested. A small flock of birds was diving and climbing within the ring of barrier shrubs that surrounded the beds. They flew up toward the glass ceiling stories overhead as James slowly stood. He noticed a fresh set of clothes folded neatly at the foot of his bed and gratefully exchanged his dirty, ragged ones. When he arrived at the table, he found Akil and Luno cheerily enjoying a large breakfast.

"The sleeping prince has risen," said Luno, holding up his flagon. James was relieved to see that Luno hadn't gone and done something rash when he'd discovered that Akil had performed a sleeping incantation on him.

"You've no idea how much I would pay to have been there when you simply strolled into the council meeting with James in tow. The look on Alvaro's face must have been priceless."

"My boy, you have viewed my memory orb twice now and seen Ilixo's reaction with your own eyes," replied Akil.

"Aye, but there is something to be said for actually experiencing an event versus simply viewing it through a memory orb."

Akil took a sip of his tea as he watched James shovel several mouthfuls of food down his gullet. He looked over to Luno and found him also watching James. Both men's air of jubilance had turned solemn. James finally sensed the eyes upon him and looked up from his breakfast.

"We've come up with a plan," said Luno. "It's the craziest bloody thing I've ever heard, but I think the old codger may have discovered a way home."

27

the battle beneath la passerelle de cel

The path out of the black abyss was arduous, but James made better time than he would have had Luno been traveling with him. With a combination of earth-bound incantations and incantations in the language of The Never, James managed to make his way up and out in less than half a day.

James stood in the center of Adelphi's main street. He was alone, but he knew it wouldn't be long before she appeared. James strode slowly down the cobbled stretch and under the passerelle de ciel. Farther down the street, a figure stepped from between the buildings and walked toward James. For a moment, he thought it was Gai…but something was different. She was too tall, too lean, her skin too dark. His heart leapt and sweat speckled his brow. Kilani.

As they drew together, it was clear by the look on her face that her mood was anything but cordial. There was no warmth or relief in her eyes. The pair stopped an arm's reach apart.

"You're all right," he said, unable to suppress a relieved smile.

"Of course I am," she replied, her inflection like melting ice over smooth stones.

"I've come to take you home. I've discovered a way, Kilani. I've found Akil, and he's told me how to get back."

"Why would I want to leave?" asked Kilani in that same melodic and unfamiliar tone.

"Kilani, your children await your return. You are a prisoner here. You must come with me."

"My children are here," she said, gesturing. Several of Gai's lieutenants rounded the corner and stood watching from a distance. "I can come and go as I please. I am no prisoner."

"Kilani, those are not your children," James said, fighting to remain calm.

These boys are my children. Gai brought them to me. She brought them here where they are safe — where we are safe from that terrible world from which we came. The only danger here…is you."

"Kilani, those boys are not your children," James repeated. "They've been here since I arrived. They are not as they appear. They tried to kill Luno."

"But they did not kill Luno. Luno lives. You, however, managed to kill one of them." James could see the anger in her eyes, her clenched fists, her defensive posture.

"That was purely self-defense. I did not intend to harm anyone."

"He was my son and you killed him. Murderer!" she spat.

"Gai has ensnared your mind with her magic, Kilani. You must come with me. We must get away from Gai."

Before he had time to react, Kilani's clenched fist struck him square in the jaw. The power of the impact lifted him from the ground and sent him flying several feet until he landed with a spine-jarring smack on the curb. Kilani had always been as strong as the men in their group, but this newfound strength was different. She walked slowly toward James.

"You killed my son. You deserve to die," she said, closing the gap between them. James's jaw and back throbbed. As he rose painfully, Kilani landed a combination of punches followed by an arm toss that sent him hurtling through a shop window. James covered his face as he flew through the panes and landed on a small wooden table that collapsed beneath his weight. Wood splinters and glass shards sank into his back as he hit the floor.

James staggered to his feet, feeling the warmth of the blood running from the injuries. He fought desperately to control his anger as he limped to the door. "Lehtinen," he muttered, extending his hands. The door broke apart into thousands of pieces, which hung suspended around the frame. When James crossed the threshold, they immediately reassembled as if he'd simply used the knob to exit. He stepped into the street and faced Kilani.

"You are under the spell of a Siren. You must come with me. If you will not come willingly, I will have no choice but to make you come," said James unsteadily. Kilani sprang at him, but this time James was ready.

"Injarjavi!" She slammed into his invisible shield and fell to the ground, bleeding. "We don't need to fight, Kilani. Come with me. Let me take you away from Gai. She has poisoned your mind. Allow yourself some clarity, and you will understand all that I tell you," said James. There was a flicker of change on her face. In that instant, James saw the Kilani he'd come to love inside the woman now determined to kill him. She scrambled to her feet and extended her hands.

"Norge!" She pushed a green ball of energy at James. It struck the shield, spreading veins of green light across it until the shield trembled and shattered. A million green-edged pieces blew away in a gust of wind. Before she could attack again, James tried his final peaceful solution.

"Apotéket." A silver fog encircled Kilani. She froze, and her expression changed from murderous to distant. James let out a sigh of relief as he stepped toward her. He extended his hand toward her bleeding nose. "Tupassari." The bleeding ceased. James reached into his satchel for a pinch of transporting powder, but before his fingers touched the fine orange sand, a force sent him hurtling through the air. He quickly oriented himself and cast a shield incantation, softening his landing. He turned to Kilani and saw that she stood in the same docile posture.

James knew Gai was near. He searched, looking up and down the street for any sign of her. The boys at the far end of the street had fled. Seeing nothing, James turned back to Kilani.

"You did not think it would be that easy, did you?" she said in a voice not her own.

"Let her go, Gai. It's me you want," said James.

A mist surrounded Kilani's hand, then faded, revealing Gai's black scimitar. James stepped back and drew his sword, thankful that, once again, he had disregarded Akil's instructions. Immediately, he felt the pull of the black castle but fought to bury it and focus on Kilani. She lunged at him with a clumsy yet powerful swing. James easily blocked the blow, but the impact rattled the bones of his arm. The searing pain that shot from his shoulder nearly caused him to lose his grip.

"Injarjavi," said James, quickly raising a shield. Kilani swung and cut through the barrier as if it were parchment. Spellbreaker steel, James thought. He sidestepped the swing and advanced up the street under the shadow of the passerelle de cel. Out of the corner of his eye, he caught a glimpse of a figure approaching from behind. He backed onto the sidewalk in order to keep both Kilani and the newcomer in sight. Both advanced cautiously. Sensing his distraction, Kilani struck again.

James easily blocked her swing and sidestepped. Catching her off balance, James shouldered her into a stack of wine barrels. She struck them hard — harder than he'd intended — and several barrels fell on top of her as she hit the ground. As he prepared to disarm her, James caught a flicker of motion in his periphery. He turned, expecting to defend himself against another attack.

To his surprise and relief, Luno ran to his side brandishing a sword of his own. He gestured down the street to Roger, Jan and Peroc, armed and hurrying in their direction. Relief washed over James as the corners of his mouth turned up in a smile. Luno ran to assist Kilani, who was struggling beneath the weight of the barrels.

"She is under the Siren's spell. Be cautious," said James, sheathing his sword.

Luno nodded. He stepped on her sword hand until she released the blade. With a smile, he reached down and picked up the scimitar. The instant he grasped the hilt, Luno was drawn away to the black castle. James saw his eyes fog over as he stood staring off into nothingness. James cursed and sent a burst of energy at the barrels still on top of Kilani. They blew aside, revealing the livid woman he'd come to rescue. She jumped to her feet.

"Reisa!" she growled, forming a ball of fire between her palms. She flung it at James, who countered with a burst of energy. The two incantations impacted in a fiery explosion that set the wine barrels alight. James could hear the hurried footfalls of his friends making their way down the street. Without looking, Kilani sent a ball of fire in their direction and a second at James.

James was able to raise his shield, but the approaching men were not as fortunate. At the head of the group, Jan raised his sword arm to block the orb of flame, but it struck his sword full force and spread up his arm. Screaming, he dropped his sword. Roger and Peroc tackled him to the ground in an attempt to extinguish the flames.

Kilani struck Luno square in the chest with the heel of her palm, sending him flying into a doorway. The black scimitar fell from his hand, and his eyes returned to their normal state of awareness. Kilani retrieved the sword just as James sent a burst of energy at her. She sliced at the flaming green orb, rendering it benign, but her poor swordsmanship left her exposed. James hated what he had to do next, but he was running out of options. He extended his hands toward Kilani.

"Lieska." Black tendrils shot from his palms and wrapped Kilani's exposed and defenseless body in a shroud of pain. She dropped the sword and staggered into the street waving her arms and screaming in agony. The sound of her screams sent chills down his spine. To his right, James saw at least a dozen of Gai's armed boy-lieutenants marching in his direction. Down the street to his left, he saw that Luno had managed to get Jan to his feet, his arm blackened and smoking from Kilani's attack. Roger and Peroc were staring gape-jawed at the crowd of lieutenants making their way toward James. Still, there was no sign of Gai.

The wooden storefront behind the blazing barrels was now fully engulfed in flames. James turned to counter the incantation he'd set upon Kilani. "Suopelon." The tendrils melted away from Kilani's body and she fell to the cobbled street. James ran to her side. He cast a shield incantation between Luno's group and the lieutenants, hoping to delay their progress. The fire was spreading, rapidly eating away at the wooden buildings on either side. He carefully rolled Kilani onto her back, trying to ignore the danger that was now beyond the shadow of the passerine de cel.

"Tupassari." Kilani's eyes shot open, and she sat bolt upright. She appeared confused but back in control of herself as she looked at James.

"What's happening?" she asked. Relief swept over James. A loud clanging drew his attention. The boys had reached the barrier and were striking it with their swords.

"We need to get out of here. Can you stand?" asked James. Kilani nodded. James slipped a hand under her arm and helped her to her feet.

"You're bleeding," she said, gesturing to his torn and blood-soaked shirt.

"It's nothing," he replied, leading her away from the attackers. As they walked down the street, she became increasingly steady until she finally shrugged away James's assisting grip on her upper arm.

"Time to go," shouted Luno. James nodded. As he reached into his pouch feeling the grains of transporting powder on his fingertips, a thunderous explosion shook the ground upon which they stood, sending everyone sprawling. James's barrier was shattered. Standing beneath the passerelle de ciel was Gai. Her lieutenants charged around her.

James got to his feet and sent several bursts of energy at the leading attackers. Each burst was deflected before it reached its mark. "Get them up, Luno," he called, not taking his eyes off the approaching horde. He sent several more bursts of energy before casting another shield incantation. James stepped back and drew his sword. To his relief, the black castle was silent. The boys crashed into the invisible barrier and again began striking it with their weapons. Behind them, Gai slowly approached the fray, conjuring a purple orb between her hands. James turned to his group.

"Get back to Harbor Town. I'll meet you there."

"We ain't leavin' ya, Cap'n," said Roger.

"You're outnumbered and outmatched," said Luno. "You cannot do this on your own." A second explosion shook the ground as the barrier was breached, but this time they managed to keep their feet. In an instant, the boys were on them. Three headed straight for James, two carrying short swords and one with a mace far too heavy for a child to wield. James blocked the blow of the first attacker, then sidestepped and ducked beneath the head of the mace, feeling the air whoosh past him as he did. He quickly lifted his sword allowing the chain to wrap around the blade. He then pulled the boy close and struck him square in the chest with the heel of his hand, sending him to the ground. He flung the mace off the end of his blade toward the third attacker who stood waiting for a moment to attack. It struck an invisible barrier and fell harmlessly to the ground. James glanced over his shoulder to see Gai standing at the edge of the fracas with a smile on her face. He turned back to the battle while making sure never to lose sight of Gai.

Despite his injured arm, Jan was easily managing two attackers with the small axe he'd brought along for the fight. Three boys encircled him, each gripping pikes and feinting. Jan allowed one boy to thrust forward, then leaned back while bringing the axe down on the pike, snapping it in half. With the blunt edge of his weapon he struck the boy in the shoulder, forcing him to drop the damaged weapon. The other two charged, and as easily as the first, Jan managed to disarm them.

Peroc stood at a distance firing arrows at his attackers, but none hit its mark. They either veered off course or simply dropped to the ground before reaching their target. In a desperate move, he took an arced shot at Gai. As the arrow reached its apex, it burst into flames and descended as ashes.

Luno had pushed Kilani, unarmed yet belligerent, back against a building and was fighting off two attackers with a long sword. James sent a burst of energy at each of Luno's attackers, but Gai blocked the incantations before they fell true. Roger, a hammer in one hand, a rapier in the other, stood poised waiting for another onslaught. Two boys lay motionless on the ground not far from where he stood.

"Poikelo ," James said, sweeping his arms together as if in a wide embrace. A gust of wind tracked away from his closing arms and swept the remaining attackers to the ground. The men quickly disarmed those who still carried weapons. The boys who were able rose to their feet and retreated behind Gai, who was now moving toward the melee. Three boys remained motionless on the ground. The street was eerily silent as she approached. Her long, dark hair was pulled back tight, revealing her smooth, high cheekbones and mesmerizing eyes. Her flowing white dress billowed out behind her as she walked.

"Bloody hell," muttered Roger under his breath as Gai approached.

"She is not as she seems," said James. "Remember that, and do not let her words poison your mind." Gai's arrogance turned to horror when she saw the motionless bodies of the three boys. She ran to the closest boy and crouched beside him.

"What have you done?" she shouted. "Murderers! You have murdered our children!" Kilani ran to Gai's side and fell to her knees. Tears streamed down her face as she carefully lifted the boy's head to her lap. The men looked on in disbelief as she wept beside Gai. After a moment, she lifted her head and looked at James through reddened, tear-filled eyes.

"You!" she shouted. "You did this! You would rather see our children dead than leave me here in peace. You are a monster!" she screamed, spitting the last word. Gai stood and stepped over the body of the boy. She deliberately made eye contact with each member of the group save Peroc, who refused to look at her.

"The first time I accepted the slaying of one of my children as an accident, but this…this is unforgivable."

"Mayhaps ye should consider the risks before sendin' kids to fight fer ye," growled Roger. Gai slowly approached him. She stepped so close that they were only inches apart. Gai caressed Roger's face. He dropped his weapons. She reached up with her other hand and drew him close, pressed her body tightly against his. A faraway look fell over his face as he relaxed in her embrace.

"No!" shouted Luno. He stepped forward and swung his long sword full force at Gai's back. Upon impact, it shattered to pieces and sent Luno to the ground. If Gai felt anything, she didn't show it. She ran her fingers through Roger's hair several times, then took his face in her hands and leaned in, letting her full lips brush against his cheek and lips. She leaned in to his ear, whispered something, and Roger smiled. For a moment the pair stood in this unnatural embrace, then Roger collapsed to the ground, motionless. Gai turned away as Jan and Peroc rushed to his side.

"Dead!" Jan exclaimed.

James felt the anger welling up inside. He fought to keep it under control. He tried to slow his breathing — tried to remain calm. He stepped in front of Gai, blocking her path.

"Inari ," he whispered.

Gai's ivory skin darkened to a pale shade of grey — the pallor of death. Her skin was scaled, her cheeks sunken. Jagged needle points replaced the perfect teeth as her lips stretched back.

"This is what we face," James said. "A Siren. Everything about her is an illusion, a trick. Her voice is poison. It ensnares the mind. It kills." James gestured at Roger. Gai transformed from monstrous back to beautiful, yet her venomous guise made her flawless face equally frightening.

"These," James said, pointing to the group of boys standing not far away, "are not children at all." He extended his hands toward the boys. "Inari. " In a flash, the innocent-looking boys changed. Their arms lengthened until they reached the ground. Their fingers tripled in length. Their legs rotated in their hips and tails extended from their spines as their skin formed black and orange scales. Finally, each sprouted a deadly looking horn from the base of its skull that followed the arc of its hairless head and ended in a cruel point above yellow eyes. "They are monsters. They are called ak kutus. Pets of the Sirens." The monsters snarled until Gai angrily swiped her hand, returning them to boys.

"What you do not understand, James, what all of you fail to understand, is that we are what you want us to be. We are what you need us to be. Our true form is irrelevant."

"If you let us go, I will give you what you want," said James.

"You are not in a position to negotiate," said Gai.

"You desire an equal, a worthy adversary, do you not? Allow me to see my friends home and you shall have it."

"Humans are far from equal to Sirens, and to think otherwise is the epitome of arrogance," said Gai. She paused, looking introspective. James wondered if she was thinking of Akil and how he had abandoned her.

"If you agree, you have my word that I shall return," said James.

Gai stepped forward until she was inches from James. She looked deep into his eyes. He could feel her tugging at his mind, but she could not penetrate his defenses.

"You believe you know my mind, but I do not need you," she whispered. "Still, there is something about you, Captain James. You are not like the others." As she spoke, her lips brushed against James's, and the dark perimeters of her irises swirled. "Here are the terms of your surrender," she said, stepping back and addressing the entire group. "I shall allow James to return one of you to your world. Only one. If James does not return within a fortnight, every human in Ak Egundiano will become my slave and those I find unworthy will be fed to my children." She gestured to the group of boys behind her.

"Agreed," said James.

"I haven't finished. Perhaps you should listen before agreeing so quickly."

"Continue," said James.

"You must travel through the black castle in order to return to your world. You may not use any other path or doorway."

"I cannot take that path. It is fraught with peril."

"Akil Karanis is a coward. He has grown old and weak. A power lies within you he could only dream of possessing. I would not send my prize to his destruction."

A shudder ran through James as he considered the path Akil had strictly forbidden. The dark key, still tucked away in his pocket, suddenly resumed its call. James had to push it to the back of his mind in order to focus.

"I must discuss it with my crew," said James.

"You have until the sun reaches the treetops," she said, gesturing to the west, "and she stays with me in the event you decide not to return." Gai pointed at Kilani.

"No," said James.

"Must another die before you see reason?" said Gai.

"I will stay," said Kilani boldly, stepping forward.

A smile crossed Gai's face as she strode to Kilani's side.

"The sands of time are falling," said Gai with a knowing smirk. "Make haste."

28

palaver

James muttered healing incantations over Jan as he lay on one of the beds in Akil's conservatory. Jan's moaning subsided as his blistered body relaxed and he fell into a deep sleep. Luno , who had lain Roger's still-warm body on a bed and covered it with a linen sheet, made his way to James's side and spoke quietly. "Will he recover?" James said one final incantation and stood unsteadily.

"He will. I was able to heal the injury although the scars will never fade." Luno nodded as the two men exited the sleeping area. "What of Peroc?"

"Because he is a native of Ak Egundiano, he cannot pass through Akil's door and into our world. I told him to return to the clearing and wait for us there with the others from Harbor Town." He paused. "Akil is not here."

"Then it is only us," said James.

"So it would seem."

They walked in silence along the flower-lined paths until they reached the black iron table that had become their meeting place. James sat heavily, Luno across from him. They were quiet for several moments. James took in the beauty around him and attempted to settle his mind as Luno closed his eyes in a state of apparent meditation.

It was useless. His thoughts kept returning to the black castle and Kilani. Always had he been drawn to the castle. From the moment he set eyes upon it, a part of him had needed it, needed to be inside its walls — to stand on its towers, to walk its battlements, to command its keep. Now he was being given the opportunity to do just that and he was hesitating.

Kilani feared the castle, above all else in The Never. Finally James had the opportunity to rescue her — to bring her home — yet he was mad with despair knowing if he chose her, she would refuse to enter the black castle. If she stayed, she would fall deeper under Gai's spell and her visceral desire to return home to her children would wane until there was no desire left at all.

Even if James could somehow convince her to go, he didn't know what lay in wait on that path — the path Akil had forbidden for fear of his destruction. If Akil fears for me, what chance do I have? What chance would anyone have? If I made it home, would I even be able to return? In frustration, James slammed his hand on the table. Rather than hitting the iron surface, he struck something much softer. Luno started at the sound and his eyes flew open.

"There is something here," said James, running his hands over the surface.

"Erakutsi," said Luno, his hand over the invisible object. Nothing happened. James traced the outline of the object with his fingers and immediately knew what it was.

"Akil's journal."

"Bloody old fool hid it with an incantation none of us would know. Typical."

James thought for a moment then centered his hand over the object. "Erak -menderatu ." A swirl of yellow mist swept across the table like a blanket revealing the journal beneath.

"What the sodding hell was that?" asked Luno incredulously.

"Many times during my apprenticeship Akil and I discussed combining incantations to enhance their effectiveness."

"That's as dark an incantation as they come. Tread cautiously, boy."

"Words are words," said James as he slid his chair closer to Luno's so they both could see the contents of the journal. Luno shot James a warning look, but he was too engrossed to notice. He opened the cover. Akil's tight, scrolling writing read:

A report of our comings and goings
A cup of tea is best to clear the mind before reading or writing
That and a stroll down a flowered path

James read the words aloud. When he finished the second sentence, two steaming cups of tea appeared on the table. Luno and James exchanged glances. Luno retrieved one of the cups and took a sip. He spat it onto the grass. "No sugar or cream. The codger always liked his tea plain."

James started to turn the page when a fourth sentence appeared.

Tea is best consumed sans accompaniment so as to enjoy the flavor of the leaf as was originally intended

James grinned as Luno read the inscription with a huff. He turned the page.

Dear James, Luno,

The two of you have, only moments ago, left to execute our plan. I must take my leave but shall return in two days' time. With any luck, the plan has succeeded and your freedom is near.

Akil

P.S. Remember, the passage of time in this place does not run parallel to time in Al Egundiano. It is seldom consistent and should therefore not be taken for granted.

Both men read the entry and jumped to their feet.

"We cannot wait for Akil to return," said James.

"We must decide now who will accompany you," said Luno.

"I have decided," said James.

"Have you?" asked Luno. "Without any discussion?"

"Aye," said James. He scanned the table.

"What are you looking for, boy?" asked Luno.

"Idazluma." A black quill and inkwell appeared. "Go wake Jan. We must leave immediately." Luno nodded and set off toward the sleeping area as James dipped the quill into the ink.

Akil,

I must travel the forbidden path. I will be coming alone.

James

In a flash of orange light and smoke, James, Luno and Jan appeared on the main street of Adelphi. There was no evidence of the battle that had taken place nor the fire that had consumed several of the buildings. The street was empty except for a flock of tymanuk hovering below the passerelle de cel that arced over the street. The flock advanced upon the trio. Both Jan and Luno reached for their weapons.

"No," said James. "They will do us no harm." The winged creatures paused in front of the men. One flew in front of the others and gestured to James. "They want us to follow them."

Before either could respond, James followed the flock across the street into the alley. One of the tymanuk stood upon a shop sign waiting for the group. As soon as James rounded the corner, it took flight and continued down the length of the alley where it disappeared around a corner.

The three men walked into the courtyard where the small garden gate led to the cliff. With a gesture, James repeated the incantation to create the stone staircase from the rock face and the men ascended, following the tymanuk. With the help of James' incantations, they navigated the rope bridge and jungle path to reach the field that surrounded the black maze. Standing in the field was Gai, Kilani beside her. Their escorts fluttered back toward the jungle in alarm. James walked toward the women and the others followed.

"What's the plan, Captain?" asked Luno.

"Play along," said James.

"That ought to be easy."

James stopped ten feet from Kilani and Gai. Kilani's eyes were glazed over, and she looked off into the distance as if she were not aware of her surroundings.

"Release her," said James.

"She is free to do as she wishes," Gai replied.

"You know what I mean. Do it or we go no further." A slight breeze brushed Kilani's hair out of her face. She blinked, and her body tensed when she saw the men.

"What is happening?" she asked, quickly stepping away from Gai. Luno took her by her hand and pulled her into their group, whispering a hurried explanation.

"Well, James, have you decided which one you will take?" asked Gai.

"Yes, I've made my decision," he said, stepping forward. "I choose Gai ak zangar."

Gai's manner changed from arrogant to angry in an instant, and her beautiful appearance flickered for a moment to her frightful true form.

"You fool, that was not part of the agreement. You must choose one of your own. I cannot travel through the tunnel."

"Can't or won't?" asked James. Gai seethed and again her appearance changed until she regained control over her anger.

"Do you not desire to be with me? Do you not desire to see Akil once again if for no other reason than to strike him down for all he has done? You are one of us. We are all trapped in this place and I offer you a means of escape. This land may prevent you from traveling through the tunnel alone but it will not stop me, and together we can successfully pass through it and whatever lies beyond." Gai was silent. For the first time, a quick-witted reply eluded her. James stepped forward, closing the gap between them to inches.

"Let us go together. You are the great Gai ak zangar. You are the last of the great Sirens, and you would know if I were trying to deceive you."

"I am not the last," she said quietly.

"Join me," said James.

"And what of your friends? Do you not wish to save them?"

"I shall return."

"Indeed," said Gai, reaching out to touch his face. Without warning, James and Gai vanished, leaving the others standing dumbstruck in the field.

29

the courtyard of the five doors

In a puff of black smoke, James and Gai appeared in the courtyard of the five doors. Caught in her embrace, James stepped quickly away. Gai smiled at his discomfort. James walked along the doors set in the bamboo wall until he reached the wooden door with the black knob on the far right, then reached into his pocket and clasped the black key. The image of the black castle flashed in his mind, but as quickly as it came, it was gone. James opened his eyes, having been unaware that he'd shut them, to an open doorway. Gai was at his side.

"Gantztu Gizaki , this way," she said, stepping past James and through the doorway. James followed. They wound their way through what felt like miles of twists and turns. James knew they were drawing closer as energy pulsed from the key and steadily increased with each step as if it were a heartbeat surging into his hand and up his arm.

Finally, Gai halted. Ahead, a berm rose from the earth no higher than James's waist. A crude stone frame wreathed a small door set into the berm. In the center of the door was an ornate ward house concealing the spring latch lock. James stepped forward and crouched. As he ran his fingers over the rough wood of the hatch, he opened the hand holding the key and looked at it for the last time.

"Your weapon," said Gai, "cannot pass beyond this point."

James looked from the key to the black sword on his belt. Before he could react, Gai pulled the blade from its sheath and thrust it into the berm, burying it up to the hilt. Frustrated, James turned to Gai and was instantly disarmed by her blank expression as she stared intently at the key in his hand.

For a moment, James considered what Akil had said about the tunnel — the forbidden path. Again the black castle flashed in his mind, and Akil's warnings faded as the desire that had plagued him throughout his time in The Never took hold. He slid the ward house up to reveal the keyway and inserted the key. The black steel slid into the keyway with no resistance. James took a deep breath, glanced at Gai, who was at his shoulder watching his every move, then turned the key. It cleared the wards as it rotated about the center post. James's entire body shook as it struck the lever, activating the latch. With a click, the door fell open.

Both he and Gai jumped back at the suddenness of the action, then stepped closer to peer into the dark opening. A bamboo ladder cut from the ebony stalks of the maze led down into the darkness. The pair exchanged glances and James nodded. He reached into his pocket, extracted a small strap of leather and tied back his dark hair, already soaked with sweat.

"I shall lead," he said. "Stay close."

He reached for the first rung and carefully settled himself on the ladder. James took one final look up at Gai. She had once again taken the form of the small boy, only now she looked terrified. James fought the urge to question her about the change. He reached up, grasped the hilt of his sword, jerked it free from the berm , and slid it into its sheath. Without another word, he began to descend. Above, he could see her step onto the ladder and follow.

As his eyes acclimated, James realized it was not completely dark. A soft white light revealed walls of white marble far off in the distance. Below was a matching white marble floor. Where the two met was difficult to discern, making floor and walls indistinguishable from each other and distance impossible to calculate.

Meanwhile, Gai had slipped to the back side of the ladder and lowered herself until she was even with James. She surveyed their surroundings. The ladder stretched endlessly far below them. Above, the light from the doorway darkened and a click echoed through the space like a gunshot, making it was clear that their path lay in only one direction.

"This is an illusion," Gai said in her boy-voice. "We Sirens are masters of illusion, yet this was created by no Siren." James nodded and continued downward, pausing occasionally to wipe the sweat from his hands. Gai kept pace, careful never to step where James's hands had gripped. From below came a rumble. Its echo bounced off the walls, increasing in intensity until the volume was deafening. All James could do was wince, as he had no intention of releasing his grip to cover his ears. The rumble stopped and the pair continued. Several rungs later, the rumble sounded again. Again they paused until the last of the noise had abated.

Down they went, losing all sense of time and orientation. Gravity began to pull across their bodies rather than from head to toe. James realized that instead of climbing down, he was now crawling backwards horizontally across the ladder. Gai, still on the opposite side of the ladder from him, seemed not to notice. James looked behind him, hoping that the change signified an end was near. He cursed when he saw only the ladder extending to infinity and heard only the rumble.

He was glad Gai was with him, otherwise he was sure this place would drive him mad. She remained silent in her boy-form and followed as James continued on. Time passed — perhaps half a day, perhaps more. Eventually James reoriented himself so he was crawling forward across the ladder. He hoped gravity wouldn't shift suddenly and pull him headfirst into the abyss. Gai progressed along the ladder as before, paying no attention to James's change in position.

On they went until James's entire body trembled from the effort, and he collapsed on the ladder. As he lay there awkwardly, he fell into an exhausted sleep and dreamed of nothing but whiteness. When he awoke, he found his jaw sore from lying against one of the ladder rungs. A thread of saliva stretched away from his mouth. As he lifted his head, it broke, swung away from the ladder, and fell but a few feet before it struck the surface of the white marble, which rippled like a still pond disturbed by a stone. James sat up excitedly. Gai perched on the ladder next to him, her legs pulled up to her chest.

"Illusion," she said.

James swung his legs between two rungs. It looked like the rippling surface was only centimeters below the tips of his toes. He slowly lowered himself until he felt his feet begin to submerge. Not a liquid — too viscous, too dense — but neither a solid. With each inch he lowered his body, his feet were engulfed in the white substance. James attempted to pull himself up a fraction and realized he could not. He struggled but was unsuccessful. Gai leaned over the ladder, once again in her woman form, and looked at James.

“Help me, damn you,” he said. She watched him for a moment as he slipped deeper into the white pool.

“Let go, James,” she said. James pulled on the rungs with all his strength, but the force against him was stronger. He lost his grip and fell.

He landed on his feet in a forest. James knew instantly where he was. This place had been seared into his memory. Arenberg. A hooded figure approached him and revealed his face. Stuart greeted his son with a smile. They had a brief conversation. James knew every word and every gesture. It was exactly the conversation they'd had the night of his father's death. James had no control over his words or actions — he was but a spectator imprisoned in his twelve-year-old body, being forced to watch the events unfold and powerless to act. James looked on as his father smiled at what his child self had said, then stopped and turned toward a sound off in the distance.

“Did you hear that?” Stuart asked, looking around nervously. An identical sound came from the opposite direction. Stuart pulled James close to him and sprinkled transporting powder over his head. Nothing happened. James could feel the warmth of his father's hand against his chest and his fast nervous breathing against his back as he evaluated the situation. How he missed his father's touch, his smell. James would have given nearly anything for a chance to embrace his father once more, and The Never had given it to him, but at what price? Could he bear to watch what would happen next? Would he have a choice?

Dark figures appeared in the forest — each of them silently moving toward James and his father in an ever-shrinking circle. Stuart sent blasts of energy in multiple directions, then took James by the hand and fled behind a large boulder. James knew what would follow. His father would admonish him not to move. He tried so desperately to refuse, to shout “No!” but couldn't. He simply nodded as his father placed both hands on his shoulders and looked into his eyes.

"It will be all right, son," said Stuart. James marveled at how calm his father appeared despite the chaos surrounding them. As Stuart turned and ran off into the darkness, James realized that was the last time his father would ever touch him. Those were the last words he would ever speak to him. He tried to reach out, tried to grasp his cloak and pull him back, but he failed. He was but a spectator. His arms remained numbly at his sides. James had played this scene over and over in his mind countless times since that moment. Every word, every sound was engraved in his memory.

Men shouted. There were several explosions and accompanying bursts of light followed by silence and then laughter, of all things. It was the laughter that always caught James off guard regardless of how many times he reviewed the memory. Completely out of place, the laughter drew James from his hiding spot deep within a crack in the boulder. He peered around the rock and saw his father in the distant clearing, surrounded by dark-robed sorcerers. Stuart was laughing, and despite the situation, James couldn't fight the smile that formed on his face. His father had an intoxicating laugh that was most often highly contagious. On this night, however, it didn't spread. When Stuart finished his guffawing, one of the men stepped forward.

"Where is the boy?" he demanded.

"Do you really think that pathetic excuse for an anti-transporting incantation could stop my son?"

"You stupid esol, this wasn't any ordinary anti-transporting incantation! It was cast by Alexander Vinokourov," another man snarled. "Tell him, Henri!"

"It's true."

Stuart paused before replying. James doubted any of the men who surrounded him had noticed, but he had. He picked it up every time he replayed the scene in his mind. At the time, the name Alexander Vinokourov had meant nothing to James.

"I don't care if Ilixo Alvaro or even the great Akil Karanis cast that incantation. Do you even know who it is you seek, or are you following commands like a dog?

"Shut your mouth!" Henri shouted.

James felt himself slowly moving back into the recess of the stone as the man shouted for the others to search the area. He could feel his lips moving as he mouthed the incantation that would blend him into the stone face of the boulder. Over and over he repeated it as the men passed the spot where he stood. One of the men stopped for a brief moment, and James thought he was found, but the man looked right through him and continued on. For the first time in the thousands of times he had relived this memory, perhaps because now he found himself reliving the actual event, James thought he recognized the man. He looked very much like Jan . James discounted the idea as he heard a voice call off the search, and they dragged his father away.

His twelve-year-old body stepped away from the boulder, bringing his adult mind with him. As he crouched in the leaves using the dimmest blue orb he could summon, young James noted the heavily trampled ground that led off into the darkness. He followed as quickly as he could without losing the trail. James was impressed at how easily his young self picked up the traces of disturbance left behind and gave pursuit.

Now James struggled to pull himself free of this memory. He reminded himself that it wasn't real. But it was real. He was here. He could feel the crisp winter air on his cheeks as he continued steadily toward his father's captors. He was being drawn in completely. Again he fought to push away. When he failed, he analyzed his situation. Why would he be forced to relive his worst memory? Akil had said the path would bring unspeakable terrors and he was right. He had lived it once and it had almost destroyed him. Now, he was living it again. Was it a test to see if he was worthy to reach the black castle? The black castle needed him as much as he needed it.

James reached the edge of the forest. The pale moon shone on the small village, its reflection shimmering in a small pond. He spotted the church, the men standing outside, guarding the door. He crouched, grasped the arrows in his quiver, and recited the series of incantations he had secretly learned from one of his instructors. Then he crept toward the church, making sure to remain in the moon-cast shadows in case his stealth and silence incantations failed. When he was close, James hid behind a wooden house, nocked the first arrow and drew, aiming for the guard who was looking off into the distance. The older James marveled at the steadiness with which he held the bow and how he released the arrow — without any hesitation. He released the second arrow before the first hit its target. Both shots landed true, and the men fell to the ground before they could cry out.

Young James darted between the buildings, passed the door, and looked around the corner where he expected a third guard to be standing. He was there, but a few paces away. James drew the bowstring and stepped around the corner. This time he paused long enough for the man's hyper-focused demeanor to melt into fear. James released the arrow, and it sank into his chest up to the fletching. He didn't wait for the man to fall.

Silently, he slipped inside the church. His father was there, at the opposite end of the building, exchanging words with the man called Henri as he paced around his captive.

"Where is the boy?" asked the man.

"You have neither the resources nor the abilities to find my son. He is far too cunning for the likes of you and your little band," said Stuart. The man drove his fist into Stuart's nose, which released a deluge of blood. James felt his twelve-year-old body stiffen and knew it was nearly time. He looked out his younger eyes at his father who, despite being bloodied and beaten, still wore the same proud smile James had seen so often during their time together.

"You fool, I have summoned Alexander Vinokourov. He will make quick work of turning your brain to mush while extracting all the information he requires." Stuart spat blood into his captor's face. Enraged, the man drew his fist back, ready to strike again.

The older James fought for control against his younger body with all his strength. He fought to keep the sound out of his throat, but the silence was broken by the boy's scream as he stepped into the light. Everyone in the room turned toward the noise. Stuart stared in utter disbelief at his son here among their enemies.

The next handful of seconds stretched out interminably as James watched through his younger eyes in horror, still fighting against the surge of energy that was building inside him. The two guards standing along the exterior walls immediately sent bursts of energy toward James. Both struck less than a foot from him and dissipated. At the same time, Stuart rose, hands and feet still bound, and shouldered Henri aside.

The veins in Stuart's neck bulged as he strained against the bindings that held his hands behind his back. Never could James recall seeing a look of such determination in his father's eyes. A third guard stepped out of the shadows at the far end of the church and conjured a fire orb between his hands. Stuart broke free of the bindings and sent a burst of energy at him.

James could feel the energy growing inside his younger body— nothing could compare to this power. The man with the fire orb sidestepped Stuart's energy burst while cursing at Henri, who now blocked his line of fire. By the time he regained his balance, Stuart had already brought down the guard along one wall and was turning to the other. Henri, regaining his balance, sent a burst of green energy at Stuart, which struck him from behind as Stuart sent his burst at the man along the side wall. Stuart fell to the floor, sliding beneath the first row of pews.

Then something happened that James did not recall despite the exacting detail in which he remembered the events in the church. He reached into his quiver, nocked an arrow on his bowstring, and released it. The arrow streaked across the church and through the neck of Henri, the man who had brought down his father. Henri stood looking at James. His eyes glazed over as blood pulsed out of his neck with each beat of his dying heart. He made no attempt to stop the flow of blood but turned and walked toward the front door leaving a trail of darkening wood in his wake. Both James and the remaining guard stood watching as he grew increasingly unsteady. He reached for the knob and fell to his knees, then pitched forward onto the floor, dead.

James saw motion out of the corner of his eye. The guard noticed it as well. Stuart was attempting to pull himself out from under the pew. Without hesitation, the man sent a bolt of fire at him. With a scream one should never hear from the mouth of a child, James released the energy that had been welling up inside him. He felt the energy surge from his hands and watched it manifest as a wave of white mist billowing outward in all directions. Everything it contacted was blown to pieces. Pews splintered, statues burst into sand, metalwork blew away like dust. James watched as his father turned toward the wave.

James felt a pull, nagging at first, but it steadily built to a considerable force — as if he were tied by ropes and being pulled to the ground. He fought it, wanting, for some reason, to witness his father's final seconds. He stepped forward against the pull and was met with a tearing pain so horrible he screamed in agony. His eyes watered from the pain, but he fought to keep sight of his father. The wave was nearly upon him, but he looked calm rather than afraid. At the last instant, Stuart lifted his head and looked at him. Despite seeing death rolling toward him, a mere fraction of a second away, the man smiled at his son.

The wave struck him, flinging him back against the wall. At that instant, James fell to his knees as the searing pain inside him became unbearable. The wave reached the walls of the church, washed up over them, and rolled back upon itself, dissipating. James began to crawl toward the spot he had last seen his father, fighting the terrible pain as he went. Every time he stopped, the pain lessened and the pull relaxed. Refusing the reprieve, he continued onward. Tears and snot flowed freely from his eyes and nose. He clawed at the wood floor with his fingers and stretched one knee forward, pulling against the invisible ropes that held him back.

James let out another scream as he pulled his other knee forward and vomited from the intense pain. His vision blurred, but he carried on, crawling toward the last place he had seen his father. Then — nothing. No more pain, no more pull. Looking behind him, James saw his twelve-year-old body lying on the floor. He realized that he was free. He stood, unsteady at first, but he quickly regained his balance.

All around him was destruction. He couldn't understand how the walls of the church remained standing after what had happened. James saw movement in a pile of rubble near the wall. How could anyone have survived? He began to pull away the pieces of splintered wooden pews. A shard of wood stuck into his hand and he cursed. Shaking his head, he stepped back.

"Tertiri Zé Manukto suomi," he said in the language of Ek Egundiano. Nothing happened. "Jaso ," James said, lifting his hands over the pile. The wood rose, revealing the crumpled body of his father and beside him the man who had cast the fire incantation. Both were seriously injured but alive.

James sent the wood hurtling into the opposite wall, still amazed that he was actually here, in this place and time. He lifted his father gently, cradling his head. Stuart's eyes opened and he smiled that proud smile James had come to love as a child.

"You came," Stuart said weakly. "I knew you would."

"Father," James said unable to keep the tears from spilling. "I'm sorry, I didn't know."

"You've come to me now. That's what matters."

James stood, his father in his arms and made his way to the back door, carefully stepping around his younger self still lying on the floor unconscious. He pushed at the back door, and it fell from its hinges, revealing the moonlit field behind the church. James crossed the field to the edge of the forest. He set Stuart down carefully against a tree.

James waved his hand over Stuart's body repeating, "Sendatu ." Stuart's listless gaze gained focus as his wounds healed, and he once again looked at his son.

"How?" he asked.

"I don't know," replied James, "but I'm here." James looked back at the church and felt a pressing need to return. He turned back to his father.

"Go," said Stuart.

James nodded and sprinted back across the field. When he entered the church again, the lone survivor had managed to pull himself closer to the back door. James felt a surge of anger as he approached the wounded man and knocked him onto his back with a kick. He placed his boot on the man's throat as he struggled. The man began to laugh, a hollow, mirthless sound.

"You find humor in death, do you?"

"Do you not know who waits in the forest? You will not escape," he said, gasping for breath. "The boy is powerful indeed but is quite helpless in his current state. Soon you will be dead, and he will be a captive." Not wanting to waste another moment, James drew his spellbreaker steel sword from its sheath and drove the blade into the man's heart.

In the forest, Stuart kept watch for the return of his son. Without warning, a cold hand gripped him by the back of the neck, and he knew instantly who it belonged to. How could he have forgotten the orchestrator of this assault? He was pulled to his feet with surprising strength. The hand released him and he turned. They stood eye to eye.

"Alexander Vinokourov, I presume."

30

alexander vinokourov

The grey eyes, Asian features and contrasting white-blond hair could not be mistaken for another. His shoulders were wide and muscled despite his age. His mottled grey robes matched the emptiness of his eyes. The sorcerer stood inches from Stuart breathing heavily and exhaling a pungency that in any other situation would have caused Stuart to wince.

"Where is the boy?" he snarled.

"I never thought someone of your stature would become Alvaro's political lap dog."

"Alvaro is a puppet, you fool, precisely as you are Akil's puppet. Now, where is the boy? I must have him."

"So you do all the dirty work, and Alvaro gets all the credit. Doesn't seem fair, does it?"

"Kalanbre -Samindu ." Vinokourov extended his open palms toward Stuart, whose body stiffened as vise-like pain surged through every muscle. A groan escaped from between his clenched teeth. Vinokourov stepped closer, so close their noses touched. The muscles in Stuart's jaw twitched like piano strings as he fought back the cries that would bring his son running to his aid.

"Tell me where he is," Vinokourov whispered, "and I won't make him watch you die."

"He's dead," Stuart said through clenched teeth.

"A lie," Vinokourov said, releasing the bind on Stuart, who fell back against the tree. "The next time I guarantee you will cry out, and I promise, he will watch you die a horrible death. If you tell me now, it will all end, and the boy will decide which road he takes. If he's half as powerful as he is supposed to be, he should have no problem resisting the enchanting words of that fool Alvaro. Where is he?"

"I am here," said James.

Stuart had seen many intimidating men in his lifetime. He thought none would ever surpass Vinokourov, yet as his grown son strode across the field bathed in white moonlight, he couldn't contain the shudder that ran through his body. James's long, dark hair blew in the breeze, revealing his lean face and blue, forget-me-not eyes — clearly no longer those of a child but eyes that would haunt whomever they set upon. The blade, gripped tightly in his right hand, appeared as if a shadow, absorbing the light of the moon into its black steel blade. He had no fear in his face as he approached the most notorious sorcerer alive.

"Who are you?" Vinokourov demanded.

"I am the one you seek. The boy and I are one and the same." James stood an arm's length from Vinokourov. "Look for yourself."

Vinokourov's eyes darted away for but a moment, and James knew he had the upper hand. The man could feel fear after all. Slowly, with a tremble only the keenest eye could detect, the sorcerer lifted his hand to James's face and closed his eyes, beginning his inspection of James's mind. James winked at his father. Vinokourov recoiled as if scalded.

"No! How is this possible?" he exclaimed.

"Through Ak Egundiano, all things are possible."

"What do you know of The Never?"

"I have been there, and I now return to set things right."

"Liar. No one returns once they are banished."

"Even as you utter those words you know they are not true. You know of whom I speak , as I know doubt and fear are flooding your mind."

"No one is ever meant to leave that place — or has the ability to do so."

"Yet here I stand." James looked down into the eyes of Alexander Vinokourov. The fear he had seen moments ago was gone, buried away. It was replaced with rage.

" If indeed you have been to Ak Egundiano and you have returned, I dare say the journey has not left you undamaged, as it damages all who return, regardless of their strength." James did not reply.

"I've come for the boy," Vinokourov snarled, "and I will not leave without him. If you stand in my way, you will die. Now, where have you hidden him?"

"You know who I am. You also know I will not give him up."

"You are powerful. I could sense that much among the closed doors and broken memories of your mind. You would be a great asset. Perhaps we should be discussing an alliance rather than pitting our egos against one another."

"If you consider leaving without the boy, I will consider allowing you to live and furthering our conversation of your proposed alliance. If, however, you insist on taking him, then we have nothing more to discuss," said James. By this time the men were rotating in ever-widening circles as Stuart stood watching.

"I'm afraid we've reached an impasse," said Vinokourov. "I cannot leave without the boy. We could leave together, the three of us, and see where the road takes us, but if you persist in withholding the boy from me, this conversation has indeed concluded."

To Vinokourov's surprise, James turned his back on him and faced his father.

"He is inside the place where I performed my first incantation. Find him and get to the main road. You can transport there. I'll meet you at our favorite spot." Stuart nodded, and James turned to face the sorcerer.

"If we are going to kill one another, let us be gentlemen about it. Although based on your reputation, I'm not sure you understand the meaning of the word."

"Rumors are often laden with mistruths. I respect my adversaries and despite your…unusual behavior, I shall afford you that same respect. I am, after all, a reasonable man."

"Now," James shouted over his shoulder. Stuart sprinted through the field toward the village. He realized he'd been blown out of his boots by the wave that had struck him inside the church as his bare feet became instantly wet from the dew. Vinokourov snarled and sent a burst of energy after him. James countered it with his own burst, redirecting Vinokourov's into the side of a house where it blew out the wooden siding and collapsed part of the roof. James could hear screams from inside.

"He will not get out of the village. My men are everywhere," said Vinokourov.

"Thirteen of them, correct?" said James. Vinokourov's eyes burned with rage as he muttered while moving his hands in a way James had never seen. On the eastern horizon, the sun transformed the night sky to a deep blue canopy in preparation for its arrival. Overhead, the moon and stars still shone brightly as an owl glided between the two men and into the forest. James sheathed his sword and set his shield incantations in preparation for whatever came next.

James heard a sound in the forest to his right but refused to take his eyes off his opponent. Vinokourov's hands stilled as he looked into the forest. James sent a burst of fire at Vinokourov as he turned away, but before the flames reached him, he simply vanished.

James looked up the hill and saw dozens of glowing eyes along the tree line. It was only when they charged that James realized what they were. Wild boar. Huge beasts, each three times the size of any he had ever laid eyes upon. Curving ivory tusks grew out of their lower jaws and bent up above their snouts, promising to impale whoever was unfortunate enough to stand in their way.

"Erori -lur ," James said, and the ground fell away in front of the charging creatures. Several plummeted into the ditch, yet most jumped over and continued their charge. James sent a burst of fire at the arrowhead formation, but the flames rolled over the animals like a summer breeze. James lifted his arms and raised coffin-sized slabs of rock from the ground, which he flung at the charging boars. Several were struck and fell out of formation, but the lead three — the tip of the arrowhead — continued on. The boar in the center, the leader, was white. Its red eyes glowed eerily in the dawn light. James fired a burst of energy, then a second and a third. Two hit their mark, but the third fell short, merely scattering earth in its wake. The white boar continued its charge, and James knew he would have one final opportunity to stop it before it was upon him.

"Dietu -ur ," he said, drawing water from deep within the earth. As it rose from the ground in a sheet, James said, "Izoztu ," freezing it solid. The white boar lunged, breaking through the ice wall. James stepped forward, pulled his blade from its scabbard and swung upward across the belly of the beast as it arced through the air. It fell to the ground, dead, a bloody swath of entrails in its wake.

James ran into the village square looking for any sign of his father or Vinokourov. He burst into the home of the bourgmestre where he had left his younger self. The interior was in shambles. Pieces of furniture, books and other debris were scattered everywhere and one wall was engulfed in flames. Seeing neither his younger self nor his father, James hurriedly made his way down the street toward the main road.

Several explosions drew his attention. James quickly turned up an alley, making for the sound. Some buildings lay in heaps. Others burned as their occupants poured outside, still in their nightclothes. James bolted past crowds toward the sound of another explosion. He rounded a corner and finally spotted the pair. His father was backed up against the white-mortared wall of a cottage. In his arms, young James was still unconscious.

"Both of you need not die," Vinokourov shouted. "Put down the boy and die like a man instead of using your own son as a shield."

"You won't kill him, you need him," Stuart said.

"I need no one. This is your last opportunity not to die like a coward."

James did not hesitate, but allowed the rage he felt to flow through his body and through his hands. The burst of energy sent Vinokourov down the alley and through the stone wall of a forge. James ran to his father and took the young boy from Stuart's exhausted arms.

"We're nearly to the road. Come," James said, running past several cottages before turning and making his way down the dirt lane that intersected the main road past a small pasture. He looked over his shoulder. His father had fallen behind. He slowed, allowing him to catch up. Together they made their way to the road. Stuart bent over, catching his breath. James looked down the lane they had traveled. Vinokourov stalked toward them. James marveled that anyone could have survived such an impact. "We must go, now," he said.

Stuart nodded and reached for the pouch of transporting powder he carried on his belt. It was gone. He looked up at his son in disbelief. "They must have pilfered it on the way to the church," he said. "You must take James and go. I cannot run any farther." Without a word, James handed the boy's limp body back to his father and walked down the lane toward Vinokourov. They met beside a dry stone wall where a lamb blissfully chewed on a patch of grass.

Vinokourov fixed James with a baleful stare. "You are powerful. But your skills are crude and no match for mine. I could teach you much. Let us work together. We need neither Alvaro nor Akil Karanis. Let us take the boy so I may get what is mine, and then we can destroy them both." The pair stood close enough to whisper as the sun's rays continued to brighten the horizon.

"And what is it you so desire that you are willing to die here today to get it?" James asked.

"Some things are not meant to be understood by anyone other than the person to whom they belong. Now, your actions have caused needless deaths here today. Let us end this destructive conflict before someone you actually care about is killed."

"I know what it is you seek. I should say, I know whom you seek," said James.

"You know nothing," spat Vinokourov.

"You have a grandson. He is about the same age as that boy," James said, pointing down the lane to his younger body. "He was taken and it destroyed you. Now, you seek to take this boy from his father in order to get your grandson back."

Vinokourov's face paled as he looked at James.

"How can you know this?" he asked.

"I know where he is. You would be proud. Serik is a powerful sorcerer." For a moment, James watched the introspection in Vinokourov's eyes. It quickly abated and his face reddened.

"You lie. I've been fed lies my entire life, and you do no different. The only way I will ever have my grandson is to take that boy," he said gesturing at young James. Now, stand aside. Refuse, and I will take him by force. If you die, so be it. I promise you this: after I take that boy and get my grandson, I will hunt down and murder the Stuart boy's family. They will pay for your interference."

James's eyes burned inside his head. His vision clouded over as the rage came. He let out a cry of fury as he drew his blade and slashed upwards across Vinokourov's face, tearing away the flesh of his cheek. The sorcerer's hand flew to his face, cradling the injury.

"How?" he cried, shocked.

James brought his blade down in an arc across the other cheek, again slicing the flesh. Vinokourov stood gripping his face as blood ran down his arms and dripped from his elbows, unable to understand how such a crude weapon could penetrate his magical barriers. James felt a surge of power and moved to strike again. Vinokourov released a burst of energy, which James easily sidestepped, as he brought down his blade, this time laying open the shoulder and upper arm. Vinokourov let out a cry as he reached into his cloak. James lunged forward to stop him from releasing the transporting powder, but the point of his blade caught only purple smoke. The sorcerer was gone.

James turned. The rising sun blinded him as he made his way to the road. Lying on the ground was the motionless body of his younger self

— still unconscious. Next to him, his father lay supine, gasping for air, his eyes fixed on the last star of the night burning brightly in defiance of the dawn. James cupped his father's face in his hands. Stuart's eyes came down from the sky and met James's.

"Son."

"Father." James washed his hand over his father's crumpled body, frantically repeating the healing incantation.

"I'm afraid that won't work this time, my boy. It is my destiny to die here. You've made me a happy man, James. Know that, and know that I am proud to be your father, every day. Now, go be the man you are destined to be. Not because I want it for you, but because you want it. Find happiness, for without it you are as hollow as your enemies. Tell your mother she is my true love. The path upon which so many have trod awaits."

Stuart fell silent as a wisp of white smoke rose from his chest, and James knew the bond of his parents' love was broken. In the end, he had been unable to change the course of events. He held his father in his arms and cried to the dawn. Down the lane, the lamb bleated as if in reply. His father was dead and his young self would spend the better part of his life blaming himself for it…unless there was something he could do. He stood.

James lifted the limp body of his younger self from the road and walked back down the lane toward the crowds surrounding the burning buildings. He felt drawn to the place he remembered regaining consciousness as a child. It was as if his body continued of its own accord. In that moment, James knew that the forces that had drawn him here would not change his future. He placed the boy's body on the ground on the far side of a burning cottage where he would later be discovered by one of the frantic townsfolk.

James started walking toward the church. He would find Akil. Akil would know what to do. As he strode down the alley, he felt a tug on his belt. He turned. No one was there. He took another step forward and again felt resistance at his waist. He pulled against it, but the resistance grew stronger, spreading up his back and down his legs. He fought against it, as he had in the church, but this time there was no tearing free, no escape. He screamed as the crushing force pulled him to the ground. It felt as if he were going to be pulled right through the cobbles. His head started to spin as the pressure grew until everything went black.

31

the black castle

James awoke in a dimly lit corridor. The moisture on the stone floor had soaked through his clothes, and he found himself shivering as he attempted to rise. His body was weak and stiff, his thoughts disjointed and confused. A single torch at the base of a staircase was the only source of light. The corridor was narrow — James could easily reach from wall to wall with his outstretched arms. Behind him, the tunnel extended into darkness. As he gazed into the darkness overwhelming dread descended on his mind and threatened to paralyzed his body. He turned and crept toward the torchlight.

"Argitu ," he said, his hands extended, waiting for the orb of light to appear. Nothing happened. James cursed. He slid the torch out of its bracket and cautiously ascended the stairs, determined to get as far away from the darkness as possible. The black stairs spiraled upward to a small steel door. James slid the torch into the empty metal bracket on the wall and held out his hands.

"Ireki ." Again, nothing happened. He let out a sigh. "Tertiri zé Manukto voriko." The door swung open slowly, and he knew he was back in The Never. Disheartened, James stepped over the threshold and into a dark room.

"Tertiri zé Manukto vinka," James said, holding his hands palm up. Rather than the light orb he was expecting, the entire room illuminated, revealing a magnificent hall. Several dozen crystal chandeliers hung over long tables, each set for a grand feast. James could smell food cooking in some distant kitchen. A long, red runner bisected the hall stretching to the raised platform upon which sat a single chair. A throne. The walls were adorned with paintings and tapestries while sculptures sat upon pedestals in niches.

James took another step into the room, this time inspecting the floor. Seamless black granite ran from wall to wall. He froze. Could it be? Had he finally reached the black castle? He inhaled deeply and shook his head as if he could shake away this reality. He stepped forward, taking everything in. Each table, set at angles to the runner like the bones of a fish, was set for ten. Each glass was filled with a deep garnet wine. Three black steel candelabras sat evenly spaced on each table, with every candle alight.

James continued past the tables to the dais. The throne was cut from the same dark stone as the floor. Swirls of grey and light crystalline sparkles broke up what would have been midnight black stone. Behind the throne hung a tapestry depicting a man clad in black armor riding a horse across a grassy field. Far off in the distance was the black castle.

James focused his attention on the throne itself. It coaxed him closer.

He became enveloped in an aura of foreboding, but the call of the throne overwhelmed all other thought. It attracted him and repelled him at the same time, but his desire could not be denied. He stepped forward onto the dais. The throne beguiled him. Soothing. Reassuring. Promising him all he'd ever wished for. He obliged and stepped closer. The throne was itself a work of art. Every inch was covered with ornate designs. Even the blood-red cushion was hand-embroidered. The overwhelming compulsion urged James still closer until finally, he sat.

The energy surged up through the throne and into his body as his mind connected to the black castle. A door opened at the far end of the hall opposite the throne. A man stepped through and hurriedly walked toward James. James knew he should be surprised to see anyone in this place, but he was, for reasons he could not explain, not surprised at all.

"Sire," the man intoned before he had traversed half the hall, "the guests have arrived and are gathered in the antechamber. Shall I commence the feast?"

"Yes, Patrick." James said. He leaned back in the throne, stroking the fur that trimmed his rich black velvet cloak . James was not the least bit surprised to find himself also wearing a hat trimmed with peacocks' feathers, close-fitting black silk breeches, and padded black leather shoes squared at the toes. The major-domo turned and clapped his hands. Large wooden doors groaned open at the far end of the hall. Two rows of guards wearing black dress-armor filed into the room and formed a gauntlet of sorts from the doors to the dais. Then, in pairs, guests approached the throne, paid obeisance to James, and took their seats. Once the last guest was seated and the outer doors closed, servants paraded in from side doors carrying tray after tray of food until the tables were covered with every possible delight James could imagine. As the last servant took his position along the wall, the major-domo turned to

James. He nodded. Patrick stepped up onto the first level of the platform, extending his arms in greeting.

"Lords and ladies. It is my honor to welcome you to the court of James Lochlan Stuart IV, greatest of all kings." The guests cheered wildly. "It is his wish that you all enjoy the feast laid before you and an evening of entertainment unlike any you will see again in your lifetime. Without further ado, you may begin." He bowed deeply.

The guests began tearing into their food while a troupe of musicians made their way into the hall. They began to play a somber song despite the festive atmosphere, but the dirge went unnoticed by the guests. The servants scrambled back and forth clearing, filling and cleaning so the guests never touched a soiled utensil or suffered an empty glass. James was amazed by the efficiency of it all, yet felt no desire to join his guests. He sat and watched as they gorged themselves on food and drink. Little was spoken as the music filled the great hall. Patrick stood with his hands clasped behind his back, nodding occasionally to guests and gesturing with a flick of his head to servants he thought were moving too slowly. When the last plate was cleared after nearly an hour of gluttony and the glasses were refilled, Patrick took another step up the platform and extended his arms. The music immediately stopped.

"I trust that you have all had your fill," said Patrick. The guests cheered. "Very good. Now it is time for the entertainment."

James sat up straighter, curious to see what form of entertainment would be provided, completely lost in the moment. Patrick nodded and two of the black-armored guards pulled at the steel rings to open the large wooden doors. Servants wheeled a large object draped by a blood-red cloth through the doors. At first, James thought it wouldn't fit through the entry but with a slight turn, they managed to wheel the red-cloaked mystery over the threshold and into the center of the hall.

Patrick stepped down from the dais and excitedly strode toward the covered object. Perhaps it was a trick of the light, but James thought it appeared as though Patrick was growing shorter as he drew closer to the covered object. By the time he reached it, its mysterious form towered over him. Patrick reached up and swiftly pulled the red cloth, spilling it onto the floor in front of him and revealing a wooden panel atop a stepped platform. The panel blocked what lay behind from view.

Patrick climbed onto the first step. He gave a signal and the troupe began to play its mournful dirge once again. The servants began to rotate the platform slowly, in tempo with the music, until the opposite side of the panel faced James and the crowd. A pair of red curtains once again blocked their view. James's palms were sweating as he sat on the edge of the throne waiting to see what the curtains would reveal. His heartbeat quickened in anticipation.

Patrick turned his back on the crowd and thrust his hands into the air, commanding the curtains to open. As they slowly parted, he turned back to face the crowd with a wry smile. He was no longer Patrick. He was Gai in boy form. James tried to stand, but found himself restrained by the throne. He fought with all his might to free himself from the invisible bonds but to no avail. He tried several incantations without result.

Behind the boy, a steel cage was suspended by a thick chain running through a davit at the rear of the platform in front of the wooden panel. Inside the cage stood Gai ak zangar in her true form. Her body was the same shape and size as her woman form, but her skin was scaled a dark blue and marbled with brindle. Her pointed ears were more bat-like than human and oriented toward the back of her head. The scales of her face and head were a shade lighter, and her eyes were larger yet equally as alluring as in her human form. She fought to free herself. She shook the bars and cursed and growled and spit and roared. The cage swung wildly, but the steel bars showed no sign of yielding.

"Here is how it will work," the boy shouted to the crowd. "This monster's cage is suspended over a shaft." A guard slid back a circular cover, revealing a hole beneath the cage. Orange and red light danced on the cage and ceiling above. "This isn't just any shaft," the boy continued. "Deep in the bowels of this pit is the molten steel from which every lock and key, every chain and bracket, every candelabra and chandelier in this great castle is forged. Even the very cage imprisoning the beast. Our great king's blade was similarly forged from this spellbreaker steel. So, as you may have guessed, despite the power this monster possesses, a dip in molten spellbreaker steel would put an end to her life and an end to the plague that has infested Ak Egundiano for centuries!"

The crowd roared their approval. James stared helplessly in a state of complete confusion. Gai in her true form caged like an animal, Gai in her boy form calling for her execution — he couldn't make sense of any of it.

"You must do something!" Gai, in her woman form, appeared next to the throne. For the first time since he'd known her, she appeared frightened.

"What is happening?" James whispered.

"I — I'm not sure. You dropped off the ladder — an instant later, I was here, somehow split."

"Split? I don't understand. Who is in that cage? Who is that boy?"

"I am in that cage and I am that boy — but his mind has been taken over by Ak Egundiano. I am here as well," she said, gesturing to herself, "but I am powerless. A mere human. My powerful body is helpless within that cage."

"I cannot help you. I am bound to this throne with no means of escape."

"You must find a way to free yourself!"

"Do not be distracted by their petty conversing," shouted the boy. "One of you will have the honor of delivering this beast to its final resting place. One of you will hold the chain that keeps this cage suspended above the pit. Should you tire or simply feel the urge to release the chain, our prisoner — this scourge — shall fall to its death."

The crowd began to chant. Fall! Fall! Fall! James struggled uselessly against the force that held him in place. He looked at the guests sitting at the tables calling for Gai's death. Their eyes were filmed in a viscous layer of blood; some bulged outward as if they might burst while others wept bloody tears that rolled down their cheeks. All were banging on the tables with their fists and chanting like drunken fools.

"Who will have the honor of holding the chain?" shouted the boy. He quickly scanned the crowd. "I think, to add dramatic flair, we should choose someone with a vested interest in the monster's survival. Don't you agree?" Two guards approached from behind and seized Gai's human form by the arms, dragging her off the dais as she kicked and screamed and fought to get away. James looked on helplessly as the crowd's cheers intensified.

"Stop this," she shouted. "You are only destroying yourself!" The caged beast roared something unintelligible, but the boy paid attention to neither plea. He pulled away a narrow strip of red fabric, revealing the chain. It ran from the top step onto the platform, around the perimeter through several steel rings, then up the davit mast where it attached to the cage. At the front edge of the platform, a single black pin secured the chain. Slack chain draped over the steps and pooled on the floor.

The guards shoved the woman onto the floor next to the pile of loose chain. She slowly stood and looked at the boy — part of her own self that had turned against her. The boy smiled, revealing needle-like teeth with bits of flesh stuck between them, and descended from the platform.

"Grasp the chain," he said.

"No."

The boy crouched over the small black pin and held it gently between his thumb and forefinger. "When I pull this, either the chain will slip and the beast will die, or you will hold the chain and the beast will live. The choice is yo— "

The woman struck the boy square in the jaw, sending him into the air. He hit the black stone floor with a smack that immediately silenced the crowd. He was motionless for a moment. None of the guards stepped forward to assist as he slowly got to his feet. His cheek was bright red and blood ran from the corner of his mouth. He looked confused, and for a moment James thought the power of the black castle had released its grip on his mind. Then the boy's confusion changed to anger and he lunged at the woman, striking her in the pelvis with his shoulder. The force was enough to knock her backwards, giving him the split-second he needed to pull the pin. The chain began to feed through the rings and the cage to drop.

She dove at what little chain remained dangling over the edge of the platform and pulled it tight. The cage stopped with a jolt, already halfway into the shaft where it swung from side to side, striking the stone lining. She strained to keep the chain taut against the side of the platform as the beast's screams echoed in the hall. The boy smiled, rolling the pin between his fingers as he looked back up at the crowd. They cheered and took up their chant once again. Fall! Fall! Fall! The boy bent close to the woman.

"Not as easy without your powers, is it?"

"You're letting this place take your mind. If she dies, you die with her. Fight, you coward!" she screamed.

The boy stood and walked along the platform. He feigned a brief inspection of the chain, stepping onto the platform, tugging at the rings, running his hand up the davit mast then reaching out over the pit and gripping the chain just over the cage. While holding onto the davit mast with one arm, he gave the chain a vigorous shake. The creature inside spat and roared and cursed in an otherworldly language. James looked on, still fighting against the invisible bonds tethering him to the throne. He was torn. If the black castle was in fact a manifestation of The Never, it would indeed want Gai destroyed, because her powers were steadily supplanting its own. It was the very reason that, on The Second Widow, he had been gifted his ability to understand and use the language — so that he could fight and destroy Gai ak zangar.

But Gai was simply another inhabitant of The Never. She was trapped like James, and she was the last of her kind. Was it right to destroy her? Why wouldn't The Never simply let her leave?

"Hear me, denizens of Ak Egundiano!" James called out in the language of the land. The chanting stopped, and everyone looked with amazement in his direction. "Long have you sought to destroy the Siren. I understand that you needed me to bring her here so that she may be destroyed. I understand that even now, within the walls of this place, you lack the power to fulfill that desire without my help."

"You doubt my power within the walls of my own castle?" the boy said in a hollow, echoing voice that was not his own.

"Gai ak zangar, release the chain," said James. She looked up at him, incredulous. "You will not die. You will rise and become more powerful than even you can fathom."

"He is lying," shouted the boy. "He chose you to come because he knew it would kill you. He said it himself."

"You have powers and abilities in this place that you have not yet realized. Ak Egundiano knows this. That is why I was gifted my knowledge — so that I could destroy you. Understand, only I can destroy you.

Ak Egundiano needs me. Do not fear. Trust in me, Gai ak zangar, and together we will prevail. All you must do is release that chain."

"How do you know this is true?" The woman's arms shook from the strain of holding the chain.

"I have seen into the heart of Ak Egundiano. Akil Karanis has seen into your heart, Gai ak zangar, and it was he who allowed me to see and understand. I understand the conflict that exists between you and Ak Egundiano, even if you do not. Every day your strength grows. You can manipulate things that should not be manipulated."

"He is a liar," said the boy.

"I have a solution that will satisfy all parties, but first you must release me," said James, looking at him. Immediately, the bonds that held him were no more. James stood, stepped from the dais, and walked toward the platform, all eyes upon him. "I shall take Gai ak zangar and return to my world. She will never return. You will regain control of your realm."

"She will destroy your world as she is destroying mine. Why would you bring this plague upon your own people?" the boy demanded in his otherworldly voice.

"It matters not. Release her now, and I will do as I say."

"Know this, James Lochlan Stuart IV, captain of the Queen Mary. You are forever bound to this place. You evade your destiny, but you cannot escape it. It is as unavoidable as death."

A bright flash blinded James for a moment. When he regained his vision, the room was as it had been when he arrived, with one exception. The woman lay on the floor near the large wooden doors. She lifted her head at the touch of his fingers on her shoulder.

"We must go," said James. She nodded and stood with James's help. The wooden doors swung open of their own accord.

The midday sun lit a magnificent courtyard as James and Gai stepped out onto the black cobbles. As his eyes adapted to the sunlight, James saw a rectangular garden bordered by styrax, viburnum and birch. Without hesitation, he stepped into the garden. The pair ducked through an arched metal arbor choked with moonflower vines and onto a white-pebbled path. Snowdrops, paperwhites, jasmine and lily of the valley bloomed in stark contrast to the black walls that rose up around them. Through the towering battlements, he glimpsed a mountaintop and thought of Kilani and their first journey to the top of Mt. Misery. He knew that he must return. Ak Egundiano was right. He was bound to this land — not by its power, but by his own will and the love he was leaving behind.

32

again

November 1901, Ireland

Akil Karanis turned west before reaching Belfast and took the path along Lough Neagh, then headed toward the Sperrin Mountains. Beside him rode Ilixo Alvaro. Gai ak zangar walked between them. They silently continued on their way until they reached the spot where, nearly three centuries prior, Akil had turned off the road and continued into the mountainside. The men tethered their horses to an overgrown shrub and walked into the narrow gap in the cliff face and up a set of winding stairs.

"This will not end well for any of us," said the Siren.

Akil stopped, extracted the Aldi Jaitsu from his cloak and flipped open the lid. A blue glow lit his face as he peered into it. He snapped it shut and continued up the stairs.

"You are correct, Lady Gai. If we do not act, none of us shall survive the Epoch Terminus.

"You will be lucky to survive this encounter. Either of you. Especially you, " she said, glaring at Akil.

Akil reached the top step and looked back into the eyes of the Siren longingly. Her cold stare spurred him onward, and he cautiously crossed under the stone archway. A freezing rain pelted the trio as they stepped onto the plateau. The surrounding cliffs had fallen away in pieces. Boulders the size of houses littered the once clear plateau.

"This way," said Akil. He stepped away from the archway, navigating through the boulders and debris.

Alvaro followed quietly, muttering protective incantations as they continued. "She is not here," he said, wanting nothing more than to be gone from this place.

"She is here, I assure you," said Akil. He mounted a pile of broken stones, muttered an incantation, and then began to speak. His voice boomed across the mountaintop. "Okon ak aintzinako, I have returned! I have fulfilled my part of our agreement, now you must fulfill yours." In response, the rain fell harder and began to mix with snow. "Lady Okon," he continued, "I have brought Gai ak zangar as you demanded. Come forth and let us speak." Still no reply came, but then a slight rumble beneath their feet put everyone on guard.

"She is here," said Gai. She leaped onto a towering boulder and began to speak in her own musical language. After a moment, a reply echoed across the plateau as if it came from the clouds. Gai turned to the men. "You must go."

"I will not leave without what I have come for," said Akil. The voice from above spoke again.

"She will give you your reward when she is ready to do so," translated

Gai.

"I will not leave without that which I have been promised," Akil repeated. The rain stopped.

"I must be getting late in years to think a stubborn fool like you would simply leave," said the Siren, rounding a boulder. She had taken her woman form as she nearly always did in the presence of men. Her dark hair blew in the wind, revealing the flawless beauty of her skin.

"Lady Okon," said Akil balling his right fist, covering it with his left hand, and bowing slightly. Alvaro mirrored the greeting. Okon glared up at Gai but did not address her.

"I see that this time, unlike your last visit, you have brought me the one I seek. And you now expect your reward," said Okon, "although by any definition what I am about to share with you is far from a reward." Akil nodded, his hands and jaw clenched, as he prepared himself for the great Siren's revelation.

"Very well," she said, glowering again at Gai before fixing Akil with her gaze. "Your great Seer's decree has long been misinterpreted for a multitude of reasons. Primarily, because all those present during the declaration were killed during the Great War . All save one. I was there when the decree was made, and I know what you do not, Akil Karanis. And as I promised, I will share it with you now. Two elements are missing from your interpretation of the decree. First, the Seer spoke of not one who would be anointed, but two. Only one will stop the Epoch Terminus. The other will be his adversary. The Seer did not speak further on this matter. Second," Okon said, exchanging glances with Akil and Alvaro, "both of those anointed must travel to and return from Ak Egundiano together."

"This cannot be," said Alvaro. Akil stood in stunned silence.

"That is the decree as I heard it. Whether or not you believe it is irrelevant. You have gotten what you came for, now be gone. I have my own business to attend to." She scowled at Gai.

"There is no time," said Akil. "There must be another way."

"You would waste even more of your precious time trying to find another path?"

"He would not survive a second time. No man could," said Alvaro.

"He did," Okon said, gesturing to Akil. Alvaro looked at him in disbelief.

"I make one final offering, and then I am done dabbling in the affairs of humans. Bring them to me, the two you believe are the ones prophesied by the Seer. I will send them back myself."

"Ak Egundiano. Again," said Akil, his voice full of despair.

"Again," replied the Siren.

CPSIA information can be obtained at www.ICGtesting.com
Printed in the USA
BVOW03s0050270415

397717BV00001B/1/P

9 780988 666856